The Scientific Romances of
J.-H. Rosny Aîné

THE YOUNG VAMPIRE
And Other Cautionary Tales

The Scientific Romances of
J.-H. Rosny Aîné

THE YOUNG VAMPIRE
And Other Cautionary
Tales

translated, annotated and introduced by
Brian Stableford

A Black Coat Press Book

Acknowledgements: I should like to thank John J. Pierce for providing valuable research materials and offering advice and support. Many of the copies of Rosny's works and critical articles related to his work were borrowed from the London Library. Also thanks to Paul Wessels for his generous and extensive help in the final preparation of this text.

Visit our website at www.blackcoatpress.com

Table of Contents

Introduction

This is the sixth volume of a six-volume collection of stories by J.-H. Rosny *Aîné* ("the Elder"), which includes all of his scientific romances, plus a number of other stories that have some relevance to his work in that genre.[1]

The contents of the six volumes are:

Volume 1. THE NAVIGATORS OF SPACE AND OTHER ALIEN ENCOUNTERS: The Xipehuz, The Skeptical Legend, Another World, The Death of the Earth, The Navigators of Space, The Astronauts.

Volume 2. THE WORLD OF THE VARIANTS AND OTHER STRANGE LANDS: Nymphaeum, The Depths of Kyamo, The Wonderful Cave Country, The Voyage, The Great Enigma, The Treasure in the Snow, The Boar Men, In the World of the Variants.

Volume 3. THE MYSTERIOUS FORCE AND OTHER ANOMALOUS PHENOMENA: The Cataclysm, The Mysterious Force, Hareton Ironcastle's Amazing Adventure.

Volume 4. VAMIREH AND OTHER PREHISTORIC FANTASIES: Vamireh, Eyrimah, Nomaï.

Volume 5. THE GIVREUSE ENIGMA AND OTHER STORIES: Mary's Garden, The Givreuse Enigma, Adventure in the Wild.

Volume 6. THE YOUNG VAMPIRE AND OTHER CAUTIONARY TALES: The Witch, The Young Vampire, The Supernatural Assassin, Companions of the Universe.

---

[1] *Le Félin géant* (*The Giant Cat* a.k.a. *Quest of the Dawn Man*) and *Helgvor du fleuve bleu* (*Helgvor of the Blue River*) will be reprinted in their original English translations in a seventh volume.

The first volume of the series includes a long general introduction to Rosny's life and works, which there is no need to repeat here; the following introduction will therefore be limited to a brief account of the stories included in this volume, which will be supplemented by a more detailed commentary contained in an afterword.

"La Sorcière," translated herein as "The Witch," was one of Rosny's earliest short stories, appearing along with "Les Xipéhuz" (tr. in vol. 1 as "The Xipehuz") in *L'Immolation* (Savine 1887). Like the title-story of the collection, it is an account of peasant life focused on the essential stupidity of the world-view of simple folk. As with several of his later works, it contends and seeks to illustrate the fact that religious faith is the parent of violence, torture and murder. Although it is not a scientific romance, I thought it appropriate to include it in the collection because it illustrates the manner in which Rosny made use of the scientific world-view and scientific vocabulary in his naturalistic works.

La Jeune vampire, here translated as "The Young Vampire," was initially published in 1920 in a series of booklets produced by Ernest Flammarion, who was then Rosny's regular publisher, under the collective title of *Une heure d'oubli* [An Hour of Forgetfulness]. *Le Trésor dans la neige* (tr. in vol. 2 as "The Treasure in the Snow") appeared in the same series. *La Jeune vampire* is manifest hackwork, but it is nevertheless interesting, in that it borrows a theme from the first winner of the Prix Goncourt, *Force ennemie* by John-Antoine Nau (Eugène Torquet),[2] modifying it for accommodation into Rosny's version of the multiverse. In contrast to his other stories, in which entities from other sectors of "the fourth universe" interact with ours, *La Jeune vampire* imagines an internal manifestation akin to diabolical possession—except that the "possessor" is not seen as actively evil or malicious, in spite of the fact that it imposes a subtle metamorphosis of its host body, which compels it to seek vampiric nourishment.

---

[2] To be published in a Black Coat Press edition.

The story was subsequently reprinted as the title story of a collection, *La Vampire de Bethnal Green* (Albert, 1935); I have not seen that version and do not know whether it actually shifts the action from Islington to Bethnal Green, but I suspect not.

The story translated herein as "The Supernatural Assassin" was initially published in *La Revue Bleue* as "La Haine surnaturelle" in 1923 before being reprinted the following year as the title story of a Flammarion collection, *L'Assassin surnaturel*. It is in much the same vein as *La Jeune vampire* and might have been initially envisaged as a booklet for the same series, although the finished text is too short for such use. As with the earlier story, it attempts to redevelop one of the classical themes of supernatural fiction in a materialistic context; in so doing, it borrows its central motif from *L'Enigme de Givreuse* (1917; tr. in vol. 5 as "The Givreuse Enigma"). It does not venture into the scientific explanation that the earlier story attempted, thus leaving its central anomaly to stew in its own implausibility, but readers who are able to interpret its events in the context suggested by the earlier novel might well find it slightly more satisfactory than those who cannot.

Les Compagnons de l'univers, translated herein as "Companions of the Universe," initially appeared as a serial in the *Mercure de France* before being reprinted by the press associated with the periodical as a book in 1934. It is undoubtedly the most peculiar of all Rosny's novels, and represents a return to the experimentation that he had been forced to stifle in order to build a career in the late 1880s. Several commentators have likened it to "La Légende sceptique," the most fragrantly experimental text of that period to have made it into print, for obvious reasons, but it is markedly different in its tone and focus. The element of scientific romance that it contains is rather tentative and seemingly superfluous, the core of the novel being a long meditation on the perversity of human sexual relationships, but readers of his other scientific romances will know that this was a theme he had developed in a moderately startling manner in a series of stories extending

9

from "Les Navigateurs de l'infini" (1922; tr. in vol. 1 as "The Navigators of Space") through "Les Hommes-Sangliers" (1929; tr. in vol. 2 as "The Boar Men") to "Dans le monde des Variants" (1939; tr. in vol. 1 as "In the World of the Variants"). Even if the latter really was written after "Les Compagnons de l'univers," there is still a sense in which "Les Compagnons de l'univers" is a kind of judgmental summary of those ideas, complete with a verdict and sentence. I have used it here as a kind of epilogue to the entire collection—a position that it warrants in spite of its manifest eccentricities.

The versions of the first three stories that I used for translation are those contained in the 1975 Marabout omnibus of Rosny's *Récits de science-fiction*. I translated the final item from the version serialized in the *Mercure de France*.

Brian Stableford

THE WITCH

"Nothing can be done about it!" cried the bone-setter.

The stable was in turmoil, horribly hot, with no windows apart from a minuscule square set at an angle, in a diamond formation. The farmer Grosse Epaule, the blacksmith, the bone-setter and Pierre Clotare watched Black patiently dying on her fetid litter. Her miserable herbivore's eyes, blue with suffering, collected the spare light, sighing feverishly. She lowed softly and plaintively, flaring her tremulous nostrils to breathe the foul air.

"But what's wrong with her?" cried Grosse Epaule piteously. "What is it? The curé blessed her yesterday!"

"What she has, I swear, for sure" replied the bone-setter, "is no Catholic malady!"

"Witchcraft!" said Clotare, curtly.

They all looked at one another pensively. Oh yes, for sure! Things had been going so badly in the region for two years!

"Lord above!" cried Clotare, rancorously. "The old shrew, the evil eye…she'll do for us all before much longer."

"Your Bertine's leg is no better?"

"Better? It's got worse!"

The cow lowed again, more quietly, her enormous pupil fixed on the four men, in supplication.

"She's looking at us like a normal person."

"My poor Black! My poor Black!" cried Grosse Epaule, with large tears on his eyelashes.

Black made a great effort, rearing up in the gloom, her breath shortening. Two large midges were buzzing around her ear. Slender sunbeams came through the gap left by the door, which stood ajar, decorating the pitiful beast phantasmagorically, and for a few seconds she steeped her confused reverie therein. Then, feeling her strength and the desirable vital vibration fade, she fell back on to the ruddy corruption and, with a hoarse sigh of resignation, passed away.

"She's dead!" howled Grosse Epaule. "There's no more justice here!"

"No," said the blacksmith, "justice is stupid."

"Must we stand meekly by like sheep?" Clotare added. "In the name of God!"

In the half-light, the horrible litter revealed wisps of sulfur and amber hair; the intoxicated tribe of midges became more numerous, and the four men resumed looking at one another with mysterious and brutish expressions.

"It's exactly 100 years," Clotare whispered, "that one of *them* was burned over there, in front of the church. My grandfather told me the story a thousand times. He saw it!"

"In those times," said Grosse Epaule, "there was justice here!"

"And how!" murmured the blacksmith.

Clotare bit the skin of his fingers near the nails. The dead animal's hide shone softly, and a gleam lit up in its enormous eye. The scars, excoriations and bald patches of its humble domestic animality were visible.

"Since it's all over," the blacksmith said, "let's go get a drink!"

Clotare was walking along the edge of a field. A yellow crescent was sinking in the west. The earth was wrinkled in large pleats; the June grain was growing tall; warm gusts of wind were harmonizing in the foliage of the poplars; and the charming voices of toads were alternating with the splashing of frogs.

Slightly drunk, Clotare struck the ground with his staff, swearing intermittently. He was solidly built, his hairless, broad and arid face shielded by the peak of a ridiculous cap, and a blue smock floated around his rustic silhouette.

"Lord God of a thousand gods!" he swore, monotonously, while the alcohol evaporated from his mouth and the crops brushed him softly. He glanced occasionally at the sickle, already red as it set in the west, adjoined to the larger Lion,[3] with Regulus resplendent, issuing a vague challenge to that scrap of Moon, so odd and pointed.

"Our Lord isn't just!" he murmured.

The harmonica of a slender stream murmured under bushy vaults. Clotare searched the gloom for the small bridge and crossed over, twirling his staff aggressively.

"*She*'d better watch out! She'll undo what she's done, or the poor man will have his own justice!"

Over the blond waves, ashen grays and black patches of the plain, pallors appeared, plastery surfaces in which rare candles flickered.

"She's at her window!" Clotare muttered, as he saw the sharp profile of two large thatched cottages at the edge of the hamlet, isolated but almost neighbors. A woman was leaning on her elbows at the window of the nearer one, coal-black in the candlelight. The peasant hid behind a hedge, very attentive, his jaws grinding, in a condensation of fetishistic ideas. "What is she plotting?"

The woman, posed behind the darkness, in the coppery aureole of flickering light, was a soft nocturnal profile, her hair falling loose about her cheeks, a trifle dreamy in the beauty of the evening.

She doesn't do anything like a normal person! the other thought—and his blood boiled. He shook his staff in a large warrior's hand while the wail of the stream, the shrill calls of crickets and the quivering emotion of the crops invited mercy and fecundation.

"I'll give you something, anyway!"

---

[3] The *fauchette* [sickle] is an asterism formed by six stars that make up part of the constellation Leo, with Regulus at the "hilt;" when imagined as part of the ensemble they form the head and forepaw of the virtual lion. The formation and conjunction have obvious symbolic significance to a writer constructing a scenario in which a peasant contemplates aggressive action.

Rummaging around on the gentle muddy slope he found a pebble; then, with a grunt, he threw it. Struck on the shoulder, the woman uttered a small scream of fright.

"That's for you…caster of evil spells!" whispered Clotare ferociously, laughing through clenched teeth.

The woman looked around for a few seconds, with the alarm of someone persecuted; then, confronted by the silence of the field, sensing a cruel *someone* lying in ambush in the darkness, she shivered and closed her window—while Clotare rounded the hedge stealthily and headed for the cottage on the other side. There was also a candle burning in his home, in the kitchen, and his wife and daughter were sitting in the corner, beside the cold and resplendent stove.

On the melancholy blueness of the walls, a cuckoo-clock oscillated heavily; the disks and ellipses of a set of glazed crockery were aligned there, along with a sequence of rural landscapes, the ruddy coronation of an emperor and the benign silhouette of a pope. There was a chest of drawers, a table eroded by patient washing and six chairs with high backs, almost church pews. The sloping ceiling was rough and full of holes, with concavities and abrupt convexities.

"Greetings!" cried Clotare.

His thin wife, with eyes like a pigeon and a neck redder and more wrinkled than a turkey's, got slowly to her feet, and his daughter—who was as pale as paper, with overly long cheeks beneath an Australian forehead—started sighing.

"Are you still feeling ill, Bertine?"

"Yes, father. My leg is burning, burning…there must be a fire inside it."

"Lord above!"

Her right leg was stiff, creaking at the slightest movement—and her father spent a part of every evening staring at that leg, indignant and overexcited, his brain prey to all manner of abominations.

"Well," he said, "the curé has wasted his holy water. I wanted to do something, though. Tomorrow, Brother Honorat—the one Maluré talked about—will come. He's famous for exorcisms. If he can't chase the evil beast away…the *other* must be very strong!"

"Oh, that one will chase the evil away," said his wife. "He cured all the swine that had been cursed in Chavres…"

The cuckoo slowly opened its little door, stuck out its ludicrous head and called nine times.

"Do you want some supper?" his wife asked Clotare.

"No," Clotare replied. "I had some ham at Maluré's.

All three of them stayed there for another half-hour—a lamentable, wordless half-hour spent in peasant misery, amid the coldness of the walls and the monotony of the pendulum. Then, as slowly and heavily as oxen, they went to bury themselves in the unconsciousness of sleep.

The following day, at about 3 p.m., Clotare and his family were waiting on their blue limestone doorstep. The charming dream of the daylight shone upon the cottages, the ripening crops and the arborescent curve of the horizon.

"He's coming!" Clotare exclaimed.

A minuscule human silhouette was scarcely visible gliding slowly between the poplars. A small hillock interposed itself, and then the silhouette reappeared, as if posed against the silver of cumulus clouds, clad in a robe longer than those of the peasant women. More precise with every passing minute, it scraped the fine fleece of a hedge, then stiff-forked willows, while Clotare ran forward to meet it.

Ten minutes later, Father Honorat came into the cottage. His robe was greasy, his eyes malign, and his belly stuck out absurdly beneath his meager and angular torso. The peasant and his wife told him about Bertine's illness—and the monk listened, impudent and smiling, while the young woman shivered with excitement and hope.

"I understand…I understand!" said the monk.

Although he guaranteed a result, however, the cure would not come about immediately. Moreover, some money was necessary to defray the expenses of exorcisms and for offerings to Notre-Dame de Malvreuse…

"Yes—40 francs…no more!"

The somber peasant went up to the first floor, dug in the secret corner where their meager savings were and came back down with trembling hands and wild eyes. He deposited eight blackened 100-*sou* coins in the monk's hands.

With a semi-cynical laugh, Honorat stuck them in his belt. "Where is the pain?" he said to Bertine.

She pointed to her right thigh. "It comes and goes, and jumps to the knee. It bites and burns, like an animal or a fire!"

"Exactly!" said the monk. "I know what it is. Sit down."

She sat down, as anxious as a dentist's client, but he remained there momentarily, his eyes blank and his irises gyrating, in order to lay down the law.

"There's no mark on the leg?"

"None."

"Good…it's as I thought."

Clotare and his wife contemplated the powerful friar with bovine stupidity.

"Put your hands together," said the monk, "and repeat my words."

Bertine put her hands together.

In a cavernous voice, he began: "O most holy Virgin Mary…no one has ever heard it said…that anyone put her trust in you…without her wishes being fulfilled…full of confidence…in your powerful intercession, O Mary, O tender Mary!…I come with a pure heart to beg you…to come to my aid…O generous, O tender Virgin Mary…and to combat the demons that inhabit my thigh…which an evil sprit has called down upon me…"

The prayer became hesitant, stammering. Clotare was leaning forward with a black expression, and the friar, his eyelids horribly tremulous, continually lowering his voice, came to a conclusion, speaking in a tone of mystery and the arcane, terribly effective upon the young girl's soul. "Now," he said, "I shall cast out the devils. Man, do you have a dagger or a sword…very shiny."

"My father was a soldier," said Clotare. "I have his saber."

"Does it shine?"

"Yes, very brightly."

"Go fetch it."

He went out, shivering, with gooseflesh all over his hard skin, and came back armed with a large cavalry saber."

"Stand in the doorway. I'll go out into the yard…and when I begin the exorcism, strike out at the air in all directions, so that the evil spirits cannot get back into the house…for they fear a sparkling blade!"

Slowly, the parents led Bertine into the roofed part of the yard. A sow grunted in its sty; pigeons showed off their sleek plumage, sparrows danced on their slender, flexible stilts, infinitely light among the bobbing fowls in the chicken-run.

The monk stood up straight, with a vague sarcasm on the mastic of his cheeks; the stolid and solemn peasant raised the large saber and tightened his jaws, sunlight glinting nimbly from the bright metal; his wife stood rigidly, pallid at the touch of the supernatural.

Then the brother's voice rose up, roaring and furious, in the mysterious Latin that confounds rustics: "*Exi, anathema, non remaneas nec abscondaris in ulla compagine membrorum…*"

After two minutes of vast silence, all four turned toward the open country, the two women in hieratic terror, their entrails quivering. Clotare was sweating, as barbaric as a crazed mystic of the dark ages, while the monk, content and surly, patted the old 100-*sou* coins extracted from the niggardly peasant with a vague snigger. Eventually, though, Bertine timidly whispered: "Will I be cured?"

"Within the week," the friar answered. And he added, with a practiced expression that defied analysis: "If you have faith."

The week having elapsed, vast clouds filled the summer sky, while the rain advanced upon the gray midday on a turbulent west wind. Clotare came into the cottage, his face savage above a doublet the color of marl. Lying beside the table where a greasy soup was steaming, alongside starchy potatoes, Bertine was whimpering miserably.

"It's worse, then?"

"It's as if something were gnawing the bone!"

The wind blew harder; the windows rattled and sheets of rain fell upon the plain. The peasant ate furiously, crushing the large potatoes with his teeth and swallowing large morsels; then he went to stand in the doorway, his eyes resentful and his mouth ferocious. The poultry in the coop clustered together in a bristling huddle, clucking softly. Silver lightning-streaks pierced the celestial cameo, the tall poplars bowing before the squalls; a beautiful peaceful rumor emerged from the crop-fields.

Clotare stared at the cottage of his neighbors—the Lastres—closed up like a cube of chalk, with red flowers in the thatch of the roof, and ducks in the garden pond, puffing out their throats of blue silk and green satin. Increasingly somber, his cheeks pale in the penumbra of his peaked-cap, Clotare raised his fist. "Witch!"

Then a clear patch appeared, cutting through the enormous clouds. A charming brightness filtered over the surface of the crops and the vacillating trees. At that moment the Lastres' door opened and a man came out, short and stout, and set off along a muddy pathway.

"He's an innocent," Clotare said to his companions. "He knows nothing about anything!" He interrupted himself with a deep breath of rage, his eyes as bloodshot as a chained dog. A woman had just emerged on to the Lastres' doorstep, her hair darker than bitumen, her eyes splendidly Iberian, lost in a herbivorous reverie. Calmly, she observed the hydrated grace of the view, the palingenesis of forms, the slow nebulous flock wandering over the occidental slopes, the fresh lazulites mounted above the silvers and sodas, the wandering barites,

18

the miry pathways, the water running down the folds in the hillsides. In the distance, her husband was marching through the clover; ewes and lambs were emerging from a farm; the pyramidal steeple of the church jutted out in front of an elm-grove.

"Great Lord above!" growled Clotare. "To think that she's brought misfortune to the whole region!"

Abruptly, the woman turned round, and the peasant met the gaze of her large eyes. Frightened, he went pale, his heavy hands trembling, furiously dreaming of a black revenge.

She bowed—as did he.

"How is your daughter?" she shouted.

"No better." Inaudibly, he added: "You know that better than I do, filthy beast!"

The woman in the short skirt, gentle and still desirable, seemed to the peasant to be a creature of the inferno and malevolence, full of equivocal science and subterranean power. She went back into her house, while the rustic lingered, thoughtfully. In that hard skull, the fetishistic history moved through prolix twists and turns, and identical phenomena; he remembered the arrival of the Lastres in the region, already two years ago, at the end of winter. He had mistrusted them from the start. The woman with the large eyes, who liked to linger in the pathways looking at the plants and the livestock, reeked of the inferno. From then on, misfortunes had fallen like hail. First the sheep: at Belloty's, Grimpart's and Lebrun's, entire flocks had died of anthrax. Then the horses had their turn, either by farcy or glanders; then came the horned beasts; then the pigs—Clotare had lost pigs himself to the diarrhea. Everywhere the vermin paused, she was sure to take her toll! Until now, however she had been afraid to attack human beings—but the stupidity of the mayor and the weakness of the curé had given her the courage, and now Jacques Bonnard had broken his leg and Michel Cacheux had died suddenly in a state of mortal sin, from having been stared at and cursed by her!

"It has to end!" the peasant growled. "Just because the curé and the mayor are stupid, that's no reason to endure witches!"

His temples were running with sweat; a formidable resolution was growing within him by the second. He saw his daughter prey to sinister powers, condemned to death—and soon, perhaps, himself!

Bands of sunlight descended, imperfectly eroded by the interposition of clouds; a weak rainbow fringed the horizon; a flock of geese was grazing on a hillside. The peasant's plan ripened.

Then he went back into his house, and for ten minutes, the thin woman with the pigeon's eyes and the haggard Bertine listened to his confidences. He growled and thumped his fists on the table; then a black mystery stiffened him, causing him to whisper—and the two females, fearful at first, but now imbued with his exacerbation, encouraged him, mingling hyperbole with his statements.

"I'm going to do it!" he said, finally.

Clotare went to knock on Lastre's wife's door. She opened it, surprised to see him there.

With a broad and false smile, he bowed. "It's for my daughter," he said. "She isn't well at all. Perhaps you could come to see her for a minute?"

Benevolently returning the rustic's smile, she replied in a soft contralto voice: "Certainly...I'll come right away."

"Thank you," he mumbled. And he preceded her, in vague triumph, in order to warn his female companions. Two minutes later, Lastre's wife arrived on Clotare's doorstep. She stopped there, apprehensively.

"Come in!" cried Clotare. "Come in, neighbor."

She went in, and saw the two women sitting at the back of the room, with equivocal expressions. As she hesitated, with the fearful watchfulness of a nervous creature, Clotare slipped behind her and coolly closed the door, turning the key in the lock. Then, transmuted, his face full of hatred, he took the woman by the arm and looked at her angrily.

"Jésus Maria! What's the matter?" she asked, gentle and inoffensive under the man's pressure.

"This has gone on long enough!" howled Clotare. "You've killed my pigs and Bernardin's and Gross Epaule's cows. You've cast spells on the entire district! But that wasn't enough! You had to attack normal human beings. That's why I want you to lift the curse on Bertine!"

The woman, without quite understanding, looked at the phantasmagorical family of fair-haired individuals, and her eyes grew wide in fear of the extended trap, while she slowly brought her hands together. With her clear profile, her southern grace, of a race other than theirs, she made them tremble even more, being in their eyes a true witch, too dark in her beauty, with excessively black hair.

Clotare shivered, and said, feverishly: "Did you hear me, witch?"

"I don't know what you mean," she replied, softly.

"I'm telling you, in the name of God, to lift the curse!"

"What curse?"

Pale with indignation, the formidable peasant shoved the woman against the wall. "What curse! Evil witch! You won't get out of here until you've lifted it, I tell you!"

A frigid, taciturn terror that combined the produce of dreams, the theater and folktales, stunned the woman—but there was incredulity beneath it all, the vague hope that it would all come out right with no harm done. Clotare shook her more roughly, though, waking her up, and she made the effort to say: "Have pity on me, M'sieu Clotare! I'm entirely innocent…I honestly don't know anything. M'sieu Clotare, I wish with all my heart that your Bertine will get better!"

Bertine, turning toward Lastre's wife with an expression of supplication, said: "See how I'm suffering. Why have you put a spell on me? What have I done to you?" Her hands were pressed together; humility tautened her excessively long cheeks and minuscule forehead. Her mother was weeping grimly, without a sigh.

"Yes," cried Clotare, "you're the cause of all our ills—will you persist in your malice?"

A superstitious electricity, the subtle influence of those tenebrous brains on her own, increasingly stifling, brutalized the prisoner, keeping her slumped cataleptically against the wall. Instinctively, like the innocents cast into the depths of jails, she ended up believing in some criminality, some ignominy of nature, some sort of original sin that merited her ordeal.

Exasperated by her silence, with a residue of anxiety—a profound fear of some necromantic trick—he cried: "Say something, then, witch!"

"I haven't done anything," she said.

"Ah! Liar!" howled Clotare—and he spat in her eye.

Then she felt an immense abandonment, a black sensation of the inevitable, a despair of ever mollifying that somber, pig-headed individual. Mechanically, with heavy tears gushing from her eyelids, she wiped away the rustic's spittle.

Indignant, feeling ferocious virtuosities blossoming within his inner depths, the peasant strode around the room, cursing abominably. The witch's perfidy seemed monstrous to him, worthy of any torture, and also absurd and idiotic, since, in the end, she would lose everything by refusing.

"You see! You see!" he said, finally, to his wife and daughter. "She refuses to repair her dirty tricks. She refuses."

Little by little, the peasant woman, initially less hard, grew exited, becoming as implacable as him, seeing, as he did, nothing but the unjust cruelty and vicious obstinacy of Lastre's wife. A brief, tragic silence fell.

"Light the fire in the next room!" the peasant finally shouted at his wife.

The mother slowly gathered faggots, and carried them to the fireplace in the other room—an old fireplace that had not been used for several years. Thick smoke spread through the house. Open-mouthed and motionless, Lastre's wife looked straight ahead, as miserable and as docile as a vanquished roe deer.

"This is the last time!" roared the peasant. "Will you lift the curse?"

"I haven't done anything," the prisoner replied.

"Ah! Lord above! Lord above! Is it necessary, after all, to submit to bodily outrage—when you have only to say a word!"

He strode back and forth, making abrupt gestures, his jaws clenched—and suddenly, he lashed out with his hand, slapping Lastre's wife three times.

"Take that! And that! And that! You'll lift it! I'll make you!"

She collapsed to the floor, sobbing dully, not daring to groan—and the peasant handed a cudgel to his daughter, howling: "Hit her! There she is! The cause of all our misfortunes! Hit her! Get on with it!"

Then, infected by the paternal frenzy, the pale girl lifted the stick and brought it down on the back of the stricken woman, heavily, urged on by her father's bellowing.

"Go on—more! Draw the good will out of her body!"

To a blow more terrible than the rest, the miserable prisoner leapt to her feet and screamed desperately: "Help! Help!"

Clotare immediately took her by the throat, cutting off her lamentation. Blue and voiceless, she let herself fall to her knees.

"You give in, then?" demanded the peasant, letting go.

"Alas!" she said. "Have pity on my misery. As true as there is a God, M'sieu Clotare, I know nothing of any curse…I've never done anyone any harm."

"Right!" said Clotare—and he stood there meditatively, in the middle of the room, calm and sinister. Then, slowly—almost gently—he said: "That's it—you refuse?"

"I'm not refusing anything. I'll do anything you want!"

"Lift the curse?"

"I can't."

"Woman," said Clotare to the mother, "have you followed my orders?"

"Yes," she replied, firmly, having forsaken all pity in confrontation with the witch's obstinacy.

"Give me the rope! The dog's chain!"

When he had the rope and the chain, without saying a word, he put Lastre's wife's wrists behind her back and tied them together. Then, crouching down, he carefully fixed the chain around her ankles, solidly. Anesthetized, deprived of her will, she did not resist, allowing herself to be bound with a frightful docility.

"A rag!" the peasant commanded.

As the gag was placed over her mouth, however, the prisoner shivered, in a violent nervous shock, a mad panic. Then he threw her on the table and, with his wife's aid, finished gagging her. When that was done, he sighed. A confused, opaque pity stirred within the ferocity of his being. He was pale—trembling, even. With his brows furrowed and his eyes lowered, he buried himself in thought for two minutes, turning over vague quibbles and primitive casuistries. Then, with another profound and prolonged sigh, his face cleared. His conscience was with him!

"Woman," he said, with a singular forbearance toward his captive, "I have nothing against you...I will forget everything if you can cure my daughter...you have only to nod your head and I will free you."

She did not move, but her eyes had an expression so soft and so innocent that he was moved, at first—and then irritated, thinking that it might be a curse.

"Don't look at me!" he said. "And since you won't...it's you who've signed your own death-warrant. Come on!"

His firm and powerful hand descended upon her and dragged her into the next room, while the mother helped Bertine to follow. In the old abandoned hearth, the pile of logs and twigs was now blazing away, full of charming bright spots and shadowy recesses.

All four of them looked at one another, with dilated pupils. A monstrousness penetrated the ambience, the magnetism of dramas of taciturn ferocity. Then, methodically, without haste, the peasant dragged his prisoner forward and threw her to the ground. He took off her clogs and tore off her stockings. Only then did she understand, in an agony of horror, and try to struggle, to roll away from the fire.

With the cold patience of a dutiful man, Clotare attached the chain that bound Lastre's wife's ankles to the old pot-hook fixed in the fireplace, and solemnly murmured: "The poor man is his own justice!"

His wife and daughter contemplated the atrocious work, hypnotized and inexorable, with the tragic conviction of a fatality, the accomplishment of a supreme justice. With these preliminaries complete, he resembled a stony Semitic simulacrum, a figuration of vengeance and impassivity.

As in the eras of torture, the condemned woman writhed in a vermicular manner, more miserable than the torture-victims of yore beneath the gag that muffled her sobs. First the soles of her feet and lower parts of her legs turned red, then all the veins swelled in frightful progression, and the somber witnesses were still unmoving. Then an odor of roasting flesh rose up, faint as yet, and the unfortunate woman's trepidations became wilder.

Clotare drew nearer. The captive's gaze was fixed upon him, and a stifled sentence rose up beneath the gag, so forcefully that he leaned over to detach the chain from the pothook, drew the woman away from the hearth and said: "Will you lift the curse?"

She signaled with her eyes and eyebrows; he was able to understand that she acquiesced, that she wanted to speak, and he untied the gag.

Then she murmured: "I will lift the curse!"

"Ah!" Clotare whispered, full of triumphant pride.

She hesitated momentarily, blinded, pulled in different directions by multiple impressions, confused hopes, terrible apprehensions and a terrible pain in her legs and feet. Then, realizing that it was necessary to speak, she stammered a few words rapidly, at hazard, punctuated by baroque syllables, and—having discovered the ruse—said: "Tomorrow morning, your Bertine will be cured!"

But Clotare would not let her get away with that. "Tomorrow!" he howled. "She who has cast the spell can take it back today as easily as tomorrow."

"I can't! I can't!" she said, in distress. "It takes time, Monsieur Clotare!"

"Right away, you hear, witch! Right away, or you go back to the fire!"

In the acuity of her terror, she found a second ruse. "I need something blessed…"

"What?" cried Clotare. "Ah! I have the blessed medallion of Notre-Dame-de-Malvreuse…"

He left the room and went rapidly upstairs. Immediately, in a supreme supplication, the poor woman dragged herself over to Bertine, and murmured humbly: "Please, my dear Demoiselle, have pity on me. As true as the Gospel, I am innocent of your pain…"

Trembling, Bertine replied: "Take away my sickness first!"

"But I'm innocent!"

"Take away my sickness!" And with an animal, invincible obstinacy, she held to that response until Clotare returned. He brought the medallion, a poor little oblong coin in silvered copper, which he showed to Lastre's wife.

"Now free her."

She looked at the pitiful relic with an infinitesimal belief that some power might emanate from it, to conclude the lugubrious portent of the cross, and she had a further inspiration. "I need free hands!"

Full of suspicion, he hesitated. He admitted, however, that the request seemed reasonable, and granted it. When her hands were free, she took the little relic gently, looked at it again, hesitated, muttered a few syllables, and then said: "You're sure that it's been blessed?"

"I had it blessed with others!"

"Ah!" she said. And suddenly, before the staring eyes of her enemies, after a further stammering attempt to mime witchcraft, she let herself go again with a gesture of infinite sadness and a faint lamentation. "I can't!"

"You can't! You can't!" roared Clotare. "That's how you mock me! Ah! Devil's witch, this time you'll pay!" He had already taken hold of her, gripping her in his formidable claws.

"Ah!" she complained. "Monsieur Clotare, Madame Clotare, Mademoiselle...the good Lord cannot want this!" But when she saw the rope inexorably taken up again, in order to bind her, she emerged abruptly from her herbivorous docility, and uttered long, loud, furious howls, which spread forth outside, into the village. Prostrate, she struggled frantically against her executioner, kicking and striking out with her feeble hands, so urgently that the somber battle remained indecisive for several minutes, and Clotare's wife had to come to her husband's aid. Then, vanquished and gagged once more, the captive found herself lying on the ground again, in front of the hearth.

The peasant had lost his magisterial tranquility; he was full of tenebrous rage, athirst for vengeance; all his barbaric virtuosity and native cruelty surged forth from the depths of his being. When, with a violent shove, he had pushed the martyr closer to the fire, he grabbed her by her hair and held her face next to the flames, with an immense desire to hurl her into them, to roast the sorceress alive.

Something retained him—the awakening of one last scruple, the terror of the definitive—and yet, he repeated to himself that the burning of witches is meritorious work.

Gradually, the temptation became irresistible; a harsh palpitation tormented Clotare's bosom, further enraged by the victim's resistance and her dolorous contortions. He gripped her long hair even harder, with both fists, and hoisted up her head, dragging it almost directly over the fire, quivering, succumbing second by second to the vision of holocaust, the vertigo of murder.

Suddenly, Clotare's wife got up, anxiously, and whispered: "Someone's coming!"

"Go and see!" he growled.

A fist hammered on the door to the yard. Clotare released his victim, and the peasants looked at one another, shivering. At the same time, a sonorous voice was raised: "Open in the name of the law!"

In the captive's burned face, the swollen eyes opened, full of an ardent, humble, frightful hope. Clotare and his wife, in dire distress, were rooted to the spot, their teeth chattering. Less conscience-stricken, shrinking back into her invalid's pose, their daughter said, coldly: "Go hide the witch in the grain-loft, Father...under the hay."

"She's right!" the rustic exclaimed. "You, wife, talk to them and keep them busy."

"Kill her," the woman said. "It's too late to spare her." Then, raising her voice and going to the door, she said: "Jesus! What's all this racket?"

"It's me, the mayor...and the garde-champêtre. Open the door immediately, or I'll break it down!"

"Don't do that, M'sieu le Maire—you'll ruin a poor family! I'll open up gladly...I've no reason not to open up!"

She started fiddling with the lock, whining: "Have a little patience...it's you who've confused me..."

An enormous blow cut her off—the impact of a beam—and the lock burst. The door was flung wide open, just as Clotare was climbing the stairs with Lastre's wife over his shoulder.

"Arrest him!" the mayor proclaimed.

Clotare continued upwards, shouting: "She's a witch!"

The mayor rushed into the house, followed by the garde-champêtre and several peasants—but Clotare was already in the grain-loft. The trapdoor slammed shut, and they heard heavy objects being thrown about overhead, pell-mell. Then there was a violent trepidation, and a confused struggle, while the newcomers pushed desperately, trying to lift up the horizontal door. It gave way intermittently, but fell back. Someone brought a small beam, and someone else brought joists; the assault became more fervent, and seemed about to succeed, when Clotare's voice was raised, resoundingly.

"It's finished! She's been punished!"

Removing the obstacles himself and raising the trapdoor, he poked his head out, his face livid, lit up by his wild fluorescent eyes.

"I've avenged the village! Take me!"

Beside the trapdoor, blackened, her tongue sticking out between her teeth, Lastre's wife was lying, strangled—and when he leaned over to examine her, it seemed to the mayor that the image of the murderer was outlined behind her dead pupils.

Epilogue

It was in November, in the main square of Malvreuse, that Clotare was guillotined, at the moment when the opals of the dawn were dying over the town. A large number of people had come, especially the people of the district, a few of whom commiserated with the condemned man. The peasant, less pale than the executioner, was exceedingly resigned, his gaze soft, attentive to the priest's words. Before the slender silhouette of the guillotine, however, he faltered, releasing a deep sigh of distress and regret for the sweetness of life, while the almoner tenderly pronounced the name of the redeemer.

At the supreme moment, however, as the murmur of the crowd faded away into a silence of horripilation, the peasant recovered his strength, kissed the priest's cheeks, and murmured: "My death is unjust. The burning of witches is a good work!"

Then he let himself go—tranquil, his lips closed, with a great confidence in the justice of Christ, and with the hope of eternal life. And the executioner did his job.

THE YOUNG VAMPIRE

I.

"There is some truth in all persistent beliefs," said Jacques Le Marquand. "I mean beliefs that relate to precise and oft-repeated facts."

"Such as witchcraft…"

"As a whole, I deny that, because it includes too many imprecise facts, and also because it varies immoderately—but modern science uses many practices similar to those of sorcerers and witches; consequently, it's ridiculous to deny that witchcraft rests, at least partially, on an experimental basis. I don't insist on that, because I've only studied the matter superficially—but what would you say if I were to affirm the existence of a phenomenon akin to vampirism?"

"Science doesn't deny it!" exclaimed Charmel, mischievously. "It merely transposes it from human beings to a species of bat…"

Jacques Le Marquand shrugged his shoulders and continued: "I knew a vampire once…in the district of Islington, in London, between 1902 and 1905—and I learned recently that she is still alive. What's more, she's married; she even has four children."

"Who will be little vampires!" Charmel interjected, gravely.

"Vampirism doesn't seem to be hereditary," Le Marquand riposted, with even more gravity.

The young person of whom I speak was the third daughter of Mr. and Mrs. Grovedale, and she was distinguished from her sisters because she was much prettier. At the time that I knew her, she was even fantastically pretty. What I mean by

31

that is that she combined her beauty with something extraordinary—I should say supernatural. To begin with, her face was exactly as white as that sheet of paper—which ought to have rendered her a trifle alarming, but, for one reason or another, didn't make her alarming at all. On the contrary, she was, as our neighbors say, *fascinating*. Evidently, her eyes, hair and mouth compensated for the excessive pallor of her skin. I don't know which was most tempting: the bush of flames that grew from her skull; her pathetic eyes, immense and avid; or her lips, as red as a *Canna* flower.

She hadn't been as pale as that for long—a little more than five years. Her mother explained that she had died— *literally* died. Two doctors had certified her death. In accordance with English custom, the cadaver was preserved for some time. On the third day, it began to decompose—which didn't prevent the fact that on the morning of the fourth day, Evelyn Grovedale revived. She presented particularities that were interesting to scientists and disquieting for those around her. Her memory was greatly disordered; she only spoke at infrequent intervals and in an incoherent manner; she showed no affection for her family. Although her intelligence was co-ordinated, one might have thought that Evelyn was two people. With respect to the present and events that followed her death she spoke in the first person; with respect to earlier events, she made reference to an indecisive personality. Furthermore, her memory only seemed to serve to guide her through life, not for any return to her past self. When she decided to grant caresses to her relatives, she did so ardently, but in a bizarre fashion.

With time, she reverted almost to normality. After some hesitation, rebellion and fear, she seemed to *accept* the story of her past, as one accepts rules of conduct or as one adopts a belief.

This is the moment to mention an abnormal phenomenon that occurred shortly after her resurrection. Father and Mother Grovedale, the two daughters and the little boy, who all had florid complexions, became paler, and languished to various

32

degrees. Her father was the worst afflicted. Her mother simply seemed tired, as did her older sister, Harriet. As for the younger daughter, Aurora, she seemed to be afflicted with chlorosis, and little Jack seemed incapable of following his lessons at school or doing his chores in the house; he was always drowsy and slept 19 hours out of 24.

The Grovedales, being unimaginative folk, made few conjectures; the family doctor manifested some surprise, but limited himself to giving various names to the epidemic of pallor and administering an assortment of pills and potions.

In the spring, all the symptoms eased. The mother and Harriet became almost vigorous again; Aurora recovered her strength; and young Jack, without succeeding in studying, slept no more than 15 hours out of 24. This coincided with the persistent presence of one James Bluewinkle, a young man built like a wrestler, who conceived an inordinate passion for Evelyn. The Bluewinkles and the Grovedales yielded promptly to the solicitations of the lovers; they were married before the end of April. They took a "trip" to the continent and came back to take up residence in London.

Following Evelyn's departure, the amelioration observed among the Grovedales was rapidly augmented. Everyone, in fact, recovered—even the child, whose ration of sleep declined to ten hours. On the other hand, James Bluewinkle acquired a "pale complexion." Endowed with the stomach of a lion, he consumed pounds of rump steak, leg of lamb, chicken or goose every day, but his vitality weakened. A succession of physicians failed to discover any cause. In the end, a homeopath had a vague intuition and prescribed a rest cure in isolation in a sanitarium in Ipswich.

The effects of this cure proved prodigious. James Bluewinkle recovered his strength. By way of compensation, Evelyn sickened and became anemic. After a few days, she sought refuge with her family—with her grandmother, since Harriet and her mother felt "uncomfortable." Aurora and the boy began to go pale again.

In their innocence, they continued not to understand it at all. They scarcely felt the slight astonishment that one feels when confronted with insignificant coincidences when, on James Bluewinkle's return, their illness vanished as if by enchantment.

You might expect that the husband would now fall back into languor, and you would not be mistaken. A month after his return from the sanitarium, he had become weak and pale again. Less candid than the Grovedales, he conceived anxieties—almost suspicions—and began to study his wife.

She led a methodical life. Her tastes were simple. She spent little; she dressed elegantly but without ostentation; she ate sparingly. On the other hand, James fulfilled his various conjugal duties fervently, but without any of those exaggerations that can sap a man's energy—especially a strong man. Nevertheless, it seemed that after Evelyn's kisses—and I mean simple kisses—he was gripped by a kind of torpor. Then, without his quite knowing how, an idea occurred to him that might well have been an *instinctive memory*.

One evening, without his wife's knowledge, he drank two cups of exceedingly strong coffee, in order to resist the lethargic somnolence that overtook him every night, and pretended to go to sleep, as usual. For a long time, nothing abnormal occurred. 11 p.m., midnight and 1 a.m. chimed successively.

Finally, Evelyn's respiration, regular until then, accelerated. At first, the young woman remained motionless; then she sat up very slowly. Bluewinkle sensed that she leaned over him. Two warm and silky lips made contact with his neck. It was a strange sensation, voluptuous and disturbing at the same time. The lips aspired something, with infinite gentleness. Gradually, he felt himself growing weaker. An irresistible numbness overwhelmed his consciousness. He knew that if he waited another minute, he would fall into a leaden sleep, in spite of the stimulus of the coffee. With a limp gesture, he pushed Evelyn's head away, and his throat taut with anguish, exclaimed: "Vile creature!"

A sob burst forth in the darkness, and when he switched on the electric lamp he saw Evelyn, prostrate on the bed, trembling in every limb.

"Vile creature!" he repeated. "What have I done to you, that you should kill me?"

Their eyes met. The young woman's pupils were quivering; her entire face expressed a mysterious terror. As if in a dream, she replied: "I can't do otherwise…I'd *die*!"

Suddenly, Bluewinkle had an inspiration—one of those inspirations that come from the utmost depths of being and are born of extraordinary contacts. He became certain that Evelyn Grovedale was a vampire.

We sat in silence for a minute, under the spell of a mystical *aura*. Then Charmel slowly shrugged his shoulders.

"What does that certainty prove?" he asked.

"I'll tell you tomorrow," Jacques Le Marquand replied, after consulting his watch.

II.

The next day, Jacques Le Marquand continued his story in these terms.

The sentiment that initially overcame Bluewinkle was one of horror and dread. Soon, though, Evelyn's tears moved him, for he had a tender heart and she seemed charming in the luminous disorder of her hair.

"It's an aberration!" he said. "You wouldn't die at all!"

"I'd die," she repeated, in a profound tone.

He sensed that she was perfectly sincere, and became thoughtful again. His conviction remained firm: Evelyn really was a vampire, but in a manner somewhat different from that related by tradition. James, who was something of a philosopher, knew that traditions embody elements of symbolism and

35

legend. In this instance, it was not necessary to believe in vampires emerging from their tombs; that was the contribution of the spirit of the macabre and popular puerility. One could believe, on the other hand, in some organic oddity, followed by apparent death—which was strictly applicable to Evelyn's case. Not only had she been taken for dead, but her metamorphosis revealed itself by an excessive pallor and by the disturbance of her mind.

"The proof that you wouldn't die," he resumed, "is that you've spent the greater part of your existence quite innocently."

"My existence!" she murmured, in a grim tone. "Was it really *my* existence?"

That question did not entirely surprise Bluewinkle; he knew that the young woman's memory exhibited singular features. Nevertheless, his attention was more excited than usual: Evelyn had never been as precise.

"What do you mean?" he asked. "Do you suppose that the Evelyn Grovedale of old and the present one are not the same person?"

She did not answer immediately. Her lips were trembling. She looked up at James with a gaze full of supplication and suspicion. Finally, as if carried away by an irresistible impulse, she whispered: "They are two different people!"

Her tone frightened the young man. He paused momentarily, as if bewildered, then said, hoarsely: "Then what? The old Evelyn Grovedale would be *really dead*…and the one that I have before me…where did she come from? It's the same body, though!"

"Yes, the same body…but *only* the same body."

"Try to explain yourself clearly!" he exclaimed, with a convulsive agitation. "The same body…and another soul?"

"Another *being*."

"The terminology isn't important. There would be a stranger living in the body of Evelyn Grovedale…a stranger incarnate therein."

"I don't know."

"How can you not know? Since you're sure of not being Evelyn, you must be the being incarnate in her body."

She shook her head, meditative and melancholy. "I can't answer you. I don't have the words to say what I'd need to say. I only know that the memories I find in this body—the memories of *before my arrival*—aren't mine. Yes, I know that..."

"How? Do you have other memories that contradict Evelyn's?"

"I have other memories."

"Of what?"

"I tell you that I don't have the words to explain them...and this brain has no images to enable me to recall my own past. They're memories of another world! They're there, apart...oh, how I sense them!—but I can't reach them."

"At any rate," said Bluewinkle, in despair, "you have a memory of the moment when you *invaded* Evelyn's body."

"I don't have any!"

James got up, and, having regained some strength with the aid of a cordial, sat down by the young woman's beside, successively enfevered by certainty and reassured by doubt. As is only natural, he sometimes wondered whether Evelyn might be mad—but if madness could explain her words and actions, it could not begin to explain the very real effect manifest upon himself.

"Explain to me," he said, fervently, "how you lived, after your death, until the moment when you met me."

"I lived on them!" she confessed. "And during your absence, as well."

With a long shudder, he remembered little Jack's pallor, and that of young Aurora.

"Then, if I hadn't come along, you would have killed those poor children!"

"No," she said, swiftly. "When one of them became too exhausted, I switched to the other. I'm not wicked...I'm unfortunate...I struggle against myself...I know that I'm doing wrong…but I also know that I'm in constant danger of death, and the temptation becomes irresistible…"

She spoke with a humble and coaxing grace, which touched Bluewinkle profoundly. He studied those eyes in which such a passionate flame burned, and said to himself: *That's not a wicked creature!* Then, seized by an ardent and somber curiosity, he said: "But what is it that you take from us?"

She looked away, hiding her face in the pillow; nevertheless, he heard her sway: "Your blood!"

He had half-expected that reply. In consequence, he was only slightly shocked, and he went to examine the place where Evelyn had set her lips in a mirror; he saw nothing but a faint—very faint—pink patch. "That's impossible!" he declared. "Blood doesn't filter through the skin like that…"

"Do you think so?" she said.

He postponed the problem until later and retorted: "Then again, you hardly eat anything. If you ate, you could give up this horrible thing."

"I can't eat much. Beyond a certain quantity, *your* nourishment poisons me."

"How did you come by the idea of absorbing blood?"

"It seems that I've always had it. I only have to place my lips on the skin. Straight away…"

She concluded with a gesture, and sighed. He no longer knew what to believe. Ideas were whirling in his head like dead leaves in a forest. As he had interrogated Evelyn, he had become accustomed to the fantastic, and no longer had a precise view of the limits that separated it from quotidian reality. There was also the darkness, the cordial, that strange and dazzling creature…he was living in a dream.

"You know that you're doing wrong. Are you repentant?"

"I have great regrets."

"So you love Evelyn's parents, sisters and brother?"

"I didn't love them at first…affection came afterwards."

"And me?"

38

"Oh! You...very much!"

He felt moved. Evelyn's seductiveness reappeared in its entirety.

"Do you consider me to be a member of your species?"

"Yes," she said, passionately. "*Wherever I come from*, I belong to *humankind*. I know that I'm a stranger in this world, but I also know that I'm a woman—and I love my new life...especially because I live with you..."

In the state of excitement in which Bluewinkle now found himself, which was comparable both to the intoxication of alcohol and that of opium, there was almost no room for astonishment. The Beyond seemed to him to be very simple, the supernatural intricately confused with the natural.

"You don't miss your other life?" he asked.

She shivered from head to toe; then, in a striking tone, she said: "I'm afraid of my other life! I sense that I underwent an adventure so terrifying *there*...that my soul was *obliged to depart*. It's inexpressible, and frightful. And what does it matter, since I love you?"

She had pronounced the last words in a voice so pure, tender and human, she was so beautiful, and her beauty so intoxicating, that James could no longer see anything but an adored wife. He seized Evelyn's head; their lips sought one another in an avid kiss.

At first it was delirious; everything was erased by an immense love...then, the strange weakness that Bluewinkle knew only too well took possession of his flesh and his mind; he felt faint. He only just had time to extract himself from the embrace.

Then he saw, distinctly, a moist redness overflowing the gap between Evelyn's lips, and red trickles on her silvery teeth.

"Blood!" he cried. "*My blood!*"

Evelyn uttered a long moan.

III.

When James woke up the next morning on the divan in the "parlor," where he had slept lethargically, it required some time before he was able to separate illusory and real ideas. Then he was gripped by a mystical dread and a bitter disgust. Pity mingled therein when he saw Evelyn again.

She was no paler than usual—that was impossible—but in a few hours, she had grown manifestly thinner. Her eyes were sunken, full of an anxious fire, and her cheeks seemed hollow. She was agitated by a continual tremor, which sometimes extended to shivering. On seeing her thus, James forgot his fears. He could not believe that that tormented creature was of an essence other than his own. And the haunting quality of the supernatural tending to dissipate, he began once again to think that Evelyn must quite simply be ill—except that the illness from which she was suffering, unknown to conventional science, had been reported in an inexact manner by tradition.

Was it curable? Strictly speaking, it could be classed among the neuroses, since, after all, neuroses confer certain abilities that are not observable in balanced individuals, and since they also often involve unusual appetites.

James tried to put questions to the young woman as methodically as possible. She replied meekly, consistently and without contradiction. In fact, once the point of departure was admitted, she said nothing absurd. She limited herself to affirming once again the fact of her anterior existence and the impossibility of expressing that form of that existence in words, or of suggesting it with the aid of images dependant on her current body.

As she was growing weaker and more feverish by the hour, James decided to obtain the advice of a physician specializing in neurology. In fact, he was distantly acquainted with the Scottish Charcot, Percy Coleman, who listened to him with all the more interest because he assumed him to be afflicted by madness as soon as he had described the first nocturnal scene—and even more so when he had described the second.

Even so, Percy Coleman consented to examine Evelyn. The young woman's spectral pallor interested him immediately, and rendered him jovial—for he had a mania for abnormalities. She refused at first to tell him anything; then, in response to James's pleading, she seemed to abandon herself to destiny, and repeated without variation what she had previously revealed.

The illustrious neurologist listened, rubbing his hands enthusiastically. "No lacuna, no fissure," he remarked. "All in place, all in order. Let's look at the machinery..."

The machinery delighted him too. The reflexes were functioning marvelously. All the organs proved impeccable.

"Delicious!" the wise man murmured, licking his chops. "Now, let's pass on to the nub of the drama."

He had a great deal of difficulty persuading Evelyn to embrace James. In spite of the brevity of the kiss, the experiment was decisive and astounded the specialist.

"A leap into the unknown!" he said, in a semi-whisper. "A plunge into the gulf! Not even a prick, and the blood passed through—which flatly contradicts everything we know about tegumentary osmosis. This little phenomenon will stir the pond for the frogs!"

His joy, muted at first by surprise, swelled his face; he looked at Evelyn with a mixture of avidity and benevolence. "Madame has acquired all my devotion," he declared. "I shall spare no sacrifice to restore her to health—none! If she requires human blood, it shall be given to her cost free!" With a little laugh, he added: "We'll club together as necessary. We have no shortage here of young men—and even young women—devoted to science."

This visit seemed to calm Evelyn at first. She consented to take peptones and a stimulant prescribed by the physician, and her attitude was meek, obliging and resigned. James was also relieved. As he knew little about medicine he had a great faith in the mysterious power of therapeutics. He promptly abandoned any idea of the supernatural; his mysterious dreads became negligible. The evening that he spent with Evelyn was, at times, quite charming. He abandoned himself to hope, and his young love came through the storm stronger than before.

Gradually, the young woman's frissons resumed. She curled up in her armchair, staring straight ahead with a sad and almost haggard gaze. She was getting visibly weaker.

"What's the matter, darling?" James asked.

"I'm tired."

He went to her and gently put his arm around her waist. She let him do it; her long hair spread around the young man's neck. When he tried to kiss her, though, she withdrew her lips.

"Never again! Never again!"[4] she moaned.

He insisted, drawing her toward him with the generous strength of love, but she resisted—and when he succeeded in attaining her red mouth, no caress responded to his own. The struggle exhausted the young woman, though. She made one last attempt to get away; her eyes closed; she smiled weakly— and then her head fell backwards. She had fainted.

He tried in vain to reanimate her. Her pulse seemed inert; the beating of her heart was imperceptible; no breath was exhaled through the parted lips…

Then, in desperation, James sent for Percy Coleman.

The neurologist appeared at about midnight, accompanied by a gigantic adolescent with auburn hair and a complexion the color of York ham.

"Hulloo!" exclaimed the scientist, tapping his companion on the shoulder. "Here's a rude fellow for you—a glorious

---

[4] Rosny has "Never more!"—which might be a calculated echo of Edgar Poe, but I have assumed that it is simply an imperfect command of the English idiom. I have made similarly slight adjustments to one or two of the other phrases Rosny renders in English, but most of them are entirely satisfactory.

servant of science. He's not the sort to be parsimonious with a few armfuls of blood."

The fellow agreed with an infantile and colossal laugh.

"The young lady will need a healthy appetite to tire him out," added Coleman, to whom the evening port had communicated a generous gaiety.

He was taken to Evelyn's bedside, and understood at the first glance that the situation was serious. The stimulus of the port evaporated on the spot. He leaned over the young woman and sounded her chest with a stethoscope. As he did so his cheeks stiffened and a keen disappointment appeared in his sharp eyes.

"My God!" he muttered. "That would be a damnable loss to science and Percy Coleman."

"She isn't dead!" cried Bluewinkle, gripped by terror. "Tell me that she isn't dead!"

"No, she isn't dead," the practitioner replied, "but she's sunk into a diabolical lethargy—and we'll need a large slice of luck to get her out of it."

IV.

In spite of the ingenious care of Percy Coleman, Evelyn's lethargy persisted for several hours. Toward dawn, however, after a long application of induced electric current, a movement of her eyelids was perceived, soon followed by an almost-imperceptible heartbeat.

"She's *coming back*," the neurologist declared, mopping his brow—for he was sweating like a stoker. "Can we keep her, though?"

James had watched that interminable struggle against death, miserable and powerless. All sentiments other than love, pity, hope and despair had disappeared from his soul. He almost forgot the strange scenes enacted between himself and his poor wife. At the doctor's words, he started convulsively, and precipitated himself toward Evelyn.

"Stop!" said the doctor, peremptorily. "She hasn't as much strength as a newly-hatched pigeon. The slightest clumsiness could snuff her out—and you're in a state of frightful clumsiness."

In addition to the young giant, two interns had come; they carried out all of Coleman's instructions with celerity and precision.

"Enough current!" said the latter. "It's time to regulate her breathing."

The older of the interns inserted fine flexible tubes into the sick woman's nostrils, connected to a complex machine that the second intern started up by means of a lever. Percy regulated the speed by means of summary indications. After a few minutes, a regular palpitation of the chest was discernible; then Evelyn's eyelids opened slightly, and her eyes, as if impregnated with darkness, moved feebly from side to side.

"We've brought her back from abyssal depths!" whispered the neurologist. With a perplexed expression, he watched that abnormal body return to life.

While taking pride in his methods, particularly the artificial respirator, he felt that he was surrounded by a vast hazard. Every action was a risk—and Evelyn's awakening, far from facilitating the task, rendered it more awkward. He had no idea what to do. The young woman's weakness seemed excessive, and did not seem to be entirely natural. An intervention was indispensable—but what intervention?

Gradually, the shadow had quit her pupils. Evelyn could see again. First of all, she perceived the doctor leaning over her, then one of the interns—but these images seemed to leave her indifferent. As soon as she distinguished Bluewinkle, her lips trembled, and she was heard to whisper "Darling!"

"Bother the man!" muttered Coleman, in a low voice. "He's making her agitated…excessively agitated! We'll have to put him into a cell for 24 hours…what did I say!"

Evelyn's eyelids had closed again; a dolorous crease appeared between her eyebrows; then her breath seemed to slow down.

The neurologist continued soliloquizing. "Blood! It's blood that she needs! I'll bet 1000 pounds to a guinea." Addressing himself to the colossus, he said: "David, my lad, take off your waistcoat and roll up your sleeve."

The other obeyed, calmly and methodically—but then Percy was seized by doubt. Should he inject blood into the invalid? Or was it necessary for her to extract it directly from its source?

In itself, the injection seemed preferable, but in exceptional cases, Coleman observed the principle of rejecting logic and holding strictly to proven methods. Now, Evelyn had never absorbed blood indirectly…

He replaced the syringe that he had just taken up, examined young David's arm and applied Evelyn's lips to the place that he judged most favorable.

The effect was prodigious. The eyelids reopened instantly, and the pupils became animated; then her breathing accelerated. Scarcely a minute had gone by, and already one had the impression that energy was returning to the exhausted organism in waves.

Meanwhile, James Bluewinkle had moved surreptitiously to the bedside. At first, an ardent joy appeared on his face—but as he watched Evelyn's resurrection, another sentiment was born, which made his limbs shiver: the idea that his wife was drawing life from the veins of another man rapidly became unbearable. He leaned over; his jealous gaze encountered Evelyn's…

With a long sigh, she thrust the arm of the young colossus away and turned her face to the wall. As on the previous evening, James heard her murmur: "Never again! Never again!"

Attentive solely to the movements of his patient, Percy Coleman took no account of the psychology of the drama. He thought it a slight delirium, or simply a reactionary phase. "We'll start again in a little while!" he declared.

A sob replied to him; the young woman's shoulders shook convulsively; then she turned round abruptly and extended her arms to James. "Forgive me!" she said, in a faltering voice. "I didn't know what I was doing."

Exasperated, Coleman authorized the young man to draw nearer with a gesture. Evelyn embraced him desperately, stammering words that were tender and enigmatic by turns. Finally, she allowed herself to fall back, stammering: "I could have been so happy...why is it impossible? I can't do it any more...I have to go back. Oh, my darling, it's so terrible...so terrible!"

Her speech was becoming increasingly indistinct. It was in an exhalation that she breathed: "Farewell!"

"She's fallen back into the abyss!" exclaimed the neurologist, furiously. "That was well worth the trouble of five hours hard work..."

James had sunk to his knees beside the bed, like a guilty man—and a desperate one.

"Get out of the way!" cried the physician, rudely. "Perhaps there's something to be done other than weeping..."

The examination to which he devoted himself brought his exasperation to a head. Evelyn was in exactly the same state in which he had found her before midnight. At first, that state appeared to be stable, but Percy soon formed the impression that events were moving on. Life was decreasing with every passing second; after ten minutes, the most delicate observations ceased to reveal any sign of it.

"This time," he muttered, "there's only one more thing that we need, and that's a miracle...and what miracle, eh, David?"

He waited a little while longer, patiently renewed his investigations, then he took a very slender tube out of his medical bag, full of a transparent liquid and sealed at one end by a fine membrane, which he pierced with a needle.

"The last shot!" he said, peevishly.

He inserted the tube delicately into a nostril and waited. Gradually, the liquid took on an opaline tint.

"That confirms it!" the neurologist muttered. "She's on *the other side*...and it's a damned shame!"

James had collapsed, sobbing. Then he shoved Coleman away brutally. Leaning over, he stared at Evelyn steadfastly, in a dolorous stupor. Suddenly, he was seized by a tremor; his pupils dilated and he cried out, in a strange voice: "Look! Look! *Since she died, she has become less pale.*"

V.

Coleman, who was making ready to leave, with the indifference of the practitioner and the acrimony of the disappointed scientist, turned round, shrugging his shoulders—but as soon as he had looked at the cadaver, he had to yield to the evidence.

"Marvelous!" he muttered. "This woman is a mine of anomalies!"

In spite of the double lassitude of a sleepless night and continuous work, he spent another half-hour carrying out various experiments. They told him nothing.

"She's gone, irremediably!" he reaffirmed. "I'll come back later. For the moment, I have a brain as thick as suet pudding. I'll send a fresh intern, if you want."

"I don't want anything!" James Bluewinkle replied, churlishly. The presence of the neurologist and the others had become unbearable. If he had given in to his irritation he would have thrown them out.

"All right," said Coleman. "I'll send him all the same— at about 10 a.m. And you'll see me again before noon, of course. You mustn't only think of yourself, young man—you must think of science."

James was full of a boundless scorn for science and scientists. He sat down at Evelyn's bedside and did not give

47

another thought to Percy or his acolytes. At any rate, they did not take long to disappear.

For a good hour, Bluewinkle remained deeply immersed in grief and remorse. Beneath his muscular envelope, he concealed a sensitive soul, inclined to the malady of scrupulousness. Not only did he exaggerate immeasurably the small wrongs he had done Evelyn, but he added others to the list that were imaginary. In particular, he accused himself for not having been able to reassure the young woman, and even more for the furious impulse of jealousy that had taken possession of him while she had been drawing life from David's veins.

"I killed her!" he sobbed. "She was better than me."

Through the mirage of memory, everything that had seemed abominable to him now seemed touching. Poor creature! Gentle, fearful and tenderly submissive, she reproached herself for the grim fatality that condemned her, as if it were a crime. She would have liked so much to live like other people! What pity he ought to have had for her! And now…

"Forgive me, Evelyn!" he whispered. "It wasn't you, but me who didn't know what I was doing!"

He had lifted up her white hand; he placed a long kiss of grief and repentance on it. The little hand was cold, but singularly flexible. Moreover, no trace of rigidity showed in her face. Only her stillness was funereal. It also seemed to the watcher that Evelyn was even less pale than before. There was a kind of sketchy tint, a sort of *rosy dawn*, on her slender cheeks and temples. At no time had Evelyn ever seemed to him so charming, even in the dreamy hours when summer sunsets had attenuated the lividity of her face.

Gradually, an unfamiliar emotion mingled with James's disturbance. It was a slight oppression, the sensation of a breath, of a mysterious *aura*, and then an indescribable *envelopment*, the passage of some imponderable vortex.

"I'm not alone!" murmured Bluewinkle, suddenly. "Something redoubtable is happening here!" He had never had such a sentiment of the immense and profound life that envelops feeble creatures. Shivering, he was convinced that an extraordinary event had just occurred.

At first, his certainty remained in a "formless fog." James was like a man who hears the distant rumor of a multitude—it draws nearer; one knows that it signifies something; one perceives obscure words, plaints, threats, objurgations...

That was how James perceived the invisible drama.

Suddenly, it all became clear, and, covering his face with his hands, he stammered: "Evelyn is *no longer* dead!"

He shuddered like a tree in a storm.

His agitation lasted barely a minute. It was followed by a strange calm, which did not lack sweetness. James resumed contemplating Evelyn. She was still motionless, but the *rosy dawn* was accentuated. There was now a gleam in her cheeks comparable to that of snow on mountain peaks at the moment when the alpenglow[5] is about to disappear. There was no doubt in James's mind; he waited, with a hypnotic faith, for the young woman to wake up. Already he seemed to perceive a vibration of her lips—and he experienced no astonishment when the rhythm of her respiration elevated her rib-cage.

"Evelyn!" he called, in a muted voice.

She did not wake up immediately. She seemed to be sleeping profoundly and calmly. When he had called her several times, her eyebrows contracted; she ended up opening her eyes.

He was immediately struck by the expression in those eyes—a particularly innocent, even naïve expression. Besides, there was something in her entire face that James had never discerned in his wife's face.

"What's the matter?" he stammered.

---

[5] Rosny inserts a footnote here to explain that the alpenglow—*Alpenglühn* in the original—is the name given by the Swiss to a glimmer that sometimes reappears on the mountains after nightfall.

She looked around in alarm, without seeming to see Bluewinkle. Suddenly, though, a blush of modesty invaded her cheeks, and she exclaimed; "Where am I? Why am I here? My mother…"

That voice troubled James tenderly. He was gripped by a kind of shame. "Don't you recognize me?" he said, extremely softly. "I'm James—your husband…"

"My husband!" she protested. "I'm not married. Oh, sir…if you're a gentleman…fetch my parents…"

She spoke with a passionate vehemence and sincerity, partly concealing her face under the bedclothes. James genuinely felt like a stranger; the respect of his race for womanly modesty filled him with a sentiment of unbearable embarrassment.

"My darling," he said, "it's three months since we were married by the vicar of St. George's. Surely you haven't forgotten…"

She did not reply. Her forehead contracted; her gaze had become interior. Then she whispered: "That's strange! I recognize you, and yet I'm sure that we've never met…and yet…I see you…oh, what a dream! What a frightful dream!"

Nothing could surprise Bluewinkle any longer. He was literally adapted to the fantastic. As if he were asking the simplest thing in the world, he asked: "Are you the real Evelyn Grovedale?"

"Am I the real Evelyn?" she said, dazedly. "Who else would I be?"

"I don't know…I can't tell! I assume that you're Evelyn—but have you any memory of what has happened to you in the last six months?"

At first, the young woman's amazement seemed to increase; then her brow furrowed. A shudder of terror shook her entire body.

"Six months?" she murmured. "Has it been six months? I don't know…but I remember now…I've been away…far away…in a frightful place…"

VI.

These words bowled James over, and filled him with a frenetic curiosity. They were, so to speak, *the heart of the mystery*. Whether they expressed a reality or an illusion, they bound Evelyn's destiny and his own destiny together with a thrilling intensity.

"Forgive me," he said, in a voce that was both hoarse and soft, "if I'm tiring you or tormenting you—but it's my duty to question you. Your future and your happiness are at stake. Everything that you say to others and to me, even to your mother, will appear so strange and so incredible that your liberty will inevitably be threatened. No one will be ready to believe you. I alone am capable of hearing you indulgently, trustingly, with the most ardent desire to know the truth—so I implore you to suffer my presence for the necessary time, and to answer me without reticence. It's absolutely necessary!"

She listened to him, gravely and sadly, reassured by his tone and his gaze.

"I want to!" she said, with a slight shudder.

He reflected. His excitement was disciplined; he had recovered the self-control that Anglo-Saxons possess almost to the same degree as the Japanese, and combined the methodical mentality of his race with a mysticism amply justified by the circumstances.

"You say that you don't know me," he continued, coolly. *"Are you sure of that?"*

"Quite sure," she replied. She too was forcing herself to be calm; her tremulous lips betrayed her agitation.

"Consequently, you don't admit that we're married…you don't admit that we've spent nearly three months together…"

"I'm absolutely certain of the contrary."

He opened a cupboard and took out a wad of letters and a large piece of parchment. "Here are the letters you've written to me," he said. "Here is our marriage certificate."

She inspected the letters avidly, and then the certificate, trembling with emotion.

"I recognize my handwriting!" she said, in a stifled voice. "I even recognize the text of the letters—but it wasn't *me* who wrote them!"

"Your parents, your sisters, your brother, your friends—everyone, in sum—will confirm that you are my wife. Everyone will tell you that you have lived in this house since our marriage. Try to summon up your memories; try to look into your inmost depths…"

She uttered a sort of moan. "I swear to you that I have never been your wife."

"Consequently, you don't remember any of the events of our engagement or of our life together?"

"I remember perfectly the events of *your* engagement and your life with *someone else*," she replied, alternately going very red and very pale.

"And how can you remember that?"

"I don't know. It's within me, like a dream…like something in which I might have participated in a strange and mysterious fashion…or, rather, like something that might have been combined with me, by some kind of supernatural intervention."

Large droplets of sweat were covering James's forehead. "You can see that other person in your parents' house, then" he went on, "before the vicar of St. George's, and, finally, in this house? You also know that I've been ill and that *she* was the cause of it. You know that she fell ill in her turn, and that she was cared for by a doctor…you must know the doctor's name?"

"Doctor Percy Coleman," she breathed.

"My God!" he exclaimed, raising his hands toward the ceiling. "Is it possible that you have such exact memories of another person, and of a person that you have never seen? Doesn't it seem infinitely more natural to believe that the person in question is yourself?"

"More natural, perhaps…untrue, definitely!" she cried, in a tone of such certainty that James started—but he had resolved not to take any account of his impressions.

"Can you tell me the approximate date when the last terrestrial events that you remember occurred? I mean, your memories concerning the true Evelyn Grovedale."

She reflected for a few seconds, and replied: "I don't know whether it was the 27th or the 28th of March, exactly— but the 28th at the latest."

James went to fetch a *Daily Mail* that was lying on a table, and showed her the date. "October 2, 1903!" she exclaimed, in amazement.

"Consequently, for more than six months *you have had no consciousness of yourself.* Isn't that absurd?"

She was breathing hard. A glimmer of distress sparkled in her dilated eyes.

"I've been *out there* for six months, then…" she said, dejectedly.

"But think about it: your body was here…everyone will tell you so."

She remained bewildered. A fearful expression covered her charming face, and the furrow that was hollowed out between her eyebrows testified to her mental tension. "It's terrifying," she stammered. "But how can it be helped? I've been away for six months, then, and my body didn't go with me!"

"And your body was alive!"

She hid her face and uttered a sigh. "Poor creature that I am!"

"Come on," James murmured, with the utmost tenderness. "Can't you tell me *where* you've been?"

"Alas, no!" she sighed, trembling from head to toe. "I would search in vain for a way to tell you, or to give you the slightest idea. It resembles nothing that you know, nothing that my body knew. It's a frightful place, where I never ceased to suffer."

"Were there other beings there?"

"There were all sorts of beings."

"Including human beings?"

"Beings like me." A sort of glimmer passed over Evelyn's face. "Yes…like me…*as I was out there!* Beings that resembled human creatures, and yet were different. Oh, I sense now why my body remained here."

There was a pause. James felt that he ought not to prolong that poignant interrogation any longer. Given the invalid's state of weakness, that would have been cruel.

"You need to get your strength back," he said. "I'll call a doctor, and I'll also ask your parents to come. Nevertheless, I would still like—and, on my honor as a gentleman, purely for your own sake—to ask you for a favor. Since you know what has transpired between me and *the other*, you're not unaware of why I initially consulted Coleman—well, I'd like you to consent to apply your lips to my hand for two or three minutes, and to do you know what."

She hesitated, her cheeks invaded by a pink flux; then, touched by Bluewinkle's respectful attitude, she nodded her head.

"Nothing…absolutely nothing!" said James, when he took his hand away. And, examining the young woman's lips, he added, with a long shudder: "*It was a different creature!*"

VII.

A quarter of an hour after Bluewinkle's telephone call, Dr. Coleman arrived in a state of vehement agitation, which he did not take the trouble to hide. He brought the giant David and a plump girl with chubby cheeks, who displayed dimples whenever she smiled deep enough to bury banknotes in.

"By God and General Kitchener" he exclaimed, "you're not playing games with me? The young lady is really alive?"

"She's alive," James replied.

"David!" cried the neurologist. "This is enough to make all the occultists in the Empire sick with joy. But I shan't believe any of it until I've seen it." Addressing James, he added: "Is she weak?"

The young man made an evasive gesture.

"She must be weaker than a fly in November," Coleman affirmed. "I've brought provisions, as you see." He pointed to David, and the chubby girl. "A veritable little barrel of blood!" he muttered. "It seemed to me yesterday that our interesting invalid manifested a little repugnance at drinking from our friend David. Modesty, eh? She'd doubtless prefer a feminine liquid. By Jove! Annie won't miss a few glassfuls!"

"I don't think Evelyn has any need of that," said James, exercising constraint.

Percy darted a suspicious glance at him. "You haven't got in before them?" he exclaimed, in a reproachful tone.

"I would have done had it been necessary, but…"

"Good! Good!" sniggered Coleman. "We'll soon find out." He had been frowning, but as soon as he saw Evelyn, his face cleared. "Good day, my joyous phenomenon, my delicious anomaly!" he said. "Bless your heart!"

He drew nearer, with the air of an angler who fears seeing some extraordinary fish escape, and gently took hold of the young woman's wrist. "76!" he exclaimed, after a pause. "A pulse as regular and as healthy as my chronometer!"

Her heartbeat and breathing turned out to be no less regular. Percy observed as much with a mixture of satisfaction and anxiety. "Too bad! She's absolutely normal, this morning…and yet, her complexion…where has she stolen this color?" Gradually, his face became sullen. He scowled even more when he had finished his examination. "This is stupid! One would think she's just anyone…"

"At any rate," David remarked, "she seems devilishly weak."

This observation brought a hopeful smile back to Coleman's lips. "That's true," he said, rubbing his hands together. "It's high time to restore her strength." He leaned over amiably. "Would you prefer David or Annie?"

A vivid blush covered Evelyn's cheeks. "Neither of them!" she whispered.

"Neither of them?" said Coleman, irritatedly. "You're off your head. You need to get your strength back, I tell you. Annie, my bonny lass, lend us your arm…"

Annie produced a round arm, pink and plump.

"Fresh as a spring, and as healthy as Highland air!" said Percy, in an insinuating tone. "Ah, you'll get your strength back!"

But Evelyn turned away.

"She *can't*, any longer," James put in, having watched the scene without saying anything, in order to confirm his own conviction.

"What! She can't do it any longer!" exclaimed the neurologist, whose face had gone purple. "Are you making fun of Percy Coleman? I can't answer for her life if she persists in this absurd refusal!"

There was a pause. Coleman strode back and forth, his eyes gleaming. James waited, desirous of a conclusive solution, while David and Annie maintained the ruminant attitudes of two young dull-witted Anglo-Saxons.

After walking for a minute, Percy recovered his self-composure. "Madame," he said, with as much softness as he could put into a naturally harsh voice, "what I ask of you is indispensable. Before prescribing remedies and a dietary regime, I need to know where you're up to. You need to understand—and I'm sure that you'll obey!"

A small frisson shook Evelyn's shoulders. Then she turned round, with a slight air of resignation, beckoned to Annie and applied her lips to the pink arm.

"That's a good girl!" said Percy, tenderly.

When Annie withdrew her arm there was a reddish mark there, but neither the examination of that mark nor the examination of Evelyn's mouth revealed the slightest trace of blood. Coleman's disappointment was terrible. He looked alternately at James and Evelyn, as if he were looking at a pair of crooks or fraudsters. He ended up saying, in a choked voice: "There's *nothing left*, then? She's no more ill than David and no more abnormal than Annie? And for that I've broken promises to the Duchess of Mousehill and Lord Fathead? That's disgusting! It's disastrous. Goodbye!"

He hardly needed to slam the door.

Scarcely had he gone out than the maidservant came to announce Mrs. Grovedale. That excellent creature came in with an impetuosity that belied her voluminous build and threw her arms around Evelyn's neck, while James withdrew discreetly. It was only necessary to see Mrs. Grovedale for five minutes and hear her proffer a few sentences to understand the innocence of her soul. Evelyn returned her hug fervently and kissed her tenderly, but she quickly came to understand that it was impossible to confide in her.

"Darling!" cried Mrs. Grovedale, breathlessly. "Poor little thing! My little flower! My love! You aren't ill?"

"Just a little indisposed. And father?"

"Father's in Liverpool, my little turtle-dove—something to do with nickel. He won't be back for a week."

Words without number sprang forth from the old lady's lips—English words, duller, more insipid and more incoherent than the words of a Botocudo.[6] Evelyn listened to them as one listens to the chirping of a sparrow; they reminded her of the immense and delightful simplicity of childhood, but they confirmed her decision to keep her redoubtable secret to herself. Pensively, she let the maternal voice run on; she could respond at random, without any fear of being called to account. Evidently, James was right. Everyone to whom she confided her adventure would think her demented. One is always alone in the world, but, for having touched the Beyond, she was more alone than others! Bluewinkle alone was capable of understanding…and so little!

---

[6] An Amazonian tribesman.

She sighed, while Mrs. Grovedale made her drink a cup of beef tea[7] brought by the maidservant. Then she fell into a melancholy reverie. What should she do? What was destined to become of her? She was both a maid and a young wife at the same time. A part of her being incontestably belonged to Bluewinkle. The part in question conserved memories that made Evelyn shudder, and which she found revolting. Her marriage seemed to her to be a violence perpetrated on her person during a profound sleep—but, in spite of everything, James was not guilty of any crime! She wanted him to be, though; she was overwhelmed by shame at the thought of this stranger who knew her so intimately and who did not know her at all!

Several times, she was on the point of begging Mrs. Grovedale to *take her home*; every time, she recoiled from the idea of furnishing the excellent creature with explanations. She could have lied, but lying disgusted her. She finally allowed her mother to leave without having made a decision; then she had the chambermaid help her dress and lay down on a chaise-longue to wait for James.

When he appeared, Evelyn's anxiety increased to the point of becoming intolerable. He was extremely embarrassed himself. They both felt even further apart than they had before Mrs. Grovedale's visit, but James had not recovered the dread and disquiet inspired in him by *the other*; this one appeared to him to be younger and more charming—*virginal*. And he was subject to a passionate infatuation.

She felt humiliated, galled and full of resentment—all the more so because James' physical appearance was to her liking.

---

[7] Rosny inserts a footnote to explain that "beef tea" is a kind of soup, although that is not quite correct as a description of Bovril, which is what Evelyn would probably have been given to drink.

"It's atrocious!" she said, eventually. "It's impossible—utterly impossible—for us to live together. It would drive me mad!"

VIII.

James listened sadly. He understood, sensing how shocking the situation must seem to her, and was bizarrely ashamed himself, as if he had treated her dishonestly. All of that only increased his passion for Evelyn. That intelligent young man—but straightforward in the bluff British manner—experienced sentiments more complex than a Parisian trained by refined company and overly subtle reading. It was the fault of circumstances. It could not be helped that he had made love to that charming body; it could not be helped that the body in question had been "rejuvenated." And there was a considerable attraction—an innocent temptation, but both equivocal and invincible—in the fact that Evelyn was both his wife and another woman. One may be Anglo-Saxon to one's fingertips, but one retains the ancient instinct of patriarchy all the same.

After all, he thought, *it's really her that I thought I was marrying! She belongs to me at least as honestly as my fortune!*

He was too much a gentleman to assert his rights. He replied deferentially. "You're free. I'm incapable of exercising the least constraint upon you. But after all, you don't know what you'll think and feel in future. I respect your first impression, which is noble, but it's not possible to undo what's done; there's no reason to think that the situation won't end up imposing itself upon you. I am, after all, your husband. And of all possible solutions, the most honorable…"

She interrupted him with a feverish gesture. "The marriage is void! Even if I loved you—and I believe that to be impossible now—I could never live with you without a new marriage!"

59

"Listen," he said. "There are many ways to arrange things and await developments. Since you don't want to live with me, you can return to your parents, or you can live alone in our home. I'll find the necessary pretexts. I'll go traveling. But what I ask you humbly is to see me occasionally, in company with your family, if you wish, or meet me in public places. I have an absolute need to *try my luck*."

"And why do you want to *try your luck*?" she asked, bitterly.

"Because I love you."

"You didn't love the other, then?"

"I want to be sincere: I loved her. But understand me rightly: I loved her as one loves almost everyone…without knowing her well—and with a certain horror…quite natural, don't you think?"

"Yes," she agreed. "Quite natural. Except that you know me even less well."

"Well, I don't think so. The details of your character certainly escape me, but I sense your pride, your purity, your horror of deceit. That's the core of a moral nature! Finally, ever since humans have existed, something has *dictated* that we also love other people for their physical nature…that's much older and much more powerful than we are. It's a law! We ought to accept it."

This argument was too well adapted to the English mentality for Evelyn to find anything to contradict it. She lowered her head, and repeated, meditatively: "We ought to accept it!" She continued: "So be it. I can't refuse to see you occasionally. I'll do it dutifully, on condition that it doesn't last too long."

"You can fix the time yourself."

"Would three months be sufficient?"

"Yes," he sighed. "Three months will be sufficient…"

There was another pause. Bluewinkle had got up to look out of the window. His heart was heavy. More than anything else, the idea that Evelyn would leave their home was unbearable. Eventually, he said: "You're still too weak to move house. This is what I propose. I'll leave on a journey this morning. The cook and the chambermaid are excellent creatures, on whose good conduct you can depend. Your family can come to see you as often as you wish. Thus, everything will be correct and comfortable."

He is, after all, a gentleman, Evelyn thought. And she offered him her hand—but as soon as she touched his fingers, she blushed deeply; the same shame and rancor that she had felt so violently a little while before seethed in her breast.

The little hand was swiftly withdrawn. James left the room, pensive and miserable. He made preparations for his departure, and did not see Evelyn again all day.

They were dismal hours. He was prey to that *inert* chagrin—if one may put it thus—which ravages men of the North so profoundly. At the same time, he suffered mentally. His state of mind would have been abnormal for any man; it was intolerable for a young Anglo-Saxon who had always lived under a regime of moral discipline in which even the unexpected scarcely gave rise to any contradiction. He was frightened by the bizarre aspect that each of his regrets or desires assumed, and the implications that his slightest actions took on. All of that added to his regret at leaving Evelyn, and made him feverish. At times, he had a desire to depart for the ends of the Earth, to bury himself in the white deserts of the South Pole or the sandy deserts of torrid Australia.

At dusk, he called for a cab and went to bid adieu to his companion. He found her lying on the chaise-longue, still somewhat weak, but so fresh and so bright, with her beautiful child-like eyes, that he felt overwhelmed by love.

"Farewell!" he said. "Be happy."

"How can I be?" she said, in a soft voice.

He felt a chill in his heart. He could not help thinking it unjust that this creature, who was so obviously akin to him, did not love him at all, while the other, who had come from the depths of the Beyond, had loved him.

When he was in the cab, he leaned out of the window. Evelyn was there, behind those windows!

If she would only move the curtain aside...

He hoped for that; darting a long glance of appeal at the casement—but there was no movement.

The hackney plunged into the mist.

IX.

James embarked on a continental tour. Meekly, he visited the museums, monuments, theaters and landscapes that his guide imposed on him. He inscribed the market value of famous paintings, the age of churches, the height of towers, the breadth and depth of rivers, the cost of hiring carriages, the population of cities and the importance of ports in a travel journal.

These efforts scarcely distracted him at all.

He thought about Evelyn Grovedale while the guardians of tombs or temples were giving him precise information about heroes, saints, relics and the apparatus of worship. He also thought about her while the apothecaries of Poquelin were waving around their vast syringes, Phaedra was enticing the son of Theseus or the swan was towing the boat of the mysterious Lohengrin. Even the champagne could not succeed in numbing his pain.

He terminated his voyage in Florence, whence he returned directly to London, just as melancholy and even more amorous than when he had left.

He had given notification of his return and the time of his arrival. A thick yellow fog blanketed the city, through which one could see a small red Sun, like a blob of sealing-wax.

Evelyn was sitting beside a fire of Wallsend, a bituminous coal that burned slow and hot, throwing off long flames apt to give rise to daydreams. She was, in fact, daydreaming, full of her young, sad grace, illuminated by her long hair, in which the shades of wheat- and oat-straw were mingled.

She seemed less nervous, but much more resigned. James's presence did not seem to displease her overmuch. In fact, it almost amused her. So they talked, softly and monotonously, of the innocent things that British conversation involves. Evelyn remained distant, though.

As he was about to withdraw, she said: "I mustn't abuse your good will; I'm planning to return to my parents' house this evening."

"That would make things very difficult for me," sighed Bluewinkle. "And what will you tell them? It would be better if I lived on the first floor and you took the ground floor. You wouldn't see me, except for a few minutes every day. I'll use the pretext of business matters and eat in town."

"That would be terribly inconvenient for you."

"Not at all! What would inconvenience us, while we can't reach a definitive resolution, is a separation that would be incomprehensible to your parents and everyone else. I beg you to think about it, at least for a few days."

She knew that he was right. She was fearful in advance of her mother's candid questions, and especially of the discontentment of Mr. Grovedale, who had a keen and almost tragic sense of respectability.

"Since you wish it, and it inconveniences you less than my departure," she said, after gazing pensively into the long Wallsend flames, "I'll stay here for a while longer."

A fortnight went by. As James got up earlier than Evelyn, it seemed natural for him to take the tea, eggs, bacon, toast and orange marmalade of the first meal alone. He lunched and dined out.

To keep up appearances, Evelyn granted him conversations that she found less disagreeable than she had feared. Little by little, they returned to discussions of their incredible adventure. It was, in truth, the cause of their separation, but it was also an exciting secret—something that rendered their destiny unique among all human destinies and made them accomplices of a sort.

Evelyn knew perfectly well that she would be able to tear herself away from that honest overgrown boy, but every time she thought of the possibility of being his wife she blushed like the Comtesse Aimée de Spenssi, of whom Barbey said that "from her forehead, cheeks and neck to the nacreous parting of her golden hair, all was infused and inundated with a vermilion blaze."[8]

Evelyn had now completely recovered her strength. She went to see the good Mrs. Grovedale, young Harriet and young Jack on a regular basis. Her health had never seemed more solid; her complexion could compete with the freshness and glow of a baby's—one of those dazzling babies who roll in the emerald grass of Hyde Park or the verdant squares of the West End. She began to suffer abrupt fits of illness, however, most frequently early in the morning, but sometimes also in broad daylight, in the middle of a walk, while reading or visiting.

One afternoon, Mrs. Grovedale, seeing her very pale and unsteady on her feet, became agitated. "You're not well, you poor little thing!" she exclaimed. "You've gone as pale as that saucer." She spoke emphatically, waving her arms like a windmill. Evelyn confessed to her bouts of illness.

As she listened to her, Mrs. Grovedale gradually passed from dread to hope. "Darling," she said, in an inspired expression, "I think it's time you saw a physician—or perhaps you'd prefer a female doctor?" She was almost smiling—she had a comically tender and mysterious expression. Seeing that Evelyn did not understand, she shrugged her shoulders. "What do you think?" she said. "We'll go right away—we'll go to Mrs. Tinyrump's—it's on the other side of the square. Mrs. Tinyrump knows all about ladies' troubles, and...oh Lord, how I'd like..."

---

[8] Rosny provides a reference to *Le Chevalier des Touches*, a novel published in 1864.

She did not say what it was she would like, and drew Evelyn beneath the oaks and copper beeches of the square to Mrs. Tinyrump's residence.

The lady was at home. She had hair the color of a fox's coat, the muzzle of a hamster and an affable smile. She instantly understood Mrs. Grovedale's telegraphy and interrogated Evelyn, who had gradually become very pale.

An examination was deemed necessary; Mrs. Tinyrump carried it out minutely; then she shook her head with a sibylline expression, and said: "One can't be sure, Mistress—not yet! But I'd swear…" She lowered her voice to offer her prognosis, and Evelyn began trembling from head to toe.

When James came home that evening, he came to make his customary visit. He saw the young woman slumped in an armchair, her face moist with tears and her eyes full of an inexpressible despair. "What's the matter?" he asked, solicitously.

"Oh, it's so horrible!" she moaned. "So horrible…!"

She burst into sobs, her face leaning on her arm, and he stood there, anxious, astonished and curious. As she did not respond to his questions, he decided to wait.

Finally, the sobbing ceased. There was a long silence. Nothing could be heard but the murmur of the fire, the muffled chime of a church clock and the rolling of a cab in the street outside. Bluewinkle contemplated her flexible, semi-recumbent body, the scattered tresses of her hair and her white neck, which was occasionally shaken by a tremor.

"Well?" he resumed, gently.

She raised her head. Her mouth was grimly set, her face haggard, her large eyes full of a feverish flame of terror. Suddenly, she said, in a low and concentrated voice: "I'm afraid…I'm going to have a child!"

As he leaned forward, gripped by an obscure joy, she cried out, in a delirium of terror: "Another woman's child…a child of the other world!"

X.

For three months, Evelyn led a frightful existence. She had the continuous sensation of being prey to mysterious and hostile forces; she knew the fears of sad creatures who, in long-gone centuries, had believed themselves to be possessed by demons. More alone now than before, her malaise seemed to have no remedy, and those who loved her the most—even her mother—were totally incapable of understanding her pain. There was no one but James!

For several weeks, his presence was intolerable to the young woman. She did not even offer her hand to him any longer. She listened to him in silence, prostrate; she scarcely said a word to him, on his arrival and departure—and her aversion increased on the days when she had a sharper sense of her own injustice.

After the third month, the affliction and the disgust persisted, but they were mingled with resignation. Evelyn yielded then to the need to confide in someone that is a dominant and irresistible trait of social beings. She explained the nuances of her torture, and tried especially hard to make him understand the struggle that was going on within her, in which she so clearly discerned an extraterrestrial influence.

"Oh!" she cried, one evening in February, when London was deep in snow. "I feel so sharply that I'm condemned, and a slave."

He listened with a patience that never wavered. While watching the silvery flames fall through the gap in the curtains, he ventured to say: "It's your child too, though!"

"No, no!" she said, vehemently. "It's not my child!"

"Think about it," he went on. "Perhaps it wasn't, to begin with, or only slightly—I don't know! But it's more so every day. For many months, has it not been nourished by your blood? Isn't it your strength that sustains it—your life that gives it life? Think of everything that it will have received from you, when it finally sees the light of day!"

These words made an impact. She remained thoughtful for some time, and then objected—but with less disgust and bitterness: "Isn't that worse?"

"Perhaps, if it were an abominable creature—but why should it be abominable?"

"Because the *other* was!"

"No!" the young man replied, forcefully. "She was strange, undoubtedly, but I can assure you—and, by consulting the memories that she has left in your brain, you can convince yourself—that she was a good creature, worthy of being mourned, and even loved!"

"That's true," Evelyn murmured. For a few minutes, she felt almost reassured—but she suddenly went white and her lips quivered. "And what if the child is a vampire?" she cried.

James went pale in his turn—for, as time went by, he felt himself increasingly subject to paternal tenderness. "That's not likely," he replied.

From that evening on, Evelyn no longer exhibited any aversion. She received him amicably; their conversations were sometimes prolonged for more than an hour. Winter passed and spring sent its petty enchantments to weave the leaves of trees and the corollas of flowers; the equinoctial storms roared in the chimneys. Then the date approached that would mark a double deliverance for Evelyn.

It was the end of May. The evenings were interminably prolonged in the London firmament; Big Ben, atop the Houses of Parliament, scarcely sounded the hour twice between the last glimmer of twilight and the silvering of dawn. Evelyn spent one frightful night, when her entire being was racked by tortures…and in the morning, a little boy uttered his first cry. Except, instead of being red and frog-like, like his peers, he was fantastically pale, and his features were already thinned out.

"What a love!" cried Mrs. Grovedale, at all hazard. "And the very image of you, darling!"

That was true, but Evelyn did not see the shape of the face; she was terrorized by that pallor, which was truly *not of this world.*

"A phantom!" she whispered—and she dared not take the new-born in her arms. However, her fatigue was so great, and she felt such a sense of deliverance, that she sank into sleep. It was a very long sleep, scarcely interrupted by a brief awakening during the evening.

The next day, when she woke up, she perceived a young woman who came to pick up the child and offer it her breast. "Mrs. Tinyrump doesn't want you to nurse," said Mrs. Grovedale. "You need to get your strength back."

Evelyn made no response, hypnotized by the spectacle of the little mouth, which had gripped the nurse's dark areola. Tense minutes went by. The thin face was seen to tremble. The mother gradually felt herself overtaken by a subtle and profound joy. Eventually, she said: "Give him to me!"

The nurse held out the new-born. Evelyn never stopped gazing at the tiny lips. She was smiling broadly, her heart palpitating with happiness: the lips were full of milk.

James had been waiting anxiously since the previous day. When Mrs. Grovedale had shown him the baby, he had been shaken by a great tremor; he recognized that prodigious pallor only too well. Confronted by the frail creature, he felt the dread and horror that had afflicted him before Evelyn's *return.* He spent an anguished day and a miserable night; his heart was full of tenderness for the child, as it was full of love for the young mother. It was the moment of destiny. If the poor mite could only nourish itself on blood, what kind of life would he lead? Undoubtedly, it would be necessary to resign himself to losing Evelyn forever.

He was thinking about these things when the chambermaid came to clear away his breakfast, which he had not touched, and said to him: "The mistress would like to speak to you, sir."

He dared not go down right away; he was like a gambler who hesitates before risking his stake...

When he went into the bedroom and saw the baby in Evelyn's arms, he breathed more freely. The young woman's face was peaceful, her eyes bright and devoid of fever. When James came closer, she whispered: "He's a child like any other!"

With an imperceptible gesture, she pointed to the nurse, who was sitting at the back of the room; for the first time, he felt a frank pressure respond to his handclasp.

Pleasant days followed. In the generous light of June, to the perfume of the pollen and verdure that rose up from the garden through the large bay-windows of the bedroom, he gradually felt the supernatural adventure becoming more remote. Terrestrial life gripped them again and consoled them; the evil past became a dream.

One afternoon, when they had talked for longer than usual, sunset took them by surprise. A furnace lit up in the distance, among the trees; flocks of birds, flying through the gaps between buildings and walls, settled on the branches, among the shoots, and on the crests of roofs, whistling cheerfully.

James had taken Evelyn's hand—and, as she did not withdraw it, he said to her in a low voice: "Why won't you be my wife?"

She did not reply immediately; she was meditative. A simple and naïve energy animated her; she knew that she could live for a long time with the tender, overgrown boy, but she sensed obstacles rising up within her, and she sighed.

"I can't give you an answer yet."

They reached the month of July. Apart from his fantastic pallor, the child remained normal. The nurse, who he had almost frightened at first, became affectionate toward him. He rarely cried. He had large gray eyes, a trifle flat, which already seemed to recognize people and objects. James, who adored him and Evelyn, in spite of resurgences of dread, was attached to his singular little person. "He's not like other children, though," she sometimes said to Bluewinkle.

He affirmed the contrary and—good Anglo-Saxon as he was—he forced himself to believe it, as a matter of paternal duty, for love of conformity, and perhaps also because he sensed that his chances of being loved by Evelyn depended upon it.

Their intimacy grew firmer. One morning, when he said something affectionate to her, Evelyn replied: "But you know that I don't consider myself to be your wife. What can we do to get married?"

He tried to reason with her. He showed her that they were married in the eyes of men and that, in consequence, their mutual consent was sufficient for the marriage to become real and irreproachable. She would not give in; she had a pathological need for some sanction.

James racked his brain for a solution to this bizarre and irritating problem. First he thought about a divorce, followed by a new marriage, but that solution required lies to which Evelyn would never consent, and which the young man also found repugnant. By dint of reflection, he came up with another idea.

"Wouldn't it be sufficient," he said, "if a priest *confirmed* our marriage?"

"Yes," she replied, "that would be sufficient."

James then went to see the vicar of St. George's, with regard to whom he resigned himself to disguising the truth. By no means a subtle man, the vicar understood that it was a matter of an eccentric woman who was excessively scrupulous. He was an overfed clergyman, inclined to indulgence by the temporal requirements of religion.

"We must not pass judgment on our neighbors lightly," he said. "Scruples are appropriate to elite souls. What you ask is not specifically provided for, but it's not prohibited. The fee, of course…" He coughed and looked at Bluewinkle.

"The fee is not a problem," the young man replied, placidly.

This response having a decisive virtue, Evelyn and Bluewinkle appeared before the vicar of St. George's, who gave them a jolly little sermon on the duties of marriage and concluded: "Evelyn Grovedale has already been given to this man, in this very church, and James Bluewinkle has taken Evelyn Grovedale into his care. They have promised to take one another, for better or worse, and to love one another for richer or poorer. I remind the wife that she must obey her husband, and the man that he must protect his wife; may the Lord's blessing be upon their marriage!"

After which James poured three pounds sterling, seven shillings and sixpence into the right hand of Mr. Blackfoot, pharmacist and sexton.

The beautiful weather tempted them to take a cab all the way to Epping Forest, where Old England retains immense oaks and fabulous elms. They wandered beneath the heavy branches, sat down on the hospitable moss, consumed roast beef, Yorkshire pudding and ale in an old-fashioned tavern— and that evening, turning toward the setting Sun, before giant clouds in which fables, legends and chimeras sparkled, she was the virgin who allows her hair to fall upon the shoulders of her beloved, and he the conqueror who carries away the gilded fleece.

There were mornings and there were evenings. The past was behind them, like a dream; James wondered whether all of it, in fact, might have been a dream.

One morning, as he was thinking that, Evelyn still being asleep, he saw the nurse on the back garden steps.[9] She was gently rocking young Walter, whose glaucous eyes were looking at the trees with a terribly meditative expression.

James felt a pang of affection for the little creature, and took him in his arms. He walked across the lawn and the baby gradually began to smile: a smile that astonished James. *It's*

---

[9] Rosny inserts a footnote here: "A great many houses in London have a small garden in front of the street façade and another garden on the side of the other façade."

certain, the father thought, *that the boy isn't like any other child…*

He felt a quiver of anxiety. The days of yore returned. He saw the first Evelyn and her livid face. He relived the maddening night on which he had discovered the secret. Then he found himself next to the dying woman again; he saw the strange cadaver…

What if Walter hasn't only inherited her pallor?

He had stopped beside a privet. His eyes met the attentive gaze of the baby, and the idea occurred to him of carrying out an experiment. He introduced the tip of his ring-finger into the pink mouth. Immediately, the lips closed. James experienced, albeit feebly, a sensation that he knew well. He waited for two minutes—and when he withdrew the ring-finger, there were delicate pink droplets.

"He's a vampire!" he whispered.

And he trembled with fear.

He was not mistaken. Young Walter Bluewinkle is indeed a vampire and, for a long time, his father has not confessed that to anyone, even to Evelyn. He is, however, an inoffensive vampire. He merely enjoys the ability to suck blood through the pores of the skin, without the skin suffering any damage. He also has an exceedingly precocious intelligence, which is attracted to the mysteries of the Beyond.

Percy Coleman, whom James was finally obliged to take into his confidence, when the infant fell ill, would not trade Walter for "a church made of gold." It is said that the neurologist owes a prodigious discovery to the young vampire, which he will soon reveal to Old England and which will turn biological science upside-down even more profoundly than radioactivity revolutionized physics and chemistry.

THE SUPERNATURAL ASSASSIN

This is a strange place! thought Frédéric Maldar, as he skirted the Slave marsh in the decreasing light of dusk.

A livid vapor emerged from the waters, amid the algal archipelagos, and the old marsh wore the same appearance as in the times when the men of old had given it the name that had been handed down for thousands of years. One divined the swarming of viscous, sly and ponderous organisms buried in the mud, on watch in the sub-paludal forests, or engaged in the battles of those that devour and those that are devoured.

In the era when Suffren[10] led his victorious fleets against the masters of the sea, my great-great-grandfather lived here. There were six brothers, one of whom fought in the Americas. Why haven't we been back for two generations? I'll renew the tradition, though…

He walked on, burdened by a latent anxiety, which gripped him every evening at the hour when that corner of the planet quit the light for oblivion. This evening the anxiety was increased. Two or three times, he thought he had seen someone following him through the woods, and he was reminded of the robbers who had terrified the region for six months. The memory weighed upon his back. Since then, however, there had been no place more peaceful, or more likely to induce a liking for the melancholies of dusk, for which he had a mystical affection.

The sensation of a presence was attached to a mysterious dread, which came from within himself. To dispel these sinister feelings, he gazed through the extended hands of a pine-

---

[10] Pierre-André Suffren (1726-1788), generally known as *le bailli de Suffren* [the bailiff of Suffren], having been granted that title in the Order of Malta, distinguished himself in naval conflicts with the English in the Far East.

grove at a forge in which violet metals were melting. It really was a forge, with a scarlet furnace, a forge of the Cabeiri,[11] hollowed out in a cloud, in which mountains of iron were hammered as it was devoured by the immense and imponderable night. A fable? No...no more so than the marsh...no more so than Frédéric Maldar. It would last for an hour, Maldar for a few seasons, the marsh for a few millennia—and all three of them would have been a tiny moment in the eternal metamorphosis...

The marsh was still there when the daylight was no more than a fluorescence lost in the sea of darkness. A menacing odor floated over the open water; the woods on the bank became thicker—and Maldar saw Altair, Vega and Capella denounce the enormity of the world. With every passing moment an atom of fire completed an illusory figure, which the inordinate variations of suns had not modified since the days of the Chaldean herdsmen, the priests of Egypt and the sophists of Hellas.

A shiver ran down his spine; standing between two rocks, a man was watching him—there was no possibility of his being mistaken, in spite of the gathering darkness: a man of rather tall stature, leaning forward, who changed his position two or three times as Maldar walked on.

The walker patted the Browning in the inside pocket of his jacket—but when he was no more than five or six meters from the rocks, the silhouette vanished. Frédéric was curious and he moved forward more rapidly. He could see nothing beyond the gap but a plot of land planted with short grass, extending as far as the marsh; the woods resumed thereafter.

---

[11] The Cabeiri were obscure deities whose worship was primarily associated with the Aegean islands of Samothrace, Lemnos and Imbros; their celebratory rites involved a mystery cult whose reputation grew over time—to the extent that Alexander the Great was rumored to be an initiate, and the Argonauts were said to have sought its protection, on the advice of Orpheus.

The last remnant of twilight faded away; coming out in gooseflesh, Maldar had a presentiment of some enigmatic and redoubtable peril.

There was no longer any but a vague luminosity woven by the stars in the black ocean. Nothing was distinguishable, within a range of 20 paces, but a willow tree in the form of a man—but Frédéric was sure that the *other* was still following him.

Eventually, a long beam of light pierced the night, and three lighted windows appeared beyond the bridge of Herbeuse. A dog barked joyfully, a maidservant appeared in the doorway, and Maldar was overwhelmed by a placid cheerfulness.

"The sunset was striking," remarked Cécile Maldar, plunging the ladle into the soup.

The brother and sister had a strong family resemblance, although he had fair hair while she bore vast infernal tresses; their eyes were similar, broad and narrow, the color of jade, with pupils that were dilated in the gloom.

"Yes," he replied. "Striking…very striking!"

In the luminous room, sitting next to this girl with the Gallic features—whom he had watched grow up and to whom he was attached by all the roots of habit—before the white table and the aromatic soup, he forgot his anxiety. Provided with a healthy constitution, he enjoyed the meal, which reminded him of so many other meals, the sweet and restful pauses of life. There as a small pike with a voracious mouth, well-seasoned, tender and firm.

"One may eat this tiger of the rivers without remorse!" he said, laughing.

"And that panther, the trout!"

"It's curious that these aquatic carnivores are tasty, while felines…"

A plum tart was judged delicious; then there was a cigarette, and a small but penetrating cup of coffee. Because Maldar had received the fortunate gift of a lack of foresight and

Cécile never paid any heed to all-consuming time, they savored the pause to the full.

Later, he found himself alone in the library, while she gave orders and checked her accounts.

The books were there, some of which went back to the era of Franklin, while others had been born into the 20th century. Maldar chose *The Voyages of Captain Cook* and a novel called *Gaspard of the Mountains*,[12] but he did not open either of them.

The twilight had returned, and a slight anguish squeezed Frédéric's throat, while he felt singularly irritated with himself. At times, his self seemed to be rising up savagely against itself, as an internal hatred unfurled, inexpressibly: Frédéric detesting Frédéric! That happened to him occasionally, but not with this intensity, and he was surprised by the internal battle. It eased, though; the twilight vanished and he was glad to find himself in that room, whose windows were furnished with iron bars.

Then he grabbed *Gaspard of the Mountains* and went to dwell with him in the Auvergne. Sometimes, he broke off; he liked to imagine the characters, the locations and the circumstances. Then he resumed the exploration with a little thrill of pleasure.

After an hour, however, he abandoned *Gaspard* and began to accompany Cook in his astonishing journeys. It was not the first time; as an adolescent he had formed a bond of faithful friendship with the incomparable rover of oceans—but he had never followed him more closely, first aboard the *Endeavour* across the Pacific, through the Friendly Isles to New Zealand and New Holland, to set out again into the Indian Ocean, and then on the *Revolution* and the *Adventure*, to travel

---

[12] This must have been the first volume of Henri Pourrat's *Les Vaillances, farces et aventures de Gaspard des Montagnes*, published in 1921; it eventually ran to four volumes, the last being issued in 1931.

the immense Pacific again: Tahiti, New Zealand, Easter Island, the Friendly Isles, the New Hebrides...

On the way back, he sailed not far from Antarctica, his audacious soul doubtless dreaming of setting a course for the South Pole.

That evening, Frédéric followed the king of the sea to the Sandwich Islands, along the coast of the near-isle of Alaska, as far as the Arctic ice-cap. The end was near. Having returned to the Sandwich Islands, that mighty man, who had brushed with death a hundred times over, perished under the hands of obscure savages.

What journeys! Maldar thought. *What flights in the unknown, impossible now on the shrinking Earth. Everything was enormous for the frail ships that drew their energy from the elements themselves. With what virgin poetry those men could nourish themselves, when their imagination was powerful!*

Closing the book, he contemplated Cécile, who was reading a book on witchcraft.

"Frightful!" she said. "How people have suffered at the hands of other people!"

"They suffer still, sister! Have not millions and millions of men just endured frightful tortures for four years? How many were burned alive, showered with flaming liquid? How many howled in distress on the bare ground? And out there in the Far East, no torture has been conclusively abolished."

"A nasty subject of conversation!" she said, throwing the book away. "Let's console ourselves with Gérard d'Houville[13] in the enchanted forest."

She took refuge in her dream, while Maldar, having read enough, considered the human cave in which books, paintings

---

[13] Gerard d'Houville was the pseudonym of Marie de Heredia (1875-1963), the daughter of the famous Parnassian poet José-Maria de Heredia, the wife of Henri de Régnier and sometime mistress of Pierre Louÿs. She was best known as a poet, but also published some fantasies for children.

and engravings had accumulated for three generations. Through one of the open windows, between the iron bars, a meadow was visible, like a glaucous lake in the moonlight. A stream elevated its undine voice, further weakening the weak voice of the poplars—and Maldar felt the anxiety return, prowling around him like a she-wolf in the forest.

"Why is a human being never at peace?" he said impatiently. "At this tranquil hour, it's absurd that I'm condemned to presentiments. My mind ought to be like my body, which is feeling no pain, nor any malaise."

He got up and walked around, for walking was his recourse against anxiety and suffering. Passing from the library into the dining-room, he conceived a desire to see the garden by starlight.

Opening the little postern, he heard the consoling melody of the stream, and perceived an orange quarter-moon, sinking among the constellations, between the copper beech and the extended hands of the pins. The grass, scarcely oscillating under an imperceptible breeze, distributed a fresh odor, and the little round hill was visible whose profile must have been identical to the one it had displayed to some Medieval watchman or a Gaulish hunter prowling through the night.

How old everything is...and how young! he said to himself, his eyes fixed on the cracked and cratered star that intoxicates the souls of dreamers and guides poachers through the pitch-dark forests.

He advanced beneath the arches of ash-trees, as far as the mildewed wooden footbridge, while a vast violet-tinted cloud loomed up in the west and covered the Moon.

The shadows deepened, vaguely grayed by the stars—and Maldar stopped, a little tired. A rustle made him turn his head; on the bank of the stream, half-hidden by the osier-bed, he perceived a human silhouette. Anguish gripped him again, and he called out in a hoarse voice: "Who goes there?"

The silhouette recoiled, and vanished into the osier-bed.

Shivering, Frédéric peered into the darkness.

When he went back in, and locked the door, in the lamplight and peace of home, he set about reflecting. The anxiety was still lurking within him like a nocturnal beast; was he confronted by an enigmatic reality or was he prey to a hallucination? Both hypotheses seemed disagreeable to him, but he would still have preferred the former, full of horror for those of a nervous disposition...

After half an hour of conjectures, he tried to get back to *Gaspard of the Mountains*, but his attention wandered, and evaporated, to the extent that he abandoned the book and started walking again.

"What's the matter?" Cécile asked him, alarmed by his somber expression.

He tried to smile. "Nothing precise...and too absurd for me to try to explain..."

Inevitably, she thought he might have had bad news, but she remembered the mail arriving that morning; it had not troubled Frédéric, and he had no relatives or close friends in the neighborhood.

Again, she asked: "You're not feeling ill?"

"No, not at all. Don't worry, my darling. It's nothing, I tell you...ideas...nothing more."

Frédéric's voice was troubled, as if hazy; Cécile looked up at her brother, gripped by a vague anxiety, but he seemed so calm—and he really had calmed down, in spite of a confused malaise in the darkness of the unconscious and vegetal life.

He picked up *Gaspard of the Mountains* again, and wondered whether he might have been influenced by the book, which featured a phantom of sorts—but he had read 100 dramatic stories without experiencing any troubling nervousness, let alone any hallucinatory consequences.

Besides, out there on the edge of the marsh, when the *other* had appeared, Maldar's imagination had not been haunted by anything he had read.

He thought that he would have difficulty going to sleep, but he fell asleep as soon as his head touched the pillow. For a long time, his sleep was profound, dreamless and without any starts…but an hour before dawn, he suddenly woke up.

As he always did in summer, he had left a window wide open; through the bars, he could see the blurred silhouette of a tree, which he knew to be a Hungarian linden, and the sparkling embroidery of Orion, Regulus and Aldebaran on the violet velvet of the night sky.

Frédéric's heart was beating violently; his entire body was distressed, and he had a sharp sensation of a presence. Sitting up in bed, he peered into the darkness; he could vaguely make out chairs, an armchair, the porcelain stove, the chest of drawers and the pale scintillation of the mirror-fronted wardrobe.

"Nothing!" he stammered, to reassure himself.

The anguish persisted, and all of a sudden, he was certain that he could see a human silhouette in the doorway of his dressing-room. Then, with a trembling hand, he turned the dimmer-switch. There was nothing there but the furniture; in the pregnant silence of the night he could not hear anything but slight frictional sounds and the innocent, muted melody of the stream on the other side of the house.

He hesitated for about a minute, then he drew his revolver and leveled it.

It was no dream; the exterior door of the dressing-room was open, although he had, as usual, closed and locked it. Someone had come in—but from where, and how? All the windows were fitted with iron bars, and the door had not been forced.

"Or else," said Maldar, in a tremulous voice, "it's a slender creature, which came into the bedroom first…or I really am hallucinating…and a somnambulist into the bargain!"

He examined the windows; a mystical fear chilled his vertebrae; he had to make an enormous effort to go out on to the landing, having switched on the electric light in the corridor, which was controlled by a commutator on that floor.

Revolver in hand, he went downstairs slowly, scrutinizing his surroundings.

Suddenly, the electric light went out; something brushed past Frédéric; he felt something pointed prick him rudely between his shoulder-blades...

He tottered, fainted, and rolled down the stairs.

He stayed there for an indeterminate time. Cécile, whose sleep was healthy and profound, had heard nothing. When he came to, it took him a few minutes to realize that he was lying on the floor. His memory vacillated, in the petty swirl of a vertiginous awakening; it reorganized itself, bringing him back by degrees to the point at which he had been struck. Then, frightened and miserable, he stood up and headed for the nearest light-switch. The light came on and showed him the corridor, the three doors of the main entrance, the kitchen and the dining-room.

Maldar heard himself murmur: "What can it mean? What can it mean?"

He felt a slight twinge of pain in his back, but would have been able to believe it a hallucination if, on the one hand, he had not perceived a dagger on a step, and, on the other hand, he had not brought his hand back red with blood when he placed it between his shoulder-blades.

He had evidently been struck from behind, then, with the aid of that dagger, whose blade was stained red—and yet, his assailant had not returned to the attack. What did he want? Was he a thief, an enemy, or a madman?

Mechanically, Frédéric went into the dining-room, where he lit the lamps, then into the library-drawing-room, and finally into the kitchen. He found all three entrance doors and the shutters closed and bolted; it therefore seemed probable that the nocturnal visitor, who might well have come in during the day and hidden, might have got in through a first-floor window or the roof...

Having made these observations, Maldar was astonished by his self-composure. He felt strangely reassured; he was convinced that the wound was slight, not dangerous at all, and that no danger was menacing him *now*. It was in this state of mind that he went back up to the first floor. There, too, there was no trace of breaking and entering, nor was there any in the attic, to which he went next. The attic, which was very large, was only connected to the outside by two hinged skylights, solidly barred and sealed by means of an ingenious catch.

"In sum," he concluded, "no one has come *into* the house since it was locked up."

To make perfectly sure, he tried silently to open the doors to Cécile's bedroom and those of the domestics. The doors resisted; as usual, the women had turned the keys. Thus, only one conjecture remained possible: the malefactor, if there was a malefactor, had been in the house when Maldar and the servants had undertaken the evening closure.

"But in that case," he exclaimed, "he's still here!"

He felt a thrill of fear, cold and harsh, which quickly faded away. Maldar was on the point of summoning Cécile, but he decided to examine his wound first, which he did with the aid of two angled mirrors. It seemed slight, and was certainly not deep. He felt so reassured then that he was about to go back to bed, after having washed the wound as best he could with Pond's Extract[14] and put a compress on it—but he thought that if *he* were still in the house, as seemed to be the case, Cécile and the maids ought to be warned. He therefore resigned himself to waking the young woman up...

Maldar's story worried and astounded her, without causing her to lose the courage that came naturally to her. "We must search the house again, from top to bottom," she said.

---

[14] Pond's Extract was a patent medicine derived from witch-hazel, marked by the American entrepreneur T.T. Pond after 1846. It had, however, virtually disappeared by the time the story is set, by which time the company Pond had founded had restyled itself as a cosmetics manufacturer, whose key product was a cold cream.

For extra protection, she lit candles, and then—with Frédéric's Browning at the ready—they went down to the ground floor. As Maldar had already seen, all the doors letting out on to the road and the garden were doubly sealed, by locks and bolts; the shutters, also closed, had evidently not let anyone through. On the first floor, save for the door to the corridor, everything was in order. Undoubtedly, someone could have got in through the window that Frédéric left open at night, for reasons of hygiene, but that window had solid bars, so close together that a child of seven could scarcely have squeezed through.

"It wasn't a child that I saw," Frédéric remarked. "It was a man, almost as tall as me."

Cécile went to knock on the maids' doors. In order not to frighten the simple girls, she limited herself to mentioning suspicious noises; in any case, the inspection of their rooms produced no further enlightenment.

"If you didn't have that wound in your back, I'd think that you were dreaming," she said, when they were alone again.

"I would also have had to have a fit of somnambulism!" he retorted.

Cécile examined the wound in her turn. It was superficial, situated close to the fifth vertebra, and it was evident that it must have been produced by an arm striking horizontally.

"Which ruins the extreme hypothesis," Frédéric remarked, "that I was able, in a hallucinatory crisis, to strike myself..." And he pointed to the dagger abandoned by the aggressor.

They did not go back to bed until they had exhausted all the imaginable conjectures.

In the morning, they notified the doctor in Favrègues, the town on which the Maldar dwelling was dependent, and also the town hall and the gendarmerie. The gendarmes discovered nothing, and went away vaguely suspicious. The doctor, an old practitioner of some skill, examined the wound, looked at the dagger, and concluded: "An exceedingly feeble blow! A hesitant hand…or that of a child."

He listened to all the details of the adventure, which appeared to interest him keenly, and eventually said: "It's highly reminiscent of an affair of the other world—which was called the Beyond in the 19th century. If you're not mistaken, and checked all the means of entrance rigorously, only some kind of phantom would have been able to get into your house."

"Do you believe in phantoms, Doctor?"

"I don't know. When I say *a phantom*, I'm expressing myself badly—it would be better to say *a spirit*."

"Are you interested in occultism?"

"Yes…but only slightly. Of occultist literature, which is so numerous and so varied, I've only read a few old books, among the most celebrated."

"Occult theories have always inspired a repulsion in me—although they have sometimes troubled me strangely."

"We don't know anything—or, at least, scarcely more than that fly, which, having landed on my hand, is evidently unaware that it is at the mercy of a being as formidable from its own viewpoint as a colossus as large as a mountain would be to us. It doesn't know—and we don't know. On the day when the facts of the Beyond are clearly revealed to us, perhaps they won't seem any more surprising to us than the prodigy of our bodies, in which millions of nervous fibers coordinate the revelations of the external world. For myself, I'm almost sure that innumerable invisible entities are moving around us; the universe seems much more logical and coherent to me thus than if I suppose spaces empty of energy and devoid of life."

"We have no other resource than ourselves and the reportage of experience."

"That's simple and complete wisdom. In your case, the interpretation of experience appears to present some difficulties. Enough! With the gendarmerie on the one hand and your own research on the other…would it be disagreeable to you if I devoted myself to a few investigations of a psychic order?"

"Not at all," said Maldar, smiling. A short while later, the idea caused him an obscure repugnance, but the doctor had already posed a number of precise, but subtle questions, and he continued: "All the same, it's not natural, since you have no enemies, and since nothing has been stolen. I might suspect a crisis of auto-suggestion—but it's impossible that the blow struck between your shoulder-blades, given the manner of its delivery, could have been self-inflicted."

"No, no!" Frédéric protested. "I've always been normal."

"Yes, undoubtedly!" agreed the physician, who was skeptical on this point, and very inclined to believe that the finest human machines are easily put out of order. "Besides, even if you weren't normal, I can't see how you'd have been able to intervene in the present instance. We must set that conjecture aside. One might also hypothesize the intervention of a madman, but in that instance, his appearance and disappearance would be no more conceivable than that of a criminal..."

The doctor considered his thumbnail thoughtfully. He belonged to an exceedingly hairy category of humankind; two tufts, like hanks of thread, sprang forth from his ears; his beard possessed an extraordinary density; his hands produced a fur the color of iron; and his entire body was probably covered with an abundant pelt. Golden-yellow eyes, flecked with jade, gleamed beneath his enormous eyebrow. He took out his watch and said: "The wound isn't at all serious; you have no need of me. I'll come back to see you regardless, if you'll permit it—but not as a quack."

As the doctor had anticipated, the wound healed rapidly, and Maldar spent a few weeks in complete tranquility. The judicial inquiry, conducted by subordinates, revealed nothing; the doctor held to his initial conclusions.

To begin with, a certain nervousness persisted in Frédéric; in the evenings, especially, he suffered minor crises of anxiety, which were exacerbated when he found himself alone in his bedroom. Because one gets used to everything, though, he was almost completely reassured a fortnight later.

The adventure remained incomprehensible, but it seemed increasingly unlikely that it would ever be repeated. Having recovered his customary good humor, therefore, he devoted himself peacefully to his studies, his reading and his walks. A great walker and agile climber, he sought out solitary places, which gave the impression of the world's recommencement that mountains, especially, invoke.

Sometimes, however, he wondered: *Was I dreaming? Is it possible that such an absurd thing, with an air of tragic mystery, should have happened to me?*

Then, if he was alone, he experienced a small frisson. However, he asked the question with increasing infrequency, even in an abstract form. And one evening, when he was browsing the book on sorcery again, he said to himself: *Soon I won't think about it ever again.*

He resumed reading, but he felt a dull anxiety that ended up making him set the book aside—and then he had some kind of fit of anger, almost hatred, directed against himself.

"There really are times when one seems to be one's own enemy!" he muttered.

He was alone. Cécile was busy giving orders to the cook, and, as the windows were open—as they were every evening of that fine summer—he could see the meadow, the garden, the pines and the beeches, and hear the innocent melody of the stream... A third of the Moon was roaming among the stars. The odor of freshly-cut hay penetrated in gusts, like a swarm of perfumes.

"It's good to be alive," Maldar said to himself. "It *ought* to be good to be alive!"

By virtue of saying these words aloud, it seemed that the anxiety evaporated. He went to one of the windows, which was a primitive sort of bow-window, and looked through the branches at a fragment of the Milky Way, remembering the pleasure he had taken in gazing at it when he had been 20 years old.

Moths brushed his face, an animal went by, its body elongated like the body of a stout serpent—a weasel or an otter—and a dog barked in the distance, at the eternal enemy that dogs scent in the shadows…and other dogs replied.

"*To lie beneath the sky, like the astrologers,*" Frédéric intoned, "*and listen dreaming, beside bell-towers, to their solemn hymns borne by the wind…* Come on!"[15]

He picked up a soothing book, *The Illustrious Doctor Matheus*,[16] and it seemed to Maldar that time was now flowing with a naïve gentleness…

Nevertheless, when he found himself in his bedroom, he took care to unhook an automatic pistol from the display, and a hunting-knife. He put these weapons in the drawer of his night-stand and lay down…

A bad dream woke him up. He could hear his heart beating with extreme precipitation. An abundant sweat covered his upper body and neck, and a vague fear tormented him. He looked avidly at the window, from which a silver trail of moonlight expanded. There was a light touch…a pale form…and, turning round, Frédéric saw a pale form at the back of the room, next to the porcelain stove, opposite the display of weapons.

"Who goes there?" he cried, in a voice that was loud and broken at the same time.

The hammering of his heart was becoming intolerable. Although his hand was trembling like a twig in the breeze, he succeeded in opening the drawer in his night-stand and grasping the automatic pistol. At that moment, the mysterious being—the same one, Frédéric was sure, as the other night—took down a weapon from the display and extended its arm…

"Wretch!" growled Maldar.

For a moment, both of them took aim, and the two shots rang out almost simultaneously. A bullet embedded itself in

---

[15] The lines Frédéric is quoting are from Charles Baudelaire's "Paysage" in *Les Fleurs du mal* (1857).

[16] *L'Illustre docteur Mathéus* (misrendered as *Mattheus* in the Marabout text) is by Erckmann-Chatrian, and was first published in 1856.

the wall above the bedhead. The unknown visitor took a step forward, turned, and collapsed on the floor.

Maldar turned the dimmer-switch; no light sprang forth. Then he was gripped by an immense oppression, such that he thought that he was going to faint, but he overcame it, and found the box of matches and the emergency candle. A faint light was added to the vague light of the Moon.

Frédéric wondered whether he had the courage to get up. He peered into the semi-darkness where the man's body had to be, but it was hidden by the footboard of the bed.

Painfully, Frédéric set his feet on the floor; then, with the pistol in his right hand and the candle-tray in his left, he moved forward. Before he had rounded the bed he saw *the other*…and, leaning over and directing the candlelight, paralyzed by fear, he uttered a feeble plaint.

The man lying there, dressed in a simple chemise, was— save for an indescribable pallor, the strange, phantasmal pallor of mist—the very image of himself.

A minute ran by before Maldar dared to move. He leaned on the bed, shivering, his teeth chattering, his eyes crazed and staring. At times, he could no longer see anything, deeply buried in an immeasurable darkness; then the cadaver reappeared, the fantastically livid face…

The dead hand still held the revolver taken down from the display: a light revolver loaded with old cartridges.

The terror and the horror dissipated slowly, and Frédéric heard himself say: "Where did he come from? Why did he attack me?"

He dared to take two steps forward and lean over. He made out a little round wound in the man's forehead; that was what had killed him.

Even more than the other corpses that Frédéric had seen, this one was empty and flat, simultaneously derisory and terrible. The eyelids were closed, the arms stiffly extended alongside the torso and the lips slightly drawn back over the translucent teeth.

At that moment, there was a knock on the door.

Frédéric opened it, after observing that the door was locked, and saw his sister, who had hurriedly put on a dressing-gown.

"What's happening?" she demanded. "I woke up with a start...it seemed that someone had fired a rifle or a revolver..."

"It was me who fired," said Maldar, softly. "Me...and him."

"Who's *him*?" she exclaimed, alarmed.

"The man...the one who attacked me once before."

Her pupils dilated by astonishment and fear, she advanced nevertheless into the room, and suddenly perceived the cadaver. Her hands began to tremble, and she was shaking so violently that he put out his hand to sustain her. Then, in a dream-like voice, she said: "Have you killed him?"

"What could I do? He fired first."

"It's terrible. And yet...yes...he looks like you."

"Doesn't he?" sighed Frédéric. "And still the same puzzle. How did he get in? Both doors were locked; it's physically impossible for him to have slipped through the bars on the window. I was at his mercy...it was by chance that I woke up and saw him. He took that revolver from the wall-display, at the same time as I grabbed the automatic pistol. All in all, it's enough to drive one insane, isn't it?"

They remained silent momentarily, full of horror, dejection and anxiety.

"It's almost morning," said Cécile, finally. "We have to notify the mayor." As she turned round, she saw the cook and the chambermaid standing in the doorway. The former was already old, with a rustic face, the other very young, with an immense head, a bovine face and the hands of a laborer.

"We heard," said the old woman, whose magpie eyes displayed a slow but tenacious curiosity, while the younger seemed astounded, "so we came..."

When they had seen the cadaver they uttered dissimilar screeches, in which fright was complicated by the obscure

89

satisfaction of being involved in an adventure. They calmed down and their surprise diminished, tonight's drama evoking memories of the other drama, which they had discussed at length with the neighbors and tradesmen.

"It's the same!" whispered the old woman. "Should we summon Legouvent and his son—it's almost the time when they get up?"

Maldar acquiesced with a nod of his head, and a quarter of an hour later, Legouvent, his son, his mother and two daughters were licking their lips over the sight of the corpse. Legouvent's son agreed to go to the town hall, and his younger daughter to the gendarmerie.

"It would be as well to fetch the doctor," said Cécile.

For anxious, ominous, mysterious minutes, having locked the tragic bedroom, Frédéric and Cécile waited in the early morning, whitened by mist. There was a gaiety in the air; the grass sparkled; wings fluttered; everything advertised the ardor of life.

The physician was the first to appear, his eyes at a standstill, his face buried in his beard. "Eh?" he cried. "The same adventure?" He looked at Frédéric and Cécile obliquely; they were vague, nervous and pale.

"Similar, but worse," Maldar sighed. "I've killed him…"

"Killed! Damn!" said the doctor, lasciviously. "Self defense, I presume?"

"He left me no alternative but to kill or be killed."

Curiosity sparkled behind the doctor's spectacles and in the bare fraction of his face. "Do you know any more?"

"Not at all. As on the previous night, I was taken by surprise…*he* was there, in my room…inexplicably…both doors locked and bolted…"

"We shall know, all the same—with the aid of these gentlemen." He turned a gravely ironic face toward the newcomers: two surly gendarmes, not yet fully awake.

One of them, a brigadier, grunted: "It seems we get called out a hundred times for the same thing…"

"Would you like to see?"

They followed Maldar, followed in his turn by the physician; the brigadier, having put on a show of examining the room, bent over the cadaver.

"That's odd! How did he get in?"

For the physician's benefit rather than that of the gendarmes, Frédéric told the story.

"He couldn't have got through either door…or the window," the brigadier affirmed, testing the bars one by one. "You're probably mistaken…you forgot to lock something."

"I don't think so!"

"He's not a phantom!" said the other, with a faint snigger. "The proof's there!"

"Perhaps he's a phantom all the same," said the physician. He had approached the body in his turn, and he put out his hand to touch it.

"Nothing should be moved!" exclaimed the brigadier.

"Don't worry, brigadier…such as it is, so it will remain…but look!" He took hold of the dead man's arm, lifted it up, uttered an exclamation in which amazement and dread were mingled, and let the arm fall back. Then, standing up, very pale, he said: "It's not a man!"

From anyone but the physician, the gendarmes would have greeted that declaration with a derisory disdain, but they knew the old man, who had been involved in numerous accidents and more than one crime.

"What is he, then?" enquired the brigadier.

"I don't know—not yet! It's too early to make any presumptions…but try the experiment, brigadier. Lift up the head a little—you'll see that the man has *almost no weight*."

The other listened wide-eyed, while a chill of fear ran down Frédéric's spine.

"Come on, doctor—you're not making fun of us?"

"Try it! Try it!" the doctor repeated, in a peremptory tone.

For a long time, dead men had not intimidated the gendarme any more than the intimidated hospital interns—he had seen so many! Nevertheless, he did not approach this one without a tiny frisson—which became a long shudder when he had raised the head and let it fall back.

"Oh—that's unusual!" he stammered. "Frightening, even! Then again—I hadn't noticed before—look at his face, and Monsieur's!"

That mystical horror arose which, diversifying according to the soul that experiences it, awakens all the forms of fear.

The room was locked, and one of the gendarmes was stationed in front of the house, while the mayor, the physician and Maldar gathered in the library-drawing-room.

The mayor, a red-haired man of prehistoric appearance, declared: "The Beyond exists!"

"What do you mean?" demanded the physician. "Evidently, there are in this world, as there are in the so-called other, many things that we can't understand…and many more that we can't even perceive…but in this case, what is the Beyond?"

"Simply what we call the other world," the mayor replied, "since the other…up there…can't be a man…it's another sort of living being…what honest folk call a ghost or a phantom."

"That's precisely what isn't certain," said the doctor. "Perhaps that being is of *our world*."

"Then the Beyond is among us?"

"I think it must be, in some fashion…as it must also be elsewhere…but if I dare say what I think, it's not from a terrestrial Beyond or an interstellar Beyond that *he* came…"

"Where did he come from, then?"

The physician did not reply. He stared straight ahead; for more than a minute, he seemed hypnotized. Then, in a low voice, he continued: "There are several ways of imagining the occult world…and that world is doubtless very diverse. I neither deny nor affirm what you call the Beyond, but I'm almost certain that *the individual up there* originated here…and from very close at hand…"

"I don't understand."

"Have you noticed the strange resemblance between the dead man and Monsieur Maldar?"

Maldar shuddered violently. He was pale, and very tired; he felt an immense void within him, and a strange grief.

"Everyone has noticed it," the mayor replied.

"Well," the physician continued, in an even lower voice, as if afraid of his own words, "the individual up there is an emanation of our host. It's his double...the nocturnal combat was a man in conflict with himself...and the man almost perished..."

The three men looked at one another, astounded—but for all three, plunged into the same atmosphere, there was the same evidence.

"It's incredible, though!" the mayor eventually murmured.

"But isn't the entire adventure incredible?"

"I'm beginning to understand," said Maldar, thoughtfully. "The great discontentment that I've always felt with myself, which became hateful at times...that was the conflict...with *him*."

"Doubles aren't immortal, then?" sighed the mayor. "Or not quite...?"

"Don't we have proof to the contrary here?" the doctor went on. "I assume now that they're formations of our self, endowed with life an individuality. Their personality is almost always confused with ours, but we've just seen that they can separate themselves, to the point of becoming our enemies, even violently. I wonder whether many actions accomplished against our interests might not be explained in this fashion...including certain suicides!"

Frédéric remembered evenings when he had *detested* himself so strangely, when a part of his being had raised itself up so savagely against the other...

Then, an immense regret rose up within him, as if he had lost someone very dear to him, accompanied by a muted fear.

"Can I live without him?" he moaned. "Will my life not, at the least, be diminished?"

93

"I have a suspicion," the physician replied, in a whisper, "that another double will be born within you before long, to replace the one that is dead."

COMPANIONS OF THE UNIVERSE

I.

I was thinking about my impending ruination when Madame Donatienne brought breakfast.

Madame Donatienne is plantigrade animal in her gait and in her body, but not in her head, which is akin to that of a buffalo, of which she has the smoky eyes. Her air of bewilderment is fully human. Provided with jutting hips and massive feet, she is resistant to anything.

I admit to considering Madame Donatienne, with disdainful indulgence, as an inferior creature—a mandarin sentiment. It is said, and plausibly, that humans mark their superiority by the slowness of their growth. Pigs, however, which resemble us, do not live long and grow with an inconceivable haste. Horses and bulls reach adulthood within a few seasons. We take 20 years to get there—whence, according to those who know, comes our relative longevity; but the stupidity and rapid development of a tortoise does not prevent it from living for centuries.

As for Madame Donatienne, I happen to know that she had grown without haste, and her physique augurs a long existence. To know whether she was of equal or greater value than me it would be necessary to deprive us of our human support network; in a virgin forest, born of mute savages, would she not be the superior animal?

As one comes into an inheritance, I have received the treasure of culture; centuries of tradition enrich me. None of my thoughts emerge from a natural individual; my instincts are deformed. I am that strange creature, a social man. Had I been born in Germany, I would speak German, would possess German patriotism, German tradition, German ideas, habits, gestures, aptitudes, and even German instincts. Had I been adopted as an infant by an Australian tribe, I would believe in my totem, and would be a person of the Stone Age. I would devote myself innocently to anthropophagy if I had uttered my first wails among cannibals, and if, by some miracle, gorillas had taken me in and raised me, I would be a sort of gorilla.

It is frightful how "interchangeable" a human beast is! An ant, a bee or a termite is allotted its function once and for all within the ant-hill, beehive or termitary; as a human, I might have been a mason, a laborer, a typographer, a cobbler, an electrician, a tanner, a house-painter, a mariner, a scare-crow, a judge, a grocer…I have had a choice of a thousand estates, each of which would have equipped me with a profes-sional mentality.

For her part, if Madame Donatienne had been brought up at the Oiseaux,[17] receiving the most delicate education and possessing the advantages of a fortune, she would have been the companion of refined creatures, finally shaped into an ele-gant lady, at least in regard to manners.

While I tried to imagine Madame Donatienne as a wom-an of the world, or a savage lost in the depths of the woods, she arranged the coffee-pot, the bread rolls, the butter and the jam in an appropriate manner.

Natural man and social man contemplate precious ali-ments with equal pleasure, both moved—in much the same way, I suppose—by the delightful odor of coffee.

"Monsieur," said Madame Donatienne, "are the mines of Lens sound?"

"Solid, Madame Donatienne—black and solid."

"My cousin, who works for a broker, says that I ought to get rid of my francs—they're going to fall to a sou. Can I risk the Lens shares, then?"

---

[17] The Ecole Notre-Dame "Les Oiseaux" is an institution founded by Parisian nuns in 1598, originally for the education of girls from poor families, although it was eventually colo-nized by the rich.

"Your cousin knows better than I do."

"Monsieur just said that they're solid."

"People will need coal for a long time yet."

"The English strike will be good for Lens, then—so I'll buy!" She placed her hands flat on her bosom before adding: "It's tragic, Monsieur!"

"As you rightly say, Madame Donatienne."

"Isn't it?" she proclaimed, proudly. "I'm glad to see that Monsieur agrees with me. I say it to everyone: it's tragic!" Inflated by that word, which appeared to her to be almost supernatural, she stood back, evoking, by means of her pose, the image of innumerable actresses.

Madame Donatienne served coffee very hot, thus rendering my slight morning drunkenness more efficacious. It is necessary to praise unreservedly the raspberry jelly recommended by Monsieur Victor of the Maison Corcellet; it is probably the best that I have tasted since the invention of jam.

A chaffinch, which had sung one morning during my childhood, started to sing again; desert islands surged forth, followed by a mundane beach on which semi-naked women were sleeping in the Sun; the star Capella displayed itself in the enchanted night when Helen joined me in the Casino gardens: a universe of desires revived the drama of unsatisfied desires; then the fumes of the coffee evoked a confidence both primitive and subtle, from which the human animal and the interhuman man[18] dissociated themselves at intervals.

---

[18] As will gradually become clear, Rosny does not mean the same thing by "interhuman man" as he does by "social man;" he imagines human identity as a tripartite hierarchy, with the "interhuman man" being intermediate between the "animal" or the "primitive" self and the "social" being. Its intermediacy should not be confused, however with the intermediacy of Freud's *ego* between the *id* and the *superego*, as a conscious entity committed to negotiating between the extremes and settling their disputes; Rosny's "interhuman" fraction is an independent bundle of impulses and appetites, sometimes al-

A disagreeable shock, followed by a contraction of the diaphragm, brought me back to my probable ruination doom.

I have behaved like an imbecile! Did I not know that it was necessary to appropriate dollars, florins and pounds? Short-sightedness, nonchalance and a little patriotic gullibility. At the end of the day, I am what I am. It's necessary to reconcile myself to not being able to climb up on to my own shoulders.

In a species, the role of the primitive individual is considerable, even dominant. Had I not known the danger as well as so many others, and, like them, the means to limit it? I had more capacity for success than the dense Laval or the slow Varail; the social man had counseled me, but the indolent savage had carried me away! And it would lead to ruination!

Theoretically, the spirit of invention should have extracted me from business—for when all is said and done, although stupidly smitten with art and vain metaphysics, I was also an inventor. That is a gift, to such an extent that it is necessary to attribute a more than average influence to it. It is impossible, here, to neglect a *third aspect* of humans—a heredity determined by the herd, too complex for the first ones who stood up on their hind feet: in a word, faculties that are imperiously personal and innate, and which sometimes taxed our social ancestors.

Madame Donatienne cut these cogitations short.

"It's Madame Malvaines," she said.

Yveline! Redoubtable memories! With her, sometimes energetic, sometimes enfeebled to the point of semi-consciousness, but always present, the most intoxicating era of the past appeared. I know full well that that Yveline had simply appeared at the right moment, that another might have had the same significance, perhaps even more profound, but at the end of the day, *she* was there. It was to her that the illusion

---

lied with one or other of its neighbors but essentially following its own agenda.

was attached, she to whom the fables of the second age had initially attached.

The garden, the swing…I shall always be oscillating before the catalpas in flower, hugging her tightly, those woman's lips always attached to a boy's lips; it will always be the most ardent memory, the cunning, redoubtable and magnificent awakening…nothing but those lips, nothing but that kiss. The next day, the big girl had been taken away.

In the human forest, someone else must have had that which I did not know how to take, according to the ritual: Yveline plays by the rules.

She entered in her customary fashion, which is furtive; her blank face recalled the other face, with more delicate cheeks—which lasted for an instant and then disappeared forever, after the first moment. There was no longer anyone but the woman of 30, with dewy eyes, amber complexion, grape-red mouth and light brown hair. You would have found her desirable; she sensed that, and wanted it.

Yveline lives on the wing, with no more idea of the management of money than the resolution of theorems. Until the end, her companion, now ruined, had provided the pretty woman's expenses. Since then, she had devoured the crumbs, heedlessly, confident that everything would work out. Her luxury is taboo; a providence watches over her—and it will doubtless be sufficient, to chase away temptation, to tell her, once and for all, clearly and brutally, that I have become a poor man. What could be more frightful and more contemptible?

Here she is. She has not needed recourse to artifice to conform to the stereotype of 1926: an elongated, flexible, flavorsome human female, her gestures suggestive of a sensuality all the more profound for being reticent. And here I am, victim once again of the mirage. You might believe that the beauty of her eyes is intrinsic and not merely a function of the form and movement of the eyelids…

A surprising fable that the centuries have consolidated persuades us that eyes are beautiful in themselves, to such an extent that we attribute to them everything that they owe solely to their petty ambience of muscles, skin and hair—without the play of which the most splendid would be the equal of the ugliest, and often inferior thereto.

While Yveline stands there, I populate her eyes. It is they, initially, that fascinate me, although I am sensible to the complexion, the redness of the lips, and even the nose—a rather grotesque appendage, but hers is small and delicately pale, with sensual nostrils.

There is hidden desire in her—perhaps more strongly than in me. Few gestures to make, but what perils! In that tall daughter of Sun-bronzed races, with Bedouin eyes, the primitive being and the human being are clearly delimited, with scarcely any traces of the intermediate animal. I imagine that she has hardly brought into the world any instincts but those of the most ancient eras, prior even to the tribal—but an extreme aptitude for imitation, a keen receptiveness, have helped her to assimilate all interhuman superficiality: all the mimicry, the elegance and the rituals.

The sensation rends me permeable; my three natures are mobilized by desire, and I have turned my gaze away from the brown hair and the white neck. She has seen; she draws nearer, perfumed like a fresh flower; a few gestures and the coveted body would yield and I would plunge into the ardent darkness—but I know only too well to what I am exposing myself, and exposing her: an abuse of trust!

Luckily, temptation retreats to cower in the depths of its cave; I shall brave it again this time. This too she guesses. Then, with a sigh, she says: "I've come to talk to you about Denise."

That is my ward, the daughter of Yveline's husband, to whom I am distantly related. Yveline loves her unreservedly. I love her too; she belongs to the race of defenseless creatures, a more seductive race than the combative ones. Without Yveline and me, she would be prey to carnivores.

"She'll soon be 15," sighed the visitor. "Have you thought about that? She's getting prettier every day."

"It's up to you to think about that, Yvo! I mean, to protect her from the Devil—I don't know anything about that."

"The Devil hasn't yet got his claws into her! It's a matter of completing her education. It's me who doesn't know anything about that. You've sometimes talked to me about her aptitudes, and said that it's necessary to cultivate them. Do you think that will be useful? I see nothing in it but fatigue, perhaps overwork. Isn't it sufficient for her to be seductive?"

"It's necessary, my love. It's a double-edged sword. For a Denise without resources, with her gullible nature, beauty is an even greater peril. She doesn't know how to exploit it, my dear, to make good use of it either for attack or defense. And Denise is, indeed, without resources."

"We've come to that."

"Poor as your arithmetic is, you know full well that your fortune is lost. I don't know how I'll get out of it myself."

My words fell into the void; there had not been a single day of tribulation, in the monetary sense, in Yveline's life; the ruination that people were always talking to her about was contrary to all reality. "You'll get out of it all right!" she affirmed.

Was it necessary to show her the abyss? I still did not have the courage; I tried to persuade myself that it was so as not to introduce despair into that improvident soul, but I knew that I was lying and that I was pusillanimously hoarding that mutual desire to which I did not intend to yield and what I did not want to see vanish…

"Yveline, you're only a cork on the waves! You have no idea of the battles raging around you, no idea of the pitfalls. Every move we make puts us in danger. We're constantly on the point of being devoured."

"Then what good does it do to think about it?"

That's true enough. What good, in truth, would anxiety, dread and somber anticipation do her? She has saved them up, refusing to give way, for fear of tomorrow, to any insomnia.

Even now, her attitude is probably the best one. How she drifts through her softly lit, minuscule and enchanted universe!

"I'll think about it," I said, finally. "I'll talk to Denise, and we'll see!"

"We'll see!" Yvo repeated, almost pensively.

The charming rhythm of her throat accelerates; her eyes, dangerously languorous, seek mine; she whispers: "I'm thinking about your garden in Chennevières...do you ever think about it?"

Desire flares up again, mounting to red heat. Yvo's mystery calls to me, its voice profound, ferocious and soft. All the stronger for seizing me unexpectedly, temptation finds me almost disarmed. Furtively, Yvo has drawn closer; her flesh-flower scent is more powerful. If she dares to cross the sexual line, by however small a margin, I'm lost.

She does not dare—not yet, at least; fortunately, adverse images come to the rescue, and words too, which emerge like incantations. "That's a long way away...in the night of time!" I say.

"It was yesterday...I can still see the yellow roses, as if they were there..."

She can evoke at her leisure! I've found my equilibrium. She undoubtedly perceives that, for she suddenly takes her leave with a patient smile—a smile that abandons nothing, which extends over the vast future.

"Who can tell whether she might not succeed?"

I stiffen myself, determined to resist, but I know the cracks in my fortifications. To spend my life with her, or even long years! For she would not release the morsel. She would not make any mistake, would cling on with a frivolous and invincible gentleness. The worst tyranny of all, the grip of a perfumed liana!

I have the password, though. Why the devil shouldn't I use it. On the day when I show her that I am, in her sense, really and completely ruined, everything will be settled. But it's not merely to keep that detestable desire in reserve that I'm temporizing, it's also in order not to accept that destiny overtly. Demonstrating it to someone else would seem to render it irremediable...

Deep down, I hope, desperately, that the warranty of my reputation will get me out of it...

The illusion breathed its April breezes; the golden apples sparkled in the fabulous garden—but the *flow* was interrupted again by Madame Donatienne, bearing another piece of paper.

"It's the nasty gentleman," she said. "Will Monsieur see him?"

The piece of paper bore the words: *Dear friend, it's absolutely necessary that I see you; my present and future depend on it. Gontran Réchauffé.*

He came in with an unpleasant and suspicious expression. His greasy waistcoat and the profound wrinkles of his elastic-sided boots were suggestive of the kind of company he kept. In an excessively narrow face with a cement-like pallor, two dolorously aggressive eyes were shining. His skull, with its back-combed hair, was fitted to a large and clumsy body. Réchauffé naturally inspired mistrust, and knew it.

"Excuse me," he muttered, extending his pauper's hand. "Perhaps you're busy?"

"I'm only working intermittently."

I felt pity for that great tramp, mistreated by fate, who rubbed people up the wrong way on occasions, but whose chaotic brain had surprising glimmers of intelligence. The primitive individual had submitted to massive reduction, and yet the social individual had not adapted itself.

"I'm obliged to come begging," he said, bitterly. "You knew that already. My raft won't touch land, and is dragging me toward the abyssal depths. Does anyone know whether or not I have genius? Myself, I don't know anything—nor do you! Do you know the old Duchesse de Mérannes?"

"I don't know her," I said, astonished by the question, which seemed irrelevant to me, coming from Réchauffé, "but I've been to her house..."

"Your father went there often."

"More assiduously than her son...my father was a sort of man-about-town..."

"I need an introduction to the Duchesse. Her son-in-law, the Comte de Mesles, who is interested in archaeology, has need of a secretary—more precisely, a man to find and file documents. My line of work...I excel at it...I have a flair for it. If you talk to the lady in the right way, she'll persuade the Comte—and I'll be able to earn a crust. I really need that!" After a strange grimace, which bestialized his face, he looked at me with a challenging and wretched expression.

"I'll gladly do as you ask, and I'll try to bring it off."

"Good! You're still the best...certainly better than me, which isn't difficult!"

"That means nothing. There's no common denominator for such things."

Réchauffé suddenly exclaimed, in an exceedingly sharp voice: "Oh, I know full well that it's connected to the deceptions of morality, complicated by the maladies of the imagination and the ambushes of speech. It's frightening, what speech solidifies! The whole story of what we believe in, with the aid of what doesn't exist in itself, but for which we create an existence collectively. When I say that you're the best, that simply means the most cordial. Between you and me, there's a qualitative difference. I don't attach any Manicheism to it..."

He talked in a roguish, pedantic, disenchanted manner, with annoying leaps. Incapable of inspiring sympathy or compassion, everything about him could only offend, discourage or consternate others, according to circumstances. Powerful in Rome or in the Middle Ages, he would have been capable of ferocity—mental rather than physical ferocity. In our time, he would have made a bad rich man, egotistical and sardonic, with brief charitable impulses.

"Well," he resumed, lowering his head and speaking with a cold rage, "that's not all. I'm literally starving, hungry every day. I'd like to eat my three meals a day for a week, like a mason, at a wine-merchant's."

Hatred ravaged his face, while a rightful distress made him as hoarse as an animal. Because I had known him since childhood, I was gripped by compassion, and, after a short pause, slipped a few pieces of paper into an envelope.

Réchauffé took possession of it as if he were tearing it away from me, and shamelessly took out the banknotes.

"There's something I wouldn't have done...I'm a rougher beast than you! And that moves me more than I would have supposed, you know...for two pins, I'd weep..."

He shook my hand convulsively.

"I know my worthlessness; I'll never do anything that will get me out of poverty...unless by chance I have—and I haven't verified it—the gift of talking to the people: then any other capacity becomes useless, and perhaps harmful. Oh, you don't know the anguish of knowing that one is powerless, when one has been idiot enough to think oneself superior." He started to laugh, acidically and discordantly. "Superior! To think that I'll always come back to that, that I'll always be haunted by that misery—for in the end, what good is it? Why should one be superior? How natural it is, the more-or-less latent hatred of the ugly man for the handsome one, the weak for the strong, the sick for the healthy, the man of the herd for the man of genius! How natural and—the word has no real meaning—how just!"

"Yes, but these words also reveal our intellectual prejudices."

"Of course! How many words spring from that! Who is capable of conceiving a fact without misrepresenting it? Misrepresentation is already so great among savages, it was surely endemic in prehistory—but all the same, savages oppose a fairly simple reflex to brute facts. We, on the other hand, tend to bury everything in the double sack of fable and abstraction, thus creating a whole other nature. When that nature is created, humankind will have nothing to do but disappear..."

"Taking the second nature with it?"

"Not at all! An emanation of the unreal, that nature will become real!" Gontran Réchauffé studied the carpet with a haggard expression, while his hand swept through the air. "To create the real with the aid of the unreal—that's the essential work of life. I say *with the aid* of the unreal, not *out of* the unreal. Reduced to itself, the real would always be the same. Life introduces the necessary anomaly: an anomaly that becomes more complicated as various sorts of creature emerge; they are its products, but they produce a new power within it…at each step, the part of the real diminishes. When abstraction has become universally excessive, when the entire contents of the given are reduced to fable, a nature is added to nature. Understand, moreover, that that nature was implicit in the other; otherwise, it would not be able to appear. A mysterious energy mingles the concrete elements with *the instruments of metamorphosis*—instruments of which, in our petty scheme, humans are the final word."

"That's what you've been working on?"

"That's it," Réchauffé declared, with ironic emphasis. Gripped by a sudden suspicion, he added: "You won't say anything to anyone?"

"I promise—although I don't know anyone who could cut the ground from under your feet!"

"One never knows. But let's get on. Think about the Duchesse, and thank you—oh, honestly and sincerely, for *I'll be able to eat!*"

I watched him leave, sadly. In the jungle, he would not have had time to grow up, fatally destined to serve as prey; in social life, he still had a slight chance…but so very slight!

That poor man's misery brings me back to my ruination.

Ruination! For the wage-earning animal, who toils away in a factory or grunts and groans in the dirty fields, my ruination would be comfort: two meals a day at a modest restaurant or an inn; a room; tobacco; the occasional trip to the cinema; and a good suit…even if money were always short. For if one sank completely, that would be true ruination, that of Réchauffé, hunger or the petty prison of the wage-slave. And why should I escape that? Deserving, undeserving…the herd, the elite...I am at the supersocial level at which none of that matters very much, any more than justice, equality, traditional or modern morality...

To tell the truth, I no longer have any profound belief, or any mystical respect. Law, religion, tradition and progress hardly affect me any more than a deer or a wolf. A refined Beyond has brought me back, in a sense, to a *tabula rasa*—but with one important difference: I am so thoroughly socialized that the primitive brutality has almost disappeared; I am incapable of actions that laws or customs deem criminal. So I ignore the temptations that lead to the slightest infraction; I would not even go so far as to make a false declaration to the fiscal authorities, with the certainty of impunity. Entirely without any faith, ritual or code—merely by simple mental reflex.

Even my affective and aesthetic sentiments have been "cleared" of the greater part of the mysticism transmitted by dead human beings and created by living ones—at least, I don't attribute more than a mediocre belief and a fugitive reality to them. And yet, I'm subject to fairly strong influences, transient tributes of enthusiasm, admiration and even veneration for certain works and certain glories—but enthusiasm, admiration and veneration are mere extensions of my psychic activity; even as they transport me, I retain the sentiment of their vacuity. I like them as I like fresh air, tasty food, the delight of a healthy body and, in addition—almost intact—a desire for women and, voluntarily or involuntarily, the myth of love with which that desire has been enveloped, diversified, ennobled and humanized in the course of millennia.

Let's get back to my ruination. Bogged down by my habits, I shall find it hard to bear. It will take me a long time to get used to *living within my means*. My consumption of dreams—metaphysical, scientific and aesthetic meditation—is considerable; it takes up most of my waking hours. An active life is an abomination to me.

I also need a minimum of physical comfort—a moderate but imperious demand. Demand! What a mockery! Whether I die of poverty, accidentally, of illness or decrepitude, doesn't it come to the same thing? I have no more right than the little ant crushed beneath the boot of the unconscious stroller. Humankind would have given me far more than my share, if there were shares! It is unaware of whether I suffer or rejoice, and, to tell the truth, apart from a few enlightenments, I am equally unaware of it. Humankind seems to me to be abject and admirable, brilliant and incredibly stupid, and much more cruel than generous.

Nature? For me, it's myself. The air that I breathe, the water I drink, the nutrients I absorb and with which I *make the man*, the Earth and the stars—all of that has no consciousness of or concern for my vague existence. We take from the universe that which we need to live, and we also take from it that which we destroy; the universe is unaware of it.

All of that does nothing to resign me to poverty. It disgusts me; it frightens me, like pain, like a desert. A supplication rises up occasionally, antique prayer—an absurd and pitiful plaint addressed to some unknown person, the obscure mystical rumor that vibrates beneath negation. The man of totems, of fetishes, of Zeus, Yahweh, the Crucified, the Roman Church, reappears in the fog of the unconscious. Sometimes, I cry: "Lord, have pity on me!"

The cry takes shape, which makes me smile; I taste the cold joy of despising myself, not for that inoffensive return, but for my cowardice—and how vain and infantile that scorn is, in its turn!

Perhaps I can fight. For, at the end of the day, I have an authentic gift, much more favorable for not being superior. I don't suffer when it comes into play. It is exercised almost nonchalantly, at the whim of a sort of inspiration; *I invent as one dreams*. That must be a resource. Doesn't my Multiplex Recorder give me a chance? Won't my Radiant Microphone soon give me another?

Yes, but when?

Is the doorbell replying to my question?

Madame Donatienne announces: "It's the little man with the goatee…"

"Show him into the drawing-room, Madame Donatienne."

The little man with the goatee, whose long-sighted eyes are magnified by his spectacles, is sitting down comfortably when I come into the drawing-room. He is Guillaume Ferrand. His social role is to conduct various business affairs on behalf of others. He is, for the moment, my road-beater; he is trying the chances of the Multiplex Recorder, groping for capitalists.

He greeted me with the cold gravity that is his way of compensating for the deficiencies of short stature and a bad complexion.

"We are perhaps," he said, after a few preliminary remarks, "on the brink of success."

Because he was not much inclined to illusion, these words could not help exciting me.

"You've found a backer?"

"Better than that—one of the three partners in the firm of Ruthven and Bullerton."

"I don't know Messieurs Ruthven and Bullerton."

Guillaume Ferrand raised his arms in a gesture of astonishment and irony. "One of the largest metallurgical companies in the United States. Monsieur Bullerton is interested in your patent."

Hope surged forth, young, agile and fresh. "In what sense is he interested?"

"In a business sense, naturally."

"I realize that—but has he made you an offer?"

"He proposes to buy your patents once he has examined the invention. He's an engineer himself."

"Good! He wants to see the apparatus working. I'm at his disposal. But if he's satisfied—and he will be—what will he do?"

"As I've just old you, he expects to buy the patents from you."

"To buy them outright?"

"If you agree."

"I've told you that I'd rather retain an interest in the exploitation. I'm holding to that!"

"Yes, yes," Ferrand replied, with a hint of scorn. "That's for discussion. At any rate, Bullerton won't baulk at a considerable price—100,000 dollars, for instance."

100,000 dollars! The prospect is too beautiful! And, the fetishistic man reappearing all of a sudden, I touch the wood of a table while affirming: *That'll do nicely!* Fear takes hold of me—the human fear of losing that which one does not have. I reply, however, in a phlegmatic manner that astonishes me, and in which I take a childish pride: "We'll arrange a meeting for Monsieur Bullerton to examine the machine, and we'll discuss the terms then."

Guillaume Ferrand looks at me, also anxious, gripped by the fear of losing what he does not have...

"100,000 dollars! The price doesn't seem sufficient to you?"

I have the audacity to reply, disapproving of myself strongly: "I'd also like a small percentage of the sale price."

"I won't hide it from you that that will be difficult," Ferrand went on, anxiously. "These people don't like anyone to know about their profits...they like to maintain business secrecy. Commercial tactics, Monsieur, are more complicated than the tactics of warfare!" He concluded, in a resigned voice: "Anyway...you shall see Monsieur Bullerton."

With that, he took his leave—with a certain resentment—and left me melancholy, with gnawing worries. Until the interview with Bullerton, my restricted circumstances would loom up before me, would pursue me in my sleep, and would mingle remorse with my cogitations.

And what does it matter? I asked myself, already feeling shooting pains and disturbances in my diaphragm. *Nothing can be done about it. If Bullerton doesn't want a partnership, I'll have to give in…*

This Bullerton, lost in the universal chaos, as abstract an hour ago as an algebraic symbol, takes on a concrete form—as concrete as the means of social existence, still nine-tenths abstract. Apart from the Bullerton created for my usage, will the other—the actual one—have a capital influence on my destiny?

The affair penetrates to the utmost depths; I have to resist that—all the categories of myself are already counting on it dangerously. It is as fateful as the circulation of my blood, and my will, awkward by nature, will only use it to add more force to the turbulence.

11 a.m.! I'm lunching with Juliane—*alias* Juliet. I have to change my jacket.

II.

Juliane always keeps me waiting. That's the rule. She believes in it; she has made it a directive of her existence, especially with respect to me. I'm so accustomed to it that I would experience a sort of anxiety if Juliane appeared right away.

At the back of the drawing-room, in a little armchair that fits my hips exactly and is very comfortable for the elbows, I wait.

For a long time now, I've been oblivious to the blue-and-silver wallpaper, the bric-a-brac of Regency, Louis XV and Empire armchairs accumulated by Juliane's husband, and the sometimes-skewed paintings hanging on the walls: a fake Poussin next to a Carrière; a dubious Delacroix next to a Picasso; a vermicular Cézanne beside a minuscule Ingres.

I'm trying not to think about Bullerton, but he keeps coming back as persistently as a wasp, taking me to America, to the shores of Lake Erie, the sources of the Missouri, the abattoirs of Chicago and the canyons of Arizona.

111

An abrupt reaction: Bullerton disappears! I sink down into ruination, more sinister than before, full of hitherto-unperceived pitfalls.

The real presence of Juliane buries Bullerton beneath the floorboards.

I give and receive a kiss whose tenderness is equal to that of thousands of other kisses. Juliane, nicely dressed and nicely made-up, is not beautiful, but almost pretty. Nature manufactures those like her by the gross: black hair, neatly gathered into a pony-tail, held away from the head, unostentatious black eyes, lips whose native color is concealed by lipstick, white and neatly-formed teeth, thin neck, regulation torso, narrow hips and medium-sized feet.

She is young, healthy, as sensual as necessary, wheedling but not very quarrelsome. For the most part, she is worth as much as many beauties, and as such, she pleases me. It's a very restful love affair. After four years, I can't see any reason to cancel the lease.

In Juliane, the primitive and the interhuman are well equilibrated by social heredity. She comprises an honorable quota of desires, none of which is morbid—just enough mysticism and amorous mirages to color her existence.

Here she is, with the scent of fresh flowers, smiling with contained ardor. "It was our anniversary on Thursday!" she murmurs. "Four years, my darling—that was yesterday!"

At this moment, she is charming, with a little—not too much—of the little girl about her, and very affectionate; she has a full complement of illusions, for it is in love, naturally, that she concentrates her native and ritual energies.

"Do you remember how much you loved me, then?"

I force my tone slightly to reply: "I still love you."

That's enough to make her radiant. "Oh! Truly, darling...still? The little house...the lake...the beautiful evening...and that violin playing in the distance."

Our memories do not correspond exactly: I model mine on hers. That first night, so clear to her, appears to me in a mist. I can't hear the violin, and the lake is invisible.

"We were going up the avenue. Oh, when you took me in your arms, when you took me into the pink bedroom…"

The pink bedroom? I could as easily see it green or violet, but for the sake of argument, I adopt Juliane's color.

"How impatient you were, darling! We could see the park through the open window. I was afraid. You reassured me; you were so gentle, so tender—a woman never forgets that!"

Touching, delightful and ridiculous Juliane! What reality could contend with that fiction? She has made it an extension of her person, and will carry it in her dry bones when she is old.

A door opens; we're no longer alone. The individual who has just appeared is her husband, an old stick with a lantern-jawed face and oily blue eyes. He knows *and is content*. His wife scarcely exists, but he holds on to the association of fortunes, cemented by a child. The two of them have resolved the problem of parallel destinies elegantly.

Jacques Davenal likes me even more than Juliane. He understands the game of intimacy, and his door opened to me so benevolently that I understood the relevant influences and weaknesses. No competition to speak of and, on Juliane's side, a timid reserve that put on a virtuous face, which seducers have little desire to breach.

Save for his indifference to Juliane, Jacques is a vagrant of sensuality. Any woman at all. He does not hide it, as cynical in love as he is conformist in his lifestyle. Our liaison suits him, and its duration amazes him. He suspects that, on my side, it is based in inertia, but he knows the forcefulness with which Juliane creates her mythologies.

"The minister's in trouble!" he cried. "One more patch-up—and it's all over!"

That's it, then—my ruination is definitive! Unless Bullerton…

Jacques and Juliane will scarcely feel the effects of the collapse; they've heeded wise advice. Their funds, for the most part, are in safe havens. Davenal is anxious nevertheless: "There's a possibility of public disorder…revolution, even…"

"No, not that!" says a strident voice. It's the first guest, a strongly-built man on sturdy legs, as hairy as a bear, with massive jaws and sunken eyes the color of raw leather. "No revolution," he continues, having bowed to Juliane, "not even a collapse. A steep fall for the franc, but it will bottom out."

"Where?" Jacques demanded, mockingly.

"Perhaps at one sou…to rise again afterwards. Not much higher, I agree…three sous, four or five perhaps! What do you expect? The country can't keep feeding a debt of 400 billion in gold, even though it's rich—very rich, fabulously rich…and so elastic! The best human rubber!"

Jumisy is no mean prophet.

"England's debt is no less," Jacques remarked.

"She has other guarantees—primarily, the American guarantee. An English-speaking country can't be allowed to go bankrupt, even partially. Strictly speaking, the Americans are hammering the British themselves, and won't let anyone else hammer them. Then again, character and necessity…"

Other guests: two women of approximately the same age and plainness; one young and pretty, but nothing more; one old virtuoso, a prince of the cello; one poet; one paleontologist; one physicist; one metaphysician; one essayist; one worn-out newspaper columnist; Ambroise Ferral, the man I like better than any other; and, finally, Marcus, who arouses all the primitive hatreds in me.

Almost all the male diners are pretty well-known in their own areas, for Jacques likes to assemble elites.

The columnist, talking about a soirée at the American ambassador's, raised the crinoline question: "There were some skirts there that were abruptly flared, beneath a long flat bodice—mere sketches of crinolines. Abominable!"

"Couturiers have been mounting an offensive on the crinoline for four years!"

"They'll end up making it compulsory—folly always triumphs among women. Besides, I think the crinoline, as it was worn under the Second Empire, with an *ad hoc* bodice, had its charm. Do you remember that play at the Variétés, with the elegant restoration? Those white stockings, neatly tailored, and dancing crinolines—my God, a pretty woman in that, would be suggestive!"

"Provocative, rather!" cried an angry female septuagenarian. "I can assure you that the grace of women came into its own then, and it was as pleasant to see them walking around a salon as in the street."

"And take note that a slim woman still seemed slim, if the writers of the period can be believed. In an old issue of *L'Illustration*, there's a fête at Compiègne...the illustrator depicts the empress, magnificently crinolined, in the midst of hyper-inflated ladies, and the text accompanying the image remarks things of this sort: 'the empress, like Diana the huntress...' With that vast contraption around her hips!"

"All the same," said the essayist, "the slender fashions of today are very seductive. I prefer them to all the fashions of the past."

"What! Little Louis XV chambermaids!"

"Ah!" sighed the septuagenarian. "The Directory had dazzling evening dresses...and at certain times, large velvet skirts..."

"I'm in favor of *all* fashions!" Jacques proclaimed. "Even puffed sleeves, even flaps, even hoop petticoats. It's necessary for women to undergo incessant metamorphoses."

"Oh yes," said Ambroise Ferral, "let's magnify the legend."

Marcus was watching Madame Lancerot with the amethyst eyes. He was on the track, and nothing would distract him.

Someone at the end of the table announced a fatal crash in pearls: "Fine cultured pearls will inevitably sink wild pearls...the oyster, which produces the one, produces the other. No structural difference, same substance, same formation, same appearance..."

"Remember that in the Antilles, we have incomparable waters for pearl-oysters. One can make hundreds of millions...and no one, save for an obstinate old man...the Japanese are paying dear for a concession there!"

A voice like a cathedral organ proclaimed: "We can talk to the Americans by wireless telegraph; tomorrow, we'll be talking to Melbourne. In ten years, we'll be able to go around the world in four days."

"It's frightful!" sighed the poet.

"Frightful?" cried a bell-tower voice, astonished.

"Hideous, Monsieur. The reduced Earth will be nothing but a miserable machine for nourishing human beings—so small, so paltry...so contemptible, in sum! Think how magnificent and frightful it was when it was necessary to imagine a demigod to slay the Nemean lion, when Job disputed with Yahweh, who crushed it with the vastness of the seas and the Leviathan, how vertiginously beautiful it was when the conquistadors set out in their cockle-shells, when travelers got lost in its virgin forests...infinity! And now, sinister melancholy!"

"Would you prefer, Monsieur, the little torches that the stars once were to the immense heavenly bodies swarming in boundless space?"

"Passionately! What have the stars to do with us now? Inaccessible, they are devoid of interest. Terrestrial space, that was what was delightful: the unwonted mystery into which, nevertheless men could penetrate. Oh, to sail along the coast in an ancient trireme, to pass through the Pillars of Hercules and find oneself confronted by an ocean without limits! Can such an intoxication be compared to the cold excitement of being confronted by a nebula? A star 25 million times larger than the Earth has less effect on me than the paltriest star of the Hellenes!"

"A meager vision!" cried the physicist. "For the stars will not always be inaccessible. Like the Argonauts in the little interior sea, our astronauts will sail the interstellar oceans. That's not a chimera! Within a century, we will be familiar with Mars and Venus; within two centuries, our conquista-

116

dores will reach Saturn and Jupiter. All that, which seems insane to us now, will be as real as Cook's voyages to the antipodes, or the expeditions of our aviators. What will remain of the infantile poetry of the Ramayana, the Bible and the Odyssey?"

"They'll remain touching and beautiful!" Ambroise Ferral put in, in a soft voice. "In the human imagination, countless marvelously contradictory imaginative products are stacked up. The past is within us; far from disdaining it, we shall love it all the more. What would we be without the miracles of tradition? Poignant evocations of those caverns in which humans carved their visions and beliefs in stone! The charming seduction of Rama! And the voyage of the Argonauts, or the less mythical one of Hanno, and the incomparable legend of Prometheus, the force of Ezekiel, the bitter splendor of Ecclesiastes. Could you be insensible to the epic of Roland? When the little stars rise in the evening, I look at them with the gaze of the Chaldean patriarchs *at the same time* as that of the modern era, which knows that they are frightful furnaces in which the Earth would melt like a blob of wax in a hot oven. Venus is a charming celestial night-light as well as a world similar to our Earth, and I will sing the praises of the evening star with de Musset, or even *Twinkle, twinkle little star* with an English child, while wondering whether there are creatures living there, as ferocious as ours, condemned to devour one another, or, by contrast, growing fraternally, each according to its species..."

"You will admit, however," said the physicist, "that astral poetry, such as science dispenses to us, is the most beautiful!"

"The most grandiose, at least. One day, we shall miss that astral poetry, as you conceive it, when it is replaced by that of a universe even greater, to which stars and nebulas stand in the same relationship as the world of the ancestors does to them..."

"Greater? While conceding that it is infinite? That infinity envisages many times the number of our stars..."

"But then, our stars, even in infinite number, are only one imperceptible existence within the universal existence…"

"I don't understand that," said the physicist. "How can an infinity be surpassed?"

"By an infinite number of infinities," said Ambroise Ferral, smiling.

The physicist shook his head, and the conversation shifted to Jane Mirval, who, young, beautiful, beloved, famous and rich, had demanded a revolver to cure so many evils.

"Is there any particular cause of despair in our era?" said Jacques. "Never, I think, have we seen so many young creatures, heaped with riches and glory, dying voluntarily."

"Cocaine?"

"Universal agitation?"

"The aftermath of the war?"

"Perhaps an ever-more-lucid consciousness of the frightful pitfall. As human sensitivity increases incessantly, everything that surrounds us becomes more terrible. Each of our movements is perilous; the death-knell never ceases to reverberate in our breasts. Can we take a step or make a gesture without risk? Does not every heartbeat coincide with the death of one of my peers? The day before yesterday, I saw a lithe and lively young man crossing the road; a car swerved, and he lay there uttering frightful screams, broken. 20,000 individuals perish like that every year in the United States. A million others are injured—and that's only one among countless dangers. Do you remember that greengrocer killed in his shop, struck by a bullet that a murderer intended for a rival? The enemy is swarming among us. Who among us can be sure of not being struck down by his own particular disease, of not suffering for years, of not being eaten away by cancer or devoured by tuberculosis? That's how it is! Perhaps it was worse on the savannah, in the cities of the ancient world, among medieval brutes, but, less taxed than we are by deadly foresight, their sensitivity was also tempered by the ambient ferocity."

We listened, reproachfully, to the gaunt man with the hollow eyes, placidly making his speech. He interrupted himself to take some *foie gras*, muttering bitterly: "Creatures capable of eating flesh are condemned by the same token! Any abomination is explicable as soon as one dares to devour dead bodies. We're living in hell."

I watched Marcus, who was sitting next to the pretty girl. He was making advances already. I think I would have found him repulsive had I been a woman, but that was perhaps further proof of his seductiveness. I'm really quite perspicacious—intuitive, even—but, being deprived of feminine tastes, like so many of my friends, I'm unable to estimate of what the sexual charm of a Marcus consists. I only know that the charm works. He plays it to perfection, endowed with infinite patience, conducting research with an ardor equal to that of great experimental scientists, and never forgetting the rules of the game.

I had the impression that the pretty woman knew how to defend herself; that impression was confirmed by Marcus's attitude. No one adapts himself better to circumstance. He practices mimicry masterfully. Such base intelligence does him a disservice with respect to some women, but how well it serves him with respect to others! Besides, when he senses that an obstacle might be insurmountable, he stands aside with genuine indifference; there is no man less tempted by the impossible. By way of compensation, for the possible, however arduous it may be, he deploys an insectile obstinacy.

Outside of his capital passion, Marcus would appear obtuse, inept in pleasures and even more so in anything that brings the cerebral machinery into play. One could say—and it is strange in such a man—that he is as incapable of discerning the bouquet of a wine as the quality of a mind. In male company he is distracted; he has a strange air of lassitude and nostalgia, while maintaining the affectionate and repulsive politeness that he practices instinctively, as if on principle. His perfume, light and discreet, repels me like a stink; his smile irritates me, as does the oblique movement, which pleases so many women, even more so.

Jacques still had a smoking-room. The conversation became more cheerful there, and Marcus only put in a momentary appearance.

"You must tell me more about this universe that you were talking about just now," I said to Ambroise Ferral.

"Would you like to have dinner together on Wednesday? We can talk about it, if it interests you."

"How could it not interest me…coming from you?"

"Until Wednesday, then."

Miguel, the essayist, was talking about cinema artistes and their fabulous fortunes. "The secret of universality and multitudes," said the writer. "A Douglas Fairbanks, a Mary Pickford or a Charlie Chaplin speaks to the entire world, within the same fortnight. They have the privilege of fairy tales or the Thousand-and-One Nights: *ubiquity*. On the same evening, Charlie is *live* in Paris, in London, in Berlin, in Madrid, in Naples…it's really him, grimacing simultaneously in 100 cities, his gaze meeting myriads of gazes from one end of the Occident to the other. In sum, he's a god!"

"A happy creature!" the romancer complains. "While our great Laveral, who is worth 1000 Charlies, earns less in his lifetime than a furrier."

"Happy? I want proof of that. Max Linder, Claude France and Régine Flory aren't the only stars of stage and screen to have committed suicide.[19] Humankind has somber

---

[19] Max Linder (1883-1925) was by far the most famous of these cited suicides. The first actor ever to create a continuing character for a series of silent comedies, he was an important precursor of Charlie Chaplin. In 1911, he was the highest-paid entertainer in the world, but his career was decisively interrupted by the Great War. Although serving in a non-combatant role, he was seriously wounded, and never fully recovered; he made a valiant attempt to pick up his career in Hollywood but failed; in 1923, he married an 18-year-old girl who had borne him a child; they made a suicide pact, which they brought to a successful conclusion at the second attempt. The German-born

turns, and I think people become more unhappy as they accumulate gains on Earth. A frightful ennui, a boundless fear and a sinister awareness of annihilation devour them in the end…and it's a death they deserve…"

"Because they sin more than other animal species?"

"No, because their moral death is attaining its marvelous destiny. The miracle that began with the first masters of fire is completed by a psychic miracle. It would be ridiculous, after having created a new nature, after having constrained the energies of life according to human custom, to die of material decadence like the reptiles of the Secondary Epoch. Human beings ought to die in despair, terrified, at the height of victory; they ought to die of having been the greatest creator that life has fashioned on this planet."

"Why terrified? A heroic, stoical death would be finer."

"Oh no—that would be a poor death. Death is only magnificent and complete in the most frightful anguish—anguish without malady, anguish without injury, or any other physical torture…"

"Not according to me!" jeered a rubicund 40-year-old. "You're too ambitious Monsieur. Humankind will end ignominiously, as it has lived, as all creatures live…and I'd rather believe that the last men will be more unconscious than the men of today; I'm happy to imagine them sufficiently brutalized not to suspect that their species is ending. Shall we talk about young women for a while?"

---

actress who used the stage-name Claude France (Jane Wittig, 1893-1928) gassed herself. The French singer Régine Flory (1894-1926) enjoyed considerable success in England before being found shot dead in the office of the manager of the Drury Lane Theatre in mid-show; although her death was eventually written off as a suicide, the police initially investigated it as a murder, and it is not entirely obvious that the official verdict was correct.

It was nearly 4 p.m. when I arrived at Yveline's house. She had changed her clothes, now being clad in Chinese crêpe with thin blue and yellow stripes on a silver-gray background, and an even shorter skirt—which, as soon as she sat down, rode up above her knees. Her stockings were almost flesh-colored, with a golden sheen.

In this new costume, the hint of the Bedouin had gone; the male of the species is very sensitive to these metamorphoses, which make a multiple personality of the same woman. Although she appeared more seductive than in the morning, I was less susceptible to the temptation. She did not seem to notice that; she struck a pose whose power she knew, leaning slightly backwards in her armchair, flexibly, melting into it, cool in her skirt, whose petals she thrust back with a mechanical gesture.

"What have you been doing since this morning?" she asked.

"Nothing, except lunch…at a friend's house."

"That might be a great deal. Do I know them?"

"Slightly—the Davenals."

"Ah!"

She was not unaware of what I was to Juliane, and her lips expressed a disdain that she pretended to suppress, but which she intended me to divine: a gesture intended to annoy me. Yveline did not know how indifferent it left me.

"They're old friends, aren't they?"

"We've been friends for five years."

She perceived the impossibility of saying anything more, and that impossibility frustrated her to the point of irritation. In effect, she wanted to get her teeth into Juliane in some way and tear her apart. I had a desire to open the floodgates, if only to see Yveline set off on a false track, stamping in the void—but the game might have become dangerous and I continued to keep the open secret.

"What about Denise?" I said, to let loose the dogs.

"Oh yes, Denise…" She hesitates, direly annoyed, but finally goes in search of Denise.

This tall, neat girl is unfinished. Her gestures are not "complete," her gait is provisional, her grace in suspense. She will certainly be seductive. She has the complexion of the most beautiful blonde marquises, a neck that, once finished, will be delicate and voluptuous, and slate-gray shining eyes from beyond the northern seas, with a precious naivety. It is sufficient for her hair to be a frank blonde, as fine as such hair unfailingly is, and fleecy. She has the dazzling teeth that everyone has nowadays, and a mouth whose lips reveal fine scarlet blood.

If one accepts the "canons" of race, she would almost certainly be a beautiful Scandinavian, nuanced by a more southerly climate. Already, I deem her highly desirable—for others than myself. For the contents of the vase, it is necessary to wait. In the meantime, a few characteristics are clear and enduring. Of the hereditary savage, she retains the vivacity and fervor of a Redskin: a healthy flesh resistant to wastage, which will keep infirmity at bay until the end of maturity and dispense a robust old age unless some external evil intervenes. Continuity in sentiments, no lack of energy in action—a dangerous tendency, of which creatures should be proud.

Of social heredity, she retains an aesthetic perception of moral tastes more noble and subtle than Yveline's, and an artistry in pleasing others that has shown her to be superior to primitives since infancy. That heredity has transformed brute confidence into generous candor, and an idealistic and mystical naivety. Her present environment has infused her with the Catholic faith, a rather vast conception of space and time, developed her musical virtuosity, and provided her with the countless notions that even a mediocre creature acquires from the immediate ambiance and the traditional ensemble.

Ill-equipped to earn her living, devoid of cunning or any venality, inclined to give freely of her wealth and her trouble, she is at the mercy of her beauty and grace—sources, according to circumstance, of fortune, misery and degradation.

She stands up straight before me, in her short dress of pale gray crêpe with silver embroidery. An enchantment animates her features; she exhales a perfume as fresh as rose-blossom; beautiful dreams surround her. The charming rustle of her skirt will intoxicate young men; she symbolizes the most delightful produce of human history, and also the furious wars, the solvent voluptuousness, the birth and death of nations. Each glance that I dart at her brings back a flood of images and rhythms: a spring in the woods; a streak of silver in the moss; a little house lost in the mountains; heather on a hillside; equinoctial winds; April showers; a wreck cast up on an island; Easter bells; a woman's voice in the dark; a hind crossing a clearing.

Scarcely warmed by the illusion, I give way to the imperious call of heredity, recklessly admiring little Denise, ready to bloom. I am not made for her, nor she for me, but at the end of the day, at the sight of her, love—both abstract and concrete—addresses itself to the entire audience.

What should I say to her? I know so little about her—the dissimilarity of cultures is so great. At Denise's age, boys become unbearable. Although the differences in "receptivity" render girls more tolerable, all conversation with them is nothing but a deceptive game, painful for people of my sort. It is, however, necessary that I make a start.

"What sort of things do you do, Denise, and what do you think about?"

How I wish she were able to talk! What happens inside Yveline, or even inside Juliane, is of little or no interest. In their commonplace, interchangeable souls, there is a flux of "conventional" sensations and sentiments, without choice or relief. In Denise, the aristocracy of choice is beginning: distinct dreams, innocent poetry, and, for what it may be worth, a conception of things that is, if not entirely personal, at least personalized.

"Always the same things," she replies. "Reading, in English and German, music…"

"Well, what books are you reading, or about to read?"

"*La Petite soeur de Trott, À l'ombre de la Croix…*"[20]

"Do you like those books?"

"Yes…very much."

"That's good, Denise…very good, in fact."

There was a rosy tint in her young cheeks.

"And what about music?"

"Anything that I can play…" She points to the piano, on which there is a pile of "select pieces," ranging from Bizet to Beethoven, Grieg to Wagner, Lecoq to Hervé or Offenbach, and even from Rameau to Haydn.

"Do you prefer music to reading?"

"Oh, yes…yes!"

That is the cry of passion—a refined, hereditary passion. What could music mean to a man of the Lacustrian era, or even the Greeks? An adventure as prodigious as an interplanetary voyage, more prodigious than the epic of the caravels! Poor primitive sounds: the indigent thunder of the lion, the lamentable voice of the buffalo, the senile croaking of frogs, the summary fluting of the nightingale. Since the year 1000, what nebulas of sound, what constellations of melody—an entire universe, imponderable and boundless—have been created by the pitiful vertical beast…

"Don't you have any preferences, Denise?"

"I dare not!"

I know what she means—a sentiment of weakness, a fear of being unjust; any preference is hazardous and presumptuous, if not cruel.

"That's very good, Denise…and yet, it will be necessary to choose, in order to know and play better."

"I'll never know anything much, godfather."

---

[20] The first title cited is a notable fictional examination of child psychology by André Lichtenberger, first published in 1898; the second title has been used more than once, but the intended reference is almost certainly to a book by Jérôme and Jean Tharaud, first published in 1917 and reprinted repeatedly thereafter.

"Why not?"

"I don't know…I sense it…"

The response sounds clearly; no false note, no camouflage of vanity. Denise probably has no ambition, or, at least, only an infinitesimal dose thereof. Any insistence would be awkward. Her gift is real, but its amplitude is immeasurable. Probably, like the majority of creatures, she will not live up to the promises of her childhood.

A short silence, which troubles me. Will it ever be possible to chat to Denise, or will she always remain as remote from me as a Chinese or a Samoyed? Will I be able to see the interior being emerging from her splendid candor, to penetrate the recesses of that consciousness like the beautiful mountain valley whose memory still intoxicates me?

An old lady with the profile of a shrew has appeared, reminding me that it is Yveline's day for receiving visitors. I want to leave, but I stay—torpor and inertia. The old lady emits her rancid anecdotes, gnawing away at one reputation, dribbling over a second, until others come to the rescue, old, mature and young, reinforced by a 40-year-old with the jaw of a lamprey. She is the only one not bored, alternatively fascinated by Yveline and Denise.

For half an hour, a nullity of remarks, equivalent if not identical, on the subject of native women. Tea and *petits fours* bring a measure of animal ease.

I am abruptly jerked out of my persistent torpor, as if I had been hit by a truncheon. Everything becomes terribly exciting: *Marcus is here!*

What a fine flood of hatred! My three natures participate in it, each one dominant in turn. In a flash, I am the savage armed with a hatchet or a club, a duelist, a magistrate, a clever psychologist guiding his adversary's maneuvers. Actions and circumstances whirl around, sketchy and overlapping. The furor cools down, dominated by anguish and pity. Denise is vanquished; she is the prey; Marcus extracts a frightful pleasure from her, wearies of it, and throws her back. She flees,

126

degraded, humiliated and—I grind my teeth—still amorous for the disgusting conqueror.

The anguish and pity become tepid in their turn. Coolly, I watch Marcus, astonished to see him here, partaking of the tea while clandestinely "evaluating" Denise. That he has written her name on his hunting list is impossible to doubt. He will come back, he will prowl around with inexhaustible patience, always on the lookout, adapted to any circumstances; he already desires her, in his brutish manner, which heads directly for the target.

In following his desire so closely, I abuse Denise in a melancholy manner. Her youth, her purity and the peril of such a seduction cannot stop Marcus. He is replete with audacity, as with endurance. He is a great champion: victory at any price, but also the intrinsic passion of the sport. A poet, moreover, in the cruel and artistic sense, with subtlety and virtuosity—and also a tactician, skilled in calculation, the choice of terrain and moment, an expert in flank attacks and turning ripostes...

With a forcefulness that astonishes me, I want to save Denise. The threat is distant. Besides, many escape, either by virtue of their nature, which is antipathetic to that of Marcus, or because his notebook is overloaded and he has too many pieces in play.

He has not yet made any headway with Denise and he will need a good deal of time—if he succeeds—to dissipate the atmosphere that protects her; he is not even making any impact on Yveline, who is preoccupied with *our* memory. I have room for maneuver, therefore, time to prepare the separation. I shall not say anything to Yveline yet; to make her conscious of the peril would determine a situation too precisely, and I'm counting on its vagueness.

Seated in a corner, I watch Marcus with a cold and lucid rage. None of his gestures are indifferent to me; they're the gestures of an enemy—an innate enemy—of which I have a photographic perception, and the importance of which I exaggerate.

Not a minute passes during which he ceases to exercise his vocation. Two or three times, he finds himself next to Denise; his voice, the charm of which exasperates me, makes remarks that seem neutral, but are preparatory; he does not neglect Yveline, who is worthy of being added to his list...

At times, I knock down or strangle Marcus, then, the gesture becoming civilized, it is before four witnesses that the fine point of an épée or a pistol-shot destroys the adversary. Oh, how my three natures desire his death, and how vain it is to struggle against that desire. I can repress it, envelop it with description, but I know with what carnivorous joy I would welcome the news of his disappearance. In helpful circumstances, would I go so far as to kill him? No. Between murder and myself the distance seems unbridgeable. But the images are there, so vivid that my heart beats feverishly—and the power of images is unlimited.

I thought that he would stay until the end, but he has not even stayed for an hour; as soon as he has crossed the threshold, there is a fresh joy, the matinal joy of the gilding of woods.

The departure of Marcus has cleared everything up. Denise is liberated; life extends immense and pure. Such a charming atmosphere envelops Yveline that I dare not risk a tête-à-tête. There is an astonishing exaltation of nerves gripped by lucid intoxication, a euphoria that makes anticipation vanish and ambushes disappear.

III.

It was an hour ago that the tooth began to hurt. It is, fundamentally, a wise tooth. Twice, already, it has sounded the tocsin. The dentist has put it under observation. I don't think he'll save it; a palpitation of ill omen affirms that disease will triumph over his science. I carry my pain far and wide; it activates rather than hinders cogitation, but it envelops thoughts with a ferocious atmosphere.

Suffering would be pleasant, if it did not surpass certain limits, either by its intensity or by persistence and repetition. A brief and violent pain has its charm. A moderate pain, for a few hours, is rich in information. A pain that comes back incessantly is simply execrable. The prognosis ought not to be dire, but life without any suffering at all would be utterly insipid!

(More than any metaphysical argument, pain, like joy, inclines me to see a component of contingency in the universe.)

Nevertheless, to what frightful excess will pain not go? I think about my brother Adrien, stifling for months on end, mortally; of that wretched woman whose facial neuralgia devours her for entire days; of the martyrs afflicted by earache; of those whose intolerable crises of faith draw them ferociously down to earth, or are tortured by the colics of *Miserere*...

There is not enough autonomous suffering. It's also necessary for accidents to break our bones, tear our flesh, scatter our entrails, condemn us to perish by fire, to be buried alive, to sink into homicidal water.

Is there a moment in time when the threat eases? What a miracle it is not to die of fear! A miracle more astonishing still: joy, or simple tranquility!

The tocsin sounds more loudly. Rage becomes almost intolerable. I walk more rapidly; *I rescue myself*—I wish I could walk through walls.

Native horrors are insufficient for human beings. The sensuality of impending suffering is born in them. All the evils that they fear become delectable as soon as they are able to inflict them on the weak and the helpless. The art of torture, incessantly extended, has a marvelous complexity; human genius reveals itself there as subtly as in art, science or metaphysics.

Thrilling epics of torturers, evocative tragedies of victims! All humankind becomes complicit. Only a few escape the original sin of cruelty. Perhaps none at all, in ancient times. How many children have you known who were exempt? How many men, in fact? You, who would not kill a fly, who are moved to pity by the slightest plaint, are you sure of having none of it, or of not having had your share? I've seen you, avid for tragedies, reading tales of torture with suspicious ardor...that's a symptom! To be sure, you've escaped, you've combated the virus stubbornly, your hand has been innocent for a long time and doubtless always will—but I know that you're jealous. How many times have you dreamed of committing violence upon a rival; to how many evils have you subjected him? You'll begin again tomorrow, or you'll cease to be ardent, you'll only be half-alive...although these bestial images can never cross the boundary of the self, never springing forth into the not-me, they're sure signs! Furthermore, your peers are lost in a countless multitude of ferocious beings.

The bell is still ringing. If only I had a soporific! But I have nothing, and all the pharmacies are closed. O for an injection of morphine, or merely a little laudanum...is it possible that that little bone, afflicted by a spot of decay as broad as three pinheads, can cause such a racket? To look at it, well caparisoned by enamel, it seems just like all the rest. It's solid, capable of lasting a quarter of a century, but it will be necessary to sacrifice it, stupidly...

"I shall torture and flay Jubit of Hamath like a tree," Shamaneser IV inscribed in granite.

And Sennacherib wrote: "I killed the rebels and crucified their corpses." Then he wrote: "I heaped up the corpses of their soldiers like trophies, and I cut off their extremities. I mutilated those that I captured alive, like wisps of straw, and to punish them, I cut off their hands."

What roasters of men the Tyrians and Carthaginians were! What a magnificent executioner, the Roman State. But perhaps it is China and Western Europe, from the barbarian

130

invasions until the 17th century, which deserve the prize for torture. Nevertheless, the most uncouth nations, nomadic populations and savage clans had beautiful refinements: the cross; the man flayed alive, thrown into boiling oil, subjected to the torture of the saw—the patient is sectioned, lengthways and sideways, often with a wooden saw; the pyre; the hacking of the condemned man into little pieces, which lasts for hours— the unconscious victim being ingeniously revived; lapidation; bellies filled with stones and spices, then sown up again; skulls squeezed slowly until the brain oozes out; human beings cast into dungeons and oubliettes, buried alive or walled up; the wheel, quartering, the strappado, red-hot irons; suspension by the wrists or the thumbs, fingernails torn out, fingers reduced to pulp, crushing under blocks of stone; pincers, boots, the sawhorse, the spider, cutting off breasts, the tongue, the nose, the ears, teeth burned through the cheeks, blinding, the red-hot mask; death by ferocious beasts, such as the lion-executioners kept by kings of Assyria.

There were epidemics of torture. Thus, in two villages in the region of Trèves, all the inhabitants except for one couple were delivered to the executioner as witches. In the town of Bamberg, 600 condemned individuals, after having screamed in the hands of torturers, were delivered to the flames. The Bishop of Breslau employed eight executioners. One of those tormentors, exhausted by labor "that exceeded the strength of a single man" recruited deputies.

A 13th-century law specifies, with regard to witches: "They are to be burned or subjected to whichever ill-treatment the judge thinks the worst and the most cruel, for they have denied Jesus Christ and have given themselves to the Devil. Those who hide them or give them aid shall be justly condemned and their heads cut off."

I have opened the book of torture; I read at random:

"The pincers were heated on a brazier. The executioner seized them and nipped the torture-victim in all the places prescribed by the judgment. The right hand was placed in the fire and held there until it was entirely consumed; on the stump, meanwhile, as the flesh was detached and the bones were charred, the executioner continued to pour burning sulfur…

"When the hand and the wrist were utterly destroyed, the executioner began to fill the wounds with boiling oil, molten lead and wax mixed with molten sulfur. The torture proceeded very slowly in order to prolong the suffering of the condemned man for as long as possible…

"Now, the horses were whipped…but they could not pull him apart. They were whipped as hard as possible, and an hour passed in useless effort.

"Suddenly, one of the noblemen mounting guard, seeing a horse completely exhausted, which was refusing to advance in spite of the terrible blows of the whip, leapt on to his mount, detached the horse and attached his own, which he roused with forceful thrusts of his spurs and his crop…

"Weary of waiting, the executioner seized a cleaver and severed the muscles of the dying man, who expired…

"Mad with rage and pain, the horses set off in every direction, carrying off their bloody trophies…" (G. Verdène.)[21]

Men, my brothers, frightful victims, monstrous torturers!

No respite. Two gnomes are striking hammer-blows at the roots of the molar: a flood of pain shakes that bone, which I imagine to be granite, because it is called a rock, and delivers it to tortures which, far from inciting me to resignation, evoke

---

[21] The reference is presumably to the journalist Georges Verdène, although the quote must be from a newspaper article, as it seems unlikely to have come from any of his published books. The description is obviously of the execution of Robert Damiens, who attempted to stab Louis XV in 1757, albeit with a weapon exceedingly ill-fitted for an assassination; contemporary accounts were endlessly and lasciviously recycled in both fiction and non-fiction. Rosny may well have found the sad story of Rebecca Lamp—which became famous because her letter is one of the few surviving documents written by an accused witch—in the same source.

all the terror of existence, the vision of miseries without number, prowling around us in myriads, like tireless phantoms.

The more I complain to others, the more tiresome my suffering becomes.

(One might think that the arterioles have ceased beating. The rock is tranquil, the pain withdraws with muffled paces.) What pity I have for you, Rebecca Lamp, who lived at the same time as Georg Pferinger, the burgomaster of Nordlingen who, with doctors steeped in demonic science, Conrad Graf and Sebastian Röttinger, resolved to exterminate witches...

You were married to a government official, the wife of the treasurer Peter Lamp. Because your name was pronounced in the course of a witch-trial, you were dragged from your house in the absence of your companion. The torturers took possession of your fragile body. Conrad Graf and Sebastian Röttinger, the savant men, watched your torture and directed it. Weak and sensitive as you were, you resisted unspeakable torments for two sessions. Finally, exhausted by agony, you gave in, O poor woman!

I do not know how you wrote this letter from your prison, your body broken, or who transmitted it to the treasurer:

"My chosen one, my treasure, if I must, in spite of my innocence, be separated from you, may my lamentations be before God for all eternity. I have been forced to speak, I have been so martyrized, and yet, I am as innocent as God in Heaven. If I knew the slightest thing, the merest shadow of this affair, I would wish that God would forbid me Heaven.

"How my death will hurt you, my beloved treasure. Alas, my poor orphans! Send me something to enable me to die, otherwise I shall perish in the fire.

"How can God permit such suffering? Why have I been subjected to such injustice? Why did God not want to hear me?"

The husband wrote to the judges (thus risking torture and death):

"I hope and I believe and I am certain that my wife has never had the slightest idea of all that has been heaped upon her, for I affirm on my conscience and on the testimony of many virtuous people that my wife has always feared God, that she is virtuous, honorable, fervent and modest, and that she was always the enemy of the Evil One and his works, by which she was horrified..."

But the savant men Graf and Röttinger knew their business! Torture was applied with a more terrible rigor, and you were eventually burned alive on September 9, 1590, poor little Rebecca Lamp!

Everything is calming down. Only a painful shadow of the racket persists. Some other evening, the optimist shall have his hymn, but tonight is black. The voice of Ecclesiastes declaims beneath the stars. The world is an ocean of threats. The jungle is no more formidable where, every night, myriads of creatures are eaten alive. Heaven, Earth, all the misery of human beings and beasts weighs upon my bones: the boundless sepulcher is open within me and around me.

My thoughts horrify me and the beating of my heart terrifies me; I am as naked as the day when I emerged from my mother's womb...

Yes, I know: tomorrow, I shall know youth again, but tomorrow does not console me at all; tonight, I am as old as if I had lived through all the ages of man.

IV.

I have finally met Bullerton. It has been necessary to annihilate the image that I had formed; the real Bullerton has nothing in common with the imagined Bullerton. I attributed to him the tall stature and sloping shoulders of Anglo-Saxons; his height is mediocre, his shoulders square, his hair is a smoky black; his eyes are dark brown, his complexion the color of dead leaves, and his lips as violet as a black man's. His teeth, which I had matched to a horse's, are small, the color of fine pearls, embedded in jaws that are reminiscent of the jaws of a hyena. Imperious, naïve, cunning, bold, summary and nevertheless complicated, savage and organized, mystical and cynical, honest and thieving according to the occasion, strictly faithful to his word—thus he appeared to me, during the interview.

In the commercial sport in which he engages with cold fury, he thinks himself master of his destiny and is, in himself, a very poor man, without support, chaotic, with depths of bitterness of which he is unaware, which he has misunderstood once and for all and which he will misunderstand until he is claimed by the scleroses and congestions that, unless he dies prematurely, he will not escape.

The engineer accompanying him almost realizes the Bullerton before the encounter: the equine teeth, the sloping shoulders, the tall stature, the glacial blue eyes, the narrow face, the cleanly-cut temples and the elongated skull.

Bullerton perceives, with satisfied amazement, that I speak English tolerably well. After preliminaries that aggravate an ill-contained desire to be brief, he says: "Look here, if your machine is good, I'll take it for 200,000 dollars, but Monsieur Ferrand says that you want a continuing involvement. I must tell you that that's not my custom—no, not at all. It's a hindrance, excess baggage..."

"Not necessarily!"

"What do you mean, not necessarily? Do you mean you'll give it up?"

"No. I think that it isn't necessarily a complication."

The primitive pulls a face, which expresses incomprehension and slight astonishment, but the social being quickly resumes a composite impassivity—a mixture of Indian and Anglo-Saxon impassivity. "Why?" he says, in a trenchant voice.

"What annoys you is the possibility of an intervention in your business affairs, isn't it? I can renounce any such intervention in advance."

"How?"

"By relying on your honesty. If, for instance, I asked for a dollar for every machine sold and if I let you determine my credit yourself, you would only have to cast an eye over your accounts at the end of every year to determine the sum due immediately."

He does not reply immediately, evidently disconcerted and wondering whether my reply might conceal some exceedingly subtle ruse. Finally, he says: "You've thought about it? You'll renounce absolutely any verification?"

"Undoubtedly."

"You'll trust us?"

"Entirely…and I'm quite sure of your honesty."

"You can't be."

"All right! Then I'll take the risk. Businessmen run such risks continually—in the Stock Exchange, for instance."

He reflects further, then, raising his eyebrows, says: "That's okay, but I don't know if I can give you a dollar; I'll know that when the machine has been built in my factory."

"According to my calculations, the retail price will be something of the order of 200 dollars. That's not important. Let's say half a percent of the sale price."

"Why the sale price?"

"Because I don't know exactly how much profit you'll take. You ought to prefer that."

He smiled—a truly child-like smile—and even laughed briefly: "Yes, that's right…I *ought* to prefer that!"

I am able to take account, confusedly, of how an American human machine like Bullerton differs from a French machine of a homologous kind. I sense that the environment has created centers of particular reaction. The compartments of the self must be more watertight. The capacities of absorption and resorption appear to me to be very different, so far as I can judge by means of a confused and doubtless fallacious intuition. I think of it in terms of constraints that, for certain faculties, determine limitations of growth, acting like incomplete nutrition, or even denutrition.

Bullerton must have beliefs inoperative in his inner being, which determine ritual actions and periodic gestures, punctually executed with cold indifference. By contrast, domestic instincts stir in the utmost depths, which he has never attempted to define, and which he would deny with the utmost sincerity were they pointed out to him. Correspondingly, a desire for liberty, which is nothing but a desire for isolation, is entirely dominated—I imagine—by a discipline born of his environment and also from a need to flee the frightful interior voices...

His voice cuts through the brusque and various meditation: "Let's see the machine..."

He has risen to his feet, as has the tall engineer. It's the latter who interests me now. His type is more common in England than America. According to that affiliation, he must possess racial instincts clearer than Bullerton's, delimited like his flattened temples. Born to conform, inclined to all rigors and all *accepted* disciplines, but refractory to others, I suppose him to be quite servile and quite free at the same time, aspiring to a social milieu comprised of companions of both sexes with high foreheads, narrow but adventurous ideas, indeterminate but intense dreams, in which, beneath the ice, a lava of lyricism is sometimes confined for an entire lifetime.

Religious by nature, with a cold ardor and a disparate logic that carelessly conciliates the worst absurdities and the strangest antinomies, he will likewise conciliate his sectarian aspirations, which comprise congregation and the possibility of living, for some years, the solitary existence of a sentinel or a scout. All in all, a meticulous, honest, clear-sighted, pragmatic professional, in whom Bullerton can have complete confidence.

While cogitating, I have started the machine working. The engineer, who has subjected it to a preliminary scrutiny, examines its operation. Impossible to tell what he thinks. His

137

face is wooden, animated solely by the gaze concentrated on the machine.

I have no need to be anxious. Everything is in order, everything will work. All the same, I am anxious. There is such a thing as luck—a fundamental mystery complicated by traditional mysteries. If I had a totem, my nerves would invoke it…

"All right!" the engineer says, eventually.

He stops the apparatus, then starts it again, examines it analytically, and repeats: "All right!" A vague smile, a broad smile, put two little creases at the corners of his mouth. "That was to be expected, according to the plans…but experiments are always necessary…always."

"Everything's in order, then?" Bullerton asks.

"Yes, everything."

Bullerton thrusts his hands into his trouser pockets and asks: "You're still holding out for your royalty? Even if we raise the purchase price?"

My diaphragm sinks, then stretches; my mouth is dry; I'm afraid of losing everything by being obstinate—but already, with the rapidity of a reflex, my reply has sprung forth: "Yes, I'm sticking to it."

"In that case, you'll have a firm response in three days," Bullerton concludes.

I'm sure that if I had renounced my royalty, the business would have been concluded on the spot.

They've gone. A gambler who has risked too much, anxiety bores into me. If Bullerton refuses, if the deal comes unstuck, what folly will I have committed? I want to continue the bargaining, and even move toward the door—but he must be a long way away.

Then again, no! It *will not* be a folly. He'll accept, or, if not, I'll only have to fall back on his original offer. Without a doubt the machine is sound, and there are other Bullertons on the planet.

There is already a profound manifest difference between the plant that makes a plant with mineral substance and the animal that makes an animal with the plant, and a lesser, but appreciable, difference between the sheep that makes sheep out of grass and a wolf that makes wolf out of sheep. Nourishment, therefore—first mineral, then vegetable, and then meat—moves progressively away from its origin. There must be analogous degrees, albeit less clear, in psychic nutrition.

We know nothing at all about the elements making up instinct, but we can be sure that they exist. It hardly matters what they are in the animal itself, for psychic life, however rudimentary it is, *the body is an environment*. Numerous gradations are imaginable; it's a science yet to be created. As regards animals, at present, opaque darkness; as regards humans, feeble glimmers in the night. (Take note that if science always rests on the simple, it almost always extends to the complex.)

We have seen that in humans deprived from the outset of a human environment, intellectual nutrition remains purely animal. The immensity of social psychology has disappeared. Nothing but a mute creature, into which not an inkling of traditional treasure has penetrated. The different estates of humanity offer an almost direct verification. In spite of the destruction of races, in spite of the invasion of occidentals, transforming the ambiances, an indefinite gradation reveals itself within modes of intellectual nutrition.

I try to imagine Bullerton born in France or Italy; I adapt our cultures to his face, to his gaze and gestures. His eye lights up, his replies are more prompt, his decisions less firm, his bitterness less secret and his moral estrangement metamorphosed. A miracle of intellectual and social nutrition!

I have more difficulty with the engineer, but, thinking of Pierre Curie, his tall stature, his blond and elongated skull, his gentle intransigence, the engineer becomes malleable; he metamorphoses into a Frenchman, nourished in a milieu of Berthelots, Poincarés, Pasteurs and Bertrands…

The doorbell rings. It's Juliane. Bullerton and the engineer vanish into the mist.

V.

She is bringing me my ration of love—a meager ration. I am an undernourished lover. The social provisions, the intoxicating fables and the interhuman imagery were dispersed a long time ago.

Beyond the protocol, it has become, for me, primitive love. With her, from the viewpoint of passion, I am little more than an animal—a slightly cruel animal, with abrupt impulses that scarcely surpass the impulses of the species. Let's not disparage those impulses; they comprise the fount of creativity, already inflated by a brusque, wild, sometimes ferocious poetry—a poetry of desire and primal conflict. They are also Iliads, the battles of stags for hinds, the pursuit of the tiger scenting the tigress, and sometimes Odysseys, like the voyage of a sturgeon in pursuit of the chosen female, across 1000, or 2000 kilometers, to fertilize the abandoned eggs, outside her, in the waters of a river...

Today, the animal is peremptory. Juliane is welcomed ardently, not because she is Juliane—any woman could fulfill her mission, better if she were pretty. The obscure lair of the woman, the creative pistil, would suffice by itself, and could even evoke, without anything else, those days of spring and autumn in which the tempest blows over the city.

Anyway, Juliane brings a certain décor. I know that she likes to be dressed for a party—pretty stockings, a suggestive skirt, charming perfume. Thanks to that superfluity, she is a shadow of interhuman love—the eclogue, the roses, Helen, Philis, Célimène, Manon, "the strange flowers on the shelves," "the happy lovely girl, fearful and wild"[22]...

---

[22] The quoted lines are from Baudelaire's "La Mort des amants," in *Les Fleurs du Mal* (1857), and from an untitled verse in Victor Hugo's *Les Contemplations* (1853).

She simulates the women that I shall never have and brings back the Juliane of yesteryear, when I molded her in the image of my dreams, when I equipped her with mystical grace...

I'm on my knees. It's good to stay there and wait. The antique desire throbs. So familiar, so unfamiliar. Juliane smiles, then becomes serious, curls up, puts her face to my neck and receives or gathers a bunch of kisses...

In her, idealized love is dominant. Tradition, conformist fables and clichéd phrases all form a thrilling and heated reality.

"Do you love me?" she murmurs.

I have no difficulty in replying, sincerely in the simplest sense: "Yes, darling."

"I know that...I can feel it!" she continues, while her breasts move like a dove's...we're made for one another...everything should bring us closer together..."

That will be her theme, until the end. She has arranged the elective affinities for her own usage...

Waiting becomes impossible. I carry Juliane away. We're in the depths of the woods...

She gets up again with her mirages; for me, it's a matter of reflux, melancholy, unslaked desires and bitterness.

Springtime, eclogues, poets, primitive passion, all flee to the antipodes. I listen to Juliane chattering as I listen to the falling rain. She glorifies us, stretches us out, searches within us and finds prodigious reasons for love.

I think about the forms that it might take among my friends, in Bullerton and his engineer, in Madame Donatienne, in Yveline, in my concierge and the embittered Gontran Réchauffé.

Did Bullerton know, in his early youth, some vertiginous flirtation, with the terror of *breach of promise*? I try to imagine him giving a kiss but, not succeeding, fall back on the stiff, timid engineer lowering his long face and his mouth with equine teeth. What strange ideal and far-fetched excitation attract him?

And Madame Donatienne? Why should she not have had her tumultuous love affairs, given a man who excited the pleasant and sumptuous qualities whose substance she has exhausted in the feuilletons of Emile Richebourg, Xavier de Montépin or Jules Mary?[23] Momentarily, she appears, prey to Aphrodite, rolling her wide eyes in sacred delirium, her heavy limbs trembling and her soft bosom in uproar.

Of them all, it's Gontran Réchauffé once again who brings forth the most fantastic images. What becomes, in the intoxication on a kiss, of that narrow face the color of cement, that sticky hair, those dry, perpetually-peeled lips and those moody eyes?

Yveline! A complete metamorphosis. The grotesque has disappeared. An insinuating sensuality changes the rhythm of her gestures, the poorest of which becomes magnificent, or at least mingled with an excitement that camouflages its ridiculous sweep.

While Bullerton, the engineer, Madame Donatienne, Réchauffé, Yveline, Marcus and the gorilla in the depths of the forest file past, Juliane squeezes my hand and murmurs languorously: "We have the same ideal!"

Is it inevitable that, one day, she will take her fables elsewhere? I can't think about that without terror and pity. If she could liberate me from the difficulties of a break-up! Oh, she wouldn't suffer at all! After all, she's dear to me. A placid but resilient affection ties me to her. She sets me on edge sometimes with her misinterpretations, the absurdity of her

---

[23] The three named *feuilletonistes* were the titans of the medium in the 1880s and 1890s, all of them specializing in sentimental fiction; none of them extended his career significantly in the 20th century although Mary did not die until 1922. Madame Donatienne presumably passed through her twenties while they were in their heyday, although she must be in the region of 60 now (i.e., in the early 1930s).

mirages, but she hardly ever irritates me. All the same, the paradoxes are obvious. Neither of us chose the other; it was a mere matter of circumstance and convenience. She was there. Infinitely adaptable, she was waiting for someone or other. Black or red, the roulette ball decided—and it was me.

Certainly, to begin with, I succeeded in transfiguring her, in giving her color, savor and relief.

"I can't imagine," she murmured, "that we'll ever be together. Oh, if only *he* wanted…"

What a terrible thought…but I'm certain that *he* will never want. Where would he find a situation and a wife as favorable to his comfort and his flings?

"Isn't that so, darling?"

A shake of the head satisfies her; she amplifies it, dilates it, makes it into the story of an entire existence.

"Oh," she sighs, "I have everything, since I have you, since I'm sure of you. I would be ungrateful to God if I dared complain, but it would have been so pleasant to travel together. Do you know little Marvaux? She's gone back to Egypt, sailing up the Nile as far as the second cataract. I envied her; I can see us sailing like that—I have a passion for the Pyramids…"

"*Crocodilum habet Nilus…*" I murmured.

"Is that Latin, my love? *Crocodilum* must mean crocodile…"

"The very same, my love." As she looks at me, questioningly, I translate: "It means: 'The Nile has crocodiles…'"

"Are there still crocodiles there?"

"Far away, perhaps, in the desert, but not in Egypt."

Good old Pliny! He knew that the mongoose takes advantage of the moment when the "hummingbird" is cleaning the crocodile's mouth to introduce itself thereinto in a flash, penetrate into its belly and devour its intestines; he describes, with such charm, the war between dolphins and crocodiles and the combat of the elephant and the boa constrictor—a combat in which both perish, the boa choking the elephant and the elephant crushing the boa. What poet has more innocence, what child a more marvelous credulity?

He would be a gold-mine for storytellers, if they knew of him. The marvelous story of elephants leaving the forests of Mauretania to adore the rising Moon on the shore of the river Amulius! Purified by ritual ablutions, they add Moon-worship to that of the Sun and other stars. They even understand religions other than their own. They only consent to embark on a sea-voyage if their driver swears to bring them back to their homeland. Honest, prudent and equitable, they understand languages, love glory and, when their memory is recalcitrant, get up by night to repeat their lessons…

Does one not see elephants ready to disembark at Pouzzol, frightened by the length and narrowness of the wooden bridges by which it is necessary for them to reach the shore, walking backwards, in order to give themselves illusions regarding he length of those fragile roads?

6 p.m.! Our love is chronometric. Juliane is dressed and I'm ready to go out.

"Will you come with me?" she implores.

"Yes, dear."

In the taxi—for she does not use her own car for our meetings—she huddles close to me. "Every time, I imagine that it's the beginning!" she says.

The game of memories again, the evocation of an adventure with which she means to fill heaven and earth.

"Do you remember that autumn day? A chimney came down just in front of the car—the wind was terrible! I was frightened, so frightened! And it was so good to be leaning on your shoulder…"

I only have a confused memory of it, but I think about the fine equinoctial winds of my childhood, immense gales over the sea, and Juliane's words are lost in a tempest until the moment, soon arrived, when she leaves me, in front of a perfumer's boutique—for she insists, in spite of her husband's utter indifference, on keeping up appearances.

While she walks away—her silhouette charming, after all—I think admiringly about her evocative ability. For five years, she has not ceased feeding the flame. Everything converges on the fable; perhaps, like reality, her rudimentary poetry far surpasses the poetry of the greatest poets, perpetually exalted, magnified and rejuvenated.

I remember an adolescent girl, ecstatic, her soul hanging on the lips of a popular violinist, who was singing as he played. Every word transported her; every word was new; the spring was every spring, the birds, the mystery of all nests, the violets, the prettiest dreams of perishable humankind. Far from rejuvenating it, the most original images would have tarnished, deflowered and misted that enthusiasm...

The antique taxi comes to a stop; I'm going to see Ambroise Ferral again, and it's captivating in a fashion very different from seeing Juliane again...

He's there, leafing through an old book.

"It's a book on light," he says. "It's absurd and seductive, but the author's theory is even closer to the latest theory—that of photons and processions of waves—than it is to the wave theory. Once more, in fact, light condemns us to revise our ideas."

His profile is somewhat reminiscent of a dromedary, with his elongated face and tawny hair. In his face, the broadness of the forehead and the large dark eyes, give him a reassuring expression of strength.

"We lack," he says, "an initial *local* foothold in the interatomic and interstellar worlds. The present laboratory apparatus cannot suffice. I believe I have an idea, but it's costly...and besides, shall we ever know?" He sighs, then smiles. No one has an odder or more charming smile. "If I had 100,000 francs," he continues, "I'd put my idea into action."

"I'd put them into action too," I say.

"You have an inconsiderate confidence in me," he goes on. "I have a right to speculate on myself, but not to let you speculate."

145

"I have a right too, especially if 100,000 francs becomes a relatively negligible fraction of my assets—something on the order of a tenth, for instance."

"Bah! Didn't you tell me that you were expecting to be ruined?"

"What if, on the other hand, I were expecting to make a fortune?"

"Are you joking? From what I know about you, you might be. But without exaggeration—we'll talk about my idea later—I think I can tap you for 500 francs for Chavres…I'll tap myself for an equal sum, and we'll fix him up. He's a child of genius lost among men."

Ferral is poor, entirely dependent on his salary at the Sorbonne.

"Fix him up how? He's delightful, but outside all the familiar fields."

"Not the field of the stars. When he works, he's a very capable observer. I've almost obtained the assent of Graivil to take him on at the Brétigny observatory…and Chavres will be happy…yes, happy. I'm only fearful that Graivil will pinch his discoveries, for he's inclined to do that, and we know he's capable of doing it recklessly. Chavres is an incurable visionary. He's dining with us this evening…" Ferral started laughing. His abrupt, disconcerting laughter was accompanied by a strange grimace: "We're going to conspire; I shall propose the greatest conquest that mankind has ever undertaken…once the 100,000 francs is found."

I stare at him, not without astonishment.

Chavres arrives at that moment, agile, furtive and as thin as a starving wolf. I haven't seen him for three months. His eyes are hollow, his skin taut over a diminished face; he has suffered, gone for several days without eating. It's not the first time. He lets himself descend, then endures the privations with a savage resignation.

Duped by destiny, the primitive is reduced in him to a minimum: hardly any defensive instinct, no animal flair. The interhuman is lost in the imaginary, and does not defend itself by any social cunning. He wanders around the city like an inoffensive beast in the savannah.

Amicable, generous, drunk on ideas, improvident, imprudent, frightfully honest, he requires an entourage that frames him by constraint, and the authority of some superior friend who can dominate and steer him. He has genius, as Ferral said, but sporadically, with gaps, enveloped by a zone of naivety with areas that are uncultivated, if not inept. In consequence, he works at hazard, passing from fever to inertia, sometimes sinking into a marshy brutality from which he shoots out like a meteor. Everyone can despoil him of his intellectual wealth, as of his money.

"There you are, miserable insect!" says Ferral, severely.

"Excrement of the Moon!" murmurs the other.

"It's high time that you were reduced to servitude! Henceforth, you will follow the route that Alberic and I show you. If not, your stupidity will kill you."

Chavres shrugged his right shoulder, and then his left, alternately. "I know that I can't be proud of myself," he says, "but I can no more be submissive—except to you, Ambroise. I'll willingly obey you, as well as Alberic, if he cares to command! In sum, make of me what you will, on condition that you don't put me anywhere that requires exact, monotonous and continuous work." He spoke with humble pride. Hunger and suffering were still weighing upon him, having been too brutal this time; the soul is breathless.

"You shall live with the stars," Ferral continued. "They are waiting for you, and your passionate impulses will be sufficient to the task, perhaps more, for your discoveries will be exploited and you won't get any credit."

"So what, Ferral? Are you one of those people who believe that it's important that the name of Galileo, rather than another, should be attached to the discovery of the law of gravity?"

"I'm one of those, yes—but not every day."

"In the end, what does it mater? If I understand you correctly, you intend to place me in an observatory."

"Yes, at Brétigny, with Graivil. He's a good fellow, full of cunning and will, *at the least*, associate himself with your discoveries. A half-share, but he might appropriate the best of them. I'll try to make sure that he doesn't go that far."

"Ambroise!" Chavres cried, with a sheepish laugh. "Here you are, opening the gate of the Garden for me…the Garden of the Seven Rivers.[24] I wish I were able to bless you. What evenings I shall spend there—a nocturnal animal by all instinct—with the flock of worlds!" He had grabbed both Ferral's hands, and was staring at him with child-like eyes.

"We must eat though," said Ambroise.

"I should say so!" says Madame Ferral, who has just emerged. She is thin, tall, ascetic, pleasant to behold, like a beautiful saint in a missal. She's Ferral's "other half," the source of his salvation, his support and his child—a distracted, imprudent child, whose steps must be watched, and from whom it is necessary to take away the cup of bitterness. There is no trace in that love of the aggressive spirit of women who play the part of a man. Nothing would annoy her but an enemy, and Ferral has no enemies.

A strange stew, from which Ferral extracts tender beef, sausages, lard and lumps of meat, which we eat with black bread. An apple cheesecake, strawberries, cream, a little rosé wine and Turkish coffee. It's the traditional dinner in the Feral household and I'd be disappointed if he served anything else; I never eat anywhere else with as much pleasure.

---

[24] The Garden of Eden had only one river, although it subsequently divided into four; this reference might be to the "seven sacred rivers" of India, to which Rosny refers in several of his other works, but the cosmological context makes it more likely to be the seven "rivers" cited in the *Zohar*, one of the volumes constituting the Qabala, which are closely but enigmatically linked to the seven firmaments and the seven planets.

The weather is mild, and the windows are open. Because there has been a terrible crime—two young men murdering an entire family—we are talking about robbery and murder.

"It's dangerous," Chavres said, "to attribute the majority of crimes to some cerebral deformity, illness, degeneration or anomaly. I believe that the general run of criminals are men as sane and normal as anyone else. That many criminals have vices it would be puerile to deny, but those that we categorize as honest by virtue of their judiciary record have no fewer. The abnormal, the degenerate and the sick who commit no crimes or even misdemeanors are legion. Often, they're creatures of an essential probity and generosity.

"The majority of men remain normally inclined to theft and predation; the number of those among the righteous who would have recourse to murder, without the constraint of the environment and the fear of punishment, is enormous."

"And what's astonishing about that?" I said. "Man has scarcely emerged from a normality in which robbery and murder were practiced in all innocence, in which it was as natural to kill a man as a roe deer.

"Brute instinct, which permits the formation of vague families, signifies nothing insofar as human life is concerned. Doesn't anthropophagy, which is endemic throughout the world, show us quite clearly that the flesh of man is assimilated just like the flesh of any other prey. Belated and obscure traditions eventually protect, for what it may be worth, the lives of people of the group, but only of the group—a protection that would have been virtually worthless without vendettas: murder redeemed by whatever prey, whatever weapon. A murderer could repossess the dead man's wife; among the barbarians, a sum of money was agreed. And what were human livestock, the slaves, among the peoples whose culture is venerated by us, the Greeks and Romans? What was the serf for the town-dweller or the mercenary?"

"And so," Chavres went on, "the gendarme, the judge, the prison, even the guillotine, are salutary…"

"Less so, however, than the constraints of the environment, the educational games designed to give murder a monstrous and frightful image."

"Yes, it's always necessary to have recourse to fictions! We turn our backs in vain on the mystic gridiron, fall back into the mystical..."

"The monstrous and frightful image is destroyed without overmuch trouble when we encounter the illegal," murmured Ferral. "There are other images, just as fictitious—for our criminals, ignorant of the primitive code, are contraband primitives."

"With what facility the non-conformists obtain their recruits! Nothing struck me more, at one time, than the confessions of murderers or thieves, in which one sees, as soon as temptation is offered, a fellow honest hitherto, agree to participate in a burglary or a murder... The story of our two scoundrels is endlessly repeated. Sins of complicity are as routine as sins of love..."

"Ferral," I asked, as we left the dinner table, "what universe were you talking about the other day?"

"It's to talk about that that I invited you this evening. You know that, for a long time, I've been a rebel against the nihilist conception of interstellar and interatomic spaces. It's become my obsession. If I didn't mention it to you any more, it was because I was seeing a means to demonstrate experimentally the self-differentiation of those spaces. The more I thought about it, the more naively anthropocentric the conception seemed of a universe almost all of which was a sort of nothingness, devoid of existence from the phenomenal viewpoint. Most people suppose it to be undifferentiated, in which case nothing happens therein, and nothing can happen therein. The undifferentiation is immutable. The undifferentiation, or homogeneity, cannot have any properties, for all properties suppose a difference. Take note that a scientist, while believing in the homogeneity of interstellar space, can write, with astonishing candor: 'A very active medium is presently po-

150

sited, which is not empty but impalpable, but which displays its activity in multiple ways, for, *in accordance with its own laws*, it transmits action from one particle to another.' But a little further on, he writes, baldly: 'The universal substratum is unique and homogeneous.'

"It's truly formidable! When one thinks that the molecules, atoms and corpuscles of our physical elements are not in contact with one another, that they are only sensible to us by virtue of the space that separates them, that it is from that space that they rebound, that that is what guides the luminous radiations, one wonders how it is possible that men, not only of intelligence but of genius, dare to affirm the homogeneity, the quasi-nonexistence of that prodigious medium.

"I am also quite sure that an idea so rudimentary cannot be admitted for long. We are on the eve of a new conception of the universe, more grandiose, relative to our universe of stars and nebulas than that one is relative to the thesis of a universe of which the Earth was the center."

"Our universe of stars is practically infinite, though," Chavres remarked, "and perhaps authentically so."

"And if it is," Ferral exclaimed, "the stars and the nebulas are comparable, compared to the totality of space, with the molecules of a few grams of soda dissolved in all of our oceans! The distance that separates our Sun from the star Alpha Centauri is so vast that the Sun occupies less space therein than a sardine in the Pacific Ocean. We can, in consequence, my friend, imagine an extra-sidereal universe—or, rather, universes. I maintain that every region of extent corresponds, on average, statistically speaking, to a quantity of existence equal to that of any other region of equivalent grandeur. An immense number of existences must occupy the spaces that separate the stars, not to mention the spaces that separate molecules, atoms, protons, electrons and photons. I conceive of these existences being formed, like ours, of infinitesimal elements, sometimes scattered, sometimes forming ensembles: one can thus envisage, between two stars, trillions of trillions of worlds, whose existence escapes us because the reactions of their elements offset one another from our viewpoint. Instead of one almost empty universe—since stars, nebulas and radiations only occupy a negligible fraction of it—why not a universe fully occupied, existent everywhere? That universe seems much vaster than the Copernican universe was by comparison with the anthropocentric universe of our distant ancestors—an abstraction made from a few Greek precursors."

"Your universe," said Chavres, "is indeed infinitely grander than the universe conceived thus far."

"For 50 years," Ferral went on, "but above all since the end of the last century, our science has got closer and closer to etheric elements. With the proton, the electron, the photon, Planck's quanta and de Broglie's 'material' radiation, we're approaching the infinitesimal limits of our universe; we're at the point of discerning some 'modality' of universal reaction. For a long time, that reaction has been apparent to us: in admitting that molecules, atoms, protons and electrons are *not in contact*, that they're separated by extents that are very considerable by comparison with their smallness, we've been forced to agree that *every energetic event* manifests itself by the intervention of the ether. For, if the corpuscles are not in contact with one another, it follows that we aren't in contact with anything, that no object is in contact with any other. Don't forget that, when two billiard balls collide and rebound, none of their elements has been in direct contact with any material element of the other, that the entire reaction is accomplished by universal space. We have no real relationship with anything except that space, which I shall continue to call the ether. Contemporary science is beginning to specify these relationships, increasingly demonstrating the *properties* of the ether—and to say properties is to say *differentiation*. A few steps more, and we shall begin to define some aspect of the etheric differentiation, and from then on, the universe *existent everywhere* will be substituted for the universe reduced to a few items of cosmic dust. Now, I believe I've discovered a method of research, and I'm counting on you to develop it. It's a supplementary theory of radiation that has put me on the track. I'm counting on you two for the experiments—you have complementary abilities. Will you?"

"Are you sure that I can contribute something?" asked Chavres.

"I've only invented petty machines," I said.

"Neither one of you has shown your full measure. To bring delicate experiments to a successful conclusion, your collaboration will be priceless. Enough! You accept." And he added, ironically: "All that remains is to find the 100,000 francs."

"A very tiny sum for such research!"

"No, for the laboratory the State has allocated to me contains the basic necessities: the Phister grant has permitted it to be subtly perfected. We only need a few items of apparatus and a few materials to get things under way." He began laughing softly, and continued: "We shall be the Companions of the Universe!" Then, sadly: "But where will the money come from?"

"A fine thing!" Chavres exclaimed. "The Companions of the Universe are at the mercy of a slight financial hardship!"

VI.

Bullerton has advised me by telegram that he is coming to see me this morning. A dozen words without any further indication than the day and the hour. In principle, that ought to mean that he isn't backing out of the deal, but I force myself to be incredulous and succeed in being pessimistic. My success in that respect increases as the hour draws nearer, but pessimism doesn't obliterate hope. It creeps furtively, insinuating itself into every impression and every idea, like a penetrating odor. In any case, it reinforces my black mood rather than attenuating it, by introducing a maddening fear, an oppression of the soul of the sort to which I am liable.

153

The doorbell. 10 a.m. He's naturally punctual...

Here are the rectangular shoulders, the smoke-black hair, the mahogany eyes, the dead-leaf complexion and the small teeth encased in the hyena's jaws. The other has come too— the authentic Anglo-Saxon with the horse's teeth, the long face and skull, and the sloping shoulders.

Bullerton gets straight to the point. "You haven't changed your mind?" he says, in his harsh voice.

Here we go! In a minute, everything will be resolved. My tongue is very dry, and I can hear the hammering of my heart.

"No," I reply. "No change of mind."

"All right. We've looked at everything. The thing is possible. 200,000 dollars cash, and a half a percent per sale. Agreed?"

"Agreed."

"In that case, read..."

He has taken a sheet of headed paper from his pocket. The text is brief and clear. I cede the entire ownership of my apparatus to Bullerton, Ruthven & Co., in return for the payment of 200,000 dollars on signature of the contract and half of one percent of the sale price, payable every year at the end of January.

"Now," says Bullerton, "would you prefer a check or a credit note on the North American and Canadian Bank in New York? A credit note will give you better protection against the exchange-rate, which is becoming highly dangerous. Your choice."

I choose the credit note. Bullerton bursts out laughing. "As anticipated. Here's the paper, stamped New York. You'll have every facility at the Parisian branch."

He has become cordial, almost affectionate; laughing open-mouthed, with a "boyish" air; he comes to give me a light tap on the shoulder. "I reckon we've both made a good deal. I dare say your machine will sell very well, and you'll make a handsome profit."

When they've gone, I turn the credit note over repeatedly. An insignificant scrap of paper, which, in itself, is absolutely worthless; the words and figures inscribed on it only have power by virtue of the imponderable signatures of Bullerton and Ruthven. A fiction of fictions, which I can transform into a series at will—an enormous series of social and natural realities. Even a magic wand and unlimited wishes fulfilled could do no more.

The unreal will give me an abundance of reality. Already, those 25 letters, diabolically traced, have delivered me from a harsh struggle for existence. They have freed me from yielding to rapacity, egotism, cunning and force, from bowing down before vile, repugnant or cruel creatures. They guarantee me the almost-exorbitant privilege of choice.

Hoisted by them to a superior level, I compare myself to a warrior who only has to make a sign to have an abundance— in his case—of all the wealth of the savannah, the forest, the lakes and the rivers. Powerful Bullerton! Redoubtable prodigy of the credit of the social *faith* concentrated between millionaires.

Confronted by this prodigy, some mysterious shadow passes back and forth, which gives birth to a malaise, also social, or moral, if you wish—it's almost the same thing, fundamentally. I desire, feebly at first, then forcefully, *to have deserved my chance.*

Am I, in some manner, giving the equivalent of the fabulous favor I have been granted? Yes, if—and who can deny it?—discovery and invention are the greatest human values. What would become of the slow and cumbersome beast, so weak by comparison with large carnivores and giant grazers of giant plants, without external equipment, the perpetual leverage upon the environment?

Will my apparatus not augment that leverage in its turn? Will it not supply a new dominion over substance and energy?

It is always too low, the reward of those who multiply human possibilities: not the hundred millionth part of what the coarser conquerors cost—the leaders of every expansion, the

155

merchants, the manufacturers, the money-handlers…a drop of water in a river!

Come on! I can take this money without scruple.

Good, evil! Let's not be Manichean; let's not exaggerate anthropocentrism, the transfer to the absolute of elements of conservation, extended across the generations, and then to the ant-hill. The basis is always the search for good pasture or the immolation of prey. While the bee and the ant are emasculated to the profit of the community, a man keeps his organs intact and maintains his personality. In conserving the primacy of the self, one conserves, *ipso facto*, the transformable energies, the spirit of discovery and invention.

To refuse a windfall like Bullerton's, even if it were gratuitous, instead of being the profits of an invention, would be to go against a *necessary* norm. And if it's necessary, all the same, to hunt for a scruple, isn't it sufficient that I am able to help Ambroise Ferral, Chavres and Denise, not to mention Gontran Réchauffé? The tax of altruism will be paid!

VII.

While I'm daydreaming, my dog Taureau bursts out of the next room. He's hideous. The head of a toad, an opaque muzzle, heavy and formless, the chest of a hippopotamus. I admire his jaws, his terrible teeth, his stocky strength. He's one of those bull-terriers whose stature surpasses that of wolves—but what wolf would stand up to him?

He's a first rate fighting dog—stubborn and extremely brave. Four individuals like him could defeat a tiger. His soul is surly, ferocious, vindictive, candid and affectionate. This formidable warrior is a slave, a mystical slave, but only to his masters. For others, benevolence, indifference or hostility. He knows the law: the home defended, the passer-by respected. Grave and implacable, he only attacks by order, or in defense of the master and his possessions—but he can make mistakes.

At night, he becomes frightful. In total, a heterogeneous combination of the most ancient instincts and a fragmentary but perfect sociality. Slow and ponderous, his intelligence risks being misunderstood. It is real, capable of increase, served by an elephantine memory. The scar of an injury is indelible—but no ill-treatment is injurious coming from the master. I think he is proud, full of an obscure scorn for human or animal multitudes, but devoid of vanity.

We are looking at one another. His eyes are the color of old bronze—globular, pure and puerile. There is something strangely nostalgic in his toad-like face, and occasionally, the skin of his forehead creases over the granite bone. One caress, and that head is rested on my knee. Taureau breathes more rapidly...

Oh, the mystery of origins! How much stronger than a man Taureau would be, without the fraction of the world that man has tailored in his image! In the night of time, Taureau, your ascendancy was conquered long after fire, wood, stone, horn and bone. Man was already the great artist of the Magdalenian, and your ascendancy was still free. Then, Taureau, your life, along with that of the ox, the pig, the sheep and the horse, was placed in the service of the frightful vertical beast.

Now, I find it strange, Taureau, that the servitude in question has had, in sum, such meager consequences. For, to what the people of the Stone and Bronze Ages accomplished, the illustrious peoples of Egypt and Assyria, Hellas and Rome and the frightful Western Europe of the last millennium have, in truth, added very little. So very little! We have limited ourselves to directly multiplying the number and sometimes the variety of individuals, and massacring the species that were still free. Isn't that inconceivable, Taureau? Can one not say that, *in that sense*, the genius of the Stone and Bronze Ages is extinct? Although the physical world continued to be "humanized" in a marvelous fashion, they merely repeated what the Lacustrian cities had done in respect of the "humanization" of the organic.

We know full well, dog with a toad's head, that naturalists, anatomists, physiologists, biologists and therapists have each, in their fashion, with increasing subtlety, studied, some the healthy beast, some the sick beast and some the dead beast, and tortured your peers frightfully, along with guinea-pigs, rats, mice, rabbits, calves, sheep and birds, in order to discover more about the subterfuges of their mechanisms or the secrets of their brains…but that's work of a different kind than that of domesticators.

I dream, Taureau, of a closer relationship between human beings and the vanquished, involving a relationship with myriads of species, the creatures of the sea, the innumerable society of insects. An entirely new and inexhaustible science will be born, which will, moreover, give us incalculable wealth. Enough to occupy a legion of minds for millennia.

Having explored every corner of the room with his nostrils, Taureau came to a halt, raised his head and demanded a mark of my friendship. I put my hand on his hard head. Because it was not meal-time, he contented himself with this almost abstract demonstration, and licked my fingers with his thick tongue. Then, in response to some obscure signal, suspecting the eternal enemy that dogs have suspected for centuries, he growled, turned his eyes of bronze to my face, and settled down.

It's then that Torquemada appears, a Persian cat, still young, with eyes of pure gold, untainted by green or gray, clad in thick gray and silver hair with a blue sheen, and equipped with a sumptuous tail. Torquemada knows the limits of his own strength, the power of humans and that of Taureau.

Without submission, without answering calls and without obeying orders like Taureau—in sum, as wild as the environment permits—he accepts, not laws, but rules. Taureau goes as far as worship; Torquemada scarcely sketches affection. The caress that he accepts is physical; it interests his skin and his vertebrae. Taureau has some concept of alliance and tenderness. Taureau's gaze, so primitive in one respect, is clearly social in another. Torquemada's gaze, ardent, wild and equivocal, is a purely individual gaze. There is an exchange with the dog; there is only a truce with the cat.

On principle, Torquemada arches his back and Taureau creases a severe forehead—but the law is formal; Torquemada is taboo. He walks past the bull-terrier disdainfully, ignores my presence and takes inventory of the furniture.

Still young—four months—he searches dispassionately for the secret of things. An open drawer: he goes in, he sniffs, he moves into the shadows of the depths, and suddenly leaps out, attacks a thread, scales my table and, without upsetting anything, circles around books, a tall flower-vase, a carriage clock, lifts up a newspaper under which he slides. From that light cavern he stares at me with eyes of fire—golden fire.

It's an invitation to play. I advance a hand; he shrinks back into his retreat and reappears when my hand is withdrawn, disappears and reappears again, until he decides to leap on to my knees, where he demands a caress with a faint *miaow*. I pass a hand over his blue back, over the little skull, tickling slightly, which he likes. He half-closes his eyes and, if I stop, gives the order to continue with a little thrust of his paw. At intervals he plays, seizing my hand, biting a finger. All is tact and grace, not a single attitude that is devoid of charm, not a single gesture that is devoid of elegance. The most flexible humans are gauche by comparison, the prettiest women clumsy.

When he has had his fill of games and caresses, he starts ignoring me again, crosses the table, climbs up a bronze bust on the mantelpiece and attains the top of a bookcase. From there, he contemplates the open window momentarily. He is almost at ceiling height, but today, Torquemada does not want any obstacle to stand before him. One bound. His forepaws grip, but his hind paws slip on the glass.

No matter, victory is necessary! With a gymnastic readjustment, the little cat attains his goal, and there he is, solidly established, standing on a surface so narrow that the slightest false movement would precipitate him on to the floor...

The return is accomplished in three acrobatic leaps...and suddenly, the little cat becomes a little tiger. His entire body quivering, his ferocious eyes full of desire, his claws ready to tear apart the prey, here he is in the pitiless forest. The little cat imagines the bloody universe, the wild beasts that devour and drink the blood of victims still full of life. But what, then, is the prey? Only that large fly, whose evolutions Torquemada's eye follows with frenetic passion. It is sufficient to awaken instincts; the feline's breast swells with voluptuous cruelty.

The fly comes and goes, zigzagging, as ignorant of Torquemada's presence as of the ends of the Earth. With a boundless imbecility, it bumps into the glass repeatedly. If it settles there too low down, nimble as it is, Torquemada will surely be able to catch it.

In the face of this unknown danger an even more unknown providence emerges. I have taken the side of the fly—and when it finally stops jigging about on the window, still too high for Torquemada to reach, rearing up on his hind legs. I'm ready to intervene.

I was an expert fly-hunter at one time; if this one settled on the wall, I could capture it with a gesture learned in childhood, without doing it the slightest harm, and release it outside...

The maneuver is more difficult on a window, risking culmination in murder. Better to fall back on the old method of the drinking-glass—I always have one within arm's reach. It's done! The fly is a captive. In its transparent prison, set on the table, it is recklessly agitated at first, then calms down and settles...

Torquemada, eyes on fire, is still watching out. He has attempted a few paw-thrusts against the glass, which my hand is protecting. And there is the mystery of transparency, which has not yet been entirely resolved, any more than the mystery of reflection that sometimes stops him in front of a mirror in which he attempts to join his image, where his actual muzzle comes into contact with his fictitious muzzle...

The fly smoothes its wings and seems, at times, as if it wanted to tear off its head, which its feet cause to oscillate, and which is only held on by a thread.

How much closer we are to one another, Torquemada and me, than the fly is to us! For now we can see it in its entirety, perceiving the details of its marvelous little angled legs, no broader than a handwritten line. How nimble and clever it is as it trots on its minuscule limbs, and as it flies, faster than a racehorse, as rapidly as a bird...

For the fly, we are only confused shadows. It is unaware of me, a frightful giant, to the point of landing on me, wandering over me, even making its meal there...

The alarming world of insects, which seems like another planet is, save for that of microbes, the most redoubtable to humans. Tomorrow, tigers, lions, pythons, grizzly bears and polar bears will be nothing but a memory—but the insect will persist everywhere, taking its share of our nourishment, the ruin of legions of agriculturalists, causing entire countries to go hungry. Innumerable in the grasslands, in the crop-fields, in forests, in gardens, a host devouring leaves, flowers, stems, roots and fruits, it does not hesitate to take its nourishment from our dwellings, and even from our flesh—mosquitoes, fleas, lice, ticks, chiggers and gnats treat us as prey, all the more terrible for being ignorant of the power of the enemy they are attacking...

Without man, they would be the lords of the Earth. Compared with them, the most frightful carnivores become negligible. What are the achievements of birds, compared with those of social insects?

If it were not for the error[25] committed in some remote and unknown era, long before our ancestor appeared on Earth—that irreparable error—who knows whether the insect of today might not be the uncontested sovereign of science and industry, the master of the Earth? But that error immobi-

---

[25] Rosny inserts a footnote here: "An error doubtless independent even of intelligence."

lized it: the workers no longer possessed sex; sex was reserved to those that were *unaware*, the parasites of the city that could not transmit the *individual* faculties of nourishers. Then, everything stopped. Thousands of centuries went by without bringing any significant change to industrial life, while the lighter of fire retained that power of indefinite transmission, *the genius of the individual.*[26]

"Monsieur," Madame Donatienne has just announced, extending a visiting card, "there's a lady…"

On the little card I read: *Francine E. Servane.*

What the devil can that lady want with me? I only run into her once or twice a year, and we've hardly exchanged 20 words…raffle tickets for the lame, the orphans, the blind or the deaf, holidays for little girls, assistance for teenage mothers?

With my consent, Madame Donatienne shows in Madame Francine E. Servane. Terribly seductive, with features assembled unmethodically. Teeth that are made by the gross—white, yes, even bright, but badly set—zigzag lips, fleshy and cock's-comb red, eyes like those offered to you by myriads of shopgirls, unpretentious eyebrows, an abundance of undisciplined, vaguely wavy, dark brown hair, a strongly tanned complexion that gets darker at the eyelids. Tall, flexible, agile, built for running—a young human she-wolf, wild in the flesh, bridled by conformism.

The ensemble assaults the senses, awakens sensuality in the tepid and excites it in the ardent. A hint of musk, of aphrodisiac perfume…

"You're probably surprised to see me?" she says, in a hoarse, dull, mysterious voice.

"A little."

"Am I disturbing you?"

"Oh, not at all!" And, stupidly: "On the contrary."

---

[26] Rosny inserts another footnote: "I mean varied and variable genius, the indefinite multiplicity of aptitudes."

It's true, though. I'm quite content; I breath in stormy air, which inflates me, and I'm already dreading seeing her leave.

She gives voice to a sly little laugh. "Oh! You say that."

"I think it too."

"Oh! Really…"

She looks at me boldly, but she obviously knows how to beat a retreat and leave you stranded, ferociously. She needs—at least I imagine so—continued play, reserving her options…but I sense that she's worth the most patient and ruinous play. After all, perhaps it's something else—with that face, one can hide countless instincts.

Indeed, the bold gaze turns into a timid, almost virginal gaze. A slight creasing of the eyelids has transformed the physiognomy. And the teeth, momentarily menacing in their red frame, have become invisible.

Not easy to decipher! It would require time and a good deal of intuition.

"Well," she continues, in her mysterious voice, "this is the purpose of my indiscreet visit. I've been told that you're a great friend of Dr. Valestre, of Vichy. If that's true…"

"It's true."

"Good! I'd be grateful if you would give me a few words of introduction to him. I'm nervous of first meetings with unknown doctors. Introduced by you, I wouldn't be entirely a stranger to Monsieur Valestre…"

A trifle bizarre but, after all, explicable.

"When are you leaving, Madame?"

"In three days…"

"I'll write to Valestre today, and I think I can assure you that he'll give you an excellent welcome. Valestre's an honest and conscientious fellow, in whom one can put one's trust. Very knowledgeable too, sure in diagnosis, taking a keen interest in his patients' wellbeing."

"Thank you, thank you!" she says, in a warm tone, with a smile so soft that her physiognomy is transfigured once again. Ah! She has many facets.

"Do you know Vichy?" I ask.

"I'm going there for the first time."

"Everything that invalids require, and others might ask for, is concentrated there in a small area. A few steps separate the springs, the baths, the clinics and the so-called pleasure spots, which are numerous."

"Do you go there often?"

"Fairly often."

"For health reasons?"

"No, I have a mania for memories; I make pilgrimages to every place that has left me a few."

"It would be very nice if you were to come."

I am sure, for half a minute, that she is challenging me—then the "virginal" expression brings back the doubts.

"My word!" I say, vaguely.

Indecision. She gets to her feet, and extends her hand to me—a small hand, yielding at first, then firm when she grips mine. Even her hand is multiple.

Nothing more now than the slight odor of musk and that sort of ghost that lingers momentarily after the departure of someone to whom one is not indifferent. Her image has taken hold within me and fixed its trace there.

The brief visit prefigures the event, and, already creates the predestined adventure, the tumult of the elements, the clouds, the tempest, the clash of antlers, the waves of the shipwreck...

Simultaneously, moonlit parks, white châteaux at the ends of driveways, odoriferous coasts...ruinous decors, resuscitated images, poetic mythology, minuscule universes, gigantic universes of stars...everything unfurls, in a torrent of dreams, desires, sublime amours, brutish amours, because a silken skirt and an odor of musk have passed through...

How many other women! Those whose eyes no longer see, those whose young eyes are on fire, those on sarcophagi and those in books, Semiramis, Mimi Pinson, Madame de Récamier and Mary Pickford, my Aunt Julie's blonde hair, and, dissolved in the profound earth, Jeannette with the immense eyes, the little milliner before the phosphorescent waves—her hand in mine and the scent of the sea?—Mathilde with the charming feet, the pure voice of Marie, in the shadows, the bare forearms of the notary's wife, Noëlle's lips, in the Church, the pursuit of Lucie across the meadow, and always, always, the kisses on the swing…

The living are as distant as the dead, all as fabulous as Helen of Sparta.

The desire to go to Vichy increases—and what's more, it's necessary to get away from Yveline. This is, I think, the time at which she is most dangerous. It seems that, without being fully aware of it, she is getting ready for a decisive assault. Isn't it the prelude to the last, the ultimate, attempt? How I desire it—and how I'd regret it!

This morning, Yveline pales before the human she-wolf that I can meet again, if I wish, wandering in the park or in front of a spring ministered by ancillary nymphs.

Are desires disposed in zones? Their disorder is maddening. They appear at hazard, indifferent to the time of their birth—as if they were on the same plane, or as if they were mixed up at random in the water of time. No one knows how they perpetuate themselves, what signals call them forth, or whether they involve an element of "inscription," like the sounds of a phonograph. However, the old recall their childhood more clearly than their youth, and their youth more clearly than their middle age; one imagines successive layers, the more recent destroyed before the earlier, deeper ones. And perhaps none of it has any basis in reality.

VIII.

I have been in Vichy for a week. All the hours of vigilance belong to the adventure. I am obedient, in a docile manner, to the commandments of the primitive species and the transposed species. Once again, the universe is new. The emotions are magnificently dressed. Around the young human she-wolf I have assembled the fetishistic apparatus. Analysis does not depreciate anything, and even helps to discover more subtle elements of renewal.

My candidature has been accepted, but I have not yet been elected. Francine-Hélène, sure that she can lead me as she pleases, even exaggerating my weakness and her own strength, is savoring the joys of a burning impatience. She will extend the route as long as she can, but she is at the mercy of a surprise.

For her, sensuality is not an accessory; the primitive power is in suspense, not combated but exasperated by the social additives.

I only have the superiority of presence, combined with an element of inclination. If someone else were to appear, clever, quick and more to her taste, it would only require an opportunity to eliminate me. Because I'm not in any doubt about that, I'm trying to hasten the skirmish that will give me the upper hand.

I've succeeded in embellishing Francine magnificently. My imaginative power brings a kind of perfection to her entire person. Her large eyes are becoming prodigious, her lips so sensual that my whole flesh is excited when I pause to contemplate them; her gait has become the gait that Saint-Simon causes me to imagine of the Duchess de Bourgogne.[27] She walks on clouds, sewing them with the salt of sensuality.

All my senses are in love. When the faint odor of musk comes in with her, I swoon; when she sits down, oh, how I long to kiss her little feet. The other evening, she left a handkerchief in the hall; I spent half the night cherishing that handkerchief, caressing my neck and breast with it, sniffing it with

---

[27] The reference is not to the philosopher but his antecedent, the Duc de Saint-Simon who wrote his memoirs of Louis XIV's court between 1691 and 1723, offering detailed descriptions of the courtiers, including the cited Duchesse.

the passion of a wolf in pursuit of a she-wolf, but also with piety.

For, frantically carnal as it may be, my love is as idealistic as befits my degree of culture and my ancestry. I deify Francine, prostrate myself before her "double," who accompanies me everywhere; I recite the most beautiful verses that my memory has amassed, and fragments of prayers or litanies; thus mingled with my religious memories, she causes me to breathe the incense with which I intoxicated myself as a child; she stifles the hideous aspects of life, to the extent that, while believing, I jeer at the fiction of the God of bounty and love...

A thousand vestiges of superstition have reappeared—presentiments, omens—I would believe in the pronouncements of a card-reader, I touch wood, the number 13 has become ominous again. On entering a church, I plunge my fingers delightedly into the holy water, I make the sign of the cross with a sort of exquisite mysticism; and in the morning, on getting up, my hand seeks the fetish-locket suspended around my neck...

It wouldn't have taken much for her to give in. I had slipped surreptitiously into her room—we were lodged on the same floor of the Radio Hotel—and we were chatting sporadically. Neither of us was capable of following a train of thought. More often than not, she asked a question, I tried to rally my wandering thoughts; when I replied at cross purposes, we tried to laugh. She laughed, moreover, in a charming fashion; her voice, slightly hoarse and mysterious, is the messenger of obscure promises...

She was wearing a very light jacket the color of cigar-ash, which opened over a scarlet Chinese crêpe dress, with silver embroidery.

Sitting in one of those rectangular but deep leather armchairs that come from America or Bavaria, she had the brightness and the lightness of a giant flower; she was as terrible as the Shulamite.

I loved her so much, perhaps more than I had loved any other woman—or, at any rate, more *integrally*, with all the nuances of my realities and my dreams. The formidable need to possess her, to be one with her, the masculine fury, did not diminish in the least the sweetness that enveloped her, like an emanation of the divine.

I interrupted myself in mid-sentence, incapable of containing myself any longer, and I knelt in front of her, imploringly.

"Francine!"

Oh, one word—the word that one seeks at that moment, which one wants to be as fresh, as new, as the verdant hillside: the word that penetrates to the utmost depths of being!

"Oh, Francine, how I'm sickening for you...and how fearful I am..."

"Fearful?" she said, surprised and charmed.

"Fearful of losing you before even having possessed you."

I plunged my face into her lap, into a fabric as fine as a camellia petal; I breathed in the brutal and magnificent mystery hidden by that frail barrier; prostrating myself, I started kissing her feet frantically...

She was in my arms; our breasts were palpitating against one another, my lips indefatigably caressing her hair, her neck, her ear-lobes, her eyelids, but always returning to the red fruit, the wild fruit that causes us to confuse devouring and love.

Bewildered, without instinct drowning out thought, I admired the beautiful fury that possessed us and the obscure will that, far outside ourselves but with our ardent complicity, had us under its sway. I was perfectly well able to perceive the derisory animality in the gestures of delirium, the encounter of mouths, all that rudimentary and rhythm-less mimicry—but that perception, far from causing my excitement to decrease, increased it in a singular fashion and only made the fables, the enchantment and the miracle more resplendent.

I don't think Francine mingled such cogitations with her emotion. She was content to savor its phases, with a perfect consciousness of the importance of the prologue, which dissuaded her from yielding too quickly to the call. She even took care to make me aware of it. "Not yet!" she whispered, after a long clasp. "It's so nice to wait…"

In spite of the reckless voices demanding an immediate sacrifice, I was of the same opinion. Carried away by the demon, however, I replied: "I implore you, Francine, full of grace…"

She burst out laughing: a throaty laugh, hoarse and voluptuous: "The Lord isn't with me!"

"You're making me suffer."

"So much the better…it's necessary." I must have had a pitiful expression, for she went on, hiding her face in my bosom: "Just a few more days."

"That's a promise? You won't break it?"

She raised her head and looked me full in the face: "I'm honest!"

In spite of her passion-dilated eyes, in spite of her amorously swollen lips, she suddenly looked like a little girl—and it was surely a little girl who pressed herself against me, curling up and murmuring: "You'll love me for a long time, won't you?"

She's the first one who didn't say "forever."

IX.

I have met the enemy. An enemy, whatever might happen—a fundamental enemy, whether or not he does me any harm—my rival, and the real or virtual rival of all the ardent males who find him in their path.

It was at the Celestine spring. He had just taken a glass of water from a pretty waitress, and he was looking at her obliquely, with a wild and sly expression. Already, she was manifesting some slight emotion, which no one would have noticed, among those who did not know Marcus. She scarcely had time to notice it herself, solicited by a flood of visitors to whom it was necessary to serve the salutary water. Was Marcus thinking about seducing even that poor girl? He must think about it when confronted with every female endowed with any grace, without any class distinction. In this case, though, it was probably just "exercise."

The animal was dressed in a rather gaudy manner: cigar-colored trousers, a blue waistcoat, lighter and brighter than sea-blue, a slightly tilted gray-brown hat and a shirt of a shade whose seductiveness I could not deny. He must, to say the least, have been shod by a boot-maker who was not only called "Master" by his servants but by his courtiers and some of his clients. A stupid, insolent churl, a cunning thief who had ended up having a boundless admiration for himself.

Marcus emptied his glass in three gulps and his eyes made a rapid inventory of the women present. As chance would have it, the majority were ugly and the remainder scarcely passable. It was then that he spotted me, and immediately caressed me with a smile. "What a fortunate meeting!" he said, delightedly. "How are you?"

A flood of hatred and dread overwhelmed me, and a veritable panic shook my vertebrae and viscera rudely. Without any transition, I saw him next to Francine; in a lightning-fast film, all the phases of a seduction. Already, their bodies were about to melt into one another.

"Not bad," I said. "You?"

"A little run down…"

As he had nothing to say, having a flat and monotonous mind, we exchanged empty words for a while, and were not long delayed in separating.

Full of sinister presentiments, I thought that Francine belonged to the race that would accord Marcus the highest valuation. Only love for someone else could armor them. A little while before, I had been almost sure of that love. Now, it appeared faint, vain and inconsistent—a mere mist. I knew full well that it was absurd, and I repeated that to myself without obtaining any armistice from my imagination or my nerves.

All morning, I was as agitated as an inexperienced adolescent, and often as naïve. Emotions do not age. The childish and the adolescent reappear with nuances that memory is incapable of suppressing.

Marcus caused all the adversaries I had fought at school to surge forth, along with the adjutant at Montargis, and the captain who commanded my company at the front in Lorraine, Valbert, who had stolen little Eulalie from me—the most delightful and the most tragic scenes, the most indifferent too, the most ridiculous and far-fetched. At times when the plurality, the evaporation of the self, becomes so manifest that one begins to doubt the reality of any individual existence, the same self also reveals the most powerful condensation, the most compact personality.

At midday, the tumult began to ease, and when I was on my way to the Casino, where I was to have lunch with Francine, the flood became calm. The young woman had the benefit of a surfeit of love; in a few minutes, I added to her all the graces that would normally take an entire day.

The food was excellent, salmon-trout and guinea-fowl; the light delicately sculpted Francine's face, which was made-up in a masterly fashion and heightened by a slight touch of rouge. Francine only uses as much make-up as her Iberian features require.

We pretend to chat, but we only exchange a few amorphous remarks. Already, our familiarity is sufficient for that not to bother me at all—and for her, it's her native tongue, outside of the supremely intimate moments when she exhales overused words on which tone and essential reality confer the fresh novelty of April foliage.

"Francine," I say to her—I've scarcely thought of anything else—"it's today that we're going to the country…"

"Oh! Really!" she says, astonished—or pretending to be.

"You promised!" I say, in a low voice.

"Are you sure?"

"You swore on oath!"

We look at one another intently; I sense that the same cloud that is blurring her vision is blurring mine. Come on! Our instincts are in accord; the same rhythm is vibrating our fibers.

"Since I swore!" she says, in a languid voice.

That was when Marcus appeared. Pausing for a quarter of a minute in the doorway, he saw me and he saw her; his cunning eyes caressed her...

I ought to have been more anxious than before; I was less so, and in a different manner. Impressions of a higher quality accompanied it, characterized by an increased lucidity.

Marcus advanced slowly, and as he passed close to our table he bowed, and looked at Francine again. His covetousness was so evident that no words could have expressed it with such precision, refined and bestial at the same time. Oh, how I would have liked to slap his face! But I answered his smile with a smile...

Francine's face revealed an almost imperceptible emotion—which, at any rate, must have been so slight that she was probably unaware of it. But it is not so much the intensity as the nature of an emotion that is important. That one "had a future." It would be up to Marcus to develop it gradually, unless Francine's love for me proved to be an insurmountable obstacle. I did not believe that, and would not have believed it even without the corrosive power of jealousy.

I returned Marcus' bow without offering him my hand. He went to sit down at a neighboring table.

We were on the coffee, and Francine, voluntarily or otherwise, did not look in Marcus' direction.

My precautions had been taken the previous evening; a car was waiting for us.

I have long been familiar with this old inn, which is condemned to an imminent death followed by an odious metamorphosis. It is falling apart. Its façade is pitted all over by mason wasps. Black ivy covers the left wing, a wild vine is scaling the right. Worm-eaten shingles cover the roof and a population of pigeons lives there happily, under a perpetual threat of which the creatures, half-wild and half-domesticated are totally unaware.

An unmagical spectacle, which will become enchanted in the machine of memory.

Even Francine, as we climb the crumbling front steps, becomes momentarily distant, while I say to the waitress who comes running, in a peremptory fashion: "A room..." And I add, automatically, with a silly little laugh: "We'll eat when we've changed our clothes."

The hostess, whom I know, comes to escort us herself, and here we are in this white cage, in which I'm counting on spending one of the most triumphant hours of my pilgrimage.

Francine has not flinched. She stands still, inspecting the surroundings with a vague mistrust, perhaps a secret anxiety. "It's charming," she murmurs. "It's clean and bright and scented with lavender."

I only have a vague perception of the walls, covered in red and green pastoral wallpaper, the white bed and the garden that is a fragment of Old France: an aviary full of birds, fruits and flowers...Francine occupies the foreground of the world. She is redoubtable.

Her tall silhouette, her short skirt, her old-silver jacket opening over embroidery and lace, the abundant vegetation of her hair, her beautifully round neck, and, most of all, her magnificently pale face, her eyes, which seem even larger, darker, more fabulous...

Is that a dream, or is it reality? It's reality *now*, and it will be the internal, immortal reality, later. I hope for that with a delightful savagery and an inexpressible refinement. Francine becomes beauty itself, sensuality, genesis and the vast future; her perfume is the supreme promise of my destiny...

I have not forgotten that she is a woman like countless others and that our adventure does not include any element of originality. But here is a breath of glory bearing me away, the force, the energy, the victory—and Francine becomes the joy of joys, the immortal flower, and also the source of brutal desire, frantic, implacable, which passes through the forest of nerves like a cyclone...

The terror that she might escape me! The possibility of not having her, now, frightens me like death. My triple humanity is concentrated on that petty form of flesh and blood, and the dream that I experience, composed of dreams accumulated in the lair, in the horde, in the tribe, in ancient cities and cities infested by prodigious industry, renders the rest of existence bleak and insipid.

Ah, Francine! I have seized her in my arms. Her mouth has never been so alive; we have prolonged the strange caress of the kiss.

She consents. Now we are accomplices. The same tumult roars in our arteries. The same ardor, which seems inextinguishable, precipitates our movements, with a formidable need to be one and the same flesh...

We almost are. There are seconds when the caress seems a conjunction, when I am in Francine as she is in me...oh, why is it so brief? Why is that singular agitation extinguished at the very moment when it extends towards infinity?

Francine turns her head away and hides her face, distant, mysterious, pale, exhausted and shaken by tears. An entirely physical pity moves me, mingling with the song of victory, which, in being the most banal, nevertheless remains the greatest, the most profound and the most marvelous.

"You'll love me forever," she murmurs. "Forever!"

The cry of long feminine servitude, and also of those who languish in limbo. It requires time, the promise of protection, and the instinct persists, beyond the need, as love persists without fecundation. When she turns her pathetic face toward me, I create new graces for her, which are added to the beauty of her languid eyes.

Her value has, therefore, increased further. But suddenly, it decreases. I see Marcus again, and Francine's almost imperceptible emotion—a seed that will probably never germinate. Virtual or real, however, it touches the heart, and Francine is already entering the future in which we will mean nothing to one another. It's not so much jealousy as a lamentable sensation of nothingness.

But she puts out her arms, half sitting up, and the living whiteness, that strange human whiteness, so distant from animal nudity that it seems to be a projection of the inner being, momentarily chases away that unwelcome future. I revive in her, and then there is the melancholy marked of old, while Francine seems to have acquired a new energy.

She's no longer pathetic; her mouth is laughing and her eyes are joyful. And she embraces me, coaxingly.

"I'm hungry!"

I believe that I'm hungry too.

"We'll eat here, then," she says, pointing to the wooden balcony invaded by mauve wisteria flowers. "That balcony's nice!"

A red-headed girl I could easily believe to be descended from the Riparian Franks brings us maslin bread, butter fresh from the churn, strawberries and cream. From the utmost depths of being, another sensuality rises: the sensuality of devouring, the source of all the others. Here, the drama punctuated by ferocious joy metamorphoses into a naïve and tender comedy. The foodstuffs seem innocent, amiable, full of some mysterious grace of odor and taste. One no longer perceives the hard work of their origin, the seemingly peaceful struggle as cruel as the content of teeth and claws. Agriculture, husbandry, tool-making: implacable realities that annihilate or degrade natural life everywhere. The laborer in his field, the worker in his factory—what, compared to them, are the boorish carnivores? Pitiful tigers, poor damnable elephants, unglamorous bisons, the frightful world of work has condemned you. No more place for you on this planet where you once reigned. A puny mammal, as slow as an ant-bear, in making use of factory production, is going to annihilate you.

"It's delicious," Francine murmurs. "I prefer this simple fare to all the masterpieces of chefs…"

Simple! Simple, these strawberries due to so many stubborn initiatives; simple, this wheat enriched by the efforts of

100 generations; simple, this divine coffee...oh, ingenuous Francine!

X.

An admirable week. No other events than those issuing from ourselves. For neither the décor, nor the occurrences, nor our gestures and words, had any significance. There was only what we drew from our own substance, for our triple natures.

Crudely welded together, we have nevertheless remained strangers, even stranger to one another, in a sense, than before. Stranger still to one another because the known fraction, as it increased, had caused an even greater unknown fraction to appear.

It was the era of the "mysteries of the couple." Francine drew, in her wake, a world as real as it was imaginary. Dull humans only perceive the multitudes hidden within them in times of tempest, sexual tempests most of all.

Blissfully unaware of the vanity of my effort, I sought to penetrate Francine mentally as I had penetrated her physically...but I only encountered the accessory, the "expressible." The accessory being a function of intelligence, not—or hardly at all—of sentiment, I only succeeded in establishing the psychological mediocrity of my lover. In that respect, she was one of the herd, almost to the same extent as Yveline or Juliane. I knew, however, that she had more complex depths *beyond*, denser than theirs, more exciting to frequent. If she did not have the genius of sentimentality, as Denise probably had, at least she had talent. And here and there, with the joy of the miner finding nuggets—or, rather, of the Christian who thinks he has discovered some vestige of the divine mystery—I found *something*, of which I could not succeed in forming a definition or an image. It stood out against the obscure background creative of sensations like a patch of phosphorescence in a cellar. I experienced a dilatation of being then, which inflamed my desire and my worship.

My worship? A cult assuredly refined by all that centuries of human labor had assembled therein of forms, terms, rhythms and ideas.

When Francine had left me, I loved to open one of the church books of which I had been fond in the time of belief, which still touch me, shot through as they are with the vibrancy of childhood and nascent puberty.

"He whom the Earth, the sea and the Heavens adore, the Lord who governs the triple machine of the world, was carried in Mary's womb...a young girl, full of heavenly grace, received in her loins the One who regulates the movements of the Sun and the Moon, the Sovereign Creator who holds the entire world in his hands..."

I wished then that Francine might bear a child, and I perceived the innumerable sequence of women of whom she was the issue.

And when I read: "Thou who art the mysterious rose who hast filled the world with the odor of thy sanctity, thou who art the morning star..." a softness expanded within me as marvelous as on the day when, in the depths of the woods, I had seen a nest full of golden-throated chicks—and the divine evening when Jacqueline, on the doorstep, looking at constellations as pure as the water of fountains, had sung the "Song of the King of Thule"[28] in a low voice.

Without these "additives" love would stabilize or come apart much more quickly. Two pigeons can love one another tenderly, but from the initial pairing on, stabilization begins. For the bull, the heifer has no personal existence, nor the bull for the heifer. Before, and even during the mating, they ignore one another; afterwards, they do not even have anything to forget. Stabilization or immediate rupture, the emotions accumulate and dissipate in no time at all. It's possible that they

---

[28] From the third act of Charles Gounod's opera *Faust* (1859).

are, during that interval, as sharp as they are for us, at least in certain species and—who knows?—even sharper in others.

They still remain brief in uncultured humans—save for exceptional individuals—but are already prolonged by the importation of interhuman images and probably also by some social heredity combined with brutal heredity.

In our milieu, the elements of prolongation abound; we obtain those beautiful periods of instability, which can entertain emotion, intoxication, fear and joy for weeks, months or even longer periods, and which feed jealousy with an inextinguishable aliment—concentrating, in sum, the best and worst of our being on a single creature.

I am a man and a faithful animal. I am like that by virtue of the natural persistence of my inclinations; I am also like that by virtue of a horror of causing suffering. The two tendencies explain my long relationship with Juliane. It will depend on Francine whether our love is eternalized...she can make me fast if she wishes, to the extent, if she has a firm desire, of anchoring me in marriage—of which, however, I have a horror. I anticipate that she is the one who will break it off, or at least let it go. And that will be no bad thing.

Another fortnight has passed. My mistress's cure is officially terminated, but we're lingering in Vichy.

How blissful these days have been! My religion of love has attained its highest splendor. I have magnified Francine to the point of prodigy; I have exhausted all my strength adoring and devouring; I have humiliated myself in frenzies of joy. I have known the glory of a god.

Jealousy has only come in brief fits, from off-stage, like the phantoms of the dusk. No retrospective jealousy. I have, however, been subject to the need one has of torturing oneself with a woman's past. Even Juliane—in a larval state, to be sure. And how much more with others! An exclusively human malady, perhaps, born of the word, but *directly* derived from male conflict. Males that fight for females (any females) are

178

abundant, but retrospective jealousy requires speech—the strange power of one being to transmit the past to another. Is there nowhere to be found, though, a male that scents the past when a female is not a virgin? It seems not, but who can tell?

At any rate, I have paid no heed to Francine's past; I have situated her in the present, if not entirely, at least forcefully enough for the Francine before me to fade into unreality...

My jealousy had but one form: the form of Marcus. Very subdued. He was, however, still in Vichy—and he had even contrived to be introduced to Francine, although the frisson of the first day has not been repeated.

In that phase, Francine was wholly devoted to the new *amour*. The threat was lost in possibilities, of which none was then probable. In any case, Marcus was concentrating his resources on wearing down a young Rumanian woman. As we would soon be leaving Vichy, I had no other anxiety than the permanent anxiety stirring in the depths of joy. It was dormant—but at the first sign of trouble, it would wake up, inflated with poisons.

Now, Marcus had settled matters with the Rumanian—and, according to his code, as soon as the surrender was complete, he began preparing for the future. The future was Francine. I never found out how he laid the trap, but one afternoon, I caught him talking to Francine on the terrace of the Casino. He was standing up; she was sitting down.

I was in a favorable spot, invisible to them but able to see them. At intervals, she turned her head, on the lookout. The gesture was full of significance—the gesture of someone fearful of a witness, so instinctive that she scarcely noticed it. She did not imagine that there was the slightest infraction, even less so because Marcus was nothing to her but a passer-by today, and perhaps an "acquaintance" tomorrow.

Was he attracted to her? I don't know, but he acted; he imposed his atmosphere, he "engraved" his image—and I had never seen more clearly, even more clearly than him, what

179

intuition guided him, and how his movements were adapted to his task.

I was close enough to hear what they were saying; I almost admired the facility that he had in talking in order to say nothing. That useful faculty stops the gaps in a conversation, the awkward hiatuses that arise between a man and a woman. The rhythm and inflexions of his voice had an abundance of charms; it was Marcus's birdsong.

At any rate, he did not linger. He has to know how to calculate the duration of initial approaches. When Francine was alone, she lowered her head, and I had the impression that it was then that Marcus acted with the greatest efficacy.

In the same way that I had suppressed the desire to appear during, I suppressed the desire to appear after; anything that disturbed Francine would hasten the fatal march.

Then, all cunning, threat, energy and struggle appeared vain to me, derisory and miserably humiliating. Swollen with passion and worn out by sadness, I took my pain for a stroll along the river.

The principal current of jealousy is, I think, that of defeat. One is vanquished. The enemy has conquered your property, and that living property, palpitating and *consenting*, he will use for his pleasure.

To see the body that you received with so much fervor receiving the other's body just as ardently, is the entrance to the void. Nature is rejecting you and the man is humiliating you. In addition, it is here, in the coarse and magical lair of procreation, that imagination is subject to its most frightful, most thrilling and, above all, most bestial surges.

I walked, gripped by homicidal furies that wrung my heart and made me shrug my shoulders, mortally sad and mocking myself unmercifully, full of pity and disdain for myself. Stupid insect, derisory little creature! Yes, but what a universe! You are within me, innumerable stars, formless nebulas, frightful interstellar spaces; you are within me, oceans, lakes and rivers; within me, mountains and forests; within me, vanquished animality and bruised humanity.

My entire universe palpitates for you, Francine—and envelops Marcus with hatred!

You have never penetrated me more profoundly, and yet here you are, deflowered. The divine falls away in tatters. Everything with which I have ornamented you crumbles. I multiply your beauty tenfold; nothing remains but a woman still desirable, re-entering the herd...

Thus I walked, in a delirium or a dark lyricism punctuated by analysis. In fact, my reason had never acquiesced to the beautiful extravagances of love, never believed that Francine was any different from myriads of pretty creatures, or even that she was equal to many, finer, more brilliant, more harmonious or even more sensual.

My reason made a list of my hyperboles, but the torrent of passion drowned it like a frail flower.

That reason did not slander the charm that had transported me beyond myself, and congratulated me for not having listened to it, knowing only too well that, in that magnificent moment, it could only be harmful. Now, its influence would be salutary. I forced myself to submit to it; I agreed with it that it was necessary not to disparage either the adventure or Francine, and that perhaps Marcus would not succeed.

Here, instinct mocked reason; it knew full well that Marcus would carry her away; it had a certainty that far surpassed analysis. And again, the feeble barricade crumbled. Hyperbole stirred in the shadows...

"If you would like to," Francine said to me, an hour later, "we can stay in Vichy for a few more days."

"Isn't it sufficient that you would like to?"

Blows are always delivered in an unforeseen fashion. I naturally imagined that Francine was already in a hurry to surrender herself. I alternated angry consent with dreams of a ridiculous struggle. Throughout, I assumed that all attempts at constraint would be in vain, or that they would be accompanied by violent quarrels. Any woman struck, bruised and bloody may return to the person who has chastised her, but it is not the rule. Either desire, like a river, refuses to flow back toward its source, or the old desire mingles its flow with the new desire.

The blow had not been too hard. I was tired of ferocious images, weary of jealousy. I listened to Francine talk, replied to her as a phonograph might have replied—but when I caught the scent of her flesh and her pleasant perfume, a flood of sensuality rose up. Was she still mine? Would I find her, not rebellious but cooled down? I had only to reach out my arms and, with the same impulse, we would sink...

In truth, that was a great consolation.

From then on, I don't know what anxious curiosity mingled with the jealousy. What would she do when Marcus took possession of her? For my reasoning self and my emotive self assumed that that denouement was inevitable. Would she reject me or hang on to me? And if she hung on to me, would my caresses be of a secondary order, or would they equal Marcus's caresses?

There were, inevitably, moments in which it was me who broke, but I did not let myself be taken: I would accept, for some time yet, whatever Francine wished to give me, the feast or the crumbs. The appetite that I had for her would take time to fade away.

You'll take his leavings, then! I cried to myself one morning, abruptly seized by the worst fury, humiliated fury, when the image of Marcus naked, at the most ridiculous and the most revolting moment, surged forth with savage violence.

I've never been more scornful of myself, while assessing my scorn as utterly absurd.

Already, nothing remained of the fables assembled around Francine. On the contrary, I now reduced my mistress to a level beneath the normal, and denigrated all the categories of her being. A melancholy pleasure accompanied this demolition work—but I was no less sensible of the attraction of that decried flesh, and the social individual found perverse savors therein.

Francine submitted with such good grace that I sometimes began to doubt that Marcus was making progress, and then, the scraps of the illusory woman reappeared in the wings.

Chance delivered me from my uncertainty. It happened one evening, while I was taking my anxieties for a walk. The hotel in which Francine was staying is situated opposite the park. The apartment has two large French windows, which open on to a balcony.

I was coming back from the river, and I came to a halt, my eyes fixed on the French windows. They were closed, or standing ajar, with the curtains drawn—light curtains, which permitted the silhouette of the occupant to be seen when she moved in front of the electric lamps...

There were two silhouettes! It was impossible to mistake that of Marcus, any more than that of Francine. The carriage of a person is as characteristic as his face. I had arrived at the fateful moment. The battle was engaged.

Marcus had taken one of Francine's hands; she pretended to withdraw it, but he did not let go. He drew my mistress slowly toward him; her resistance visibly weakened. Finally, he held her in his embrace.

She hesitated—how they hesitate when everything is in revolt! Marcus began kissing her hair and her neck, and sought her mouth. She refused it for some time, but the die was cast; the mouths met amorously...

Then, the resistance increased. Francine was too wily to squander the preliminaries, and also to surrender herself in a place where I might appear at any moment—and Marcus was too experienced not to know that he would have to wait until the third act. If he prolonged the contest momentarily, it was because that was also in the rules, and surprises are possible— of which it is then appropriate to take advantage.

Finally, having established that Francine intended to control the phases of the adventure, he beat a retreat.

A few minutes later, Francine was alone.

My personal drama was less bitter than I had expected; the armor-plating thickened, and if jealousy uttered a few loud roars, and the instincts leapt up, as was only right, the machine of reasoning was fully functional.

In spite of the ferocious impulse that thrust me toward Francine, I forced myself to undertake a preliminary consultation. It lasted five or six minutes; it approved my desire, while demanding that a scene—which could only be favorable to Marcus—should be avoided, which I took care to swear several times over.

When I went in, Francine shivered—almost a start—but it was brief. In such circumstances, even the most stupid person knows enough to "let it be." Francine combined her natural resources with the resources of the laboratory. At the sight of her, meanwhile, fury hurled itself against the bars—but did not take long to lie down again at the back of the cage. Implacable desire was dominant, spurred on by jealousy.

"I wasn't expecting you," said Francine, in a blank voice. With admirable aplomb, she added: "I'm glad that you've come!"

If that was false when she said it, I'm sure that it was true when I looked her in the eyes. She recognized the gaze of sensuality; her flesh, vibrant with Marcus's kiss and still in love with mine, dilated; I saw the intoxicating movement of the throat, raised up by an evident sensuality.

And I locked the door…

"Oh!" she said, as she got up again. "I love you so much, darling! I love you so much!"

I imagine that she was sincere. All the energy of memory combined with a kind of remorse and the joy of being unsuspected.

I was astonishingly calm. The jealousy died away; I felt that it would only awaken torpidly from now on, for increasingly brief intervals. Besides, the last illusions attached to Francine were falling like autumn leaves. She was scarcely more now than a desirable female; her image alone would reassume, later, a part of the splendor with which I had camouflaged her.

She even descended, initially, lower than her actual rank—for, after all, she was classed above the multitude.

That day, I only recognized in her the physical refinement, in the sense of ornamentation, attitudes and gestures, of a beautiful woman of the people. The excess of the depreciation constituted the brightest element of my vengeance; I stripped her bare instead of striking her...

Later, she would be raised up slightly, if her flesh continued to accommodate itself to mine.

XI.

It was last month that I left Vichy. The rhythm of my sentimental life has relented. I know, without it troubling me, save for a few slight twinges, that Francine has given herself to Marcus; I also know what she does not suspect—that he will soon reject her, with the brutal indifference of a child. She always welcomes me warmly, and takes a troubled delight in deceiving both of us.

Marcus must know the truth as well as I do—with the result that, fundamentally, she alone is deceived; that doesn't displease me at all.

I've seen Ferral again. I had assured him before my departure that I had the means to obtain the apparatus indispensable to an attempt to break into the universe.

Ferral is trying to bridge the gap that must complete the hiatus between light and the primitive corpuscles. He does not believe that their formation requires the extreme temperature and pressure that people imagine. Besides, pressure and temperature can be limited to the infinitesimal. In favorable conditions, the universe will furnish them if one can only discover the necessary lever.

Already, Ferral has obtained impressive "preliminary" results: the dissociation of helium, among others—which, if developed, would put new energies in fragile human hands. The dissolution is still capricious; Ferral is trying to render it constant.

In this battle against the universe, my role is secondary. Ferral claims that I "mount" the experiments more skillfully, more surely and more rapidly than him. In our association, he is the creator. The faculty of realization has not been refused to him, as to so many great mathematicians, but he goes astray and loses time, and his hands do not have the agility of Chavres' or mine.

When the time comes to rest, we talk about our experiments and the tricks by which we expect to "put one over" on nature.

Afterwards, the chat wanders; dreams race away. There is no more universal man on our plane of existence than Ferral. The events of social life or the life of an insect, the ups and downs of minuscule quotidian existence, are no more indifferent to him than the convulsions of the masses, the pleasures of the arts or the evolutions of the stars. When his mystical eyes—there are few as vast—fix themselves on empty space, he reminds me of a cenobite immersed in prayer. He runs lightly through the regions of metaphysics, attracted by all the forms of the unknown. He has clear—empirical— beliefs, but also innumerable beliefs "in the mist."

"Without the pressure of hypothesis," he said, the other evening, "without the religious impulse toward possibilities, would humans even have attained the civilization of ants?"

"Yes," I said. "The experimental loses itself in the hypothetical like a river in the sea. Religious faith and social faith, modes of body and mind, popular metaphysics and abstract metaphysics! Even verified science has its dogmas, hasn't it? Scarcely a generation separates us and those who *believed* positively in the wave theory, and the indivisible atom. Even

186

today, how many scientists solidify the abstractions of time and space!"

"Time and space can also be narrowly accommodated, mathematically, to the experimental...and they're also prodigious extracts. Imaginary as a volume, a plane or a line might be, volumes, planes and lines are the surest supports of experience—and, better still, they verify it. Without their incomparable collaboration we'd still be something like the stone-carvers of the Magdalenian or the Lacustrians who built houses on stilts. With the abstractions of metaphysics and the dreams of religions, we enter frankly into the domain of fiction, sometimes totally. *Pure* metaphysics only reaches a tiny fraction of men, though. If, however, they mingle fraudulently with popular mystics, their role becomes more considerable. As for religions, considered intrinsically, what incomparable creations of human reality! Certainly, metaphysics plays its role therein and phenomenal reality is called to its rescue, to the point that, in the past, *for all men*, religion was not separate from general knowledge.

"Fetishistic influences, magic, gestures, formulas, rites, sacrifices, actions, gods and the One God—the entire, immense and vertiginous domain of the unverifiable—have regulated, and still regulate innumerable social and individual destinies."

"And will never cease to regulate them!" Chavres interjected.

"That's quite possible! As a child and adolescent I was maddened by the spectacle of humans surrendered to the frightful mix of religious beauty and hideousness. Certain peoples, such as the Romans, scarcely conceived of spirits or gods except as species of ferocity, perfidy and caprice."

"What effort!" exclaimed Chavres. "They had 20,000 or 30,000 invisible beings, which they had to propitiate according to precise rituals...I'm thinking about those formulas that it was necessary to repeat 27 times, spitting every time, and those beans that people had to throw behind them, for incessant consultations...and the sacrifices! Jupiter demanded white oxen, Vulcan liked russet animals, Ceres pigs…there was a god that presided over an infant's first cries, one who taught it to drink, another to eat; a god for cleaning up, another for the dung-heap; one for sowing, one for harrowing or weeding…"

"You could continue until tomorrow morning," I said, "and until the end of your life if you wanted to list all the rites, the formulas, the sacrifices, the spirits, the gods…and the saints! Think of the immensity of Buddhism, Brahmanism, Mohammedanism, Totemism, Fetishism, ancestral cults… enough to fill myriads of books…"

"Oh, but they exist! Theses on the Quran alone cannot be counted, and that's only a poor literature compared to that of religious India, not to mention our Christianities. There's enough to occupy 20 compilers for a lifetime in sacred dances, from the leaping priests of Rome to jungle dancers."

"The splendor of the imagination!" murmured Ferral, admiringly.

"What choice would a natural man make, suddenly confronted with the diversity of religions?"

"If primitive, I suppose that he'd rally to some native cult. If he were inclined to enormous imagination, to the fraternity of humans and animals, Buddhism or Brahmanism would seduce him. If he were a little less quintessential, throwing the animals out into the external darkness, he'd be a Christian, a Jew or a Muslim."

"Sacrifices!" murmured Ferral. "Sacrifices! How they alarmed me once! What frissons of horror I had when I was 16!"

"The idea was so powerful that it extended to divinities. Prometheus, Jesus…"

"The *sacrifice* of the Mass…"

A long pause, Chavres surrendered to the strange sensuality of the pipe and Ferral plunged into abyssal depths.

"All the same," Chavres said. "The mystery!"

"It's one of the numerous illusions of anthropocentrism," Ferral murmured. "There is no mystery external to us. What escapes us in the universe is no more mysterious in itself than what we think we know. Our human limits are meaningless in confrontation with the unlimited. We would only have to be constructed differently for our present mysteries to disappear, wholly or partly, and for a fraction or the whole of our knowledge to become mysterious. Those who only admit mystery provisionally are victims of another kind of anthropocentrism; they hope that we will end up possessing a key to the universe—a hope that, among other absurdities, assumes a simplicity hidden beneath complexity, which is capable of explaining the complexity..."

"The unknown fraction is diminishing, though!" said Chavres.

"It is increasing. That is the function of knowledge. Every time we increase knowledge, we glimpse a vaster region of the unknown. I mean *the unknown suggested by the known,* not the absolute, baseless unknown, which is more properly called the unknowable. A child's unknown is limited by the mentality of the child; the unknown of an Australian aborigine is proportional to his rudimentary knowledge—rudimentary compared with ours, but immense I suppose in proportion to that of a kangaroo. In the same way that the visible universe increases as we improve telescopes, our unknown develops along with our discoveries."

"Will there be a limit to human discoveries?"

"I imagine that it's inevitable, and that the limit will announce the extinction of our species..."

"But where are the iguanodons?" caroled Chavres—and he added: "Ferral, we shan't penetrate the mystery of the execrable and magnificent romance of terrestrial life. I mean, of course, the anthropocentric, not to say zoocentric, mystery. I don't know why the two most gripping aspects of that mystery are still, for me, the reptiles of the Secondary Era and our abominable humankind. What an endeavor, those monsters, the largest of which concentrated more living substance than a thousand of our peers! I can see them distinctly, swarming on marshy ground, beneath a nebulous sky—it's frightful, Fer-

ral…admirable and grotesque. For so much life, accumulated in a single one of those creatures, culminated, it seems, in an infernal stupidity!"

"Stupidity!" I exclaimed. "It was undoubtedly genius, by comparison with trilobites! I'm stunned with admiration by the emergence of the feeblest glimmers of intelligence. Those immense machines would not have been able to live without some ingenuity, and without cunning…and what a marvel cunning is! Take note, as well, that we have nothing for which to envy the Secondary Era in terms of colossal lives. Our blue whales and sperm whales are too often forgotten: those champions equal, and sometimes surpass, the Secondary champions. Furthermore, they've attained a higher grade: their warming apparatus is more perfect and they're mammals!"

"Alas! Will the little vertical beast let them live?"

"You don't like human beings, Chavres?"

"I hate them, I am scornful of them and I adore them! Ferocious and magnificent little beasts! Creators of a world…and I mean a *world*: a world between the so-called organic and mineral worlds…"

"I believe in the life of the mineral world!" I said.

"Me too," Chavres riposted, "but that's another story. I believe, with a few others, that between the mineral world and the cellular world a new world has been born…how fragile, how perishable…but, when all is said and done, new. It was born in the days when humankind's first fires were lit, or the first tools were shaped. Between the animal and the water, the atmosphere and the rocks—stone, dust or mud—something had arrived that would grow immeasurably, and very rapidly. It was only yesterday that our ancestors began their humble industry. Between them and us there's at least five hundred times fewer centuries than between them and the Iguanodon—and see how the power of machines surpasses the strength of sperm whales, elephants and tigers by such an extent that those giants have become derisory. They might as well not exist any more! But that's still nothing but power, at the expense of concentrated intelligence…to the extent that the fac-

190

tory worker is stupid by comparison with his machine…and to the extent that we hear the voice from beyond the grave and constrain expansion to extend our word indefinitely, to carry it into the clouds or into the polar deserts! Yes, it really is a new world, a world that is neither mineral nor vegetable or animal…which is truly *something else…*"

Chavres was getting excited, and Ferral looked at him, smiling.

"What a partisan you would have made, Chavres, in the times of Arius, the Albigensians or Calvin!"

"And who knows," Chavres went on, "whether that world might not be the milieu in which the kingdom will be born which, in future, will succeed the world that human beings have ruined so terribly?—a more subtle kingdom, less basely submissive to expansion, more agile in its increase and vaster in its intelligence. Some little-known writer[29] has sustained this thesis and imagined the primitive elements of that kingdom—I think he called them the ferromagnetals: the actual elements will, I think, be less simple, not in their manifestation, but in their structure."

"For myself," Ferral said, "I can willingly believe that our successors will be organisms more fluid than ourselves…perhaps purely energetic…"

We remained pensive for a while, then Chavres resumed speaking: "Science, after all, only knows *the past…*"

"What do you mean?" I asked.

"As it must!" he replied, showing his sparkling teeth. "We can only know that which already exists. Now, we cannot doubt that, within our universe, and in all the universes of which Ferral speaks, completely new things must occur! On this planet, no animal world existed in Archean times, unless it was a world animated in a fashion different from ours. Then, there were only water, oxygen, nitrogen, carbon dioxide and various other elements out of which the animal world would

---

[29] Rosny, in "La Mort de la Terre" (tr. in vol. 1 as "the Death of the Earth").

191

be constructed. What science, even one as superior to ours as ours is to the knowledge of toads, could have foreseen the roles to be played by those elements? What science would have predicted the formation of trilobites, when the trilobites did not yet exist, or that of mammals before the mammals, or merely that of present day humans after the fugitive animal in the trees? The universe has only one constant: it possesses the capacity to become other than it is—and that capacity escapes science. My imagination is overwhelmed by the successive appearance of fauna and flora…what am I saying? It's already overwhelmed by human beings creating the world about which we're talking."

"Since a living world," said Ferral, "almost a human world, was able to spring from a mineral world—which, I believe, is also animate in its fashion—one can almost take it for granted that entire universes, different from present universes, might spring from the unsoundable depths."

"What can we call that," Chavres asked, with a mystical air, "if not creative power?"

XII.

It is one of those days when coincidences proliferate; I have received, in a matter of hours, visits from Francine, Yveline and Juliane.

Francine was the first to arrive. She was dressed in melancholy—melancholy suited her—her mouth bruised by an unslaked desire. Her tall frame, flexible and agile, was abandoned to nonchalance. She was bringing me, I had no doubt, a brand new deception. Had Marcus replaced a rendezvous with a note or a telegram? Did she suspect that notes and telegrams would increasingly replace her conqueror? Not yet. She was still before the altar, steeped in mystical sensuality, taking great comfort from the thought that she was deceiving him with me—for her instinct must be warning her about the cruel

192

soul of the conqueror, of whose sins the woman was not sufficiently aware, while, sure of my benevolence, she slightly regretted deceiving me.

Today, she came in search of both compensation for disappointed desire and a fragment of vengeance—a haphazard vengeance, inclined as she was to believe that Marcus's absence was justifiable rather than admit the contrary.

So she came, offered me her exceedingly tender lips, and then, burying her face in my neck, murmured: "I've never loved you so much!"

I almost believed it. Then, not believing it, the worlds tickled me agreeably. It did not take long for them to aggravate me, even humiliate me. Generic hatred awakening, with the odor, the form and the color of Marcus, I detested Francine. But she was too tempting, with her eyes of tender fire, her gracious melancholy and her lukewarm desire, delicately perfumed with musk. I "knew" her one more time.

Unfortunately, still tremulous, she repeated: "I never loved you so much!"—which caused the odious phantom of Marcus to reappear.

I heard myself say, without really meaning to: "He'll cause you more distress yet!"

She sat up with a start; the flames in her eyes flared up again; her melancholy was transformed into astonished anger, hateful pain and jealousy—and overarching everything, an immense disappointment. It was only a flash. Her womanly duplicity camouflaged her physiognomy.

"Distress? Who will cause me distress, darling?"

The game was boring me; I replied, with a hint of impatience: "How could you, clever as you are, believe that I didn't know everything?"

She looked at me, dumbfounded, quivering with indignation. "Someone's betrayed me!" she cried.

"You betrayed yourself, poor child…and Marcus too."

She fell back, overwhelmed. Gripped by bitter grief and humiliated.

"You knew...and you didn't say anything...you *accepted*...my God! And I thought you loved me!"

"You weren't wrong, Francine!"

"No, no! You never loved me!"

"On the contrary—passionately...and, if it will give you pleasure, you have even been the great love of my life."

"Is that true?" she groaned. "Is it possible? And you haven't been jealous?" She let her arms fall slack and repeated, in a desolate voice: "Haven't been jealous."

"Very jealous," I said. "You've made me suffer terribly."

A victorious gleam immediately replaced the humiliation in her pathetic features. "You're more secretive than a woman!" She began to cry, weeping desperately, her entire being in distress.

I took her in my arms and rocked her like a child, murmuring in her ear; "Don't blame your perspicacity; my jealousy was established in advance."

"What does that mean?" she sobbed.

"That I knew in advance what would happen and I had already suffered so much when it finally arrived that I was able to control myself."

"In advance?" she sobbed. "You didn't trust me, then? You were scornful..."

"Not at all! But I know Marcus. To men, he's a vulgar animal, slightly ridiculous and rather stupid, but to women, he's irresistible. It was almost impossible for you to escape him—so I was resigned...and as I didn't want to lose you..."

A little laugh emerged from the tears. "You didn't want to lose me?" And, becoming depressed again: "Not even to make a scene!"

"I have the good fortune—it's a great one—to believe, deep down, that scenes make bad situations worse."

A long silence. Francine's tears dried up. Motionless, with her mouth agape, she asked: "Is it true that you still love me? Really true?"

"Quite true."

"Not like before?"

"My darling, would that be possible?"

"It's possible for some men."

"Not for any man."

"What about those who kill themselves rather than live without the woman who has abandoned them?"

"Those sometimes love more *afterwards*, but it's not the same love…"

"That's true. But do you love me *as much?*"

I didn't answer. She wrung her hands and moaned; "I'm so stupid! Can one be in love, when, when one is hardly jealous at all? Oh, unfortunate Francine, miserable Francine! I love you—I love you madly; I love you with all my soul."

I couldn't help saying: "But not with all your body."

She looked at me with a kind of dread, then said, in a broken voice: "It's better if we don't see one another again."

"I don't think so. There's nothing to hope for on Marcus's side; he'll certainly leave you—and soon. Marcus is too busy; one woman never holds his interest for long. As you aren't a profligate woman—far from it!—and inclined to constancy…"

"Aren't I?" she cried. "In spite of *that*…"

"Yes, in spite of *that*, which is a unique incident in your life, I'm sure."

"Oh, you can be!"

"Well, think how careful you'll be when it's broken off. You'd do better to anticipate it. I fear that it might be beyond your power—and then, like everyone else, you'll hope against hope…"

"You'll see!"

She got up, and hugged me impulsively, her eyes catching mine. "Will it be painful for you if I don't come back?"

"Yes, Francine."

"Very painful?"

"Very."

"I love you! I love you! I'll keep coming back for as long as you want. I'll be your poor dog. Oh, if only that man hadn't come! I was so happy, and I would still be so happy!"

195

She left, her voice still echoing within me, charged with that strange human creature's lamentations, uncertainty, gentle and ferocious promises. An hour earlier, she had almost pitied me, but now I'm redoubtable. She would not have suffered much from a rupture; now it will be a torture. She arrived with a considerable depth of ironic pity; she left prey to a voluptuous terror. Now the primitive being is merely the slave of the social being. Her strength is under the yoke, lashed and whipped to excess; it is humble, tamed, quivering with a pain imposed by fable.

I cannot refuse myself the pleasure of a victory. In spite of my skeptical and easily-resigned acceptance, I presented the appearance of a victim. Now I'm a victor in a contest that I judge derisory, but which the machine of the emotions takes seriously. I have certainly been pitied by her slightly—pitied passively, with a residue of cruelty. In flashes, a frisson, almost a stab of alarm; faithful, or believed faithful, what would she not have been able to impose on me? Anything, including a chain.

In the agitations of consciousness, Marcus reappeared. He remains a victor, and no revenge is possible against him. Not even if Francine had the courage to break it off herself. A mere passing fancy for him, if she left him spontaneously, he'd find that the most comfortable of conclusions. Others would succumb; already, no doubt, someone else was replacing Francine.

I ought to hate him more than ever, but the subconscious has its caprices; I hate him less. Tomorrow, undoubtedly, the execration will take hold again.

And here is Yveline. As usual, desire stirs before the tall, flexible figure, but the agitation is weak. Francine has gripped me again. And I study, with placid covetousness, the beauty who draws me back to enchanted shores. She is in a neutral mood herself. Even so, we exchange the glance that we knew so long ago, whose soft ambiguity I regretted later.

"I've come to ask your advice," she says.

She sighed and I smiled. "My approval?"

"No, genuine advice—which I shall follow." She sighs again and adds: "Perhaps."

"Good. We're getting back to normal."

"Not entirely, for I'm truly hesitant—so hesitant that one word might be sufficient to make me prefer a yes to a no—or a no to a yes. Can you imagine, my friend, that someone has asked to marry me?"

"It's not the first time."

"Naturally—but I didn't hesitate then. This time, I've been thinking."

"Do you like him?"

"No more than the others—but my notary's becoming impossible. He's warned me, with an inconceivable brutality, that I don't have enough to live on for more than six months. Six months! It's crazy, isn't it?"

"It's wisdom, ugly but definite."

"I can't believe it—it's impossible. After the six months, something will turn up."

"A miracle."

"Anyway, I'm sure the notary's an imbecile—but I've been thinking."

"So, damn it, you've been thinking!"

She bursts out laughing. "It's true that, in money matters...enough! I've been thinking...I've even experienced a certain anxiety."

I haven't told Yveline about my dealings with Bullerton; Ferral is the only one who knows about it.

"So," she says, "when *he* asked me *that*, I hesitated."

"*He* doesn't displease you?"

"No, he's good...besides, you know him. It's Hautbourguès."

"That's perfect, Yveline—more than perfect. Hautbourguès is a fine man; he has tact, he has power—a great deal of power. With him, you'd have the abundance that your beauty gives you the right to expect."

197

"Do you think so?" she murmurs, half-closing her eyes—which makes her gaze excessively troubling. "Perhaps I'll enjoy it. But what about Denise? Can I impose Denise on him?"

"It would be a light burden for him—but I'm ready to take responsibility for her."

"That wouldn't inconvenience you?"

"Not at all."

"Well, I'll think about it—don't laugh; you're annoying! I really will think about it! I won't answer before I've seen you again."

This is laden with threat. A troubled silence, like swamp-water. The same idea possesses us both, active in her, passive in me. No doubt about the desire of her inner demon. Only I can relieve the obsession.

Afterwards, she suspects, I'll be neither more nor less than Hautbourguès.

"Whatever happens, then, Denise…?" she goes on.

"Yes, whatever happens, Denise will be protected."

She holds out her hand and sighs. Our hands become dangerously linked; they are lovers; they exchange our desires, and the effort I make to break the grip is heroic.

"Naughty boy! Naughty boy!" murmurs the sad Juliane. "A fortnight without seeing you!"

After the other two, what a poor creature! Her presence oppresses and depresses me; she freezes my ideas, paralyzes my sensations, and I experience a melancholy pity for her. I think, wanly, about the fictions of beauty and seduction.

Why do Francine and Yveline appear, on the amorous plane, as superior to Juliane as a man of genius is to a man of the common herd on the intellectual plane? No precise feature disqualifies her. Her eyes are not faded, or her nose defective—it is white and straight, though small…and the nose is often more absurd, ridiculous or repugnant than the other features; her mouth is as prescribed, with healthy teeth, her cheeks not badly contoured…

Her face is dull, though, neutral and vague. She studies me, tearfully, indefatigably tender, and I realize, with terror, that she has succeeded in making me her "ideal"—in enveloping me with its elements to the point of extravagance. What a relief it would be if she could become my sister! But the unfortunate woman will retain an incurable appetite for love into old age...

No choice: it's necessary to lie; the slightest inkling of the truth would fill the poor creature with horror. In a plaintive tone I reply: "It's been a terrible two weeks, Juliane...too much work, sleepless nights, anxieties about my kidneys..." I put my hand on my back, somewhat ashamed, and with a slight desire to laugh. "It was for my kidneys, you know that I went to Vichy. The doctor forbade me any excess..."

A sigh. She understands. She looks at me compassionately, ready to spend days and nights by my bedside. Tender and generous Juliane, placid and very dear friend, I have bitten into a tastier fruit!

The goal is achieved; the lover resigns herself—and when the opportunity arises, I'll serve her up a little slice of illusion...

She kisses me on the cheek, hugs me and murmurs: "Look after yourself, my darling!"

XIII.

Side by side, the Bible and Homer. Tonight, they remind me of the terrible martyrology of sacrifice!

"3. And in process of time it came to pass, that Cain brought of the fruit of the ground an offering to the Lord.

"4. And Abel, he also brought of the firstlings of his flock and of the fat thereof. And the Lord had respect unto Abel and to his offering.

"5. But unto Cain and his offering he had not respect. (*Genesis.*)

"Then God said to him:

"Take now thy son, thine only son Isaac, whom thou lovest, and get thee into the land of Moiah; and offer him there for a burnt offering upon one of the mountains which I will tell thee of. (*Genesis*.)[30]

"1. And the Lord spake unto Moses of the Tabernacle of the congregation.

"2. Speak to the children of Israel and say to them: 'When someone enters thou shalt make an offering to the Lord; it shall be thine offering of fatted and lean cattle...

"5. Then the throat of the bullock shall be slit in the presence of the Lord and the sons of Aaron, sacrificers, shall offer the blood and spread it around, on the altar that is at the entrance to the Tabernacle of the congregation.

"6. Afterwards, the offering shall be burned, and scattered in pieces.

"7. Then the sons of Aaron, sacrificers, shall set a fire on the altar and arrange the wood of the fire.

"8. And the sons of Aaron, sacrificers, shall arrange the pieces, the head and the skin, on the wood, on the fire, on the Altar.

"9. But he shall wash the flesh and the limbs, and the sacrifice shall set fire to all the things on the Altar: offering and sacrifice made by fire that the odor shall delight of the Lord."

(I cannot help seeing the Lord, with an immense nose, sniffing that delightful odor of fat and roasting flesh.)

---

[30] The first quote from *Genesis* is from chapter 4, the second from chapter 22, verse 2. As with the preceding quotation, I have taken the parallel text from the Authorized Version. The next quote, which is a synoptic paraphrase of *Exodus* 29, does not correspond to the A.V. text in its numbering or wording, so I have improvised considerably in making the translation. With respect to the quote from *Judges* I have reverted to the A.V. text. The subsequent text derived from the *Iliad* I have translated directly from Rosny's French version.

"(*Judges* 11) 30. And Jephthah vowed a vow unto the Lord, and said: If thou shalt without fail deliver the children of Ammon into my hands.

"31. Then it shall be, that whatsoever cometh forth from the doors of my house to meet me, when I return in peace from the children of Ammon, shall surely be the Lord's, and I will offer it up for a burnt offering..."

"Everyone makes sacrifice to a chosen god to ward off death and dangers. Agamemon, king of men, immolated a fat ox of five years to the powerful son of Saturn. He invited the most ancient chief of the Greeks; first Nestor and King Idomeneus, then the two Ajaxes and the son of Tydeus, and finally Ulysses, as wise as Jupiter. Menelaus, brave in battle, came himself, for he knew how preoccupied his brother was.

"They gathered around the ox and proceeded with the sacred rite. King Agamemnon prayed: *Glorious Father, great Zeus, ruler of black clouds, inhabitant of the sky, let the Sun not set and the darkness not come before I have razed the palace of Priam, burned its gates by enemy flame and ripped Hector's tunic on his breast with my sword! Let a great number of his friends lie stricken in the dust, taking the earth between their teeth.*

"The son of Saturn requires no more, he said; he will receive his sacrifices and prepare himself for hard labor.

"When they had prayed and completed the sacred rite, they cut the victim's throat, stripped it of its skin, cut off the legs and covered it with a double layer of fat; they burned the raw flesh on the cut and defoliated wood, then pierced the entrails and held them in the fire..." (The *Iliad*.)

When humans imagine occult powers, can they see them as other than tragic or ferocious? As tragic and ferocious as themselves, as beasts or the weather.

In the forest, the savannah, grasslands or giant trees, day and night, pitfalls, hunger, thirst and carnage, suffering and sin. Water drowns, cyclones tear apart, rocks crush, thunderbolts strike, fire devours, beasts gore. The implacable belly commands; without grass, without foliage, without fruits, without flesh—death!

Whenever a confused notion of secret, invisible or inaccessible force is born, that force will inevitably be cruel, whether it is imagined in the image of humans or beasts. What can be done, save for bowing down before it, seducing it or fighting it? From the outset, signs, formulas, offerings, prayers. As the signs and formulas become more precise, magic cordons them off. On the one hand, one assaults the invisible or inaccessible, taming it by means of mysterious practices— that is a ritual attack. On the other hand, one implores it, one flatters it, one humiliates oneself before it; that is the ritual of prayer. Finally, one seduces it, disarming it with gifts—and that is the ritual of sacrifice.

All that soon becomes the prerogative of the strongest, and especially the cleverest. They live on it, provided with food, feared and admired. How could you think of refusing a salary to the sorcerer who provides you with the secret means of attaining the prey, of vanquishing or killing the enemy: incantation and magic spells? You will give him powerful weapons, precious tools, ornaments, a share of the game or the booty. In order that he will make his prayers more effective, will assist you in making your offering, your sacrifice, you will not think it too much if he claims the flesh of animals, warm furs, rare seashells or sharpened axes, will you?

Humans are too ingenious for rituals not to become, at length, savant and subtle codes, scrupulous and innumerable— and for the beyond not to be populated with vague entities that become beings in a definite sense: gods, goddesses, with a hierarchy modeled on human and animal hierarchies, culminating in a sovereign God.

Primitive ferocity subsists. Often, it becomes more terrible, richer in tortures and refinements.

When was human sacrifice added to the sacrifice of animals?

Once, in fetishistic Africa, the immolation of humans was widely practiced. Was it not the same among the fetishists of the Aurignacian, the Magdalenian and the Lacustrian eras? If the sacrifice of animals was agreeable to the hidden beings, and then to the gods, how much more so was that of human beings!

For millennia, the Moloch or its equivalent devoured victims. There was a successive host of furnaces before that of Carthage, cooking children and adults alike! The Gaulish Taran, for whom animals and humans were roasted pell-mell in the same wicker mannequin, must have been one of numerous precursors. For centuries, I suppose, people were drowned in the name of Teutates. Myriads must have perished to attract the good will of Hesus.[31]

For the gods, and for the chiefs deified by death, it was a very banal sacrifice to put slaves and women to death in order to serve the dead in the other world. Hindu sacrifice, in the bosom of a gentle race worn down by a long and subtle culture, is an example—perhaps it persists today, here and there, secretly. The chariot of the juggernaut reveals another aspect of sacrifice: personal sacrifice; victims voluntarily throw themselves under its sacred wheels to merit eternal joy.

It is Mexico, in the time of Cortez, that offers us the most striking example of how many human sacrifices there might have been among so many peoples whose history we do not know. Every year, the emperor Montezuma disposed of 25,000 "sacrificables." A vast credit in the beyond! Human blood also streamed in torrents in the Aztec temples. The

---

[31] Hesus and Teutates were the war gods of the Gauls in Celtic mythology, but Taran was actually one of their heroes, to whom no sacrifices would have been offered, with or without the aid of "wicker men;" it is conceivable that Rosny's narrator is confusing his name with that of the Norse god Thor, although the following paragraph implies that he imagines that the Gauls deified their dead kings, after the fashion of the Romans and their emperors, just as he subscribes to the myth of the Juggernaut and similar slanderous travelers' tales, seemingly avid in his credence.

priest, cleaving the victim's breast with a stone knife, tore out the beating heart and offered it to the Sun God. That evening, the sacrificers and their relatives feasted on the flesh of their victims: a family occasion of sacred anthropophagy.

I can imagine the ceremonies: the crowds, curious, ferocious and indifferent, like those Chinese crowds watching the torture of a man cut up slowly, piece by piece, while many of the spectators carry little caged birds...

In Christian times, the West saw bloody sacrifices disappear. Until then, its temples swallowed victims destined for ritual knives. The Gospel shows us the merchants of this livestock encumbering the Temple of Jerusalem; it was both a market and an abattoir.

In the end, Yahweh, having become triple, ceased to love the delightful odor of roasted flesh that had pleased him so much before. Caught up by the new fashion, even the Jews renounced throat-cutting.

Even so, the witches and heretics burned alive maintained part of the tradition of religious murder, and sacrifice retained considerable power. God continued to love suffering. Fasting, mortification of the flesh, renunciations of love and posterity, a thousand delicate tortures invented by the writhing saints, replaced the ceremony of death. Increasingly, sacrifice became a personal oblation of the victim. It was voluntarily that the elect condemned themselves to hunger, flagellation, sleep-deprivation, filth, vermin and fatal solitude, even in the desert, to the savage prescriptions of convents, to the exacting repetition of prayers.

It is incessantly necessary to undergo trials and agonies, to seek them out, incessantly in order to celebrate the power and the generosity of a Lord, a connoisseur of suffering, avid for humiliations, sighs, plaints and supplications. For God, after all, has offered *Himself to Himself*, on the cross; to His own wrath He has opposed His own torture—and every day, He condemns Himself to descend into unleavened bread, to be swallowed by myriads of corrupt creatures.

In the utmost depths, born of perpetual ferocity, of implacable devotion, of all the evils and all the agonies, sacrifice retains its power in the human imagination.

We still claim to disarm or seduce the beyond—by flattery, humiliation and suffering. Has the hypocrisy of the weak praising the strong ever reached the heights to which our Western culture has taken it? Although everything in our ritual, assumes the fundamental, unrelenting wickedness of the Lord, we celebrate his generosity, his mercy, his love for human beings.

An incomparable literature, which the human imagination conceives as the greatest, the brightest, the most subtle, the most delicate, and the most pathetic, has grown up on this dung-heap of horror, on this compost-heap of divine perversity, of sadistic omnipotence. There is nothing more penetrating than the lamentations or analyses of great Catholics on sin, redemptions, divine bounty, eternal damnation, temptation, the snares of hell, and the voluntary tortures of saints! To crown this great work: the limited number of the elect—hence the perpetual torture of almost all of those to whom the Lord deigns to give the gift of life. A few years on a planet where the miseries already far outweigh the joys, and then—forever—agony!

Forever!

"Imagine," said some Father or other, "a diamond sphere as large as the Earth. Once in every century, a sparrow brushes it with its wing. When, after an immeasurable time, that friction has worn the sphere away, eternity will hardly have begun!"

Such images as that reduced Pascal to despair. He had a horror of unending torture: a fiery gulf opened before him; the angel of torture awaited him there, and it was *for all eternity*.

XIV.

I have to go to see Denise. Wasn't it an irreparable stupidity to have assumed responsibility for her? What demon drove me to do it? What use will Bullerton and his providential gesture be to me if, delivered from my own worries, I take on someone else's?

My dread is purely speculative. I continue to envisage dark circumstances, but I scarcely take them seriously. A little money will save me from them, and for the time being, Denise can have whatever she wishes in life.

The interval between us is too great. I know nothing about Denise's inner being; she can only have a confused and false idea of mine. Even so, our errors might perhaps be benevolent. I have a considerable warmth of sympathy for Denise. When I had only just met her, she was already dear to me. In the human hierarchy, I place her well above Yveline, Francine and the plaintive Juliane.

Inclined to make her a creature of the elite, I'm ready to be enthusiastic on her behalf. A dangerous state of mind, full of mistaken judgments. What destiny might bring! I shall gain nothing by taking the tiller; there is no point.

In her pale setilose[32] dress, with her young arms half-bare, the blonde bird's-nest of her hair, her eyes changing like the ocean waves, the tall, virginal and wild Denise puts me in mind of a druidic virgin—the Gaulish forest, the ancient oaks, the mystery of carnivorous gods.

---

[32] Setilose, a kind of acetate rayon, was one of the earliest artificial fibers adapted for commercial use; the term was used as a trade name in France by a couturier who produced some classic Art Deco ads *circa* 1930, and it is presumably those ads that Rosny had in mind when conjuring up this image.

Her purity is frightening; a silvery aura surrounds her, and I imagine her, indistinctly, as a member of a noble human species, in the golden glow of an immense future.

I feel the weight of my responsibility. In giving my word to Yveline, I have almost certainly acted against my own interests. I shall not be able to treat Denise like anyone else. Secret impulses will force me to fulfill a duty to her more severely than to anyone else. I shall try to escape from it in vain. It will be as if I have betrayed myself.

That's why I'm looking at her with dazzled anxiety. In parallel, I'm proud of having a part to play in her destiny. It's ridiculous, but irresistible. I have the feeling of being, relative to her, a sort of freed slave. My body seems to me to be more coarsely woven than Denise's slender body.

I talk, without paying much heed to what I'm saying. I say something like this: "It's possible, Denise, that you'll have to live in my house for a while…unless you prefer a girls' boarding-school. You can choose."

Her cheeks become just a little rosier. It's a flow of blood, less visible in the round, frail neck and the earlobes. The charming flood evokes a profound and secret life; a line of verse resounds in my memory: "The hawthorn had put on its pink and white dress."

"I daren't choose," she said, in a voice that retained inflections of childhood. "Whatever you wish would be best."

"Does that mean that you have no preference?"

"Oh yes, I have a preference."

"You must tell me what it is."

She hesitates; our eyes meet; this time, there's an undine amid the reeds of that beautiful pool, whose green blades cast a spell, one stormy morning, on a small boy astonished and delighted by his enchantment.

"Well?" I ask.

While her little hands clench on the fabric of her dress, she murmurs. "But what about you, godfather—what would you prefer?"

"What you would prefer, Denise."

"But is that really true? In your house, wouldn't I get in your way?"

Deep down, I think that, however slight her presence might be, she would impose servitudes upon me—but I'm no less desirous of her presence for that. "That's quite true, Denise."

"In that case"—the rosy pink tinge reappears—"I'd rather go to the boarding school."

I've been stupid—and what's more, I still am. "In that case, Denise, you'll live with me, with Mademoiselle Brigitte to accompany you."

This time, the blood flows the other way; Denise is as white as a newly-opened camellia. "Thank you!" she murmurs. The words spring from the depths of her being. I sense shackles about my limbs, but, rejecting the omens of the black bird, I say: "Music, Denise—do you still love it as much?"

Velleda stands up.[33] In the innumerable multitude of sonorous waves, the waves from which the human creator has made a world, Denise is at home. "I like it more! I think that, without music..." She lowers her eyelids over her large mystic eyes. "Without music, I wouldn't be able to live!"

"But Denise, no power can deprive you of music—you have music within you!"

She emits a little laugh, as fresh as the melody of a spring in the depths of the woods. "I'm stupid!" she says.

I imagine Denise alongside Bullerton. She was already mysterious; she becomes more so. The internal unknown has grown along with her height. She has arrived at the era when *astonishment*, in creatures of her sort, approaches its maximum, while it decreases in creatures of the herd who, in be-

---

[33] Velleda was a Germanic druidess in the reign of the emperor Vespasian. She took part in a rebellion against Rome and died a captive in Rome; she became famous in 19th century France after being given a starring role in an episode in Chateaubriand's epic *Les Martyrs ou le Triomphe de la religion chrétienne* (1809).

coming adult, are complete, immured in their nature, unable to develop further.

A thousand clues lead me to sense that she is no mere bee, subservient to the hive. She will be all the more dangerous to my security. It will be necessary to witness all the disorder of the evolution of an original nature; it will be necessary to watch and undergo...

Will I remain insensible to the frightful charm that she is going to emit? I'm only a poor male, in spite of my social baggage; my three natures are fallible.

Incoherence and misery! Whether it triumphs or not, with what cunning, what detours and what infernal genius the instinct of the other world adapts itself to the innumerable conditions of existence! Far from liberating us, the word, the abstraction, the social lie makes us more subservient. The ancestor agglomerates the intersocial elements, actually exciting, spicing up and "magnifying" the generic impulse.

While I'm observing Denise, all the more anxious because she is so candid, Yveline comes in. Are they any less different from one another on the human plane, than Earth and Saturn are in the planetary world? I have difficulty detecting a single quality in which they coincide.

The desire that the adolescent Yveline aroused in me, which has never been extinguished, I would never have been subject to with a Denise; if some imperious—or rather unilateral, born of a simple condition of the flesh—circumstance had given birth to it, it would have expired the next day, and I would have been ashamed of it, as of a profanation.

With Yveline, our two imaginations and our two organisms coincide by virtue of a sudden, profound and mutual impulse. All the elements of a vivid and profound memory amalgamate, take possession of one another, with equal force, conscious and unconscious...

"Have you spoken to Denise?" Yveline asks.

"I've spoken to her."

"I'd like to tell you something else." She's emotional, in an unexpected fashion, and—a bad sign—her emotion penetrates me instantly. Her tempestuous mouth and pale cheeks make me go pale myself. "Come here, will you?"

Her voice is considerably lower than usual. I am the harmoniously beautiful woman in a little blue and gold room, populated with dreary trinkets.

Now we're face to face, and Yveline's face announces that the encounter will be decisive. I'm afraid. In a flash, my life might be enchained. An internal cyclone carries me away, even though I call the resistance of yesteryear to my aid. My will is as soft as my flesh; the room is falling apart...

Yveline speaks; it's still the lowered voice, the tempestuous mouth; the beautiful pallor of her face is making me dizzy.

"Are you prepared to take Denise in, if necessary?"

"I'm prepared to do that, Yveline."

"The thing is..." She pauses, breathlessly, in order to inhale. "I promised Hautbourguès a definite answer within a fortnight. Anyway, I've made up my mind...but I intend to *be my own mistress* until then. From the day when I've said yes, you know, I shall be *completely faithful*." A wave of rising blood chases away the pallor; Yveline's eyes dilate. "Completely," she repeats, "but, not being a young woman, I don't owe him anything of my past, do I?"

Whether it is deliberate or not, we're standing very close to one another. I breathe in a slight perfume, like the morning; I breathe into the entire woman—and our complicit hands join together.

One gesture, and I'm defeated—but is it a defeat? For someone else, Yveline's words would be ambiguous; for me, they're clear. For once in her life, and in order to disemburden herself of a unique malaise, she's contravening the rules of conformity...while she's still free...

Once her word is given, she won't betray it; she'll observe the contract with Hautbourguès as with her first companion. Her frivolity folds up unreservedly before religious and social exigency.

While the little hand trembles in mine, that certainty penetrates me like an arrow and dissipates—though not entirely—the fear of an action that I no longer have any hope of avoiding...

One more minute. Let's taste the unslaked desire one last time, the delay that has been one of the forms of my destiny. Then, one gesture, and already, everything is turned around.

The melting body of Yveline, so flexible that one can scarcely believe that it has bones, her indefatigably desirous lips, and the dream dissolves into a reality that is still a dream!

There we go! It's finished. The unknown Yveline will never reappear. Not that I know her any better, as with any woman, but *this* unknown is of the same order as that of Francine—it's not the secret of the cloud.

How can I not regret that? What impulses I owe to her, of avowals incessantly suppressed, aspirations in which aspects of adolescence were incessantly reborn! The desire for Yveline is now mixed in with the flock of everyday desires. Besides, I still desire her, and with what ardor! Her too, I think; neither she nor I will consent to the dream of a dozen years being exhausted in a single embrace.

She will spend as many days as necessary appeasing it, at least to an extent that is tolerable—and safe.

"Do you love me?" Yveline murmurs, burying her head in my chest.

Her finely-scented hair is dear to me—how sweet it is to plunge one's face thereinto! My gratitude is profound. Yveline will be my friend forever.

"Do you love me?" she repeats.

Come on! The time for nonsense has come.

"For such a long time!"

"Yes, I know," she says, with a little laugh. "I'm not blind...and I too have loved you since...that morning!"

The word reanimates the fire; the garden is there, the swing, the adolescent girl...why is it a miracle?

"What a morning! I'll never forget it, Yveline..."

Silence. Anxiety. I stiffen in the face of possibilities.

"You'll love me for a long time yet…a long time?"

Is that an assault? Is she taking up the project that she must have taken up a thousand times before? I have to risk it, though. "A long time…a very long time."

"Ah!" she sighs. "We could live together!"

I receive the blow without flinching, but with what anguish! "Yes, that would be delightful for me…but disastrous for you! He can give you 10, 20 times as much as I can."

"I'm not afraid of mediocrity."

"You don't know anything about it! I'd never forgive myself for having stood in your way…"

She has raised her head; she looks at me, attentively. There's no sign of rebellion. Her decision is made!

"Until tomorrow?" she murmurs.

Now that the fearful menace has disappeared, that tomorrow sounds a fanfare of joy and love. By the time she says yes to Hautbourguès' proposal, we shall both have exhausted a dozen years of desire—but I shall retain a fondness for that melting body, as supple as that of a handsome carnivore.

"Until tomorrow!" I replied, with a last embrace.

"Do you love me?"

"I love you."

The magnificent reality of the lie!

XV.

It's an intense period of deception. There are three of them—Yveline, Francine and Juliane—who must be charitably deceived. Above all, they mustn't find out about one another!

After all, lying is an irresistible *reality*, whose origins go back to animal life. Primitive cunning contains the embryonic elements of lying; it already has presocial characteristics, for it supposes influences and relationships between the inhabitants of the sea, the forest and the plain.

A roe deer would never have dreamed of covering its tracks if it had only encountered inoffensive creatures in the grass and the trees. Wolves would not set traps if they had not had to defeat the skill of prey animals, the panther would not lie in ambush for the innocent herbivore, and the ant-lion would not hollow out the well that it has the skill to make seem inhabited. Everywhere, superior but solitary animals know difficulties in which nature has something of the social, of innumerable interactions whose influence is certainly not a negligible quantity. It would be absurd to exaggerate this viewpoint, more so to take no account of it

In sum, everyone is submissive to the harsh necessity of trickery; it is necessary to lie about the position one occupies, the force at one's disposal, the route one is following. The struggle for existence of a red deer, an antelope, a fallow deer or a sparrow demands perpetual dissimulation, from which, for other reasons, the tiger, the jackal and the marten are scarcely exempt.

When the first rudiments of animal sociability appeared, the *elements* of deception had already made incalculable progress. It took the form of a science of traps transmitted from generation to generation. Human sociability played its part in that. The primitive traps that humans set for other humans came out of it.

As the wars of family against family, tribe against tribe and nation against nation multiplied, the lies with the aid of which the enemy will be surprised or terrified became more subtle. The art of concealing sites, erasing tracks, concealing individual and collective steps, laid the foundations of the military arts of barbarian and civilized nations. Humans increasingly learned that, although force is an important element of war, it gives way to cunning, to the extent that *deception constitutes the principal element of a useful deployment of combative energy*. It is necessary to appear stronger or weaker than one really is, sometimes to offer the antagonist the bait of a flock to be crushed or taken by surprise, sometimes to project doubt or fear by simulating a non-existent power. Thus developed a *generalized* sentiment of tutelary deception, which—fortunately—evolved beyond war and hunting.

How could the man who knew how to deceive his prey or his enemy not use such an ability to deceive his companions and profit therefrom? Lying came into the world along with the word. In substituting for realities, already so fluid as to be sometimes ungraspable, signs that could be combined in such a way as to deny, confirm, truncate, obscure, embellish or degrade the things that they represent, what an inextricable web of fictions could be added to all the fictions created by the organic and social struggle.

Before the elements of deception born of warfare, however, were there not an incalculable number of falsificatory elements born directly from our own organization? The eye that perceives light as a whole, which makes a color appear to be a motionless ensemble, deceives us for our own good, hiding from us the prodigious, *insupportable* agitation which constitutes that color. It is the same for all the senses, and even more so for the notions that science incessantly forces itself to revise, without ever having succeeded in substituting a sure reality for mirages without number.

The ironic nature that shows us the Sun rotating around the Earth continues to lure us in every direction. We can only substitute fables for fables. All that one can say is that the new fables give us more leverage on the environment, on nature, and, by virtue of that, permit us to hope that we're a little less far away from reality.

In sum, with mineral lies, animal lies, human lies, and the lies the self tells itself, how can we be astonished by voluntary lying: concerted lying, the creator of singular and powerful realities? How can we be astonished that the development of humanity involves a strange mixture of fictions imposed by nature and fictions imagined by people? The latter fictions, in the final analysis, seem to have carried us away, until now.

What interests me most of all, however, is that, in the imagined fiction, *intentional* deception balances out the other, if it does not surpass it. Those who are in possession of the strange power of developing myths have been unable to resist it. They have deliberately invented histories. The miracles of all religions are less often the result of hallucination than of trickery. It is the same for the *historical* reports of men and spirits, gods or God, and the fraudulent explanations that are the daily bread of believers of every sort.

Moreover, a desire for marvels is quite sufficient to impel humans to make up false stories, to swell the legend of a treasure of invented anecdotes. What does that impulse become when the desire for domination and self-interest are added to it?

So, humans find themselves caught, by virtue of the most subtle requirements of nature, in an inextricable web of lies—voluntary to begin with—which constitutes the principal cement of human societies.

All in all, it's no exaggeration to say that fiction/deception plays a preponderant role in both great and petty social illusions—fiction/deception becoming solid illusion with time and space, however slightly chance and circumstance favor it, whether by virtue of the coincidence of events, the coalition of beliefs or by the prestige of those who affirm it.

Where, dear children, have our paltry lies dragged me? But are they not the image of enormous social lies? Each of the four of us has constructed a microcosm in which our mutual lies are consolidated; they are hardly likely to disappear therefrom—and our memories are aggregated there as clearly, or even more so, than our sincerities. And after all, are not these chapters of our own history, infinitely trivial as they are, the image and the portrait of all human history?

215

XVI.

Denise is neither a burden nor a hindrance. Communication has been established with a disconcerting promptness. Denise's universe, after a few days of hesitation, anxiety and mutual suspicion, has appeared in full illumination. I can, as I choose, according to circumstances, provoke its extents, its variations or its uncertainties. Sexuality, which ought to obscure or mask everything, plays a negligible role, and yet makes more seductive an amity that is, on my side—and much more than on hers—(provisionally?) pure.

Denise's universe is visibly growing; I sense, with a certain intoxication, that I shall play—that I am already playing—an essential role in that growth. It was vast already by comparison with the majority of adolescent universes; it will not be subject to the relative pause to which it is subject in the majority of human beings as soon as youth takes forceful hold.

I have never taken such clear account of the relationship between the immense social supply and the creature that absorbs it. Denise's aptitudes are not passive; they precipitate her toward new ideas, and they subject them to metamorphoses that render them more assimilable *for her*. She has the key to great developments, intensity, enthusiasm, astonishment and admiration, and there is nothing more exciting than seeing her absorb new elements. Together we're making a prodigious voyage, the voyage of humankind through the centuries, the oceans, the forests, the mountains, the stars—and centuries, oceans, forests, mountains and stars are within her rather than around her.

I have never seen a vertiginous *consumption* of the universe so energetic. Better than anyone else and all the sciences, Denise makes me understand the part of the individual and the part of that humankind which incessantly offers its treasures, now inexhaustible. As in the sky, where, every time the power of telescopes increases, the number of stars is increased, so humankind, as one absorbs its knowledge, its arts and its millennia-old memories, reveals new knowledge, new arts, and new vistas of time.

Denise's mind seems limitless in its extent; everything that it adopts opens the way to further adoptions. "The eye never tires of seeing, nor the ear of hearing," says the old scribe. Denise creates—she creates from morning till evening, and during the mysterious interval of night: an unusable creation, but original—original *to her*. Myriads of men and women, as they assimilate the millennia-old heritage, are *rediscovering* that which others have discovered. Occasionally, a rare being is not only *rediscovering* but *discovering*.

The sensuality of bringing to life in her a part of the universe that lives in me is a minuscule episode in the immense series of torches which began in the night of centuries. If I had not been here, the Denise of tomorrow would not be the one that she will be. She might even be very different. Her whole environment would have orientated her toward a mental destiny incompatible with that one, and would have rendered communication between us obscure and incoherent.

How much can be introduced into a human brain— provided that it consents! Isn't it in Denise that I've had the best glimpse of the phantasmagoric game of consciousness? Infinite variety. Neither unity, nor continuity, nor homogeneity; sometimes the expansion of a drop of water taking on the dimensions of the Milky Way, sometimes the concentration of the Milky Way into a drop of water; the invasion of centuries or the contraction of everything into a second; a boundless multitude, then a desert solitude, the most powerful of realities and almost total unreality…

In the intoxication of beginnings, every idea imparted to her reappears with the gracefulness of a blossoming. A part of my social being participates in a resurrection—for if I am transforming her universe, she is transforming mine by repercussion. What I give her, she gives back to me, recreated, and by living with her, hearing her and seeing her, I rediscover a way upstream, taking other routes that I once took in following the flow. All kinds of new notions are generated within me—a world of images that needed her in order to be born, a world of impressions whose demiurge she is. What I know, I know differently, and what I feel is participating in an unknown genesis.

I know full well that there is something of that sort in every appearance of a living being. A friend can be a revelation, a mistress reanimates a thousand dying fires and can light a million others. That is the great social privilege: development by one's neighbor, one's multiform neighbor—but never, for a long time, has interpersonal development had the amplitude that it has with Denise.

There is a world in which everything comes from her, into which I can only venture as a voyager; Denise is the queen of sonorous waves. In that boundless world, the part played by nature is so negligible that it seems almost non-existent. The sounds revealed by the universe are only noises; if the birds are already more harmonious than nature, the finest chirping of the little russet nocturnal singer is only a rudimentary couplet, so very different from the first human music! But since then, what oceans of *living* waves!—oceans incessantly increased by the frightful occidental races.

Though very tiny, a Denise is saturated with waves. It's a gift, and one of the most mysterious. Up to what point is it of interhuman origin? An African, born in the most indigent musical horde and transported as a child to Europe, if he has the gift, can understand the titans of the symphony.

Almost every evening, Denise draws me into the boundless worlds of *Human Sound*. They have their rivers, their forests, their savannahs, their crepuscular skies and their fabulous nights, their lost archipelagos in the vast oceans, their hurricanes, their rainstorms and the serenity of astral solitudes after the emergence of fauna and devouring humankinds...

At least, that is how, by distant analogy, I interpret their perennially changing existences. There are times when that flow becomes frightening; one feels oneself disappear, losing oneself one drop at a time in eternity. At other times, it seems that there is the most intoxicating promise of duration...

In truth, I've never lived hours comparable to those I am spending with this adolescent girl. Close to her, at times, I've felt an enchanted peace. As much as is possible for a man corroded by anticipation, it is a happy time. When she arrives in the morning, in her bright dress, a delightful young girl lit up by childhood, what a tumult of admiration! How much dearer she is to me than the most beloved of mistresses; with what ardor I desire never to love her in any other way than I love her now—to be exempt from the frightful desire that will draw her toward the beast. I intoxicate myself with the illusion of a Denise sheltered from the baroque gestures of generation—and I'm sure that she is still a stranger to sexual torment.

But isn't that the play of an idealism with no real foundation in living beings? And behind my worship, apparently inimical to desire, won't there be the hypocritical camouflage of the flesh? Impossible to know. Human beings who have been able to produce a world in their own image—poetry, music, art, pure science—have also, and *positively*, created a transfigured love. If the primitive almost always takes command of it, it also surrenders it; its intensity can become insensible; human-sourced love exists almost entirely in the memory. How many times have I adored a lover almost in the way that I love Denise, while sensing that it is only a truce, and that the beast is ready to leap forth again.

In Denise, the beast does not exist. The realm created by man is completely separated from the animal realm.

Anyway, for the beast (emphatically crossed with the ideal) I have Francine. She has not been able to reclaim a single crumb of Marcus, who is busy with ardent pursuits. She has resigned herself to that much more quickly than she would have done if my confession had not reorientated her attitude to me. I even suspect that she can't think about her adventure with Marcus without disgust. She is able to recognize that there is nothing significant beneath the tramp's magnetic power and cannot be alone in knowing that it is an external, atmospheric seduction. When a woman arrives in the contact zone, the man loses the greater part of his influence. Then, if she has antennae—if she is not enticed by an excessive fiction, an astonished Eve—she feels her ardor cooling and is conscious that Marcus is, after all, an ordinary lover.

Who knows whether he might suspect that—whether his prompt break-ups are one of the necessities of his game? At least, by withdrawing in haste, he might leave the woman victim to her imagination, enthusiastic to recover the violent love that she still imagines that she has experienced. Thus Marcus triumphs *afterwards*, as he triumphed *before*, while *during*, he loses his prestige at a rapid and accelerating pace.

In addition, Francine, having initially missed him frantically, while simultaneously tormented by my confession, has returned to me more forcefully than I would have wished. In a sense, she remains dear to me. I haven't had my fill of her physical person, but she has not entirely escaped their wrongdoing; she exaggerates, in the frequency of meetings and their multiplication, and she repeats too often: "You don't love me any more!"

These words prick me like darts. I have diabolical difficulty replying to them with sufficient warmth. I wait for the brief sentence with an irritation mingled with anguish and the enervating dread of replying discourteously. If she could only shut up! She's delicate, though.

Why is she so little given to recrimination? Why doesn't she know that by shutting up, and cutting out half her visits, she would double the charm of her presence? If she would simply accept my days, or not want so many of them, if she only knew the value of silence, it would be so simple! But she's like those orators who, sensing that they're losing their audience, try to recapture it by lengthening their speeches immoderately—and end up exasperating it.

What a contrast with Juliane, tenderly resigned, admirably credulous, accepting the worst defeats without flinching and nourishing her love on crumbs that her imagination transforms into feasts! It's true that her love is nourished by its "elevation"—the real cause, at the end of the day, of its endurance.

This Friday was almost intolerable.

The arrival of Francine had been stimulating. Her costume and her person had a violent brilliance that would have been gaudy if not for their complementary combinations. She was reminiscent of one of those beautiful daughters of tropical countries who exude the salt of sensuality, and I spent a fabulous hour in which the imagination and the flesh enjoyed the full intensity of the adventure.

A novel charm emanated from Francine; she was new; her conquest seemed precious and incomplete. At the outset, I even experienced a shadow of the dread of the early days, when I was fearful that she might escape. She would have been able, had she identified my impressions, to strengthen the game advantageously, to taste the fever of flight and pursuit. Knowing that she was very tempting that day, and miraculously adorned, she had, I think, anticipated a lively response, but she had underestimated its value, and responded to my embrace with a passion greater than my own—with the result that we yielded without delay, having scarcely stammered ten words. At any rate, the expenditure was delightful and the aftermath as languid as euphoria.

After a period of perfect silence, with her head resting on my shoulder, she murmured: "You don't love me any more!"

She could not have said anything more inappropriate—for I loved her at the moment more than I had loved her at any time since the Marcus affair. The little sentence, as strident as a locomotive whistle, annoyed me insupportably and, with an automatic gesture, I withdrew my shoulder.

Surprised, Francine looked me in the eyes. I had tensed up all the way to my ankles; my face must have been revelatory. "One might think you were angry?"

"No!" I said, incapable of containing myself. "It's that sentence. Why do you repeat it so frequently?"

Her eyes shone with indignation and sadness; she lowered her head and burst into tears. "Because it's true—and that's why you're angry!"

Incompatible sentiments jostled one another, in a furious surge. I felt sorry for her and I was full of rancor; my hatred for Marcus resurfaced, refreshed, and I was subject to the point of ferocity to the annoyance of having been snatched, as if by a blow from a cudgel, from such a blissful moment. So I had great difficulty in saying: "No...it's not that at all...it's because..."

At that point, I lost my footing. How could I explain without offending her? It was necessary to take another tack. "I was unusually happy," I went on. "I was living in the present, with you and entirely wrapped up in you. What you said fell on me like a block of stone. It caused discordant memories to surge forth. There's no need to say any more about it."

She listened avidly. "Is that true—that you were so happy?"

"More than you can believe."

She kissed my shoulder humbly; her tears ran in floods; she sobbed, and moaned: "You're right...I've been an idiot. Oh, my sin! You can't imagine how much I detest it when I think about it—so the idea that I reminded you of it makes me want to rake myself with my own fingernails!" She threw herself abruptly upon my knees, and cried out in a lamentable voice: "Forgive me, my darling...forgive me!"

I was torn between compassion and an irresistible sensation of ridicule, so touching and absurd did Francine appear. The compassion won. I lifted her up and pressed her to my heart. She was warm, supple, moving, and I yielded, like any common imbecile, to the temptation of a woman in tears.

Scarcely had she disappeared when Madame Donatienne appeared. "Monsieur, it's the monsieur who used to be dirty and isn't any longer!"

222

"Madame Donatienne," I said, "you're going a bit too far."

Madame Donatienne stood firm, massive, attached to the ground like a leaden she-bear. "Monsieur is right," she agreed, "and Monsieur is partly to blame for it."

"I don't know what you mean, Madame Donatienne."

"I mean that Monsieur is too good—so discipline suffers. I take account of it."

"I shall be more severe in future."

She shook her bovine head, with a pitying smile. "Monsieur won't be. It's not in his nature. It doesn't matter to me, because I love Monsieur—but the others! There was a king who said that a master must choose whether to be scorned or hated. Personally, I'd rather be hated—it's nobler!"

"Show Monsieur Réchauffé in," I said, rather dryly.

"Fine!" muttered Madame Donatienne.

Gontran Réchauffé appeared. He appeared clad in a brand new fur coat, an ample frock coat reminiscent of the men of 1885, trousers the color of a brown rat's fur and shiny shoes. Within that, his long skeleton gave him away, more irredeemably condemned to a social life that reproved his gray face and his aggressive eyes. However, that face created for torment and suspicion smiled on seeing me; the orangutan hand shook mine affectionately.

"You see!" he said. "I have new fur, and I'm getting fatter." He deposited his amusing coat on an armchair and continued: "I'm eating! Every day! Three times! A prodigy, a miracle—I'm amazed by it. I'd got to the point of thinking that the three meals were a legend of the Northern peoples." He tried to laugh; the laugh did not emerge. "I've never been able to," he remarked. "There's some animal in my throat that doesn't permit it. Finally, I'm approximately happy, thanks to the Comte de Mesles, to whom you recommended me—an admirable old beast for whom, old chap, I have considerable affection. We understand one another, like a hare and a rabbit. I, Gontran Réchauffé, am the ideal secretary for that dear old goose. Provided that he lives!"

"Is he ill?"

"Only of old age—which isn't without danger. In my estimation, he might last 20 years. Oh, long may he last!" Réchauffé sat down on the edge of a chair, then straightened up like a human spring, and took a few absurd strides, beyond humanity and animality—the steps of a Vaucanson duck. "Are you working?" he asked.

"Not too hard."

"And your ruination?"

He is not someone to whom I shall confide the Bullerton secret. Outside of that business however, the stabilization of the franc and the rise in French shares had sufficiently revived my original capital for me to be able to say: "Poincaré has averted it. And if a few banknotes can be of use to you…"

Réchauffé attempted a magnanimous gesture. "No need, and I even intend to repay my debt. I've brought a down payment."

"Listen," I said, compassionately, "I don't need it."

"I know," he said, seized by the most insipid and imbecile vanity at the idea of playing the role of a gentleman discharging his debts. He had just deposited a 100 and a 50 on the table. "There you are!" he said. "My chest swells."

It did, indeed swell; he caricatured himself with frightful grimaces.

"What about you?" I said. "Are you working?"

"Incontinently, in a fever. I've reached the chapter on the primitive finality, which is nothing but energy—for energy, my dear chap, and the initial finalism, are one and the same thing."

"What do you mean by that?"

"It's quite simple. Matter being a combination of electricity, and electricity in its turn a combination of energy, the latter translates itself by means of a finalist impulse—innumerable and vague finalisms seeking a realization, but seeking blindly, with the property of combining with other tendencies. Infinitely various and disordered in principle, the virtualities, in amalgamating their finalisms, arrive at more logical formations. Logic evidently aggregates corpuscles of pure energy into corpuscles of composite energy, and those into properly material corpuscles—let's call them atoms. They continue to increase in nebular formations, astral formations, the superior formations of the physical world, and eventually in indefinite series, increasingly conscious—of which life on Earth offers one of innumerable examples."

"You believe in other life-systems, then?"

"I don't permit myself to say life, for I conceive of differences without number. In certain worlds our life would seem, to superior beings, as rudimentary as the mineral is to us. Doesn't our life already suggest to us an indefinite continuing ascension, with much groping, but also with an inexhaustible variety of structures, from primitive organisms to man? In sum, obscure tendencies create increasingly clear tendencies, increasingly clear-cut finalities. On Earth, our human finality is a maximum."

I let him go on. He lost his footing in the subtleties that he perceived, or thought he could perceive, better than he could express them. Chaotic ideas, precious stones sealed in their matrix, bumped into one another, diverged, then tended to order themselves and isolate themselves, without ever succeeding.

Eventually, he frowned, stopped, and only started again after two full minutes of a silence that I thought I ought to respect. "I'm explaining myself badly. When you read it, if I finish my work, you'll understand it."

"But it was very interesting," I said.

"No—I explained myself badly with regard to tendency."

He shook my hand hastily and stalked out like a giraffe—which permitted Madame Donatienne to show Yveline in.

That was too abrupt. It required a few minutes of preparation. I think I paled. She saw my pallor with an evident satisfaction, marked by a play of the physiognomy that was slight, but easily perceptible to me. It's certain that I shall always find her desirable, and certain too that she will always take pleasure in it.

Not only will she not forget, but she will not want to forget. Circumstances have contrived that I should be involved in the only adventure in which her frivolity was in accord with her passion. My person means little to her, but she knows how to make up the deficit. I am the accomplice of her only derogation. Consecrated and inaccessible henceforth, she will be glad to evoke me in stormy moments, perhaps to permit me superficial familiarities—but nothing more.

For my part, the temptation that I will have on seeing her will remain impure, but bridled.

"I trust that your trip went well," I said—she has been absent for several months.

"Splendid!" she said.

She attempted to display some admiration for places, monuments, works of art, but quickly renounced that arid subject to talk about her sumptuary pleasures. I did not listen to her without pleasure; I've always had a taste for feminine frivolity. It's not that I read very much into it, but excitation for costumes, jewels and puerile luxuries gives me an intense sensation of femininity, and introduces me into an intoxicating intimacy, a nature made of delightful artifice. Yveline's soul cannot conceive of itself in any other manner than dressed and ornamented like her body.

I let her ramble on, therefore, plunged into a quasi-voluptuous torpor, interjecting a word here and there.

"And how is Denise?" she finally asked.

"Denise is perfect."

"Not too heavy a burden?"

"Lighter than a hummingbird—and so restful."

"Restful?" she said, bewildered.

"Oh yes, my dear. She brings me youth and renewal—without the arrogance, egoism or exigencies of first youth."

"Yes, she's an excellent creature. Still, you have to make time for her."

"I make time for her."

"You see!"

"With pleasure…"

"I wouldn't have thought…" She looked at me, inquisitively, a trifle suspiciously, fearful that I might be in love with Denise—or on the point of falling in love.

"No, Yveline," I said.

"What do you mean, no?" she exclaimed. "No to what?"

"It's not what you think."

"What I think?" she says, almost bewildered. "And what do I think?"

"That I might be in love with Denise."

"Oh!" Yveline said. "What a thing to say!"

"That's what you were thinking."

"Well, yes. And it's a bit rich for a man to have been sure of it. And what's your response?"

"I deny it. The pleasure of being with Denise has an absolute purity."

"You, you could love her purely—that's the sort of man you are."

"I still deny it. On the day it becomes true, Yveline, I shan't hide it from you."

"You think it's possible, then?" A note of jealousy in her tone, easy to disperse.

"These things are always possible."

"What will you do if that happens?"

"I don't know."

She looked me in the face, suddenly very serious—a strange gravity that does not tally with her personality at all. "Will you marry her?"

"You're going too fast, my dear. I'm not ready to reply. It wouldn't be sufficient for me to love Denise, to take that path; she would have to love me too. Hardly plausible—and, to tell you the truth, the implausibility will probably be sufficient for me never to have anything but an amicable affection for her."

"Indeed! You think you have the strength to quantify and direct your passions!" She passed into an ironic mode—and I

227

sensed my inferiority, forcefully; had our adventure not con-tradicted what I had just said?

With my head bowed, positively confused, I stammered: "That's true. I've loved you *fatally*." The imp of perversity suddenly intervened to make me add, involuntarily: "I love you still!"

She blushed like a little girl, smiled tenderly and said, in a low voice: "I should hope so! It would be frightful if you no longer loved me *already*."

I knew full well that the memory would return, but I had not anticipated this interlude. "Yveline," I sighed, "I owe you a very great happiness…"

She sighed too, and whispered: "Love me for a little while yet…I want that so much." Her agitation was manifest.

Taking her hand and putting it to my heart, I said: "Oh, if it were still possible!"

She did not take her hand away; she even permitted me to put my arm around her, but when I tried to kiss her she raised her arm between our heads. "It's not entirely extinct in me," she said, "but it's no longer possible, and it will never be possible again…*at least for…*"

She disengaged herself gently after the last equivocal words; we remained silent.

Finally, with a victorious smile, she said: "Let's get back to Denise. What if she loved you and you loved her?"

"Put like that, Yveline, the question contains its answer. Why, in that improbable case, shouldn't I marry Denise?"

"I don't know! The fear of too heavy a burden, or rather, one that cannot give you what a woman should."

"Let's not talk about burdens. After all, I think Denise is no more than half—or rather a quarter—a coquette and won't demand luxury. My resources have stabilized."

"I don't understand, then. I thought you were firmly committed to your freedom."

"With Denise, I'd be free."

"You wouldn't have been with me?" She looked at me sharply, singularly attentive.

"No," I said. "No, not at all. You're not half a coquette, Yveline, nor half-fond of luxury. You require *everything*—and you're not mistaken."

"Why am I not mistaken?"

"It suits you so well; it's your natural environment—which renders you more charming, more tempting, more inebriating. One is what one is."

"It's not malicious, what you've just to me! Given, on the other hand, that you still love me…? Say it again."

"I love you still."

She buried her face in my shoulder and whispered, so softly that I could hardly hear it: "It's good to be loved by you."

She could not prevent my mouth running over her neck, but she stopped me quickly. "The lips are forbidden!" Then, straightening up, she said, with a tender irony: "Let's get back to Denise. You know that I love her like a little sister. I'd like to have her visit me from time to time. May I come, soon, to take her for a few weeks?" And, as my attitude betrayed my displeasure, she added: "Don't be selfish. Haven't I brought her up, in part—and not too badly, after all, in not contradicting her nature. Is that true?"

"It's true."

"Then you ought to understand my desire."

I understood it. I could not deny Yveline's affection for Denise, or that she had rights with regard to the child. "It's agreed," I sighed.

"Don't sigh. You can come to see her as often as you like—and that way, *you'll also be able to see me.*"

Oh, how she loved playing with fire!

Denise left me—temporarily—the day after next. She had not had any hesitation when Yveline told her what she planned. It was natural that she would acquiesce willingly, for, without sharing any of the young woman's tastes or penchants, she could not help loving her. I had not been surprised to see her joyful at the prospect of a holiday, however attractive our communal life was; I was glad to see that she did not leave without a certain sadness.

After her departure, Madame Donatienne, Torquemada and Taureau could not succeed in distracting me. Fortunately, there was a great deal of work to do in Ferral's laboratory. We thought we had detected the traces of unknown existence in the void, and we were working so hard to perfect the experiment that sometimes, overwhelmed by fatigue, we were inclined to hallucinate.

"No matter!" Ferral said, one night. "I believe we'll end up sending the first *effective* probe into the unknown."

We worked for another two hours. Then, having collapsed into an armchair, I said: "I'm exhausted. I'll spoil everything!"

"I'm no better," said Ferral. "It would be crazy to continue."

The ancient world of the stars entered through the open window. For half an hour we allowed our brains to steep themselves in reverie—a reverie that was quite bitter at first, but hard: almost as tiring as the work. Our minds were stubbornly anchored in the field of research. They solved problems, they re-ran experiments imaginatively, aiming for solutions that would soon have been falsified.

Then the flow relented, the surf calmed down and thought relaxed into a benevolent torpor. The old stars were the little stars of the child, the ignorant person and the savage, florets of light in a sky commensurate with the Earth.

"Ambroise," I said, "science, in its ultimate speculations, would be almost sacrilegious, if nature were divine."

"I know what you mean," he replied. "We're obstinately intent on breaking the frame, rejecting the tutelary shade that life has permitted. That's what has fixed the limits by the creation of the senses, charged with the deceptive perception of things."

"Throughout our lives, it has hidden the discontinuity full of abysses from us. We march on a path of life that is illusory but so firm that, *for our feet*, the infinitely mobile and infinitely perforated Earth…"

"We're revolutionaries!" Ferral murmured. "How much more so than the unfortunates who kill one another over vague social ideas! We're biting into the breast that has nursed us with all our teeth!"

"Without any remorse! For it's also the cause of our monstrous, our infamous destiny…"

"So beautiful, the infamous destiny…"

We fell into a coma—I mean into a death-like sleep. The Sun took responsibility for our reawakening.

This morning, I received a telegram from Yveline. *Why don't you come to join us? The manor would be happy to welcome you.*

The telegram has an exaggerated effect on me, without my succeeding in suppressing my agitation. Is it Denise's "abduction" or the desirable prospect or dread of being tempted by Yveline? There are times when that brutal departure exasperates me, others when it intoxicates me. Is it not an invitation to adventure, a bay-window open on the unknown—but what unknown?

When I left for Vichy, I enjoyed victory and defeat. The stake was precise: even the risks had a definable form. Here, deep down, there's no stake. Whatever the assumptions might be, Yveline will withhold herself. I don't want her surrender, in any case—but can I prevent my flesh desiring her?

Then again, how shall I find Denise? In Paris, I always found her the same. In a new environment, what voices have risen up within her? There are, in holidaymakers in general, definite tendencies to decomposition. Those by the sea seem to me to be the most fecund and various in sensualities; the waves are corrupting…

Because there is a hiatus in our experiments, I can leave without inconveniencing Ferral.

231

XVII.

The Manoir des Tempêtes occupies a little plateau, at a modest height, and offers a spacious view over the Atlantic Ocean. Although old, it is vulgar. It has been refurbished for the comfort of guests, and nothing is lacking there that facilitates corporeal existence.

To all appearances, my arrival is perfectly calm. Hautbourguès is there, a man in his forties, from a sturdy race, with a fine figure, whose face is reminiscent of that of Pierre-Paul Rubens. Yveline and Denise, dressed in white, almost as scantily as the nymphs of Aphrodite, are incalculable human destiny at its purest and most equivocal, its most durable and its most changeable.

Roosting on solid millions, the apparent master of the moment, Hautbourguès is an emotional man; the surrounds of his eyes testify to that: currents flow through his eyelids; folds and waves form and deform incessantly. Powerfully smitten with his wife, simultaneously jealous and confident, he must be making use of "the man with the key" or one of the other spies who work for "the tranquility of families."

He will receive excellent reports. Faithful, impeccable in her moves, Yveline will not have to admit to our secret, which will leave intact the essential property of the husband. Furthermore, Hautbourguès pleases her—she finds him *good*, and for her that meager syllable expresses the maximum of masculine valor; it is an Yvelinian ideal in which nature and artifice combine their elegances. In that sense, Hautbourguès is almost perfect. He also has abundant experience, tact, self-control and the art of talking to women.

I will not go so far as to say that she loves him ardently. Applied to Yveline, that adverb would be excessive, almost scandalous. She is scarcely able to surpass a placid affection, combined with a fairly strong measure of sensuality; I think that, in the present case, she goes that far. I don't really know whether he's suspicious of me—more than anyone else, I mean; he doesn't exactly have confidence in anyone. In consequence, he must think about my possible roles with respect to Yveline, during a very long past in which the circumstances and combinations are incalculable. He will certainly spy on us; I expect that he already has one or two reports from "the man with the key."

Yveline welcomes me in an appropriately and desirably natural fashion—child's play, even for the awkward. It's not difficult for me to do likewise, concentrating my attention on Denise, in fearful expectation of a transformation—a dread legitimate in itself at her age, but absurd with respect to her. Dangerously pure, in every sense, gullible by nature, almost superhuman in her honesty, Denise cannot be other than on the day of her departure—and I am certain of that as soon as our eyes have met. If she ever succumbed, it would be completely, with heroic frankness.

In the three minutes of the "confrontation" I thought I saw the consciousness of the two women as clearly as their faces. In Yveline, the traces of ancient feminine servitude and her slyly superabundant resistance, of variable depth. Yveline knows only too well that, in her case, servitude has always been transferred to the man. Her duplicity is a game—an irresistible one. It is necessary for her to deceive, and she takes such pleasure in it—but she will reserve the central treasure, lest the slave should devote himself drunkenly to revolution. In the meantime, she will use and abuse any ambiguity, any secrecy and any mental complicity.

Denise's instinct has not, it seems, retained any instinct of servitude. She is a free spirit—so free that she instinctively shuns any perversity like a stink. And there is, therefore, an essential part of her that turbulent age will not reach...

Days more peaceful than I had expected. The open air, the sea, the beach, mostly populated by women, the casino. Hours of intense nature, nocturnal descents to the waves that incessantly sweep away the human traces and restore a virgin-

233

al nature to the sand and stone. Nights in which the stars, by turns, are the lamps of shepherds and the monsters of scientific mythology.

I feared that Yveline might abuse temptation. That was to misunderstand her. She knows her game too well, and that it is necessary not to deprive it of savor by incessant repetition. The hour and days pass without her setting out any bait. She has the beautiful attitude of a drowsy she-cat. Then, always unexpectedly, and at the choicest moments, a reminder that makes my diaphragm quiver. Sometimes a mere glance—but so knowing! A brush, an ambiguous word, an expression...

Twice only, she has affirmed: "You still love me!"

And my entire flesh trembled in servitude.

I admit to myself that I love that equivocal game. Would it be possible not to love it, though? It lifts up the universe of the self, opens the way to creative powers. Every time, there is such a nervous disturbance that everything seems new.

One awkward factor, although slight: the presence of Denise. It seems that, with respect to her, I am committing a graver infraction than that with respect to Hautbourguès.

I tell myself that this is absurd; I believe it, but I don't feel it. In the final analysis, it's trivial; most of the time, I don't think about it, and when Denise is present, I am glad of her existence. Our intimacy is almost as complete as in Paris. Yveline abandons me to her; she admits the complete purity of our affection. Physically, that goes without saying, but also mentally; otherwise, Yveline would have a "quantum" of jealousy. She would even be scandalized. Her confidence is rather disconcerting; at the end of the day, she cannot rely solely on Denise's candor and has no reason to deem me heroic.

But that's the way it is! What suspicious soul does not have unjustified confidences? Let us fall back on instinct. In the present case, Yveline's instinct is not mistaken; there is no troublesome cloud.

It's obvious that Hautbourguès is alert, and also obvious that he is sufficiently perspicacious, and that I only inspire

234

confidence in him subject to verification. He will make, or try to make, that verification.

He is methodical in his jealousy. He acts without precipitation, without nervousness, even with ease. I'd be deceived if I hadn't had certain items of information in advance. Yveline has completed them. We're on our guard. Having known one another for such a long time, Yveline and I have a right to a certain familiarity that he cannot find suspect. Furthermore, when he's present, her attitude reacts; she is "feverish," she renders me placid.

For the meantime, it can be left to Yveline. She brings an Asiatic cunning and prudence to her little perfidies. The entire surroundings are explored in advance. Then she is always furtive and fugitive. Few words, a slight contact, a glance, a sensation that is brief and unwitnessed. I would give it up, but not her. Because she is sure of not crossing the line, she intends to prolong the pleasure of throwing the hook, with a hint of sensual ferocity.

To sum up, it's completely impossible that Hautbourguès or his detectives—male and female—will discover anything. They are contending with the imponderable; that's one excitement more, almost as powerful as the other. Yveline amuses herself madly with that mobilization of police forces, incessantly lost in the void.

Sometimes, on the beach, in the casino or in the café, she has a half-smile, and I only have to follow the direction of her gaze to discover someone, male or female, who—in spite of their best efforts—cannot completely hide their identity.

One day, after lunch, while three of us are taking coffee—Denise being absent—and we're talking about a murder committed the day before by a jealous woman in the middle of a crowd of bathers, Yveline says to her husband, with a tender smile and in a cheerful tone: "By the way, dear, you ought to change them around—they're starting to be too obvious."

Hautbourguès put down his cup, bewildered. "What are you talking about?"

"You know perfectly well. The man and the woman responsible for watching over my virtue. If they're always the same, it will end up becoming irksome, and will make us look slightly ridiculous."

Hautbourguès looked at her rather stupidly. I listened, no less astonished than him.

"It's not—my God!—that it worries me—but why such lack of skill? By the way, I'm sacking Odette. The girl takes advantage, and her role is too much like treason to be amusing."

Yveline said this nonchalantly, fixing her brightly blushing husband with a medusal gaze.

"I assure you..." he began. He stopped, not being a liar by nature, and having, in any case, been caught with his hand in the bag.

"Good!" she said, still smiling. "Perhaps, at home, it would be better if you didn't involve my chambermaids in your game. Replace them with apparatus—it's said that they make marvelous devices for recording speech and taking snapshots. I'd like you to be completely reassured as much as you would. I am, my dear, incapable of giving to others what belongs to you; I'd like to, but I couldn't do it."

With that she uttered an exceedingly soft little laugh, while looking Hautbourguès in the face. He was rendered mute by the tranquil audacity and the clarity of that attack. I assume that he was delighted deep down.

Soon, he turned an anxious face toward me.

"Oh," said Yveline, "he's such an old friend that I preferred to speak in his presence."

Hautbourguès' physiognomy passed through various contrary phases in a flash. Evidently, deeply troubled at first that the scene had been witnessed by me, he suddenly resigned himself to it and smiled at me. "After all," he said, "I suppose she's right."

"But you haven't done anything wrong!" she said, amiably. "And I advise you to continue, at least for a little while. It's no bad thing that you should reassure yourself completely,

236

and that's what I want." Visibly, she had just acquired a considerable supplement of influence upon him. "Because," she continued, "I don't forbid myself a certain amount of badinage. A woman needs pleasure—you wouldn't want me to cease to be a woman?"

I was thinking about that conversation, sitting in the park near a meager fountain, which ran so weakly that one could scarcely hear it, when I saw Yveline coming.

She was wearing a Basque costume, with an olive-green bodice and a red skirt and the colors made her seem slightly primitive.

"Oh, you're a fine player!" I said.

"Aren't I?" she said. "I have to be—but don't imagine he'll disarm for so little. I don't want that. But he'll take measures to render the espionage even more invisible than it is. To tell the truth, I could have put the detectives off the track myself."

"You like playing hide-and-seek?"

"It's so amusing." She sighed. "Oh, he can be sure that I won't give anyone *what belongs to him*, and that without regret...except..." She darted an ambiguous glance at me. "Do you still love me?"

The fire flared up amid the ashes; how sweet it would be to kiss Yveline! She's sitting very close to me...

I dart the glance of a thief around me.

"No one!" she says.

My lips have plunged into the beautiful tender neck; Yveline's bosom rises in its charming palpitation. Then she gently pushes me away.

For my justification, I ought to say that, if I thought she were fallible, I would make an effort not to be alone with her. I would not deliberately take possession of Hautbourguès' present property. What I take—the surface of what belongs to me—does not seem to me to be a harmful infraction, but something akin to the interest on a moral mortgage. And since

I believed us both to be determined not to cross the frontier, I had no inkling of remorse.

For Yveline, the question of conscience did not arise. The adventure was in conformity with her code; if she had a moment of weakness, she would settle it by changing all or part of her code. She could do no wrong, all her actions being legitimate, or becoming legitimate by virtue of their very accomplishment.

It would be abusive to conclude that she is immoral. In her light fashion, I deem her very strict, to the extent that I only attribute to her one sole infraction (ours), justified by the interminable duration of the temptation. Committed when Yveline was free, that could pass for the best means of bringing the "maximum" to Hautbourguès. Had the temptation remained unappeased, it's probable that Yveline would have loved her husband less—for, after all, she does love him, in her temperate manner, and he profits from the intermittent excitement that she grants herself with respect to me.

It's obvious that Yveline's offensive has done Hautbourguès a great deal of good. He is refreshed by it, as if his soul had taken a Turkish bath; he has thrown overboard the ill-defined suspicion that I inspired in him. His friendship, more evident, no longer confuses me and leads me to flee temptation. Yveline, who perceives that, amuses herself, perversely, in seeking it out—without any abuse.

This is a happy time. Hautbourguès takes long walks; I take abundant advantage of the mountain, the forest, the heath and the sea. An agreeable companion, who rarely uses winged words, he chooses the locations with discernment.

One morning, when the peace was complete and I was feeling the serenity of a demigod, the beast appeared unexpectedly—the lubricious beast of the prophet, symbolized by Marcus.

I would have been glad to give him a beating at any time, but that morning, on the shore of the ocean, how I desired to leap upon him! Already he was bowing to Yveline, bowing to

Denise and extending his hand nonchalantly to Hautbourguès and to me. Hautbourguès greeted him coldly, and I felt a twitch in my shoulder-blades. The primitive was howling in his obscure cavern, and my two other selves almost let him out.

Marcus did not stay long. After the polite formalities, of which his voice and gaze made an enchantment for the women, he went off to set snares. Already, however inattentive one might be, one could discern a disturbance in the flock. Old frumps and young women, trying to outdo one another, were recognizing someone who brings a formless promise, a breath of the unknown—someone who exists only for them, only thinking about them, for whom everything is vain but the desire to please them.

Do they also have a presentiment of his ferocity when he has sucked the sap of sensuality from them—the sensuality of expectation, the sensuality of satiation, the sensuality of beautiful agonies? Perhaps they are all the more intoxicated, whirling around the murderous flame!

A faltering of what I had considered the most certain thing on Earth—will Denise fall prey to his charm? Once, however, he had to beat a retreat before Yveline—but she would not be the first woman who, protected by a dominant force, having rejected Marcus to begin with, eventually shared the common fate.

Two surrounding fortifications had sheltered Yveline once: the permanent, virtually traditional, temptation and her code of rules. To succumb to the permanent temptation, while she was not yet married, she had had an imperious reason: its duration; to succumb to Marcus she only had fragile motives. Now, married, she would be impregnable. I was as firmly persuaded that she would only give herself to Hautbourguès as I was that she had not been born under the sign of multiple adventures. Ours would suffice for the remainder of her existence. But Marcus was Marcus. It was quite evident that he would try to undermine the fortress and that Yveline would not discourage him. I knew her well enough to know that she could not be restrained by advice—that advice might even stimulate a spirit of contradiction, so I refrained from intervening, and also from alerting Hautbourguès.

When required, Marcus knew how to vanquish by speed. With Yveline, he perceived that he would need recourse to tunneling. Previously, he had reckoned her impregnable, but the change of circumstances had stimulated a desire for revenge.

She let him come, consented to light engagements, taking care not to squander the preliminaries. Marcus was received at the manor, without Hautbourguès seeming troubled, while I was subjected to a stupid crisis of jealousy. It did not matter that Yveline, with my full consent, had never ceased to be my mistress; she remained mine by virtue of the sin. I wanted—how forcefully!—that the sin should *belong to me*, without being shared. At any rate, I had never been jealous of Hautbourguès, but any lover would have exasperated me mortally—and if the lover were Marcus! I woke up at night sweating in distress, with the soul of a murderer. On a desert island, would I have resisted the need to kill Marcus?

That lasted, I think, for a fortnight. I was wandering in the dark. Nothing but phantoms. The adventure was lost in the ungraspable, in furtive gestures, neutral words and banal encounters.

Then, one morning…

I am in my room, next to my window, which has a view of the lawns, the rose-garden and the park, when Yveline appears. She is walking nonchalantly, like a beautiful wild beast out hunting, which will only become animated on scenting or catching sight of prey. Her life has never known a defeat. She has always made men into what she wanted them to be—who knows that better than me, indelibly marked by her.

She seems, this morning, to be wandering at hazard, but is drawing nearer to the park. She stops to look at the manor; she disappears. The traction could not be more forceful if she were being dragged by a cord around her neck.

In an instant, I am on the lawn, on the track, but while Yveline follows her course I move under cover between the clearings. There is no décor more precious. These large trees, the tall grass, the light mist, the mossy fountain, the faun and the naiad, that ravishing woman—oh, don't tell me that the Romantics were vain! They built up a fine treasure; they brought forth a new mystery, a splendor that grabs you by the guts, and illusions all the more profound for being imprecise. With them, women became more miraculous; they sprang from new depths, and the entire décor was magically amalgamated with their dresses, their hair, their footsteps and their smiles.

Yveline wanders in the delicate, grotesque morning, a creature of legend who makes unslaked desires rise into the hearts and maddened dreams of the sons of men. My *third* nature is in control—so strongly that the primitive seems to have disappeared. The flesh of the sensualist seems dead; sublimated flesh quivers at every one of Yveline's little footsteps...

And here is the carnivorous beast. Immediately, the primitive growls in the depths of the cavern, and the second self, the intermediary, gets up, almost as wild—without, however, the third incarnation standing aside; although it is subject to the influence, it acts according to its norm.

Meanwhile, Marcus is advancing, while Yveline, as chance would have it, is close to the shelter where I am hidden.

All this is theatrical enough for my anxiety to be mingled with mockery, without being attenuated by it. There is nothing to criticize in Marcus's appearance: harmonious, precise and supple, it is already an element of seduction. The gesture completes it when he bows, and the voice perfects the petty cycle at which, from the preliminaries on, Marcus excels.

The first words confirm what the mute scene announced: it really is a rendezvous.

Yveline extends her hand; Marcus, inevitably, holds on to it, his lips lingering upon it. It rarely needs more, when the paths of approach are already traced, but with Yveline, a swift attack cannot succeed. Marcus knows that; he will talk; if his vocabulary is restricted, it includes the essentials, all the more valuable for his knowing how to use them. At the point they have reached, each of them is decided with regard to the personality of the other, or believes so. For Marcus, it does not matter; any fruit is good so far as he is concerned, although he does not give that appearance.

In superior intelligence, Yveline is not distinguished, even though she is more intelligent than Marcus. Although he does not have all the qualities she demands, he possesses several to a transcendent degree. He might therefore suffice, even to satisfy Yveline—if she were to deem herself free. I had fewer trump cards, and those that I had scarcely came from my person. Can Hautbourguès, better provided than me, compare to Marcus? Not one woman in 100 would admit that *a priori*. I thought, however, that I could identify something that would eliminate Marcus in himself, quite apart from the code of marital fidelity adopted by Yveline. But here he is! My intuition founders.

"Ah!" he sighed. "If you only knew how much I love you!"

In sum, what jouster says anything better? In any case, Yveline's smile welcomes the words with manifest fervor. As she must, she replies: "You say so!"

"Never…never yet have I loved like this!"

"Oh!" Yveline, protests softly. "You have loved a great deal!"

"That's because I was thirsty for love; I was searching…without finding; I've only ever been half in love; while you, I've sensed for a long time that you…I would be able to love completely."

She sighed in her turn, and looked at him in a fashion that I consider languorous—to such an extent that once again, homicidal fervor swept through my veins. "Is that really true?

Why would you prefer me to so many others who are prettier?"

"Oh, prettier!" he protested. "No woman is prettier, none has as much charm."

The hyperbole disappears beneath the warmth and velvet quality of the voice. Marcus simultaneously mimes and submits to passion; his authentic excitement, far from undermining his skill, reinforces it. It really is love: the love of the bull or the stallion, enlarged by the triple nature of human being; love devoid of pity, devoid of tenderness, without duration— but not without preference, and how keen it is at the moment when it settles upon the temporary chosen one.

At this moment, he undoubtedly loves Yveline just as much as I loved her in the most flamboyant days, and his tone reveals an anxiety—a well-contrived anxiety.

She recognizes that ardor, savors it and breathes it in— but as a dilettante, it seems. "I believe you," she says, in a subdued voice. "Perhaps you do love me."

"How I love you!" He strikes an attitude of adoration, without seeming ridiculous.

"Today!" says Yveline. "I'm flattered by it, I would even be touched, if I did not know you, but I do know you! Tomorrow the flame will be extinct!"

"I swear to you!"

"An honest oath. So much the worse for anyone who believes it! Personally, I want to be loved for a long time and, if there is a breach, that I should be the one to make it. I would never forgive myself for having believed you; I would hate myself for as long as I lived…"

He must be scenting the impossible; his face, which contracts resentfully before going blank again, appears almost ugly.

Yveline continued: "Don't hold it against me; know that you please me, at a distance, and tell yourself that I am absolutely incapable of deceiving the man to whom I have linked my life."

In a rage of humiliation, he said in a low voice: "Then why did you let me come here?"

"Because you're Marcus! Try to understand that." She uttered her brief laugh, held out her hand to him, and turned back toward the manor.

Have I ever experienced such a wild joy? My entire body was vibrant and singing. I could not help catching up with her.

"Yveline," I told her, "what pleasure you've just given me!"

She looked at me obliquely. "Pleasure? Oh, you were there? Hidden like a vaudeville hero...that's shameful." She laughed like a little girl. "Shameful—and I'm glad that you did it! It proves..." She let a few suspenseful seconds go by. "That you still love me! Exactly what I want..."

Because she wants it, my flesh becomes amorous again; perhaps she intends the abrupt quickening of the heart. In front of a cabin of greenery, a capricious refuge in which wisterias, virgin vines and convolvulus are doing battle, she says with a disquieting smile: "I'm tired."

I had given up. It pleased me to believe her virtuous—in her ambiguous fashion—and I did not want to take from Hautbourguès an item of property for which he was paying royally. In that nest of leaves and flowers, however, after Marcus's defeat, there was nothing but a man and a woman.

All my zones conspire together; no kind of emotion is stranger to them, even hypocrisy, auxiliary to affection. A slight odor, so charming, amalgamates her favorite perfume with the effluvia of the bindweed. I am no more than a prey to desires—metamorphic desires, fundamental desires, as feral as an autumn wolf and as delicate as Yveline's eyelids.

"Yveline, dearest!" The contents of that cry! Boundless aspiration, enraged by inexpressibility.

"Ah!" she sighed. "You love me—and how much I want that!"

Her head on my shoulder; her hair on my mouth; and very close, languorous, sensual, perfidious eyes, lips partly open over moist teeth. My voracious mouth wants hers, but finds only accessories: the cheek, the ear, the neck.

"You must tell me!" she demands.

Servile and cowardly, I obey, an amorous slave whom she neither welcomes nor rejects. She accepts the hug, the kisses, but prohibits her mouth like a fortress...

Finally, raising her arms: "I love you too." Cunning, eccentric, mysterious: "*Almost*..."

There she stands, unvanquished, plausibly invincible, a marvelous artiste of love. My arteries are still sounding the tocsin...but the deception is purely corporeal. The superior zone only participates in it to approve; it knows that it would regret Yveline's capitulation—and I am indulgently scornful of myself.

"It's wrong of you tease me like this, Yveline!"

"No. It's very good. I'm sure of myself, and I want to. Nothing more—but *that*."

"What am I, to you? Some puppet!"

"Not at all. How alive you are! Oh, it pleases you as much as me."

"Not afterwards!"

"Sometimes it pleases you anew...but I won't abuse it..." And, laughing in my face: "That would spoil the beautiful temptation, and I love it, passionately!"

She is rosy, fresh, healthy, content with life, content to reign. I forgive her—and how could I not forgive her?

Marcus is squared away. We meet him on the beach, at the casino, in the café, taciturn, smiling, always on the warpath. My congenital hatred has decreased, although it is still keen, especially in the higher regions. If the primitive male has calmed down, the human male is thinking that beautiful victims, thinking along the highest sentimental lines, are being finished by an ignoble sledgehammer blow and carrying away a frightful provision of suffering and humiliation.

I deem Marcus to be worse than a Rasputin, who was a summary animal, a mere sexual creature who left little suffering behind him. Has not a historian written: *they retired sound and happy*? The filthy monk, reeking of goat, offered straightforwardly that which the dog offers the bitch. With him, princesses and duchesses tasted solid animality—he was a warrior!—and the perversity that they mingled with it came from their side, not his. He was nothing but a pretext; they alone bore responsibility for the sin—theirs—in which he was no more involved than if they had given themselves to a gorilla.

All the same, Marcus and Rasputin exemplify different stages in sexual contagion. Is it, fundamentally, more astonishing in Rasputin than Marcus? Marcus possesses a subtle sense of the woman, a sure instinct, accrued from experience and attraction; he is almost the perfection of the genre, for a livelier intelligence, being hesitant, contradictory and clumsy by nature, would work to his disadvantage. He knows the tricks of the trade thoroughly.

Rasputin had a peasant cunning, a crude sexual energy and the renown of a "magnetic" warrior at his disposal. The most difficult thing for him was to commence his lubricious career. The Court would be his astonishing furnisher, his reserve. The apparent distance between him and ladies of proud lineage, not to mention aristocratic small fry, was enormous.

In reality, the number of women who, knowingly or unknowingly, are inclined to taste the most brutal dishes of love is not so restricted. The beast sleeps scarcely more soundly in women than in men. If everything to which they have been subjected forcibly through the ages were able to enter into their heredity, one could scarcely be astonished that they can be more attracted to the sewer than their companions. In which case, the role of Rasputin, not forgetting the favorable circumstance of this influence on the imperial prince, would be as easily explicable as that of Marcus, even though the monk was dirty and his teeth rotten. It is sufficient that circumstances aid a contagion which, in normal times, would be almost impossible.

Not without peril, Marcus continued his ravages—I'm thinking about some husband with the face of a pirate, some somber lover. Wherever he went, he unleashed jealousy. That no revolver had been fired at him during the epidemic of his crimes of passion is a miracle.

I remember one bitter senora, an incendiary beauty who exuded the salt of sensuality, welded to a tragic husband, a harsh man devoured by suspicion and by no means blind. Marcus and the senora gambled their lives; they were suspected, and the tragic man followed the trail; twice close to flushing out the game, he found himself empty-handed.

In the end, he took his wife away, saving her—and Marcus—from death.

Those who have a wife or lover to defend, those who covet, even those who have nothing to conserve and nothing to hope for, hate Marcus. Some, however, devote to him one of those surprising sympathies that do not conform to the norm: men without antennae, in whom the sentiments are reminiscent of a lottery, or homosexuals.

Fundamentally, am I so very different from Marcus? Among those who hate him, how many are virtual or effective imitators, and how many, if they were able to pluck women without danger, reprobation or difficulty, would hesitate? The beach is overflowing with males who are only awaiting the opportunity. Pusillanimity, awkwardness, inertia or ugliness, old age—not to mention impotence—stop them, otherwise...! Failed Marcuses or Marcuses without scope!

Fundamentally—if there is a foundation—he's only a little worse than they are; his only defect is taking the gamble, and, above all, of knowing how to win. But isn't that all the more reason to hate him?

XVIII.

"Denise hasn't come back yet," said Yveline.

It was time for tea, a time of epicurean indulgence for Yveline, and for me, on that odiferous ground, a time for daydreaming and hope. What hope? I don't know. Formless hope, the most desirable and the least deceptive, by definition. It requires Denise. She adds herself to the softness of a gentle light. A radiance less sharp, harsh, and violently blue rays, a Sun swelling and becoming redder, toward which one might raise one's eyes without fear of deadly darts.

Denise comes in before that time, when she has not announced some random excursion. She intoxicates herself in solitude with torrents, rocks, vegetation and clouds. That land of bathers and tourists is much safer than our suburbs or certain crapulous corners of the Faubourgs.

That day, she had gone out after lunch on her bicycle, in order to be able to go anywhere.

Seeing my annoyance, Hautbourguès said: "She's less than an hour late. It would only require a minor accident to the machine."

Whether by virtue of impatience or anxiety, I am very sensitive to lateness. With Denise, anxiety is dominant, which increases as the light decreases. The Sun swells over the ocean, a golden Sun that will soon be coppery red.

When two hours have passed, I can no longer bear it. Yveline, and even Hautbourguès, are nervous.

"Let's go look for her!" she says.

But which way shall we go? Denise could have reached the depths of Guèvres.

"We'll send out Charles, François, Aline and Marie as scouts," says Hautbourguès. "They'll ask around. Once we know which way she went, we'll each take an automobile and spread out. Anyway, we needn't worry. Denise will come back!"

The golden furnace is lower in the west.

Hautbourguès gives his orders. The two chambermaids and François must be back in half an hour, Charles has more latitude. I can't stay still.

"Well, let's go out too," says Hautbourguès.

Servants and masters, equalized, interrogate the housewives in their homes, the men at work, and strollers—tourists and locals alike. By this means, we discover Denise's *initial* direction. The automobiles are waiting for us.

"We'll go together, at first," says Hautbourguès, "stopping frequently to interrogate pedestrians and automobilists, then we'll split up."

The furnace is scarlet, ready to set. A festival begins in the clouds, a magnificent unreality filling the sky; for me, it takes a tragic form. Mingled there is a wave of youth, the resurrection of times of adventure, great departures, the rush toward the unknown, all subject to a black enchantment, joys transformed into anguish, while retaining their joyful appearance.

We go here and there, pausing. We interrogate passersby, peasants and their wives standing on their doorsteps. Some of them know Denise and have seen her pass by. The traces become vaguer; in the end, no one knows anything.

"She must have taken to the footpaths," Hautbourguès soon concludes. "It's time to spread out."

We've brought the dogs. I'm given the black Rhesus, an enigmatic dog with the head of a panther, who howls raucously rather than barks, but more often remains mute. As soon as we set off, Hautbourguès, with the aid of one of Denise's garments, acquainted him with our objective. Rhesus has practiced that sport; he knows what to do—and when the car stops at a crossroads he explores. His chances are poor. The dry ground scarcely shows any tracks. To begin with, the soles of Denise's shoes, as she walks, only exude imponderable fluids, and she might only be walking intermittently. As for the bicycle—nothing.

Rhesus, however, likes adventure. He's a fighting dog, in whom the intoxicating vicissitudes of the hunting-dog are lacking. He precipitates himself forward passionately. He persuades himself that he is on the warpath; he exercises his own genius with a sagacious exaltation—the genius of the sovereign sense that, for him, counting for more than sight or hearing, provides a consciousness of the world. In searching for Denise, a thousand odorant images arise: prey, love, danger, battle, revelry, everything is based in smell...

A pause. The twilight is expiring in a night of ash and embers. The east is covered in crêpe; the major stars are coming out and, imperceptibly, the snow of starlight is accumulating.

A vertical shadow. I interrogate the passer-by, whom the night makes almost as black as Rhesus. An obscure dialogue, which is suddenly clarified; by two or three indications, I think I have recognized Denise. The man has seen her, on a path diverging from the by-road we're on.

"You'll see a boundary-marker, which looks as if it has a crack in it, and as tall as *this*. There are two other paths before you arrive at that one, and it's on your left."

The path is hollowed out between worn and cracked granite walls—a path ripe for murder, full of ambushes, where crosses mark ancient tragedies. It is necessary to abandon the automobile and I have an acute sensation of isolation, in a mountain region, where human authority is extinct. I walk, surrounded by minerals and stars, on a pale soil, with the feeling that my journey is in vain. If Denise has passed this way, she's long gone!

For Rhesus, the night is less opaque. His lupine hearing, his nose for countless nuances, renders sensible and various that which seems monotonous to me.

He falls silent. This is his mission, and he will only betray himself in response to an order. The path comes to an end; there is a roadway along which, mysteriously, a shaft of violet light extends.

Rhesus breathes deeply in his warlike manner, and demands that I guide him. I want to figure out which way to go first.

The light is emanating from the headlights of an automobile. The car has stopped and just in front of it, a male form and a female form...the man, leaning over, is holding the woman in his arms...oh! I shiver, all the way to my bones. It is Denise and—mortal horror!—Marcus. The shock is so terrible that, at first, I am as motionless as a mineral, breathless, my muscles helpless.

He has lifted Denise up and his lips are joined to those of the young girl. Disgust, fear, an immense sensation of annihilation—a revolution of the *unique* soul, unseconded in the revolutions of life. Denise seduced by Marcus makes this night into the end of a world!

A dull sadness follows, which gives me back my muscles. Then a great leap of the heart, a blind fury, and I hurl myself forward...

My rush draws Rhesus along; he bounds forward, howling hoarsely.

Marcus, straightening up, paling in the violet light, sees us coming. I have struck out at hazard and snatched Denise away, while Rhesus knocks down the man, who moans piteously: "An accident...Mademoiselle hurt her foot...I had it bandaged in Margues...I was bringing her back..."

A voice murmured: "That's true." Only then did I notice the chauffeur, whom I know well—an equivocal individual who has been working for Marcus for a long time. As pale as his master, he had not moved a muscle to help him.

Meanwhile, Marcus and I were beginning to recover our composure. He stopped mumbling. "She wanted to get out of the car...and she fainted."

Already, Denise's lips are moving, and her throat is rising and falling, gently. Everything remains obscure, but my worst suspicion is already beginning to disperse. It had surged forth at a stroke, massive and overwhelming, effecting a total disorder of my being. I cry: "I *saw*, you blackguard!"

Marcus lowers his head silently, his eye fixed on Rhesus.

Denise came round. She stammered a few inconsequential words, recognized me, and held out her arms. I clutched her to my breast, and she murmured: "I'm glad...glad." Then, noticing Marcus, she shivered from head to toe. "Not good!" she murmured, in a soft voice. "Oh, not good."

The last traces of suspicion and the unique horror—which could only have been aroused by Denise, and before which I had become *direct*, simple, candid, with no more experience than a little child—were dying away. Oh, how good the night air smelled!

Marcus having become negligible, I addressed myself to the chauffeur. "There must be a way of rejoining the by-road to Port-Aigues..."

"It's just a matter of heading that way," the chauffeur said, extending his arm.

"Good. You can take us as far as my car, which is waiting. I'll show you...then you can pick up...your master."

"But..." the man objected, stunned.

"He'll wait here."

The chauffeur turned to Marcus. Rhesus was still beside me, ardent and ready to pounce.

"I'll wait!" Marcus agreed.

In a few minutes, we were back in my car. As we moved off, I said: "He didn't do you any harm?"

"Harm? No...I shouldn't have anything against him. He helped me, he cared for me...it was only in the car..."

Gradually, the anecdote takes shape. First, the cycling accident, the sprain, the impossibility of getting under way again, the arrival of Marcus, the transport to the inn, the wait, the country doctor, the bandage..."

As they were coming back, Marcus had made a tactical error. The game had inspired confidence, the expectation of the reward of his intervention. He had become affectionate, risked a few gestures that might have been merely friendly, then...Denise was not precise, but it could be inferred: the stimulus, the attraction of the young mouth. She had opened the door; Marcus, amazed, had ordered a halt, and Denise, having got down in the road, had fainted. By way of denouement, my arrival.

A small adventure, immense for me. No tragedy could have aroused emotions of such power, lined to the great foundations of life. Denise seduced by Marcus would have been worse than a murder. I sense that with as much astonishment as intensity: a flood of youth has risen, and to recover the "nuances" of delight that swelled my chest, it is necessary to recapitulate all the phases of my life: infancy, nascent virility, the flower of youth. What's more, these evocations are phantasmal; my emotion is new; it is not framed by any other.

Denise's universe is more complicated still. What, in essence, is that candor, that *innocence*, which defends her against actions into which others would dive head first, or into which they would at least allow themselves to be drawn? While I questioned her, I realized the disgust that Marcus, so seductive for the feminine majority, had inspired in her. He had appeared to her as a sort of beast-man, a sinuous and sickly beast, and all the more repulsive for it. Innocence? In a child, though, innocence is brutal, it does not take away any ferocious instinct, but renders them more precise, less masked by hypocrisy, less attenuated by moral constraint.

In Denise, innocence is a nobility, an initial elevation of instinct, a generosity *in all directions*, which excludes cruelty, slyness, hatred, borrowing little from education, from the present supply of the human world. Her environment is Yveline's, in which Yveline plays the essential role; so far as Denise is concerned. Yveline is the negation of innocence: as a little girl, a charming feminine perfidy was already within her; her morality arises only from constraint, conformism and a sure instinct of self-preservation.

I cannot see, in respect of Denise, any being from whom a contagion of candor might come. She has retained her essential instincts integrally: social life has enriched them, not combated them; her complex universe, in becoming more complex than that of Yveline, has made her innocence a numerous and various sentiment, the purity of which is quite unaltered.

I am happy—fantastically happy—in this little room that hurls itself through time. My happiness, as innocent as Denise and as new as spring, transforms the evening stars and makes them different from all the stars of other nights...

XIX.

For three months, we have been obstinately trying to breach the limits of our universe. We are living in Ambroise Ferral's atmosphere, but if he is the dominant presence, Chavres surpasses him in experimental detail, and material intuition, and my companions consider me superior in focus.

A fortnight ago, Chavres obtained luminous points that Ferral had predicted, and which could not have arisen, *normally*, from any of the elements or any of the forms of energy that we were using.

Ambroise paled slightly and said: "Perhaps we're really about to open a new era."

It was, I assure you, a solemn moment. *Everything* was about to be increased immeasurably. The dawn was breathing on the backs of our necks. I saw the fourth universe opening up, by comparison with which our stars and nebulas are not even what a single insect is among all the animals of Earth.

"Let's verify it," Ferral added.

It took several days to carry out the experimental check. It succeeded. We really had surpassed the bounds of human experience.

What a night! We chatted in low voices, in mystical meditation, hoping that the fragile human beast was about to discover the first of the lines that attach it to *the great all*. Our generation would only see feeble indications, the next few generations only a little more—and then, undoubtedly, according to the norm of modern progress, an explosive advancement.

What a strange emotion ours is, mingling a certain disinterest, which transfigures Ferral and Chavres, with an abstract pride, which might even exceed the sanctions of the elite. Perhaps the instinct for prey, booty and reward recurs in the hope of the cold glory of scientists, a glory restricted to a small group, scarcely perceived by the multitude, often with a long delay. Let's remember that it took generations for the great Carnot, the Carnot of the Principle, to be known even to his imitators; a century passed before his name received a faint hospitality in the dictionaries—while the Carnot of the Victory settled comfortably in books, periodicals and compendia.[34]

Restricted as it is, however, that glory is only a secondary appetite in Ferral and Chavres. They are religious minds. They delight in discovery for its own sake, in the breath of enthusiasm, rendered ecstatic by the prospect of a breach in the formidable mystery. Their *sublimated* pride rises above the purest social sentiments; it is an indication of a superhumanity, in which the need to dominate the herd is no longer found, even in its elites. It also has a solitary beauty, exceptional in its destination as if by necessity, as desirable as any, but not in a routine manner.

---

[34] The Sadi Carnot (1796-1832) who formulated the first law of thermodynamics—known in France as Carnot's principle—was a member of a family of famous politicians. His father, Lazare Carnot—a talented mathematician—became involved in the revolution of 1789, organizing the Republic's armies and designing their plans of campaign, thus earning the title "Organizer of the Victory." Lazare's younger son, Hippolyte, was a member of the provisional government formed after the 1848 revolution, and Hippolyte's son Sadi became president of the Third Republic in 1887; as Rosny observes, the earlier Sadi was completely eclipsed for many years, until the importance of the science of thermodynamics was belatedly realized.

In the bumpy and erratic march of progress, which always seems to be devoid of a definite goal, but which nevertheless contrives growth by the increase of the interhuman world—sciences, arts, metaphysics and industries *created and conserved*, situated *outside ourselves*—the likes of Ferral and Chavres play a role of the first rank, without being indispensable, for only *one aspect* of their disinterest is required to aliment the treasure. The great Faraday, in claiming a *finder's rights* in discoveries derived from his own, manifested a spirit of conquest that is even sharper in a Berthelot.

I must be inferior in quality to Chavres and Ferral.

Chavres lives in a child-like innocence, rather like a woman in that he loves *slowly*, without agitation, with a distracted fidelity. His passionate life is entirely bound up in his visionary wanderings. Victor Hugo, when young—and still fresh, I assume, for he was soon watered down—wrote: "My days progress from one dream to another."[35]

That was already only half true. A terrible realist was lying in wait for the dreamer. For Chavres, it is absolutely true; his days really do progress from one dream to another: dreams of science, of metaphysics, and also of nature—for he knows how to appreciate a place, clouds, or the rustling of foliage.

Ferral controls his dreams. He disciplines them, weaves them together solidly with the fabric of science. He loves his wife ardently, with a youthful enthusiasm that extends to the threshold of old age, and his love is unique. As he has only had one wife in his past and his present, there will only be one in his future. In her, he summarizes all women; every day he renews the finest of human vows, and his love has a breadth that scarcely exists in Chavres' idle love.

I was not born under such beautiful stars. It has never been possible for me to condense the feminine world into one single creature. Even at the moment of the most avid love, the others exist, with their cortege of temptations. Neither in mi-

---

[35] From "Enthousiasme" in *Les Orientales* (1829).

sery nor in joy, nor in the most depressing fatigue, nor shackled by jealousy, can I remain insensible to the passage of beautiful women. They are the spice of the universe; no other enthusiasm, no other poetry and no other beauty, either in the universe or in human beings, can compare with them.

All the speeches that I can make on the subject of the fable, the mirage and the incessant deceit that is love, in all of its forms, cannot freeze a single one of my desires or diminish feminine treasure in the least. Judging it *illusory* does not prevent me from seeing it as the sovereign reality.

I think about that while waiting for Francine. My senses are still impregnated by her; she still evokes the triple intoxication. That of the primary zone is dominant, but the other two zones are not negligible. All the qualities of the dream are represented, albeit unequally. In the highest zone, in spite of the ravages of Marcus, a magnified, purified image of Francine persists.

She arrives today in a blaze of scarlet. The red dress and the stormy head bring a Dionysian joy; fervent verses sing in my memory, and her perfume, sharper than usual, is suggestive of the odoriferous lands of the tropics.

The pleasure of holding her against me, of feeling her shiver and palpitate like a dove, is still new. All the same, what a fine treasure! And what have I done to deserve it? What have I done to deserve the least of these exciting creatures—even my poor Juliane...?

The pleasure is so much greater than the effort of conquest!

"I've had an adventure," says Francine, an hour after her arrival.

She adopts a modest air, belied by her eyelids, and leaves to continuation in suspense, waiting for me to ask. Teasingly, I remain silent.

"Aren't you interested?" she asked, slightly vexed.

"How do I know?" I say. "Perhaps it would interest me very much."

"Well then, have you heard of Amnès?"

"Of course I've heard of him—almost a Ford."

With a girlish smile, she deftly lets fall: "He's asked me to marry him."

Although I contain myself, jealousy returns in a rush, leaps up and assaults me. The days return when Francine was the queen of heaven and earth. My palpitations revive a supernatural past when love filled the three zones. "That proves," I say, "that he has good taste."

"Oh!" she groans. A desperate, bitter, vindictive cry. Gripped by indignation, she says: "You never loved me!"

I shall have no difficulty putting on the best possible show of denial, for, at the idea of breaking up—and of *the other*—the fury of the species rises again; as our gazes meet, knowing themselves complicit I embrace a Francine enslaved.

"So you still love me!" she murmurs, as much victorious as submissive. She whispers in my ear, almost imploringly: "You're jealous, aren't you?"

Today, I let her win. "Yes, Francine."

"Oh, I'm so happy…" A brief pause, and then the dangerous question, charged with storm-clouds. "I'll refuse, shall I?"

She doesn't take me by surprise. As little time as I have had for reflection, my argument is ready, almost in battle order.

"I mustn't intervene in the slightest, Francine. It would be inexcusable to trample on your future, since I can't offer anything in exchange for such a renunciation. Only you matter. I cease to exist."

"But you love me, and I…"

"There's no proof that you'll love me tomorrow."

"Oh!" she protests.

"Come on, Francine! You must know full well that no one can have complete confidence in themselves."

The blow strikes home; Francine literally shudders, and as it suits me not to let up, I continue: "Can I answer for myself, any more than you're able to offer any guarantee? The future, even within us, holds no certainties. What can I offer you, in compensation for Amnès?"

She weeps gently, and says in a plaintive voice: "Oh, I shall never do it again."

"That's quite possible, but this is a moment that requires absolute frankness: the past cannot die, for me! I never wanted anything from you so, I had nothing to forgive; all things considered, we were together without any conditions, without having made any promises—but I haven't been able to forget!"

She dries her tears, perhaps saving them for later. "But does *that* prevent you from loving me?"

"Certainly not!" I say, forcefully enough to convince her—and who can tell whether I didn't desire her all the more for it? "I don't owe Amnès anything."

"Then I'll still have you?"

"Almost certainly."

"Almost! Oh!"

The flood of tears threatens to resume. I take hold of Francine and cradle her. "Understand, my dear, that I cannot and must not give any answer that has any appearance of an engagement, for you or for me. Let's just talk hypothetically. If you were married today, certainly, it wouldn't change my love at all, except, perhaps, for the amount of jealousy mingled with it."

The last words please her so much that she can't help smiling. And the meeting ends pleasantly. When Francine leaves, I have the feeling that, sooner or later, she will be Amnès' wife. And what better denouement could I wish for her, and for me, if not for poor Amnès? Not that I have, at present, any desire to break it off. She's dear to me, and I'll always retain a memory of her full of charm—in spite of Marcus. *In spite of Marcus?* Is that really true? Over Yveline, Marcus's victory would have burned me to the core, Marcus seducing Denise would have been the negation of all terrestrial beauty. For Francine, it's a different chemistry, inasmuch as the affinity between us was not so much compromised as complicated, perhaps completed. Francine, with passionate remorse, went from one to the other in a sinful excitement, inflamed by her guilt, and was, with Marcus and me, ardently polyandrous—which completed her, impelling her to the extreme blossoming of her amorous personality. I possessed her more fully because she gave herself to Marcus. Complementary for her, the double adventure would have unbalanced and reduced the status of Yveline, and indelibly tarnished Denise.

If she married Amnès, she would scarcely think she was being unfaithful in coming back to me, since it would only be a repetition of actions about which nothing could be done, since they had already been accomplished. She would, alas, bring to me—perhaps even to Amnès—a Francine in her most flavorsome form.

And nothing requires me to look after Amnès, a shark of industry, a merciless businessman.

Meanwhile, Ferral doggedly pursued his course. All through the autumn, steering through a course of subtle experiments, we continually ran into reefs, running aground before indecisive glimmers. We obtained, however, manifestations beyond corpuscles, wave-sequences and photons. We believed that we had seen corpuscles and photons vanish, and from that, it follows that our existence re-emerges from an innumerable renewal, so rapid that we cannot form any sort of idea of it, without thinking about reflected images in which none is only one single image, but each an indefinite, not to say infinite series of images.

Sometimes, an idea of the false constancy of forms suggests itself to us via the kinds of flow that our language makes into objects—a river, a cataract, a whirlpool. I have spent hours, hypnotized, beside a river whose form does not show me any appreciable change—the same level, the same speed of current. In my homeland there is a waterfall that, since my childhood, has reminded me somewhat of a bearded face. Seen from a distance, that dazzlingly white face seems as motionless as the surrounding rocks.

In sum, much more so than in the past, the image of the world seems to be a variable whose variations have a vertiginous rhythm; perhaps even *the all* is composed of variations on an ungraspable theme.

When we have taken a step *beyond* our nebulas and stars, what shall we see, in the exceedingly restricted sense that the word "see" can be applied to our gropings in the dark? Very little, for sure—so little that almost nothing will seem to have changed in our cosmological conceptions. However, since the time when human progress began, we have learned to attach an extreme importance to these "almost nothings." Once, electricity, as a concept, was next to nothing; cathode rays initially went unperceived; the initial discovery of radioactivity was merely suggestive of an abnormal phosphorescence. But since then!

If Ferral succeeds, there will doubtless be objections, then an explosion of enthusiasm, a rush of researchers in the new direction. Then, what a flood of discoveries! One only has to think of the frightful metamorphosis of physics in the last 100 years!

XX.

An invisible horde of winds, originating in the wilds of the Atlantic, has hurled itself upon the city. It howls and laments; widows shake, frames creak, doors bang and bewildered passers-by protect themselves, lashed by gusts that would sink ships.

We are alone: Denise, Torquemada, Taureau and me. Torquemada is anxious; his furious eyes search for an invisible enemy. Taureau cocks his lupine ears, troubled by memories which, beyond his own life, link up with others in the chain of his canine ancestors. Both of them have recognized the voice of the original Earth, which they have never seen, from which they are permanently exiled. The ancient liberty palpitates within them—the roots of the forest and the grass of the savannah, where existence was limitless—and do I not also have a sudden intuition of the Lost World?

"We can't go back there," I've just murmured, talking to Taureau, who is looking me in the face. "We've been captured, and all your descendants, my big dog!"

Then the other voice chips in—the new voice: Denise, singing the song of the dying forest, while her fingers wake the spirits of sound. Springing from her, the world of sounds is just as beautiful as the free Earth; music is purer than other human creations, and its charm is all the more profound for being accompanied by the multitudinous ferocity of the storm.

A moving moment of existence. She renders desirable even that which was dull and bleak a little while ago. Denise, a daughter of humanity more than of nature, has no place in the forest. To construct her required numerous interhuman generations. How many new beauties had to be created in order that the heavy jaw, the thick face and the animal structure should culminate in that slender chin, those delicate cheeks and that sublime substance, in order that that subtle and versatile voice should spring from grunts! Even more to create Denise's soul. New beauties? Shall I go so far as to believe that beauty is real? I have every reason to deny it—and I do deny it. Concretely, however, I am submissive to it, like my flesh and my blood. The quibbles are mere smoke in the wind; as soon as I see Denise—and Yveline and Francine too—beauty imposes itself upon me with the same authority as the imperious force of rhythm; and how, after them, can it *feel* imaginary? Localized, rather, submissive to the same intrinsic laws as everything else.

Grass, the maker of muscles for the buffalo, is nothing to the tiger: the element of subjectivity does not establish that the nourishing herb is an illusion. It follows that Denise's beauty is no illusion *to me*. I have no need for preparation to perceive it; it is imposed upon me at the first glance. And her grace does not prevent me from shivering with primary passion in listening to the assault of the winds, in contemplating the savage rain, the source of all life, which, at the present moment, is massacring its creation.

O clouds emerged from the profound sea, clouds as white as the flesh of our children, gray as ash, blue as slate; clouds which, in the two twilights, dress more faces, and vaster ones, than all the faces on Earth, more sparkling than gemstones, more colored than flowers; palpitating, migratory clouds, which die incessantly and return to life without respite!

The spirits of sound have been killed; somewhere, a window breaks; an automobile horn sounds, like the plaint of a great wild beast, and Madame Donatienne appears. "It's Madame and Monsieur Hautbourguès and another Monsieur," she says.

"In this weather!" I cry, on seeing Yveline, her husband and a young man to whom I know Hautbourguès is related.

Yveline bursts out laughing. "The weather is of no consequence! The automobile is solid…"

"And heavy," says Hautbourguès. "If we've come at a bad time, blame Yveline. Once she gets an idea into her head, she gets carried away."

"Florent," says Yveline, "Is leaving for Tunisia tomorrow."

Without any definite suggestion, images show me this young blond with Nordic eyes and the fresh face, attracted by Denise. In Yveline's house, the manner in which he watched the young girl betrayed a lively predilection, at least. All things considered, it's probably not important.

"He's come to say goodbye to you," Yveline continues.

Young Florent suddenly seems to me to be as silly as he is untimely. He has the right to think himself a handsome fellow, in the best fashion, masculine and delicate at the same time; I denigrate him while conceding that the impression he makes is bound to please.

Meanwhile, the visitors have sat down, and the three men would remain sheepish if Yveline did not fill the hiatus of silence with masterly frivolity.

She talks about the wind, the rain, her friends or nothing at all—everything that makes excessive frequentation possible among chatty people. It soon becomes clear that Florent is here for a purpose that might still have been confused yesterday, but has suddenly become precise. His imminent departure has triggered in Yveline one of those resolutions that she is inclined to pluck "out of the air." Soon, her ambiguous words leave no room for doubt: the young man, who is ready to disappear temporarily, is being *displayed*, in order better to enchant the present and future.

This preparatory operation lasts a good half hour. It is not advantageous to Florent, who is confused, and interjects a few insignificant words, ineptly. Then Yveline says: "I want to ask you something." And, with an indefinable smile: "Not in front of them." On which I take her into the next room. "Perhaps you've guessed?" she begins.

"Would you be surprised?"

She hesitates, then, as an intermediary: "You may kiss me."

The hair, the eyes, the neck, then the feint toward the lips, which, according to protocol, are withheld. The pleasure is lukewarm—which she does not seem to notice, for she stammers, like a quivering stem: "Do you love me?"

"I love you, Yveline."

The game goes on for a little longer, the lips inaccessible, the hair in my neck; then she says, point-blank; "Can you imagine that that young man is in love with Denise?"

I must have blanched. If she notices that, she will attribute it to the pressure of her face on my shoulder.

"A good fortune, a good family, a handsome lad, of excellent character," Yveline continues. "Impossible to find better. And parental consent is assured. So it's necessary not to hesitate, isn't it?" Her cheek gently caresses mine.

"That's your opinion?"

To give me courage and justify my disturbance, which has increased, I embrace Yveline precipitately. I even pretend to be striving to attain the impossible.

"Ah!" she said, excited and cheerful. "The gate of hell. You must abandon all hope! Then it's understood, with regard to Denise?"

"But only Denise can decide, Yveline."

"Of course! But she'll accept; I'll guarantee that, since we're in agreement."

Agreement! The word burns me to the core. A sudden hatred rises from the depths, in both simple forms—the most violent—and complex ones that lose themselves in subtle shades. In the simple forms, no compromise: young Florent is brutally reduced to the adversary who must be struck down mercilessly. In the complex ones, there is a mixture of revolt and resignation.

Denise also becomes multiform. She *accepts*, and, in doing so, becomes almost odious; she *refuses*, and my heart melts with a tenderness that is exalted to the point of worship.

"Isn't she too young?" I stammer.

"Too young! You think age makes a difference! She won't know any more, relative to the marriage, in three or four years. Florent is a perfect candidate. The boy's agreeable to look at, sound, rich, of good character, intelligent, culti-vated...what more do you want?"

I admit, with a rage whose baseness disgusts me, that she's right; I also feel that I'm not taking any account of De-nise's future, that I'm virtually sacrificing it in order to keep her here.

"It's almost certain," Yveline continues, "that she won't find a better opportunity! She hasn't much of a dowry, to say the least—and our young people need money. Must she marry an old man?"

As simple as an arithmetical addition, these words grip me by the throat. Their evidence crushes any reply; my arsenal of arguments only suggests absurdities.

"I had to say that," I murmur. "Denise will decide."

"She's not stupid enough to refuse!"

Whether by virtue of an eclipse of intuition or the pre-eminence of a sentiment, Yveline does not perceive my distress, or even that I've just looked at her with hatred.

"I'll come to take Denise out tomorrow," she concludes, "and I won't have any trouble convincing her!" Ah! I resolve to fight, while she looks at me with a tender expression and murmurs: "You can kiss me…"

I would rather bite her—but it's necessary to obey; and the charming gesture, this time, is an odious one. We repeat the scene in a servile fashion.

"You may, however, warn Denise," she says, pressing herself against me…

A quarter of an hour later, I find myself alone with Denise, Torquemada and Taureau. The storm continues to fill the streets with ferocious voices, brutalizing chimneys for want of trees.

We are silent. Between us, silence is as natural as between Orientals and some Anglo-Saxons. Even prolonged, it does not trouble us.

Today, on my part, it's abnormal. I've been on the point of breaking it ten times, and every time, what I was about to say has escaped or been disagreeably transformed. And so many various preliminaries lead to extreme simplicity.

"Have you ever thought, Denise, about getting married?"

She has shivered; her dreamy expression becomes an astonished one, and she limits herself to saying: "No."

"Never?"

"Never."

"Then how do you see the future?"

"I don't see it."

"But you think about it, though."

"Not for myself."

"Come on, Denise, you have desires, wishes…"

She thinks about it for a moment, then says: "I don't want anything other than what I have."

The reply goes further than anything that I could have imagined. Stifled by joy, I have difficulty murmuring: "You're not deceiving yourself?"

"How could I deceive myself?"

Her fearful smile! I'd like to leave it at that, frenetically happy—subject to verification. I cut into the joy by saying: "What do you think of the young man who came to see us today?"

She doesn't seem to understand; her bright eyes interrogate me. "I don't know."

"There are things that one has to know."

"I don't know him. He seems just like all the rest to me."

There we go! My imprudence is unpunished. On the contrary, it is rewarded. No doubt possible; the bird is one of the flock; he has no particular existence for Denise. It would be absurd to persist. Silence. We listen to the winds—oh, how I love them; they become the essence of terrestrial beauty, messengers of space, roamers of oceans, vagabonds of deserts, wanderers of forests!

XXI.

What further trials Ferral imposes on us! One check after another—but after each check, a revelation. Without any doubt, we have surpassed our universe of stars; we are dealing with mixed phenomena, on which our ultimate corpuscles still act, but in a different way and without continuity, in the form of powerful reservoirs of electromagnetic energy.

"We're getting closer!" Ferral affirms.

Chavres, under the impulse of Ambroise's genius, is deploying an unprecedented ingenuity in mounting the experiments; even I am surpassed. And when we stop, our brains buzzing, Ferral rewards us with a fervent speech.

Several times, he has declared: "Without you, it would be necessary to give up. It requires three different mentalities."

267

Thus he nourishes our courage, as if we were hearing the voice of a demigod.

How many times have we thought that we had reached the end! Then, everything clouded over, the experiment became vague, sparse, irregular; one might think that *the all* were defending itself, playing with our paltry efforts.

Then even Ferral had his moment of weakness. He lowered his head.

"If I were superstitious, I would say that the universe doesn't *want* us to succeed."

"Who knows?" sighed Chavres.

"Yes, who knows? Has not hiatus been the very condition of the formation of our universe of stars? Without that hiatus, there would be no individual worlds, existences would be eternally confused, or, rather, would not form at all."

"The chaos of the Hellenes!"

"But infinitely, and much more subtly, chaotic."

While Ferral, Chavres and I, bouncing back, are attempting to breach the boundaries of a universe already too vast for our feebleness, my little personal adventure continues among the terrestrial adventures.

Yveline tried to convince Denise, but Denise would only consent to think about it. Prudently, my sinuous friend has granted her a long delay—so long that nothing had to be resolved until the beginning of spring. And young Florent carted his plan and his dreams around somewhere in central Asia, among people still overtly rebellious, although already conquered by the phonograph, to which no barbarian can oppose an effective resistance.

Francine had yielded to the supplications of Amnès, who, the possessor of all the powers of fairies and magicians, a pitiless plunderer of the credulous, was vanquished in derisory fashion by a little creature with no other magic than her eyes, her cheeks, her round neck and her gait. He ferried her around in racing cars, steamships and aircraft, more securely chained every day, lured as effectively as the lamentable victims of his piracy.

268

That's what I learned, as the first day of spring approached, when Denise had either to recall young Florent from Central Asia, or convince him to continue his pilgrimage.

That morning, the expiring winter displayed a pale Sun, as cold as a moon. In that indigent light, I thought with disgust about the glacial lands in which Eskimos gorge themselves on fat, for I was chilled by a horror that was mingled with a kind of hatred.

"Madame Amnès," announced Madame Donatienne, in a discreetly ironic manner.

Francine appeared—the same, unaltered by marriage, without ostentation and as dangerously seductive as ever.

"Ah!" she sighed. "Finally!"

How simple it was. Taking refuge in my arms, rearmored, her mouth avid, she offered herself so naturally that I was not astonished by it until afterwards…

"What imprudence, Francine!" That was what I said, as soon as the harm was irreparable.

"Oh, that's true!" she said, ingenuously. "I didn't think of that."

Am I Amnès' keeper? Is it up to me to protect him from Francine's caprices?

"What do you expect?" she whispered. "I've never renounced our love—and I haven't promised him anything." Because I smiled, she added: "Except before the mayor and the priest, but that's just protocol. What have they to do with it? And I didn't know that I'd pay so dear for it!"

"So dear—truly? He makes you suffer?"

"Without knowing it! I imagined that it would be more bearable. He didn't displease me before; now, I'm indifferent to him. But what a bore! At least he's happy that it's sometimes affectionate. Imagine—a man who ruins people with a smile, before whom everyone trembles, but humiliates himself like a slave before a young woman!"

"Which must, in your eyes, redeem the horrors."

"Redeem them! If I loved him, I'd love him all the more for that. What does it matter, after all? Amnès is only a triumphant swindler."

"What if he catches you?"

"He has no suspicion, and if, some day, he does, perhaps it's for the best."

"What about the fortune?"

"You can take it for granted, my dear, that the marriage contract has put me in a comfortable position. So comfortable that I might perhaps think myself richer without him than with him, by virtue of the incalculable virtue of arbitrary freedom."

"If it exists."

"What?"

"Arbitrary freedom."

"Ah! Right. Of its appearance, if you wish—that's sufficient for me."

The immemorial prostitution of the woman, in conformity with all ancient and modern statutes. From my hand, Francine would not accept a four-*sou* coin, while she will someday carry off Amnès' ransom after a divorce, legitimated by a notary. She did not even see a distant analogy with the wages of women who sell sex.

"After all," she concluded, "I've resolved to be absolutely faithful to him. Don't smile—it's sincere! You don't count." With that, she becomes aroused again, her eyes wandering. In a low voice, she adds: "Since it was like that before, nothing has changed."

She must be so close to believing it that it is as if she does believe it. And we cease to worry about Amnès.

XXII.

We have breached the fourth universe! It is morning; the first day of spring has arrived, a sour harbinger of showers, caprices, wind and rain. To us, *another* light has appeared.

Words are merely symbolic here. The radiation that springs from unknown depths is even more invisible than our most subtle radiations—gamma rays and cosmic rays. Are there living beings somewhere that can perceive it? For us, it only exists thus far in a leaden cage, in which the pretended void has been pushed as far as contemporary technique permits, but it manifests itself by indirect influences and we already know that its velocity is much greater than that of our light.[36]

What days and nights we have just lived, sustained by a sacred intoxication.

Chavres is exhausted, at the limit of human strength; I have vertigo, and Ferral, also weary, but not to the point of exhaustion, is smiling at fabulous visions.

"Ambroise," I murmur, "where will this lead human beings? Will they create a new kind of matter? Will they see further—much further—into *the all*?"

Ferral places his hand on my shoulder. "I don't know! What seems to me to be certain is that they will be able to comprehend our own universe much better. The multitude of unilateral notions will divide into two. Science will be relative to the universe, instead of being—as it still is, in essence, almost entirely—anthropomorphic."

"I think," muttered Chavres, emerging from his paralysis, "that it will be better than that. I have more confidence than you, Ambroise, in the future of your discovery. We know *something* about the universe the least different from ours, which must offer a few analogies with our astral world. What a dream, Ferral, if we perceive worlds beside, and even *inside* our nebulas and stars!"

"Can one hope for that, after thousands of years? Will the human race live long enough to succeed? Let's content

---

[36] Rosny's narrator inserts a footnote here: "When the opportunity arises, we shall publish a brochure giving the technical details that cannot be accommodated here."

ourselves with having brought forth the primitive light, Cha-vres."

"No!" said Chavres, resolutely. "No, I won't be content with so little! I intend to dream without shackles, to dream of all the possibilities, Ambroise. One never dreams high enough, or far enough!"

Ferral looked at him with affectionate indulgence. "You're a magnificent dreamer, Chavres!"

"Less than you!" said Chavres laughing. "What dreams it must have required to culminate in your discovery!"

"Mine, no!" protested Ferral. "What didn't you two have to discover before the idea became realizable? Without you, I'd have been lost in limbo."

"I've only been an instrument," Chavres muttered.

"And I," I said, "a vague amateur."

"Don't slander yourselves," Ferral said, severely. "You've both demonstrated genius."

Genius! Chavres stood there open-mouthed, and for my part, I'm sure of only having sparse mental faculties.

"Let's resign ourselves," Chavres said, in a humorous tone. "We don't know what we've done…"

I'm coming back through the streets.

The clouds swirl, pale and charming, feminine clouds de-livered to the caprice of the wind, traversed by glimmers of light as bright as a child's eyes. It's the time when the migra-tory birds begin their great journeys. Young leaves sprout, as ardent as kisses. Once again, the ancient Earth devotes itself to the youth of plants and trees.

I thought about Ferral's victory—which is simultaneous-ly, however little, mine! Denise appeared in the interstices of my reverie. The fourth universe, for sure—but am I any less perishable therein? And how I want to protect Denise!

Will she follow young Florent, to become with him, ac-cording to *Genesis*, one and the same flesh? I can't imagine Denise as a wife, in the manner of Yveline or Francine. I have made her purity, after a fashion, supernatural. She is taboo.

Whatever form my predilection might take, eventually, it does not, at present, include any dross. What woman is more feminine, though? Perhaps she is more so than any other, but in what an indefinable manner! If young Florent gets his hands on her, it will be the most ignominious, the ugliest despair of my life…

The sweetness of her actual presence! We're seated side by side, while Torquemada prowls around like a little black demon and Taureau looks at us with his large attentive eyes.

I've just told Denise about Ferral's victory and we're daydreaming peacefully, our eyes fixed on the window where the beautiful clouds are passing by.

"Madame Hautbourguès," announces Donatienne.

It's the appointed day! She's come to steal Denise from me. And as I see her advance, tall and flexible, sowing sensuality with every gesture, it's not a pretty woman that I see but an execrable serpent.

Her gaze goes from me to Denise, passing from ambiguous tenderness to placid affection.

Conventional remarks, by way of an introduction. Eventually, the redoubtable question: "Well, Denise, have you decided?"

No more breath; I am the man in the dock; I await the verdict.

"Quite decided," Denise replied.

"Entirely?"

"Entirely."

"And it's yes?"

"It's no, godmother. I don't want to get married."

My breast is positively bursting; a song of triumph rises, and the odor of enchanted archipelagoes.

"That's crazy, my darling!" says Yveline. "Such an opportunity will probably never arise again. No, you haven't really thought about it."

"Yes, godmother. I know that I'd be unhappy. I want to remain free—free!"

273

Yveline shrugs her shoulders, with disdainful pity; a wave of ill-temper passes, followed by a smile. "You don't know what you're doing, Denise! You're only a child."

"It's because I'm a child, godmother, and because I enjoy being one, that I'd be very unhappy not to be one any more, so soon."

"All right," Yveline says, resignedly. "I've done what I could, for your own good. God grant that you won't regret it."

"You've been very good, very good—too good for me!"

"No," says Yveline, suddenly becoming affectionate. "You're my little girl, my darling." She has taken Denise in her arms and kisses her with the "quantum" of tenderness that she has at her disposal, and which simulates maternity, in a shrunken state. Then: "Go away! Your godfather and godmother need to talk now."

When Denise has gone, Yveline says: "I knew she wouldn't go back on that decision. Who can tell? Perhaps, later, there'll be another chance. In the meantime, what are we going to do? Her resources are insignificant…"

She is speaking with a hypocritical gravity, while looking at me ambiguously through partly-closed eyelids.

"That's of no importance," I say.

"Oh! Really? Your finances, then…"

"Much better."

"She still doesn't inconvenience you?"

There is no need to minimize. "On the contrary. I like having her with me."

"Ah!" Her gaze is sharp, penetrating suspicious. "That might compromise her slightly." That's a blow to the solar plexus, which cuts off my breath. "Are you sure that you're not following an inclination?" Yveline continues. "Honest, I have no doubt—but, all things considered…! You're young, my dear. Too young…"

"Wasn't I young when you sent her to me?"

She draws nearer. "Do you love me?"

274

Damn! It's no time to be lukewarm. Fortunately, assured that Denise will remain—all the more surely, the more ardor I express to Yveline—I sigh: "More than ever!"

It's only half false; instinct consents to be on the right side of the barricade.

"Do you swear?"

I've sworn worse than that.

"I swear it, and then..." I seize her violently, almost brutally. "Yveline, don't tempt me too far!"

A rain of kisses, which she accepts, in torment herself, while whispering: "Oh! Quite mad!"

All the same, how desirable she is! The figure yields, the throat thrusts; we're in the cavern—are we going to violate the oath?

"That's good," she sighs.

The mouth is so close, but I can't reach it! That little red fortress is definitely impregnable...

"It's true, you still love me," she says, when the armistice arrives. "Well, what are we going to do about Denise?"

"We'll keep her, of course."

"I'll come often to take her."

"That goes without saying."

There we go—all is well. Destiny decides that she has confidence—a confidence surer for being led by instinct, and which will persist as long as I am or seem to be in love with her. A long-term investment; I shall be all the hungrier for Yveline if the desire is never fulfilled.

We are alone again, with Taureau and Torquemada.

Taureau is daydreaming; Torquemada has taken possession of an armchair and, armored and full of grace, plunges into a deep sleep.

Outside, the Sun has taken on the color that it used to have on Easter Sundays; the ambience comes in through the windows, charged with delight; the young human female breathing beside me transfigures it. It's a moment of perfect security, as if I were saturated with faith and hope, as if I believed in the *real* gentleness of the universe. And perhaps it's *one* of those days when I have the clearest perception of the monstrous abomination of existence, incessant death—death that, at every beat of our hearts carries away one of our peers, while millions of others are living out their last weeks, in the anguish of pain, and the masses struggle pitifully and ferociously for food, pleasure or love. Hunger, murder, rape, uncertainty—a rightful plaint transmitted through the generations!

Because I have beside me a small perishable form, nothing emanates from all that misery but happiness. Denise equals the universe, the stars, the immeasurable Earth, the sacred rivers, the light of the morning and the grace of summer evenings. In her, humankind loses its ferocity, its ugliness and its infamy; she is one of those miracles of purity which allows a glimpse of a glimmer of divinity in the chaos.

Afterword

"The Young Vampire" is a curious text in several ways. On a trivial level, it illustrates Rosny's tendency to publish his first drafts without revision, even when they contain manifest contradictions. As the frame narrative is forgotten and never properly closed, the whole thing could easily have been excised, but even if the author did not want to do that, it is not obvious why he left in the line in which the storyteller says that the victim's vampirism proved not to be hereditary—which could have been eliminated with a single stroke of a pen—once the climax of the story had established that it was, and uses that fact to generate a sense of closure. It is equally mysterious that his editors let the contradiction stand, given the minimum effort required to eliminate it, but they, like Rosny himself, appear to have maintained an excessive reverential respect for the produce of his creative inspiration.

Perhaps Rosny's first impulse was correct in this respect, and vampirism, as described in the story, should not have been hereditary. On the other hand, the decision to represent it as hereditary in this instance (though not, presumably, in respect of the other three children with which the frame story credits Mrs. Bluewinkle) is more interesting in terms of the possibilities it opens up. What happens to Evelyn is a kind of temporary identity-exchange between worlds, but the advent of a new mind clearly has metamorphic effects on the flesh (we can only wonder as to what effect Evelyn's mind had on the inexplicable flesh of the inhabitant of the other world) so it is perhaps only to be expected that such effects might have extended to the produce of her ovaries. The temporary exchange thus contrives the possibility of a kind of hybrid identity, akin to the kind of shared identity featured in "Dans le monde des Variants" (tr. in vol. 2 as "In the World of the Variants").

Given that the anomalous individual is subject to scientific investigation from the beginning—unlike the protagonist of "Un Autre Monde" (tr. in vol. 1 as "Another World"), who has to solicit investigation when he reaches adulthood—lovers of speculative fiction can only regret that the story stops short of informing us as to the detailed results of that investigation, but the author doubtless thought that more elaborate metaphysical speculation would be inappropriate to a work destined to be published under the heading of "An Hour of Forgetfulness," and was probably right.

It may be worth noting that the chronology of the story seems slightly odd. We are told that it takes place between 1902 and 1905, and the frame narrative seems to be looking back from some time thereafter—Evelyn has, at any rate, had time enough to have three more children. Given that the story was published in 1920, the reader's natural assumption would be that the frame narrative is set in the present. When the story switches back into the present tense at the end, however, Walter—born in 1904—is still a baby, so the narrative voice seems to be speaking from 1905, or perhaps a year later. If Le Marquand really is supposed to be narrating the story in 1920, he should be able to report on Walter as an adolescent. It therefore seems possible—as with so many other Rosny stories—that it was begun, but probably not finished, some time before its publication, almost certainly before the Great War, while Rosny was still inspired by Maurice Renard with the possibility that "scientific marvel fiction" might have a bright future in terms of critical estimation and commercial marketability.

"The Supernatural Assassin" is cut from the same imaginative fabric as "The Young Vampire," but similarly fights shy of any kind of metaphysical discussion regarding the implications of its central hypothesis, presumably for the same reason. Writers of speculative fiction have always been bombarded with editorial advice begging or instructing them to stick to the story and get rid of any speculative extrapolation into which they might have been tempted by logic or creative momentum, and have rarely had any alternative but to take it. The result of that determination is that "The Supernatural Assassin," like "The Young Vampire," is only half a story rather than a whole one, and bound to seem less convincing in consequence, but it is by no means rare for items of published speculative fiction to suffer that fate. One suspects that in this instance, as in so many others, any such extrapolative explanation would only have served to expose the logical flaws in the initial hypothesis by *reduction ad absurdum*, but that is a risk which all innovative speculative fiction runs.

Given that the story's theme echoes that of "The Givreuse Enigma" (in vol. 5), one is tempted to wonder whether it might not have been begun before the short novel in question, and abandoned precisely because the other variant was much more promising, in terms of literary development as well as potential metaphysical explanation. Although it is not as patchy as some of Rosny's other works, the tone of the opening sequence— is markedly different from that of the conclusion, and the implication that the marsh will be important to the plot is completely forgotten. It is also worth noting that the story's theme bears a certain resemblance to that of a novel by Jules Clarétie, which was serialized in the first few issues of *Je Sais Tout*—a periodical that Rosny targeted—as "Moi et l'autre" in 1905 and subsequently reprinted as *L'Obsession*. Given that "The Young Vampire" is a variation on a theme that Rosny first encountered in Nau's *Force ennemie*, it is not improbable that "The Supernatural Assassin" can also be regarded as a deliberate variation of a theme he encountered in his reading.

Those readers who regret the relative dearth of explanation in "The Young Vampire" and "The Supernatural Assassin" might well feel even more frustrated by "Companions of the Universe," whose speculative elements take under-information to an irritating extent. If the narrator's machine is to be mentioned at all, and its salvation of his economic fortunes is vital to the story, then why be so reluctant to explain what it actually *does*? To include a scene in which the narrator demonstrates his machine to an expert, without describing the device itself or the results of its functioning seems positively perverse—but it cannot be mere carelessness, because the author uses exactly the same strategy of non-specification with regard to the experiments demonstrating the reality of the fourth universe. Rosny is, of course, always uneasy in his descriptions of measuring devices and the results they yield—an unease that is manifest in "The Navigators of Space" and "The Mysterious Force" (in vol. 3)—but there must be more to his calculated negligence here than mere timidity. Perhaps he was deliberately over-reacting to editorial censure, or perhaps he thought that any technical description at all would deflect attention away from the internal musings that are the novel's real substance and philosophical core; in either case, the outcome is decidedly odd.

As a quasi-existentialist account of the narrator's management of his sexual desire and erotic impulses, the novel has the advantage of a surprising depth of cynicism—all the more surprising because so many of Rosny's earlier works had subscribed to a more conventional mythology of attraction and consummation. He was, of course, in his late seventies when the work appeared, and presumably looked back upon the influence of the erotic impulse within his life with a certain amount of regret, if not horror, but the reaction manifest in the story cannot be written off as merely mellowing. There is, of course, an element of symbolism in the juxtaposition of the narrator's quest for a revelation of the fourth universe and his desire for a confirmation of Denise's unique chastity, but the mere observation of that parallelism is not of much interest. The gratuitous insertion of sections that specifically accuse Christian religion of embodying all the crimes of corruption he had previously identified, with calculated vagueness, as sins of religion in general, extends an apparent desire to be starkly honest, stripping away veils of hypocrisy that had previously covered up his less palatable ideas, but that desire does not sit very well with the countervailing desire to treat certain matters very vaguely and circumspectly indeed.

All things considered, however, one can say of "Companions of the Universe," as of so many of Rosny's works—and of his entire *oeuvre*, seen as a whole—that its apparent flaws cannot take away from its fascination, and that it has sufficient originality to compensate for a multitude of sins. If Rosny was, as René Doumic contended, simply a bad writer, then he was a great bad writer, who never consented to retreat for long into the stolid, mediocre and deliberately unadventurous form of goodness in which so many writers find a safe haven. If Edmond de Goncourt had not consented, on a whim, to take an interest in him, it could easily have transpired that he remained forever beyond the limits of editorial toleration—but how much more might he have accomplished had those limits been less restrictive? We cannot know, but we may certainly suspect that he would have tested those boundaries, wherever they were set, and that his achievements, however eccentric they might have seemed to the conventionally-minded, would have been well worthy of interest to minds of an independent and neophilic bent.

SF & FANTASY

Guy d'Armen. *Doc Ardan: The City of Gold and Lepers*
G.-J. Arnaud. *The Ice Company*
Aloysius Bertrand. *Gaspard de la Nuit*
Félix Bodin. *The Novel of the Future*
André Caroff. *The Terror of Madame Atomos*
Didier de Chousy. *Ignis*
C. I. Defontenay. *Star (Psi Cassiopeia)*
Charles Derennes. *The People of the Pole*
Harry Dickson. *The Heir of Dracula*
Sâr Dubnotal *vs. Jack the Ripper*
Alexandre Dumas. *The Return of Lord Ruthven*
J.-C. Dunyach. *The Night Orchid. The Thieves of Silence*
Henri Duvernois. *The Man Who Found Himself*
Henri Falk. *The Age of Lead*
Paul Féval. *Anne of the Isles. Knightshade. Revenants. Vampire City. The Vampire Countess. The Wandering Jew's Daughter*
Paul Féval, *fils. Felifax, the Tiger-Man*
Arnould Galopin. *Doctor Omega*
V. Hugo, Foucher & Meurice. *The Hunchback of Notre-Dame*
O. Joncquel & Theo Varlet. *The Martian Epic*
Jean de La Hire. *Enter the Nyctalope. The Nyctalope on Mars. The Nyctalope vs. Lucifer*
G. Le Faure & H. de Graffigny. *The Extraordinary Adventures of a Russian Scientist Across the Solar System* (2 vols.)
Gustave Le Rouge. *The Vampires of Mars*
Jules Lermina. *Mysteryville. Panic in Paris. To-Ho and the Gold Destroyers*
Jean-Marc & Randy Lofficier. *Edgar Allan Poe on Mars. The Katrina Protocol. Pacifica. Robonocchio. Tales of the Shadowmen* (anthos.; 6 vols.)
Xavier Mauméjean. *The League of Heroes*
Marie Nizet. *Captain Vampire*
C. Nodier, Beraud & Toussaint-Merle. *Frankenstein*
Henri de Parville. *An Inhabitant of the Planet Mars*
Polidori, C. Nodier, E. Scribe. *Lord Ruthven the Vampire*
P.-A. Ponson du Terrail. *The Vampire and the Devil's Son*
Maurice Renard. *Doctor Lerne. A Man Among the Microbes. The Blue Peril. The Doctored Man. The Master of Light*

Albert Robida. *The Clock of the Centuries. The Adventures of Saturnin Farandoul*

J.-H. Rosny Aîné. *The Navigators of Space. The World of the Variants. The Mysterious Force. Vamireh. The Givreuse Enigma. The Young Vampire*

Brian Stableford. *The Shadow of Frankenstein. Frankenstein and the Vampire Countess. The New Faust at the Tragicomique. Sherlock Holmes & The Vampires of Eternity. The Stones of Camelot. The Wayward Muse.* (anthologist) *The Germans on Venus. News from the Moon*

Kurt Steiner. *Ortog*

Villiers de l'Isle-Adam. *The Scaffold. The Vampire Soul*

Philippe Ward. *Artahe*

MYSTERIES & THRILLERS

M. Allain & P. Souvestre. *The Daughter of Fantômas*

Anicet-Bourgeois, Lucien Dabril. *Rocambole*

A. Bisson & G. Livet. *Nick Carter vs. Fantômas*

V. Darlay & H. de Gorsse. *Lupin vs. Holmes: The Stage Play*

Paul Féval. *Gentlemen of the Night. John Devil. The Black Coats: The Cadet Gang. The Companions of the Treasure. Heart of Steel. The Invisible Weapon. The Parisian Jungle. 'Salem Street*

Emile Gaboriau. *Monsieur Lecoq*

Steve Leadley. *Sherlock Holmes: The Circle of Blood*

Maurice Leblanc. *Arsène Lupin: The Blonde Phantom. The Hollow Needle. Countess Cagliostro*

Gaston Leroux. *Chéri-Bibi. The Phantom of the Opera. Rouletabille & the Mystery of the Yellow Room*

William Patrick Maynard. *The Terror of Fu Manchu*

Frank J. Morlock. *Sherlock Holmes: The Grand Horizontals*

P. de Wattyne & Y. Walter. *Sherlock Holmes vs. Fantômas*

David White. *Fantômas in America*